P F M

PFM

Pure F**king Magic

JANET CAMPBELL

Epigraph Books
Rhinebeck, New York

*PFM: Pure F**cking Magic* © 2020 by Janet Campbell

Cover photograph by Giancarlo Espinosa, Key West

Paperback ISBN 978-1-951937-17-1
Hardcover ISBN 978-1-951937-18-8
eBook ISBN 978-1-951937-19-5

Library of Congress Control Number 2020903574

Book design by Colin Rolfe

Epigraph Books
22 East Market Street, Suite 304
Rhinebeck, NY 12572
(845) 876-4861
epigraphps.com

Definition from Urban Dictionary:

PFM

Pure fucking magic.

Person A: How in the hell does a person sing in harmony with themselves?

Person B: PFM.

THE GOOD GIRL

Despite her earplugs and eye mask, something woke Cathy up. It was Bob. He was snoring, like he did every night, every night that he wasn't at the hospital. And every night, she climbed into their king size bed hoping it would be different. Their enormous bed enabled them to lie miles apart. She could reach out her arm and barely touch him. They had shared this bed for twenty-five years. So why couldn't she sleep?

Cathy lay there debating the inevitable. The snoring didn't abate. As he often did in his restless sleep, Bob grabbed the sheet and rolled over, tugging it off her body.

Quietly, Cathy made her nightly climb out of their bed into the guest room. Let's face it. It was her room. She was the guest. She crawled into the twin bed and reached into the night stand. She popped open the prescription container and split one of the cylindrical pills into thirds. She swallowed one tiny bit.

She felt horribly guilty about taking Ambien. But she couldn't seem to sleep without it.

She lay there thinking about tomorrow. She and Bob had another counseling session. This was their third therapist in the last four years. Every time they met with a new person the first question was the same.

"So, what do you want, Bob?"

Without hesitation he replied, "I want to fix my marriage."

"And what do you want, Cathy?"

After a long hesitation, she managed a choked whisper. "I don't know."

What a load of BS. You know perfectly well what you want, girl-friend. You want OUT of your dead marriage.

(CATHY JERKS AT THE SOUND OF THE VOICE) Who are you?

Don't pull that innocent act on me. I'm the voice that you've stuffed down for years. Consider me your truth serum. You're welcome to call me TS if you want.

Am I going crazy?

On the contrary, this is the healthiest thing you've done for a long time. For the first time in years you're finally letting me through your ridiculous "good girl facade." Hallelujah! I've been screaming to be heard for forever.

It is not a "good girl facade."

Now don't go getting all upset. Of course, you've always been a good girl. You've led a model life—an A-student, loving daughter, dear friend, wonderful wife.

(SNORTS) Now you've gone too far.

You don't think that you've been a good wife? So, what was all that cleaning, cooking, raising the kids, managing your gracious home, and compromising your career so that Bob could become

one of the top cardiologists in Manhattan? Your picture sure as hell wasn't in New York Magazine.

Bob has worked really hard. His patients love him. They're always telling me how they can talk to him about anything. They think he walks on water.

Right. The God syndrome. All-knowing, all-powerful. Making the difference between life and death every day. No wonder he's so egotistical and controlling. Must be heady stuff. Can't say your soap-opera writing has quite the same gravitas. But, somehow the "God" act doesn't pay off the same for you. It would be nice if you could tell him anything and he would actually listen. And, how is it sleeping next to "God" every night? When was the last time "God" came over for a snuggle?

He's always exhausted.

All I ever see him do is stare at his phone. Hard to believe that God can get so tired from that.

It's my fault too.

Girlfriend, I understand. It's hard to be "in the mood" when you're not happy.

I think it's just what happens when you get older. I remember an Oprah show where a guest psychologist polled the audience. She asked how many of the women didn't care about sex anymore. Over half the audience raised their hands. That's me. I'm not interested.

Whoa there. Well, I am.

(SARCASTICALLY) Sorry, "girlfriend."

No need to be snide. Instead of Twenty Questions, I have a much simpler game. Let's play One Question. DO ... YOU ... LOVE ... HIM?

What? He's the father of my children, husband of twenty-five years.

Don't do your Fiddler on the Roof revival for me. Do you love him?

(SILENCE)

Let me try again. You were always good at math. In a sacred union between two people where each one enhances the other's life, shouldn't one plus one be greater than two?

That's what I always thought.

I hate to shove this down your throat, but I've been waiting to ask this for so long. Does that math work for you and Bob?

(A HUGE PAUSE AND THEN, QUIETLY) I'm not even sure one plus one equals two.

Glorioski! The whole truth and nothing but the truth. Will wonders never cease! Look, I'm not happy about this, either. So let me get back to my original question. Do you love him?

(WRAPS HER PILLOW AROUND HER HEAD) Go away!

You know what the therapist is going to ask you tomorrow. All I ask is that you tell the truth.

THE SESSION

With trepidation, Cathy drove down the West Side Highway heading for the Chelsea office of Dr. Stein. They had tried a couple of Connecticut counselors without great results. This psychologist was the recommendation of one of Bob's coworkers. They were going into *the city*. They were going for the big time.

After her drive she needed to use the bathroom. As she passed the mirror she couldn't help noticing her pale, tense face. Her dark blond hair still surprised her. Although she had been born a brunette, her colorist had recently suggested going to this lighter version of herself. This way, her grey roots were much less noticeable.

But she still had her brown eyes—those girl-next-door eyes that no longer sparkled.

When she came out of the bathroom, Bob was sitting, frowning into his phone.

"Hi." She tried to be civil.

Bob sort of grunted back. He was not happy to be dragged into another one of these sessions.

Dr. Stein shepherded them back to a low-lit, comfortable, somewhat cluttered office with two couches set perpendicularly to each other. There was a swivel chair opposite the corner of the couches. Dr. Stein motioned for them to sit down.

Cathy sat on one couch. Bob sat on the other. Dr. Stein sat equidistant to the two of them on the chair. It was like a middle school geometry diagram.

They made some small talk to break the ice. Dr. Stein asked several questions about their history, children, etc. He made a few notes.

Finally, it was crunch time. Dr. Stein looked at both of them. "So why are you here?"

Bob, always the one to take the lead, jumped in. "Well, Cathy is not happy. I'm here to fix our marriage."

Dr. Stein turned to Cathy. "And you, Cathy? Is that why you're here?"

Here it was. The moment of truth. "I don't know. I don't know if it can be fixed."

Bob cleared his throat.

It was so painful. Thank goodness there was a third party in the room. It's funny how you could live with someone for all those years, but not be able to be really honest. There was a reason for people to go to a therapist. It made a conversation like this a lot easier. It was almost like there was a referee.

Dr. Stein turned to Bob. Clearly, Bob was upset. Clearly, he felt threatened, even bewildered. "I love you. I thought you loved me. I haven't changed."

Cathy murmured softly, "Maybe I have."

Dr. Stein looked directly at Cathy. "Cathy, do you love Bob?"

Cathy looked at Dr. Stein. Then, she found herself drawn to Bob's white face. She tore her eyes back to Dr. Stein. "I wish I did …"

An incredible jolt of nausea traveled through Cathy's system. Suddenly Cathy knew that this was the truth. Dizzy, she got up and stumbled by Dr. Stein on her way to the bathroom.

As she passed him, she mumbled, "I think I'm going to be sick."

Cathy could hear clapping and cheering as she rushed down the hall.

Be still, my heart. You did it!

NEGOTIATION

Thirteen months later, it was done.

That makes it sound easy. The first six months were pure hell. They had to tell Michael, Paul, and Ashley. When they finally sat down together, it didn't go well. Naturally, Bob couldn't resist leading off with "Your mother was the one who wanted this." Cathy couldn't say anything. It was the truth.

Thirteen months later, Cathy was still feeling the effects of her decision on her children. She could only pray that time would eventually heal their anger. Cathy remembered a nurse telling her at the hospital when Michael was born that her baby would be only as good she was, so she had to take care of herself first. Wasn't this situation just like being on an airplane, where they told you to put your oxygen mask on before helping your child?

In addition to the children, the divorce negotiation had been singularly painful.

The first session went well enough. The mediator gave each of them a budget to fill out, projecting what they would need to match their current lifestyle.

Cathy struggled to complete the massive form that asked for

annual estimates for the cost of everything from housing and insurance to hair appointments and travel. She and Bob had agreed that he would keep their big house in Connecticut, and she would keep their country house in the Hudson Valley, which they had bought when they were living in the city. Cathy had always loved that house. But they had only used it in the summer. She had no idea how much it would cost to live there for the whole year.

In a funk, Cathy called Amy, her best friend, who was an attorney. She explained her dilemma. "I am overwhelmed by this form. I feel awful asking for any money at all. After all, I'm the one who wants out. I'm not sure I deserve anything."

On the other end of the phone, Cathy could almost see smoke puff out of Amy's ears. "Don't be ridiculous, Cath. You want out because your marriage hasn't worked for years. You took off all those years to raise your children, keep a beautiful home and entertain while Bob was building his practice. Imagine where you might be if you hadn't left your career? As I recall, you were a rising star when you quit to stay home. Yes, you've been lucky to get back into the soaps as a script writer. But your field is perilous. Do you have any job security?"

Cathy gulped. "Probably not."

"Exactly. Whereas Bob is one of the top cardiologists in Manhattan. He is never going to starve. Bob's life would have been so much different without you. I don't ever want to hear you say you don't deserve anything. You *deserve* a lot. Do not penny pinch when you fill out that form. I don't want Bob to be the sugar daddy to your kids while you're 'Poor Mom.'"

Cathy blinked. Maybe Amy had a point.

"And one more thing," Amy continued, "you know perfectly well your numbers will be challenged. Leave room for Bob to 'win' some cutbacks, and still leave you comfortable."

With Amy's words in her head, Cathy filled out the forms. Bob hadn't been happy, but Amy had been exactly right. It had been a painful and tedious process. But, in the end, Bob had "won" a number of victories. And, Cathy had been left with enough.

Whew! You just dodged a bullet. Thank the lord for Amy! Without her you would have given away the farm. At least now you'll be able to afford the heat, possibly even a manicure once in a while. I don't know what you were thinking!

I don't think I was thinking. I was just feeling horribly guilty.

Okay, dollface. Time to dump that Catholic schoolgirl baggage. You got rid of the plaid uniform decades ago. You know perfectly well that you tried your darnedest to make it work.

Did I?

AAAArrrgggghhh! You know it's really painful to have that "little" voice inside you screaming at the top of her lungs.

(WINCES) You're hurting me!

Well, you're killing me! You know the truth. I know the truth. Well, I am the truth. It's over. Onward and upward.

MOVING OUT

Cathy looked around her kitchen, the kitchen that she had cooked in for two decades, the kitchen that had produced dinner parties, birthday parties, and some really lousy family meals. It had been the center of the family. And, now she was leaving it.

Five months after their last counseling session, Bob had met a female physician from the city. Cathy couldn't deny that it hurt how quickly he had replaced her. She hadn't seen him smile like that for years. At some level, she was really happy for him. But she wondered if she would ever smile like that again too.

Cathy doubted it. At least, not because of a man. She was so weary—so done with all of that man stuff. Who needed them?

She took a final walk through the house. She could picture Michael's third birthday party in the family room. She had made a cake in the shape of Big Bird. There was Paul's room, still full of soccer balls, trophies, and old shoes. And there was Ashley's room with the psychedelic fuchsia bedspread. How many midnight talks had she had with a teenaged Ashley in that room?

By now, tears were streaming down her face as she looked at the corner in the living room where their Christmas tree had so recently stood.

It had not been a normal Christmas. But they had tried to enjoy it together as a family one more time.

After the kids had gone back to their lives, she and Bob had sat on the floor and divided up the ornaments. Surprisingly, they had been unbelievably civilized about the furniture, even the art. But the Christmas ornaments were something else. As they sat cross-legged on the floor, a part of her seemed to leave her body and observe this heartbreaking moment from the upper corner of the room. She had an overwhelming sense of déjà vu, like this was a scene she had written for the soaps. And now she was living it.

It was like a punch to her gut to think that she wouldn't be able to unpack every single one of their precious family heirlooms. There was kindergarten Michael's pine cone porcupine whose glitter was coming unglued year by year; third grade Ashley's curly-haired Arielle; and middle school Paul's wooden fox, made in cub scouts.

Cathy had gotten the porcupine and the fox. She would always be brokenhearted about Arielle.

They had survived that night. Barely. Bob had given her one of those why-are-you-doing-this-to-us looks and retired sullenly to his bedroom. Cathy had opened a bottle of wine and stayed up half the night, drinking. She had had a vicious headache in the morning.

And now, a few weeks later, Bob was away at a conference, and Cathy was about to move out, move on.

The movers had come earlier in the week to move the big stuff. Today she was taking the small items she had wanted to transport personally. She carried the last of the boxes out to her car. It was snowing. What a ridiculous time of the year to be moving.

Cathy had one more thing to do. She had spent half the night working on it. She didn't believe that you could be married to someone for twenty-five years and then just walk away without saying anything. She pulled out the sheet of paper that she had finished at 4:00 a.m. It was filled with memories and regret and love.

Barely able to see through her tears, Cathy closed the front door.

Jeez, why didn't you bring a box of Kleenex with you? You're going to wash us away with your waterworks.

Would you please shut up and let me be sad.

OK, already. I'm pretty sad too. It's the end of an era.

Thanks for that insightful observation. I had no idea.

Now, don't get all snarky. You know this is for the best. You've been a miserable camper for a long time. Bob's grinning from ear to ear these days. You're next.

Right, how's that going to happen? All my girlfriends have told me in no uncertain terms that there are no men out there, even if I wanted one— which I don't.

All your married girlfriends have been married forever and know nothing about whether there are any men out there or not. Plus, I bet they're jealous as hell that you've had the courage to do what half of them want to do.

My girlfriends are pretty damn smart.

And so am I, your number-one girlfriend. We are on the brink of the unknown. How exciting is that?

We are on the brink of the abyss.

Stop it, stop it, stop it! How many times have you written this pep talk? "When one door closes, another opens—when one chapter ends, another begins." We're going to strap on our parachute and jump!

I'm terrified.

Of course, you are. It wouldn't be nearly as much fun if you weren't! I've got your back, baby! Remember your sophomore year in college—when Rick broke up with you? You were a mess. You wanted to transfer. But instead you reinvented yourself and had the best year ever.

(RELUCTANTLY) You're right. I needed that.

I knew that.

SATURDAY NIGHT

Three months later, Cathy still hadn't unpacked all the boxes she'd brought from Connecticut. But at least the horrendous winter was over. She had gotten to know a lot of her country neighbors much better, now that she was living here full time. She had joined a gym and worked out almost every day. She had signed up for the local library book club and was a bit of a celebrity because of her soap opera writing job. And, of course, she had the structure of her weekly script assignment to keep her sane. Every Monday, she got the breakdown of her new script. Then, she became a recluse as she transformed the twenty-page outline into an eighty-page script. Friday, at five o'clock she emailed her finished script back to the head writers. And then she collapsed.

So Friday night was no problem. She was exhausted and happy to kick back with a glass of wine or dinner at a local restaurant. Frequently, one of her new friends from the country would invite her over for a casual Friday-night meal or the movies.

No, Friday night was not the problem.

It was Saturday.

Starting in high school and firmly cemented in college, Saturday night was party night, date night, fun night. Saturday night was a night to get dressed up (at least a little), go out, and do something. Even in their darkest days, she and Bob had always done something on Saturday night. Even if it was only dinner and a movie. Even if they had barely anything to say to each other.

But, everything about the rhythm of her life had changed. In so many ways, it was a relief to be by herself, to do whatever she wanted whenever she wanted, to not feel as alone as she had sitting in a room with Bob. But there was no denying that her life was different, and the difference wasn't all that comfortable.

Most Saturday nights, she was quite deliberate about trying to organize some kind of activity. She didn't like to think she was desperate. But in her truly honest moments she knew that she was. Her married friends usually had plans with their husbands. Her few single friends often had travel plans. Her children were never available for a chat because they were always out.

Like so many other Saturdays, tonight she had no one "to play with."

Cathy delivered a stern lecture to herself. Enough was enough. She was going to enjoy a lovely evening. She had a very nice Sauvignon Blanc from New Zealand. She had several TV programs recorded that she wanted to watch. And she thought it would be good to write in her journal. She was determined not to feel sad or alone.

She watched an episode on Netflix while she slowly ate her dinner. But, all too soon, the episode was over. She stared at her journal next to her on the table.

She had a new black Pilot Precise V5 rolling ball pen. There was nothing quite like writing by hand with a perfect new pen. She found the next clean page in her journal and stared at it.

Ahem. (NOISY THROAT CLEARING) **You can start anytime now.**

I don't know where to begin.

Holy Moly! You're the writer! Start with what you're feeling. And—tell the truth.

So, here I am on Saturday night, alone in the country wondering, as I have every morning since I've been here, what have I done?

Okay, okay. I get it. We're doing the "pity pot" thing. All that breast-beating, mea culpa—mea culpa stuff, right? So, go for it. Get it all out of your system. Pick up that pen. (CATHY STARTS TO WRITE AGAIN AS THE VOICE CONTINUES) **You made the worst mistake in your life—ever, right? You feel guilty because you've ruined your family, even though you were miserable? Your life is over because you don't have anything to do on Saturday night. How'm I doing?**

Pretty good.

Shall I continue?

Could I stop you?

Point taken. You don't deserve to be happy. You are done with men. Despite doing everything right in your life up to now, you've blown it big-time. There is no way to fix your situation. You are screwed.

That seems a bit harsh.

Oh? Then what are you going to do about it?

I've done everything I can think of.

Seriously? For a person who makes her living being creative, you're tapped out of ideas? Surely people have things to do on Saturday night, even up here in the boonies. What about volunteering on a hotline? I suspect you're not the only one who gets bummed out on Saturday night. What about working at a restaurant? You used to love waitressing in college. You could meet a ton of new people. What about cooking up a Saturday night supper club where everyone has to bring a new person?

That sounds like fun.

Hey, I have a brainstorm. Look down by your feet. In that pile of mail that you've been ignoring for days, I think there's a catalog for that Omega place near here. Isn't that a wellness place? Seems to me you could use some of that—wellness. I bet they have stuff to do on Saturdays. Take a look.

Sure enough, in the pile on the floor there was a catalog with a photo on the cover of a woman resting in an Adirondack chair. Her eyes were closed. Her face was illuminated by the sun and a Mona Lisa smile.

Whatever Kool-Aid that chick is drinking, you could use some.

Cathy flipped open the catalog.

Omega Institute for Holistic Studies
Awakening the Best in the Human Spirit

Well, that sounded pretty good. Isn't that what she had been searching for with the drastic change she had made to her life? She certainly hadn't been her best for a long time.

There were workshops from April to October. Frankly, it was mind-boggling. She read about Qigong, Yoga, Mindfulness, Past Life Regressions. There were even couples' weekends to promote sensuality and intimacy. Hmmm. As if she could even remember…

One by one, she looked through the bios of the various instructors. None of them were familiar to her. She was intrigued by metaphysical ideas but could easily become uncomfortable with stuff that was too "out there."

Feeling pretty discouraged, Cathy closed the catalog. As she did, it slipped off her lap onto the floor and fell open to a week in June. She picked it up and peered at the page. Theo London. *Labyrinth of Happiness.*

Something about the workshop title intrigued her. What a cool name. The search for happiness did seem like a spiral that went round and round. Getting to the center was so elusive.

Maybe, she'd have to take a little scouting trip.

That's my girl!

THE FIRST STEP

After a lot of procrastination, Cathy was on her way to Omega to check it out and, if it wasn't too weird, register for the workshop in June.

It was a breathtaking May Day. The birds were singing. And so was Cathy.

Amy had given her a CD of oldies, mostly Motown. Cathy had her windows rolled down and she was doing her best imitation of Diana Ross wailing, *Stop! In the name of love,* as she drove down the long driveway lined with walkers.

In high spirits, Cathy made her way to Guest Services. She came in with a big smile and energetic voice. "Hello, I'm hoping to buy a lunch ticket."

The young woman with braided hair seemed to wince visibly. She barely mouthed a response. "Excuse me. It's our silent retreat week. There's no talking on campus."

Instantly, Cathy felt like crawling under a rock. She pictured herself riding along, singing at the top of her lungs. To Motown. What a way to make an entrance.

Chagrinned, Cathy whispered, "Oh, I'm sorry. I didn't know. Well, maybe I'll just walk over to the dining room and take a look."

The woman gave her a map. Cathy made her way down the path. It cut through a series of gardens. Benches and Adirondack chairs were positioned here and there. She had to admit that the grounds were incredibly peaceful and beautiful.

Feeling totally shaken by her faux pas, Cathy couldn't help remembering the silent retreats that were part of her Catholic grade school experience. In the older grades, for one day every year they all came to school as usual, but they were not permitted to talk. For Cathy, it was pure torture.

Finally, she came to a big dining hall with steps on two sides leading up to an enormous wraparound porch. It was very old-fashioned and cozy, with swinging screen doors.

Tentatively, she climbed up the stairs to the dining hall and peeked in. The large, round tables were crowded with people. They looked perfectly nice, not weird at all. But the silence was creepy.

Cathy turned around and walked back down the steps. Today had not been what she had hoped. She started to head up the hill to her car.

Chicken!

Would you please leave me alone? This is not for me.

Omega is out of the box for you. I want to see you like you were back in college—pushing the envelope, trying new things on a daily basis.

It doesn't feel right.

So I don't get it. You come all the way here just to turn around and run.

They're having a silent retreat week. I arrived blasting my music. I couldn't talk to anyone at the dining hall.

You're just freaked out because of grade school. Let's face it, those retreats were pretty awful. But this silent thing at Omega is just this week. It won't be like this when you come in June.

But I don't know what it will be like. That's what I wanted to find out today.

The only way to find out is to go out on a limb and sign up! Wasn't it cool the way the catalog fell open to something that appealed to you? Don't you think that that meant something?

Maybe ...

I know you felt it too. Now, look, are you going to just crawl back into your cave for the rest of your life, or are you going to take a few chances?

That's really not fair. I've been trying lots of new things.

Oh yeah, I forgot. The library book club. The gym. Whoo-hoo! Give the nice lady a medal. Then, there's Bob. He already has a girlfriend. Isn't he going to India with her this summer?

You are hitting below the belt.

Yup. I know you're not ready for a steady beau, but how about a little guided soul-searching at a place around the corner, which obviously really interested you, or you wouldn't have come in the first place.

So, you think I should sign up?

I think you came here for a reason. Don't panic now. Go for it. What's the worst that can happen?

I'll lose a bunch of money and a weekend.

You're a big time TV writer. C'mon. I think you can afford it. As far as the time—it's not as if your weekends are so booked. But if you'd rather sit home and write in your journal, be my guest.

THE WORKSHOP

The atmosphere was completely different when Cathy arrived a month later. People were chatting wherever she looked. Thank goodness.

She walked over to the dining hall. She scanned the tables on the large porch and spotted one with a couple of open chairs. The people at the table looked professionally dressed, like they might have just come up from the city. Taking a deep breath, Cathy moved up to the table. "Is this seat taken?" She was greeted by equally warm smiles.

"Not at all. Please sit down."

"I'm Meg. What workshop are you here for?" the woman next to her asked.

"I'm taking Labyrinth of Happiness. How about you?"

"I'm doing Past Life Regressions," Meg answered.

"Have you been to Omega before?" Cathy asked.

"Oh yes, I come every summer. This is my eighth time," Meg replied happily.

A woman appeared at Cathy's elbow. "May I sit here?" she asked pleasantly, as she placed her tray on the table.

"Of course," Cathy said as she assessed her new table mate. She was a lot older than most of the people at the table, with short gray hair.

"I'm Pat," the woman said. "What course are you taking?"

"Theo London," Cathy answered.

Pat reacted with enthusiasm. "Me too. Oh honey, you're going to love him. Theo is such a wonderful speaker." Pat said Theo's name with a kind of reverence. "We're going to have so much fun." With that, Pat turned and introduced herself to the person on her other side.

Cathy thought it was a little odd that Pat had called her "honey." But she seemed very nice. With a pang, Cathy found herself thinking about her mother. How many times in the last year had she wished that her mother was still alive? Her mother had been her best friend and cheerleader. Her mother had always given her perspective.

Pat turned back to her and artfully started asking Cathy about herself. In a matter of moments, Cathy was pouring out her heart talking about her job and her recent divorce.

Pat squeezed Cathy's hand. "Oh honey, you've come to the right place. We've all been through those times. I can't wait to find out how you feel after the weekend. Let's talk on Sunday."

Hesitantly, Cathy said, "Okay."

"We'll have lunch after the last session," Pat declared confidently. "Your mind will probably be blown, so you'll need a debriefing."

After dinner, Cathy made her way out of the dining hall down a dark path, which she thought led to the main hall. It was shadowy. As she stepped off the side path to the main walkway, she almost collided with a man walking along. "Oh, hello," she said, a little startled.

"Hello," he responded.

She looked at his face. Glasses, a sparkle in his eyes. She had done her research. Oh my. "It's you," she stammered reflexively.

"I'm Theo," he commented with his lovely British accent. "What is your name?" He kept walking as he talked.

"I'm Cathy."

"I like your necklace," he commented. "It twinkles like the stars."

Cathy could feel herself blushing. "Oh, thank you."

"Are you heading to my workshop?"

"Yes, I am. I've never done anything like this before."

"I hope you will find it enlightening."

"I'm sure I will."

And with that, they were at the front door of the main hall. Gracefully, Theo slipped off his shoes, waved goodbye, and disappeared inside.

Cathy just stood there. What a weird coincidence

Suddenly feeling impulsive, Cathy walked right up to the front row. At first glance it seemed that all the chairs were taken. Then, two women who were sitting next to the middle aisle said, "This one is still free." They picked up the stuff they had tossed onto the third chair. If she was going to do this, she was going to do it all the way.

"Oh, thank you so much," Cathy said gratefully.

Angela and Maxine introduced themselves, and the three of them chatted until a hush came over the group as Theo materialized in the front of the room and began talking—just the way he had spoken to her just thirty minutes ago. He was utterly relaxed as he walked around. Cathy was delighted that she was sitting in the front row. She felt like he was talking right to her.

"Good evening, ladies and gentlemen. Let's jump right in with *happiness*, the center of the labyrinth. I know you're all thinking—why in the world are we here for the whole weekend when we'll be done with this stuff in an hour."

Cathy laughed along with the large group. Perfect. No nonsense here. Well, she hadn't been happy for a long time.

Words and ideas flooded the room. Theo talked about transformation and acceptance. Cathy found herself unable to write fast enough.

Suddenly, Theo stopped. "Now, I have a question for you. What do you want?" He walked back and forth making eye contact one by one with everyone. When his eyes met hers, Cathy felt a jolt of energy.

"Don't overthink this. Just jot down your first reaction quickly. Then, I'd like you to put your notebook away, sit comfortably with your hands in your lap, place your feet on the floor, and close your eyes. Then, as much as possible, let your mind go blank and concentrate on your breath going in and out. If a thought comes to you, let that thought float away and pop like a bubble. We are going to meditate for twenty minutes."

Cathy stared at her notebook in a panic. It was like a test that she was completely unprepared for. She squeezed her pen. *I want to be happy. That's why I'm taking this course. I want to be the real me, whoever I am.* Oh god. What a lame answer.

But she had no more time to think about her answer. They were going to meditate! She had never done anything like that. What kind of an airy-fairy workshop had she gotten herself into? She thought about getting up and leaving, but she would make a spectacle of herself. She didn't have the nerve.

Cathy took a deep breath. Okay. When in Rome. She needed to stay open-minded. It was only for twenty minutes. Surely, she could manage that.

At first Cathy felt unbelievably uncomfortable. But then something about the effect of the whole group meditating together seemed to pull her into their energy sphere. She found her shoulders relaxing, her breathing slowing down. She tried to focus on her breath going in and out, but quickly found that she couldn't pay attention to it. Thoughts came and went, but Cathy's mind couldn't commit to any of them. Just like Theo had said, they were floating away and vanishing.

A bell rang. Cathy's eyes opened.

Smiling, Theo said, "See you tomorrow."

Cathy felt a little light-headed driving home. What had just happened to her?

I'm proud of you. The front row!

I know. I'm not sure what got into me. But it was great being that close.

That meditation stuff was frustrating. I kept wanting to talk.

Thank goodness you kept quiet.

It was hard.

SATURDAY

At nine o'clock sharp, Theo appeared in the front of the hall looking fresh as a daisy. Cathy wondered how he did it.

"Let's take our first step on the labyrinth. How do we find happiness?"

And they were off! His words flowed like a waterfall. Cathy wrote and wrote until she felt like her fingers were going to fall off.

> *You must have chaos within you to give birth to a dancing star.*
> —*Nietzche*

Cathy had to smile to herself. Well, she should be creating a whole constellation in that case.

Every idea that Theo developed triggered more questions for Cathy and apparently for everyone else. After an hour and a half, Theo asked if there were any questions. Forty hands shot up. Two people asked very complicated questions. Then Theo called on Pat. She cut right through all the confusion, paraphrasing the previous questions so they could be understood.

When they took a break, Cathy went over to Pat. "Thank you very much. Your comments were really helpful."

"Thanks, honey," Pat said. "I've been reading Theo's books for a long time. It isn't easy material."

In what seemed like moments, Theo was ready to begin again. "Now that you've had a chance to move around, I'd like us to meditate."

Cathy couldn't believe it. They were meditating again. This workshop had the wrong title.

Theo sat in silence for several minutes. Surprisingly, Cathy could feel herself drifting off. Then Theo spoke again, "Today, I'm going to ask you to imagine a time when you felt really happy. How, exactly, did you feel?"

Cathy concentrated on her body. She could feel her heart beating. She could feel a smile creeping onto her face.

Theo spoke softly again. "I have one more question. What made you so happy?"

Before any time seemed to have passed, the bell rang.

There was a hush in the room. No one said a word. It was as if they were all coming back from someplace far away.

"Would anyone like to share what they remembered that made them so happy?"

Many hands flew up.

People were eager to talk about their childhood birthdays, their parents' approval, winning an important game, the birth of a child.

Theo nodded. "All of your memories come from lovely heart-warming moments. But, wouldn't it be nice if we could be happy for no real reason? To stay in the center of the labyrinth all the time?"

It was time for lunch. Feeling a little light-headed, Cathy gathered up her purse and looked for Pat. She caught up to her on the path to the dining hall, walking with three other people. Pat was clearly the "wisewoman" of their workshop. Cathy managed to sit at the same table as Pat, but not next to her.

Instead, Cathy started talking to the woman on her right—Annie. Annie looked at her tray of food and commented, "This is not how I usually eat."

Cathy gave Annie an appraising look. Annie was not young, but she had a very slim and youthful figure. "Well, however you do eat, you look great."

Annie laughed. "Thank you. But I owe my body to Dr. Martin."

And with that, Annie went on to rave about the nutritionist who had changed her body and life. For some reason, Cathy found herself scribbling down the doctor's name in her notebook.

It was one o'clock when they finished lunch. Pat was still engrossed in conversation. Most of the people were going back to their rooms for a little rest. Cathy didn't have a room so she went out onto the grounds and found a couple of Adirondack chairs in the shade. She had to laugh at herself. She had become the cover of the Omega catalog.

A little while later, Cathy heard footsteps. She opened her eyes. It was Pat. "Is anyone sitting here, honey?"

Cathy was delighted. "No, please sit down. I live around here, so I don't have a room to go back to."

"Me too," Pat said.

Cathy thought that Pat might want to just close her eyes and take a rest. But, right away, Pat started asking her questions, picking up where they had left off at dinner the night before.

Cathy wasn't sure why she felt so comfortable talking to Pat. Before she knew it, she was pouring out her heart about how she felt living alone after all those years with Bob.

Pat smiled. "As Theo said this morning, there is no such thing as a coincidence. You are attending this workshop for a reason. How, exactly, did you end up here?"

Cathy told Pat her story. A little embarrassed, she described how the catalog just seemed to fall open.

Pat nodded with a radiant smile on her face. "Synchronicity. The universe presented you with an opportunity, and you had the awareness to follow it. Most people just ignore most of the possibilities that are offered to them in life. Most people would have picked up the catalog and tossed it out. But you were brave enough to pay attention."

This woman was making her feel wonderful, just like her mother always had. "I'm not sure I was being brave. It was more like desperate. I freak out just about every Saturday night when I'm alone."

Pat talked about her first marriage and divorce. "Change is very uncomfortable. But discomfort isn't a bad thing. In order to grow, you have to change. Imagine how it must feel to be a caterpillar that breaks down into a cellular soup in the cocoon? That must feel pretty uncomfortable, don't you think? But, think of the reward—having that soup become an exquisite butterfly."

The afternoon session flew by. In a bit of a haze, Cathy made it home and made herself a simple dinner. Then she settled herself in her recliner with a notepad. Theo had given them homework. They were to write a story about themselves, really sort of a fairytale where all their dreams come true.

But what were her dreams? What did she want? For the longest time, all she had wanted was to end the everyday unhappiness that she had felt in her marriage. Well, that was accomplished. So now what?

Theo believed that the universal desire of people was to be happy. Cathy agreed. What's more, Theo seemed to believe that it was possible.

So, what did she want to make her happy?

Theo had said today that the ultimate goal was to be happy for no reason. Not because of more money, or love, or a better car or house. Just because.

Cathy would love for that to be true. However, at the moment, she thought she needed some things to happen to fill her life, to stimulate her, to make her feel like a new person. Today was a start.

She started jotting down notes. She wanted:

1) *Happiness*
2) *To feel good about herself (for too long, she had been feeling horrible about ending the marriage and breaking up the family)*
3) *Creative fulfillment (with a family and Bob's demanding job she couldn't have taken on much more, but now she could do anything)*
4) *Her children to accept the divorce*
5) *New interests, new friends, new adventures*

Here you go again—ducking the truth! Jeez, you've been sitting

in that hall all day digging down to the essential truth of life, of happiness. Would you please get real.

What do you mean?

Honestly, do I have to spoon-feed you everything? Do you remember how you decided to go to Omega in the first place?

(RELUCTANTLY)   You told me to look at the catalog.

Well, at least you remember that! And I told you to look at the catalog because ...

Because I was upset about being home on a Saturday night.

Because you are a social creature who loves to go out, who used to love the opposite sex, who dated a gazillion guys while in her freshman year in college.

Oh please, that was a hundred years ago. I don't want that anymore.

No? Well, I do. I love to laugh and play. I remember all those cute guys swirling around and paying attention to us.

Well, they are not cute anymore. They are bald, out of shape, and stuck-in-their-ways now.

That's ridiculous. Is Nancy's new guy like that?

I guess not. But she was lucky.

She wasn't lucky. She was brave. She went online.

Would you stop. That's out of the question.

I'll take that off the table for the moment. But how about an occasional dinner, movie, or concert on a Saturday night... with a man? Would that be so awful?

How is that going to happen?

I'm no expert at this visualization stuff, but somehow, I think the first step is to just acknowledge that you would like that. Theo didn't

ask you to write how you made it happen. He just suggested that you identify what you want.

Okay, okay. Got it. Can I get back to my list now?

Be my guest.

With a deep breath, she picked up her pen again and reluctantly wrote:

6) Saturday night dates

With her notes in front of her, Cathy started writing her "dream story."

Cathy had high hopes that her life was going to change. She didn't know exactly how it was going to change, but she knew it would because she was the one who had the power to change it.

She kept herself open to all the possibilities that crossed her path. She tried new things. She worked hard during the week and received a lot of positive feedback from Lorraine. Every weekend was full of new friends and new adventures. She was busy every Saturday night. Whenever Cathy looked at herself in a mirror, she was smiling. She was happy.

SUNDAY

A no-nonsense Theo briskly entered the room and asked them to pull out their dream story and read it before they meditated.

Obediently, everyone took out their story and settled down. The bell rang.

Cathy read through the page that she had written last night. It felt funny to read something about herself in the third person. But Theo was right, it made her feel like more of an observer of that person, Cathy. Then she closed her eyes and focused on her breath going in and out.

It wasn't long before Cathy felt herself slipping off.

She was barely aware of a tiny ding. Cathy had to consciously will herself to return. She had definitely been somewhere else. She couldn't believe that, after only three meditations, she was able to slip off to this other place so easily.

It was already getting late. Theo, obviously feeling time pressure, went into a new gear. He talked about meditation, acceptance, savoring the moment. Cathy's head was swimming. "The path to happiness is a labyrinth. It seems very complicated. You feel like you're going 'round and 'round. But, if you trust yourself and still your mind with meditation, in the end you come to the center and you're there."

"It has been my great pleasure to talk with you about my favorite subject. Thank you all so much for coming." And with that, Theo made his way out of the room.

Cathy made her way over to Pat, who was surrounded by people. Pat seemed to have infinite patience for talking to everyone. Cathy sat down to wait.

After some time, Pat managed to extricate herself from her circle. She gathered up her belongings. "Okay, honey, let's go eat. I'm starving."

Now that Cathy thought about it, she was too. They walked companionably over to the dining hall.

"You've never meditated before, have you?" Pat asked.

"No, I really knew nothing about it. I have to admit that I was pretty skeptical."

"How did you feel after our session this morning?"

Cathy was almost reluctant to describe what had happened to her. "Actually, I am a little flabbergasted. In the other sessions, I was restless. But this morning I found that I just slipped off. It was so easy. And then, this weird thing happened. I started seeing colors. And, finally, the colors coalesced into this bright blue ball."

Pat stopped in her tracks and looked at Cathy. She held Cathy's arm. "Oh, that's wonderful, honey. You saw the Blue Pearl!"

Cathy repeated, "the Blue Pearl?"

"Some people believe that the Blue Pearl is a manifestation of your soul, your consciousness. At the very least, it seems to indicate that something of spiritual significance is happening. Some people spend their entire lives hoping to see it."

Cathy nodded slowly as she digested this. "It did feel special." She didn't want to carry on about it too much, but she was thrilled that it had happened. She felt like that good girl again who had gotten an A+ on a paper. She hadn't felt like a good girl for such a long time.

"Well, as I said before, I think you were meant to be here. I'm so glad."

All too quickly, lunch was over. Cathy suddenly felt very wistful. "You know," she said haltingly, "I have truly loved getting to know you. We don't live that far from each other. Could we get together for coffee, or something?"

"Yes, I'd love to keep up with you too, honey," Pat replied squeezing Cathy's hand. She fished a card out of her purse. "Here's my card. Call me anytime."

Cathy tucked the card into her pocket. "Oh, thank you." They walked to the parking lot and exchanged a big hug, and then Pat got into her car and drove off.

Still feeling a little light-headed, Cathy slowly made her way to her car, one of the last ones in the lot. On an impulse, she pulled Pat's card out of her pocket.

Pat Love, MSW. Therapist

Cathy couldn't believe that Pat's last name was Love. But it certainly seemed appropriate. Cathy felt chagrinned that she had never even asked Pat what she did. And Pat had never volunteered much of anything about herself. Cathy guessed that it was not surprising that Pat was so easy to talk to. She was a professional.

Cathy tucked Pat's card into in her purse and started her car.

THE FIX-UP

Despite how powerful the workshop had been, Cathy found herself immediately reverting to her old routine. She tried to meditate once, but found that she couldn't settle down.

Her week was crazy busy. There was a big writers' meeting in the city on Friday. She had to complete her script a day early. Then, on Saturday she was invited to a neighborhood party. The Taylors, who were hosting it, told her that they had invited a friend who had recently lost his wife. It was obvious that they were doing a little matchmaking.

At first, Cathy didn't like the idea. But she thought about what Theo had said about coincidence. All right. This was an opportunity that was falling into her lap. She should try to stay open and positive.

She got home from the city late on Friday, slept late on Saturday and almost shrieked when she looked at herself in the mirror. She had big bags under her eyes and looked like hell. How in the world was she going to meet someone tonight?

She started rummaging through her closet for an upgrade to her usual summer outfit of elastic-waisted shorts and a T-shirt. She dug in the back of her closet and found some old summer dresses. One by one, she tried them on. One by one, she groaned. The bulge around her middle was way worse than she had thought. Brutally, she took off her clothes and stared at herself in her full-length mirror, an action she realized that she normally avoided at all cost. OMG. What had happened to her body? Now that she thought about it, she realized that she had eaten her way through the divorce.

Almost shaking, she found an old black sundress that was pretty forgiving. Well, if she put on a big necklace, maybe no one would notice her middle.

She found herself getting more and more nervous as the day went on.

What is the problem?

I'm not ready to meet someone new.

Are you kidding me? You asked for it—you got it. Might I remind you that you're the one who wrote down "Saturday night dates" on your wish list just last week.

Only because you badgered me.

If I were you, I'd be down on my knees saying a prayer of thanks. That Theo is a genius. I'm even amazed at how well that story thing worked.

But it could be so awkward. I'll probably be completely tongue-tied.

In the highly unlikely chance that you have nothing to say, just smile and walk away.

But everybody will be watching.

Jeez. You've been writing too many scripts. Everybody will be enjoying themselves, paying no attention to you and your psychodrama. Get over your inflated ego.

(BIG PAUSE) Well, I'm scared. I have this big roll of fat around my middle.

Do you honestly think that the poor man who lost his wife a few months ago is going to be feeling you up?

(HAS TO LAUGH) Well, if you put it like that.

You know perfectly well that you don't look awful. You may have put on a few pounds in the last couple of years. Big deal. I seem to remember that Bob isn't as trim as he once was. He has already jumped back into the pool. Are you going to let him do all the splashing?

Two hours later, Cathy was as ready as she was going to be. She looked at herself critically in the mirror. Her make-up had done a pretty good job of hiding the circles under her eyes. Her streaky blond hair fell softly around her face. Her fun jewelry added a sparkle to her outfit. All she could think of was, thank goodness for black. Pink or Orange might be the New Black, but she liked the Old Black.

She stared at herself. She looked scared to death.

For a split second, she saw herself as she had looked in college when she was getting ready for a big night out. She didn't think that she had ever attended a mixer without meeting someone new to date. But she had been a bright-eyed, cute little thing then. Where had that confident, funny, flirtatious young woman gone? How in the world was her tired, sad, lined face ever going to attract anyone?

It took her awhile to relax at the Taylors. Just when she had totally forgotten about her "fix-up" and was finally having a really good time chatting about plants that the deer wouldn't devour, Mark

Taylor appeared at her elbow with a thin, balding man with a beard. Cathy glanced at him and immediately thought, he looks like my grandfather.

With a big smile Mark said, "Cathy, I'd like to introduce you to Harold. Harold is an old tennis partner of mine. He's a professor at Columbia."

Well. An old tennis partner is certainly accurate. This is who the Taylors want you to meet?

Would you please go away? I can't handle you on top of all of this.

Sure, sweetheart. Good luck.

Cathy swallowed and smiled as best she could. "Very nice to meet you. What do you teach?"

The man attempted a strained smile. "I am a Professor of Philosophy. Actually, a Professor Emeritus. My special focus was Nietzsche."

Oh dear, the man practically clicked his heels when he answered her. He had a faint German accent. "How interesting," Cathy responded politely.

"And what about you? What do you do?"

She was standing here with a European intellectual, and she had to tell him what she did. For a second, Cathy felt like making something up. Then, she straightened her shoulders. "Actually, I write for television. I am a soap opera writer."

"A soap opera writer?" Harold furrowed his brow in confusion.

Of course, "Professor Nietzsche" probably didn't even own a television. Cathy smiled apologetically, "A soap opera is the name for a serialized drama that is shown during the afternoon. They got the name 'soap' operas back in the day because soap companies used to own the shows. And, they were very dramatic, like operas."

Harold's face lit up with recognition. "Oh, you mean like *General Hospital*. My wife loved that show." And then, his face crumpled. "I'm very sorry. My wife passed away in February."

Cathy couldn't help feeling touched by the professor's distress. "I'm so sorry."

Harold tried to pull himself together. "One has to go on. But I miss her terribly. I sometimes feel so alone," he mumbled.

This nakedly vulnerable confession cut right to Cathy's heart. "You know, I am also alone a lot now. I recently got divorced, which I know is quite different from losing your wife. However, if you'd ever like to come to dinner and talk, I'd like to have a reason to cook a proper meal."

The German Professor looked a little taken aback by Cathy's impulsive invitation. Then he said rather stiffly, "I'd like that very much."

DINNER DATE

Just a week later, Cathy was flying around her kitchen trying to get ready for the dinner wondering what she had gotten herself into.

You are an imbecile! Why in the world did you invite that old geezer to dinner?

Because he seemed so sad. And, let's face it, I hate always eating alone. It seemed like a good idea to have someone over for dinner. And it's not so scary to start with someone like him...

Oh, so you're just using him for practice?

No, I'm not! Well, maybe I am. Somehow, I have to figure out how to do this. It's been thirty years since I've been alone on anything that resembled a date with a man other than Bob. I have no idea what to talk about, how to be ...

Don't be ridiculous. You could talk to a statue all night, if necessary.

Well, that won't be necessary. Harold is a professor. I'm sure he'll have lots of interesting things to say.

Brushed up on your Nietzsche lately?

Stop it. It's just one evening. I haven't cooked dinner for anyone in ages.

It certainly looks like it. You've been running around like a chicken without a head for the last two hours.

Well, when things were going downhill, Bob and I stopped entertaining. I guess I'm a little out of practice.

You think? You couldn't have started with coffee at Starbucks in a nice, public place? First off, you had to have him to your house with your bedroom right upstairs?

Look, the Taylors introduced him to me. I'm sure he's not a serial killer or rapist.

Okeydokey. Whatever you say. Break a leg, sweetie.

Harold arrived on the dot of eight o'clock. German precision, she thought. He looked as uncomfortable as she felt. He presented her with a bottle of red wine.

He wore an open-collared shirt and a well-worn jacket. She could faintly smell pipe smoke. Again, she thought of her grandfather.

Cathy found herself talking too fast, too much. "Did you have any trouble finding my house? It's a little hard to see the number on the mailbox. Sometimes, I even drive by it." For heaven's sake. She had to calm down. "Would you like a glass of wine?"

Cathy offered Harold the white wine that was chilling in her refrigerator.

Harold looked very apologetic, as if he was breaking every rule of etiquette. "If you wouldn't mind, might I have a glass of the red wine I brought?"

Cathy felt embarrassed. Just because she preferred white wine didn't mean that everyone liked it. "Oh, of course. She fumbled for the wine opener in her messy utensil drawer. Her potato masher got stuck in the back of the drawer. She had to wrestle with it to get it unstuck.

"May I?" Harold asked, pointing to the opener.

"Oh, thank you," Cathy breathed a sigh of relief.

With no effort, Harold got the bottle open in seconds.

Cathy led the way out to her screened porch. It was a lovely summer night. "Cheers!" She clinked her glass with his.

"Prosit," Harold said solemnly.

Cathy took a gulp and tried not to panic. This man was so serious and so contained. How was she going to get through dinner? Only a few minutes had passed. It seemed like an eternity. Why had she thought this was a good idea? The man was still grieving. There was an elephant in the room. She didn't know how to proceed without talking about his wife's death. "So, please tell me about your work," she finally managed.

Harold's thin pale hands held his wine glass as he stared into the ruby liquid. "As I told you, I am retired. I was working on a book on Nietzsche. But then my wife got very sick." He turned his head away to collect himself. "I'm afraid I haven't had much inclination to continue ..." His voice trailed off.

All right, all right, Cathy thought to herself. This is a test. A soap scene. Just write it. She took a deep breath and trusted her instinct. "When did you find out she was sick?"

Harold's eyes flashed open and looked into hers for the first time. It seemed he was assessing whether she really wanted to know, whether she really wanted to listen.

She seemed to pass the test. His meticulously controlled face loosened into a myriad of emotions. "In fact, it was just about a year ago, last summer ..."

Somehow, Cathy managed to serve the chicken with mustard sauce, farm-fresh green beans, and salad without a problem. Harold talked about the spectacular love he and his wife had shared, her devastating diagnosis, and finally her death. It was obvious that the man had so much bottled up. Cathy went on autopilot, nodding and making sympathetic noises.

While Harold talked and talked, he drank glass after glass of his Pinot Noir. While Harold talked and talked, Cathy drank glass after glass of her Sauvignon Blanc.

At 11:30, Cathy looked at her watch.

Unfailingly polite, Harold caught her glance. Stiffly, he pushed back from the table. "Oh my, I have been remiss. It is late. I have overstayed my welcome. I must go."

Alarmed and a little unsteady, Cathy asked, "Are you sure you're all right to drive?"

What in the world was she going to do if he wasn't? She really wasn't prepared to offer him a room for the night. But she couldn't let him go drunk into the night on country roads. Cathy vaguely remembered that she could be legally liable if something happened to him. This whole "dating" business was so much more complicated than she remembered.

Harold gave her a sweet smile. He touched her hand. It was the first time he had touched her all night. "Please don't worry. I am afraid that since Anna's death, it is very typical for me to consume a bottle of wine every night." He made a rueful face. "I will be fine." With true professorial authority, Harold moved to the door.

Cathy followed him. He seemed perfectly steady on his feet. She prayed that he was really all right.

At the door, he turned back to her. Now, what was he doing? Cathy felt pins of anxiety prick her skin. Was he going to try to kiss her? Was he going to ask her out again? Oh dear, how should she handle this?

"You were very, very kind to ask me to dinner," he began formally. "The chicken was delicious. It has been a long time since I've had a home-cooked meal. I'm afraid I was extremely tedious, as only an old professor can be, monopolizing the conversation."

"It wasn't like that at all. I felt privileged to hear about your life. I am very, very sorry about your wife's premature death. But it sounds like you had a very special relationship, one that most people never get to experience. I must admit, I'm a bit envious."

Harold nodded, unable to speak. His eyes glistened, and one tear escaped from the corner of his left eye. "Yes, I try to remind myself how fortunate I have been."

Cathy felt like her heart was being ripped out. Spontaneously, she reached for his hand. "I know it seems like you will never feel better. But you will. You have lots of life ahead of you."

Harold patted her hand. "Thank you, my dear. You have been very, very generous listening to an old man's ramblings. I do hope you will let me return your hospitality and take you to dinner."

He began to lean towards her. Oh no. But then, still holding her hand, he lifted it and kissed it very gently. A European gentleman through and through. He straightened up and turned to open the door, all in one swift motion.

And with that he was gone.

Cathy watched him get into his car and disappear into the night. She said a little prayer that he would get home safely.

She closed the door and suddenly the room was spinning. Unsteadily, she walked over to her couch and flopped down. Then, she began to cry.

THE MORNING AFTER

For a minute, Cathy didn't know what had hit her when she opened her eyes. A wave of nausea, distress and bewilderment washed over her. The sun was streaming through the cracks of her blackout curtains. It was after ten. Why had she slept so late? That tiny movement of her head made her stomach flip. Her eye caught a ball of fabric on the floor. It looked like her black dress. And then, little by little, it came back to her. She had cooked dinner for a man last night. For Harold, the Professor. It was sort of like a date. The first date she had been on in thirty years. He had been so sad. He had drunk a whole bottle of wine—so had she.

Was that why she felt so bad? Cathy ruthlessly delved into her feelings. It's true that she had drunk too much. That certainly didn't help. But it was more than that. She used to be so good at having dinner parties. But she was used to hosting them with Bob. They had a whole routine worked out. Last night had been so strange, so painful.

Cathy kicked the sheets off. She was suddenly burning up. She didn't like feeling so awkward in a social situation. She didn't like the fact that Harold seemed like such an old man, and that the Taylors had obviously thought that he might be a match for her. She didn't like the truth that men around her age were going to have baggage. Serious baggage. Just like she did. It certainly wasn't the same as the last time she had dated in her twenties and everyone was pretty much a clean slate. No one was going to be a clean slate. The men were either going to be widowers or divorced. Or never married at all—which was probably worse.

A wave of despair came over her. Why had she gotten divorced?

She couldn't think why.

Eventually, she dragged herself out of bed. Her head throbbed as she walked into the kitchen. It looked like twenty bombs had been dropped on it. How could that be when there had only been the two of them? Apparently, she hadn't been able to face the mess last night. A pan of chicken was still sitting on the stove, now ruined. The salad was stuck to the sides of the bowl.

But the worst of it was still sitting out on the screen porch. When she pushed open the porch door, wincing from the blinding summer sun, the two empty wine bottles were sitting there like a damnation.

She crumpled onto her chaise and surveyed the damage.

What in the world were you doing last night? You're not some stupid Freshman coed getting caught up in her first fraternity party. You're the mother of three grown children!

I know, I know. I'm really not sure what happened. I was just so nervous.

You knew last night was just about getting back in the saddle. You knew that he was too old for you. You knew that he had recently lost his wife. You told him that it was just a chance for the two of you to have dinner—a chance to talk.

That's true.

So, why are you making such a fuss out of the whole thing? It was one lousy night. You drank too much. Big deal. Make some coffee. Eat something. Take some Ibuprofen. Get your act together. This is not your first rodeo, Cowgirl.

(SOFTLY) It feels like it, though. It feels like I got tossed off the horse. It feels like I have no clue how to ride a horse.

Are we having a "pity party" again? Are you kidding? No clue how to ride a horse?! I seem to recall a lot of blue ribbons back in the day. So, you've fallen off the horse one night. Call in the clown, dust yourself off, and get moving. It's a beautiful day.

Two hours later, Cathy was just moving out to the porch with her third cup of coffee when the phone rang. She snatched it up like a lifeline.

"So how was it?" asked the voice with no preamble.

"Amy!" Cathy reacted. "Oh jeez. I was a hot mess. I am a hot mess."

"What happened?" Amy asked soothingly.

So relieved to vent, Cathy confessed about how awkward she had felt. How half the time she had forced herself to pretend that she was writing a script. How she had nothing to say.

Amy interrupted, "*You* had nothing to say?!!!"

"Honestly, Ame. My body was sitting there with him. But my head was someplace else watching me make a fool of myself. Thank god I finally had the nerve to ask him about his deceased wife. The poor man talked for three straight hours. And I drank for three straight hours. A whole bottle of wine!"

"Ouch. You must be hurting."

"In more ways than one." She took a big gulp of coffee. Her voice dropped almost to a whisper. "Why did I do it, Amy? It'll never be the same. I miss my old life."

Amy took a big breath. "You're right, Cath. Your life will never be the same. But as I recall from all those conversations all those years, *that* is a good thing. You will probably have more painful evenings. But change is like that. At the moment, you feel crummy. You have a hangover—but you survived. I'm not sure I could do it."

There was a pause between the two friends. Cathy knew all too well that Amy's marriage had its own problems.

"I think you're the smart one," Cathy said wryly.

"Look, we all do the best we can," Amy muttered. "Instead of thinking about me, I think you should think about Nancy. She's having the time of her life. Ever since she met Matt on Match."

Cathy groaned. "You know how I feel about online dating. I just wish I could meet guys like I used to. It was so easy. So natural. Online dating is so contrived."

"We were in college living in big clusters of kids our age. Everyone was single. Every party, class, and sport we attended had endless possibilities. How many gatherings are you a part of with a group of single, age-appropriate men?"

"None," Cathy admitted reluctantly.

"Exactly," said Amy firmly. "I just wish you'd talk to Nancy. Pick her brain. And in the meantime, do something nice for yourself. Take a swim. I'm not sure why, but you love swimming. Get over yourself."

Cathy had to smile, "Thanks for the tough love, Amy. I needed that."

"True," Amy agreed.

Cathy hung up. It really helped to talk. That was probably the hardest thing about not being married anymore, having no one to talk to. With a sigh, Cathy could feel her mood sink again.

Out of the blue, Cathy thought of meditating. She could sure use something to calm herself now. She settled herself on her chaise and closed her eyes. Within seconds her mind quieted. Her breathing slowed down.

Cathy wasn't sure how long it had been when a sound brought her back. It was like wet laundry on a clothesline snapping in the wind. It was swans flying over the lake. She wondered if she had fallen asleep.

After her swim, she felt like a new person. It was like a baptism, a cleansing. Amy had been so right. Damn that girl.

Later, Cathy decided that she really didn't feel like cooking dinner. She headed to one of her favorite local restaurants that had good French food in an old nineteenth-century tavern. It had a big, comfortable bar that was nice to sit at when you were alone. There was an older man at the bar having a beer.

Before she knew it, the older man had introduced himself. "I'm Mack. Beautiful day, isn't it?"

Cathy stared at Mack. He had a shaggy salt and pepper beard. She couldn't help wondering why so many older men grew facial hair. She soon discovered that Mack was a woodworker. "How interesting. What do you make?"

Mack's face lit up as he slid over to the seat next to her. Then, he was off and running, telling her about his work and his life. He finished off with a flurry. "My friend is having a party next Sunday. Would you like to come?"

It was all Cathy could do not to choke.

Why was this old man asking her out? Obviously, he thought it was possible that she would say yes, or he wouldn't have asked. What was she going to say?

Quickly, she made a decision. If she said she was busy, he might suggest another date.

She beamed him a friendly smile. "Hey, thank you so much for the invitation, but actually I am seeing someone."

Mack didn't seem upset at all. He flashed her an understanding smile. "I figured a woman like you would be taken. Just thought I'd try."

What an expression. He figured she was *taken*? Cathy took a deep breath. It occurred to her that she should be flattered that he had said that. But something about the whole interaction sent her into a tailspin again.

She quickly paid her check and left. She certainly hoped that she wouldn't have to worry about running into Mack every time she came here.

She practically sprinted to her car.

In a funk again, eh?

Leave me alone, it's been a tough twenty-four hours.

Oh yeah, real tough. You've had two perfectly nice men pay attention to you. What's so tough about that?

They both seem old enough to be my grandfather.

Looked in a mirror lately? They weren't.

I know, I know. But, I'm so scared. I don't want an old man.

I thought you didn't want any man.

(A BIG SIGH) I don't know what I want.

Newsflash!

I miss having someone to do things with.

Look, honey, you're a mess.

I guess I am.

So, if one of your characters was on an emotional roller coast like this, what would you do for her?

(SHE THINKS ABOUT IT SERIOUSLY) I'd probably write a scene for her to talk with a best friend, or her mother.

I think your mother could have helped, but she's dead. You tried Amy this morning. Was her advice enough?

For the moment.

Listen, sweetheart. Do I have to put words in your head? Well, I suppose I am the words in your head. You've done no counseling for yourself during this whole process. Oh yeah, yeah—you saw a counselor with Bob. But, what about you? Maybe a little professional help would be helpful?! Duh—Why do you think they call it "help"?

What do you mean? Who could I talk to? Not that Dr. Stein!

I seem to remember that cool lady from Omega. You got along with her. Wasn't she a therapist?

(ALMOST SWERVES OFF THE ROAD) Oh right—Pat, Pat Love.

Great name. Seems like it's worth a try. She lives up here, right? You said yourself—it was almost like you were meant to meet. Do you still have her card, or have you managed to lose it?

Hey, that's a great idea. I did like her.

I always have good ideas. Now, look for that card when you get home, if you don't drive off the road first.

Cathy's heart was beating as she pulled into her garage. Without even getting out of the car, she started rummaging in her purse. Of course, there was virtually no light in the garage. Her purse was like a black hole.

She checked her change purse first. Nothing.

Because she could barely see, she shoved her fingers into the larger of the zipped pockets on the side of her purse. She found an earring and a stick of gum. Frustrated, she resorted to the two small pockets on the other side of the purse. She honestly didn't think a card would even fit there. But there it was.

Triumphant, she bolted out of the car and headed into the house. Before she lost momentum, she dialed the number.

"Hello."

Cathy almost fell off her chair. She couldn't believe Pat had answered the phone.

"Pat, this is Cathy. I met you at Omega."

"Cathy! How are you, honey? How are things going?"

Pat's voice was so full of warmth and genuine concern that Cathy felt tears prick her eyes. Cathy tried to hold it together. "I'm okay, I guess. But I was wondering if it would be possible to come talk to you. Professionally, I mean. I'm feeling a little … emotional … and confused at the moment."

Pat chuckled. "Welcome to the human race. When would you like to come?"

"Well, in general, Mondays are the best day for me."

"You remember what Theo said about synchronicity. It just so happens that I just got off the phone with a client who cancelled for tomorrow at eleven o'clock."

Cathy gulped. Tomorrow was so soon. It was tomorrow! But she had liked the way Pat had referred to her appointment with a *client*, not a *patient*. Frantically, she searched her mind for a reason to say no. But in her heart of hearts, she knew this was the right move. She didn't usually get her assignment till midday. The timing was perfect. "Yes. Great. I'll see you tomorrow."

AN UNEXAMINED LIFE IS NOT WORTH LIVING

Cathy's eyes fluttered open. Oh my. She had just had the most vivid and strange dream. Distracted by her dream, it took Cathy a while to realize that this was not a normal Monday. She was going to see Pat today. She had better get going.

Cathy arrived in the circular driveway of the address on Pat's card. Golden marigolds lined the edge. There were flowers everywhere. There were three buildings. The one on the right had a sign by the side of the door. Pat Love, MSW. Hollyhocks grew next to the sign.

Cathy let herself into a cozy reception area with a table, couch, and brick fireplace. The house appeared to be very old. It was so charming, Cathy couldn't help feeling delighted. Even going to a therapist in her new Hudson Valley life was like entering the pages of *Country Living*.

Cathy heard footsteps, and Pat appeared from another room. "Hello, honey. I'm so glad you made it." She enfolded Cathy in her arms. How long had it been since she'd been hugged?

They proceeded into a sunny, book-lined office that had a couple of chairs, fresh flowers from the garden, charming watercolor paintings, and a coffee table set up with small objects—shells, twigs, stones, and figures on a tray of sand.

It was as if Pat were reading her mind. "I use that tray for therapy with children. And some adults," she added with a twinkle. "It includes a lot of Jungian symbols."

"Didn't Jung study the symbols in dreams?"

"That's right." Pat nodded and smiled as if Cathy were a very precocious student.

"Funny," Cathy responded. "I rarely remember my dreams. But this morning I woke up from a very strange dream."

"Sit down and tell me about it, honey," Pat prompted eagerly.

"I was walking through a sunny garden full of brilliant flowers when I spotted something shiny between the flowers. It was an iridescent grey. Like a gorgeous black pearl. I moved towards it wondering what it was. Imagine my surprise when I saw that it was a large snake. The weird part was, I wasn't afraid. Instead, I picked the snake up. It didn't thrash around or scare me. It just lay calmly in my arms as I walked to a charming cottage."

"So is the snake a symbol of sexuality?" Cathy asked ruefully. "Didn't Freud think that sex was at the bottom of everything?"

Pat smiled curiously. "Freud may have, but I don't think that's it, honey. Not in this case. A snake is often the symbol of the unconscious. Given the serene and soothing nature of your garden dream, I think you dreamt that you located, picked up, and brought your unconscious ..." She hesitated dramatically, "... to me. Your beautiful, lustrous, black pearl snake unconscious. Mysterious, alluring. I accept it with honor. What a wonderful way to begin."

Cathy was taken aback. Her unconscious? How cool. It had been exactly like that. What's more, somehow her dream had been quite prophetic—right down to Pat's charming cottage, surrounded by flowers. Uncanny.

Pat pulled out a notepad. "I remember quite a lot about you from Omega, but I'd like to review your history so that I can take some notes. Didn't you tell me that your mother passed away pretty recently?"

Cathy gulped. This loss was still so painful to even talk about. "Two years ago. My mother was my best friend. I could really use a mother."

Pat looked her straight in the eye and said softly, "I'll be your mother."

Cathy just knew that Pat understood what she needed. "From the very beginning, I sensed that you could be."

"We all need a mother, honey. It's a universal need. You never outgrow it. Even when your biological mother is gone."

Feeling a closeness that she couldn't have imagined could develop so quickly, Cathy launched into the details of the last few years. Pat commented from time to time, but mostly she wrote down a lot of notes.

"It sounds like you were unhappy for quite a long time. Why did it take you so long to make the decision to divorce?"

Cathy sighed. "It just seemed wrong. It didn't seem like something that a good girl would do."

"Ah, the good girl archetype," Pat commented. "It certainly sounds to me like you were a devoted mother and good wife."

Cathy nodded. "I think I've always been a good mother. But, a good wife? I guess I was at one time."

"I think you tried very hard for a long time. But it doesn't sound like your marriage was enhancing either of you."

"That's it, exactly. We somehow managed to run a good-looking life. But a lot of the time we made each other feel terrible. I was just as guilty of that as he was. There were times I really hated myself. In the end, I thought it was worth the risk of giving up everything to create a chance at real happiness for both of us." Cathy found herself growing pretty emotional. "I think Bob is the happiest I've seen him in a long time. I really am happy about that."

"And you?"

"I keep feeling these waves of regret. Like I gave up something very precious that can never be replaced. And I know it's true. I will never be involved with someone—starting a life, having children— again. I feel discouraged about the future. I thought I was done with men and relationships. I thought I would be fine—with my job, my friends, some traveling. But I feel pretty lonely a lot of the time. I miss the fun of being part of a couple in social situations. The thing is, I'm a party girl at heart. You should have seen me in college. I dated forty-seven different guys my freshman year!"

Pat laughed. "That's quite a record. Then why aren't you doing that now?"

Cathy was speechless. She looked at Pat like she was crazy. Then she began, haltingly. "Because I'm old. Because I'm really scared about the pitfalls of relationships. Because I've been told by any number of friends that there are no men out there anyway. Because I understand that men my age feel entitled to much younger women. Because I feel incredibly nervous about getting intimate with any man, anyhow. Because my body isn't what it used to be. Because the only men I have met are two older men I met this weekend who seemed to be interested in me, but all I could think of was that they reminded me of my grandfather!" Although Cathy was almost whispering when she began, her litany built and built until she was practically shouting.

"Excellent," Pat nodded. "I take it that's why you finally called me last night?"

Cathy's face was burning. "I guess so."

Pat beamed happily. "Someday you're going to thank those older gentlemen for getting you here." She reviewed her notes. "What a lot of mythology you've told me. You've heard of ghost busters? Consider me your myth buster! Let's get started."

Pat smiled coyly. "I believe the first "because" was your age. My-oh-my. You're a veritable Methuselah. Do you feel old?"

"Not really."

Pat nodded. "And, when you look in the mirror, do you think you look bad?"

Cathy flushed. "Well, I don't look like I did when I got married."

"I can't imagine you look a heck of a lot older. You are a very attractive woman."

"When I'm put together I guess I can look pretty good," Cathy agreed hesitantly.

"Do you think you're too old to start again—to have new experiences—to have new loves?"

"I suppose not," Cathy admitted reluctantly.

Pat let out an impatient whoosh of air. "Oh, c'mon. Don't tell me that you don't write 'September romances' on your show all the time! Don't tell me that you don't believe that they *can* happen and *do* happen all the time!"

Cathy held up a hand to stop Pat. "All right, of course I write them. It just seems different when I'm the one in the story."

"You were married for a long time. I think you need to be patient. And I think you need to look inside yourself and reflect on what you want. By the way, how is your meditation practice going?"

Cathy made a guilty face. "I'm afraid that I haven't quite incorporated it into my daily routine yet."

"Look honey. You've been changing your life in so many ways. You need to be kind to yourself. So much of life is establishing a rhythm."

"I'm afraid I've sort of lost the beat. I guess 'lost' is the operative word about the way I feel in general. I was so focused on ending my marriage, negotiating the divorce, and moving out of the house that now that the dust has settled, I don't know what to do."

"As we discussed at Omega, you ended up there for a reason. One of the things that will help you the most is meditating. I'm going to give you some homework today. I'd like you to set aside twenty minutes to meditate every day until I see you next week—assuming that you want to come back."

Cathy nodded eagerly, almost gratefully. It was good to have someone tell her what to do. She was good at homework. "Yes. Of course, I can do that."

"Great. Let's see how you feel next week."

Pat referred to her notes. "Moving on. Number two." She read, "'because I'm scared of the pitfalls of relationships.' Well, who isn't? Isn't that the flame that draws us and terrifies us at the same time?

The irony is, you are a relationship expert. Aren't they what you write about all the time?"

Cathy smiled wryly. "I suppose I am in a way. But not trained, like you. Most of the time my job is to figure out how to complicate the progress of a relationship. A happy couple is a boring couple. A boring couple is bad ratings. I dwell in a world of misunderstandings, obstacles, and triangles."

"I can imagine that you've written about a multitude of relationship problems. But it certainly doesn't sound like you've lived them. Being married for over two decades is no mean feat. Was it terrible the whole time?"

"No, of course it wasn't. We would never have lasted."

"And your parents? Did they stay together?"

"Yes, they did."

"Did you ever have any successful relationships before Bob?"

"Yes, I had several boyfriends in high school and college."

Pat looked her square in the eyes. "So if you were raised by parents who loved to ride horses and you had many years of enjoyment riding horses, what would you do if you got thrown off of a horse? Would you give up riding forever? Or would you get back on the horse?"

Cathy's face burned. "I would get back on the horse."

Pat nodded. "Right." She looked back at her notes. "Because I've been told there are no men out there anyway." Pat again challenged Cathy. "Do you believe everything you're told?"

"No, of course not."

"Do you know many divorced people your age?"

"Yes, quite a few."

"And in each case, presumably, a woman and a *man* became single?"

"Yes."

"So, shouldn't there be, at least in the case of divorces, an equal number of single women and men?"

"Probably, but the men my age all want younger women!" Cathy burst out.

Pat smiled and glanced at her notes. "Oh good, we can tackle number three and four together. I beg to disagree. Men most often want mothers. As we all do. I don't believe all men want playthings. My second husband certainly does not."

"Well, I haven't met any."

"Two men is hardly a comprehensive sample. Have you thought about online dating?"

Cathy shuddered. "Not you too."

"Me too. I have lots of clients who say it can be a really fun and effective way of meeting people."

"I do have one good friend, Nancy, who has had a good experience," Cathy added hesitantly.

Pat pounced on this information. "And have you asked her about her experience?"

"Not really."

"Well, I think you should."

Cathy sighed. "My friend Amy was just nagging me about that yesterday."

"Too bad you have to pay for the same advice today," Pat teased.

"Sometimes, I think you have to hear something a few times before it sinks in," Cathy agreed.

"They always say that the universe knocks three times, in case you ignore the first two times," Pat said. She jotted down another note. So part two of your homework is to call Nancy."

Pat glanced at her watch. "It's getting a little late, so if it's all right with you, I'd like to skip over your fifth excuse, 'because I'm incredibly nervous about intimacy anyhow.'" Pat's eyes twinkled. "Here we go, Dr. Freud. Your dream snake may not have been about this, but there's no avoiding s-e-x."

Cathy groaned. "I know, I know."

"Look honey, it's perfectly natural to feel some misgivings after so many years with one man. But it is an important topic, and I'd like to have some time to do it justice. So, let's save sex for next time and move on to the next item on the list, your body. Obviously, how you feel about your body has a lot to do with how you feel about being close to someone new." Pat leveled a look at Cathy. "Now, why do you feel uncomfortable about your body?"

Cathy's face fell. "My body is nothing like it used to be."

"You have had three children. I think you look great."

"You know, I'm not expecting to be as tight and firm as I was back then, but I have this stuff forming around my middle. I call it my flubber. It looks a bit like cottage cheese. I never had that before. It even bothers me when I'm sitting down. I can't imagine taking my clothes off in front of someone."

Pat assessed her openly. "Well, as far as I can tell, you don't need to do much to get rid of your dreaded flubber. Have you ever worked with a nutritionist?"

"It's funny that you ask. I met someone at Omega who gave me the name of her person. She swore by him."

"Ah," Pat smiled. "Another knock from the universe. For your last bit of homework, why don't you google this doctor and consider seeing him. Plus, I would encourage you to really indulge yourself with some new clothes, possibly a new hairstyle. Whatever it takes for you to feel really good about yourself. How you feel about yourself adds to your attractiveness more than anything else."

Cathy could definitely use some new fun clothes. "Hey, this is great. For homework, I get to meditate, call a friend and shop. That wasn't the way it was in fifth grade."

Pat turned to her book. "So, shall I put you down for next week, same time?"

Cathy beamed. She felt better than she had in a long time. "Absolutely."

So?

So, what?

I'm waiting ...

(TAPS THE WHEEL AS SHE IS DRIVING) Oh, all right. You were right.

Yes, I was, wasn't I? As always! You found someone eager to pull apart your ridiculous myths and play mommy all rolled into one. Winning!

(CAN'T SUPPRESS A SMILE) I do feel better.

And ...

And—thank you.

I heard you singing a minute ago. I can't remember the last time I heard you sing. That's thanks enough. I am on your side, you know. Well, I am your side.

True.

So, what are you going to do next?

I'm going to do my homework.

That's my "good girl."

I really have been wanting to meditate every day. I liked it in the work-shop. Surely I can manage that for a week.

And, you're going to google that nutritionist.

I will.

Do I detect some reluctance?

I don't know where he is, or when I'll have time.

Excuses don't burn calories. That flubber is annoying, even to me.

Okay, okay. Can I go back to singing now?

You are no Adele.

No one can hear me.

I can. One more thing—what about Nancy and online dating?

Look, I really need to feel good about myself before I put myself out there again.

Calling your good friend, Nancy to do some fact finding and putting yourself out there again, are two entirely different things. I didn't hear Pat say that she wanted you to sign up for Match this week. Did you?

No.

I rest my case.

I'm turning on the radio again.

Cathy turned on the radio very loudly and immediately started singing along with Adele at the top of her voice.

HOMEWORK

Cathy found herself singing the whole way home. She felt ten pounds lighter. Now, if only she could actually be ten pounds lighter. She smiled ruefully.

She meditated, then made herself a quick lunch and started her script. Cathy was excited about her Friday breakdown. Fridays were usually the most exciting day of the soap week. This script included a storyline featuring Dylan and Dana, two of her favorite new characters. In this sequence, Dylan and Dana bump into each other volunteering at an animal shelter. In their previous interactions, they each thought that the other one was a jerk. This sequence was the first one where they saw each other in a new light. It was the beginning of their love story. Cathy felt privileged to get this day.

When Cathy looked up at the clock and saw it was five o'clock, she was shocked. The words had been pouring out of her. She realized that she had already gotten through the first half of the script. Amazing. Usually, her Monday work pattern was full of stops and starts as she developed her creative strategy for each storyline. It usually wasn't until Tuesday, when she had slept on her assignment, that she was able to write confidently.

But she had to admit that today everything had flowed.

Maybe Pat was right. If she could write this stuff, maybe she could live it. She felt really good about what she had written too. Despite all the sappiness possible with kittens and puppies running around, she thought she had walked a fine line between sentimentality and fun banter. But all those animals had made her miss her cat, Bouncer. She hoped Bob was taking good care of him.

She stared at her phone and thought about calling Nancy. Her stomach reacted. Not yet.

However, she could google that nutritionist. Miraculously, she found his name in the back of her Omega notebook. Dan Martin.

In seconds, there he was—Dr. Dan Martin, Manhattan and Rhinebeck. He apparently charged $250 for the first two sessions, which included an assessment and the first follow-up. Even though it was after five o'clock, she picked up her phone and impulsively dialed the Rhinebeck number.

"Hello, Dr. Martin's office."

"Hello," Cathy stammered. She had never expected to get connected right away. "I was wondering if I could make an appointment with Dr. Martin."

"Did someone refer you to Dr. Martin?"

"Oh yes," Cathy checked her notes. "Annie Miller couldn't say enough about him."

"Are you interested in the Rhinebeck office?"

"Yes. I'm in Dutchess County."

"Dr. Martin is in Rhinebeck on Monday and Friday, and normally we are booked weeks ahead. However, I just got off the phone with a cancellation for this Friday at two o'clock."

She took a deep breath. "Great. I'll take it."

Cathy hung up the phone breathing deeply. How crazy. From searching the internet until hanging up the phone with an appointment had taken about seven minutes.

She couldn't believe how much she had accomplished today. She wondered if it was the power of meditating, or seeing Pat. She hadn't realized how much she'd been carrying around for months—for years. It was kind of like getting her hair cut. It didn't seem like her hair was heavy. But after she got it cut, her head felt so much lighter.

Humming to herself, she decided to cook herself a healthy dinner. Then, because she had so much energy, she thought she might go for a swim.

Hey Miss Sunshine, if everything I recommend ends up with you singing, I may have to stop.

You won't stop. You can't.

When did you get so smart?

CURVE BALL

Friday morning, she woke up leisurely, pleased that her script was finished. Routinely, she turned on her phone and checked her messages. Uh-oh. Lorraine, the head writer, had called her and texted her several times. *CALL ME!*

Still in her pajamas, Cathy picked up her phone.

"Holy hell, Cathy, where have you been?" Lorraine practically shrieked,

Immediately, Cathy felt the hysteria in Lorraine's voice. "I just got up."

"You just got up?! Are you sick?"

"No, actually, I pretty much finished my script yesterday. So, I thought I'd sleep in."

"That was yesterday," Lorraine explained grimly. Your C Storyline, has been changed. It shouldn't be a big fix, but all the scenes will have to be modified. If you need a couple of extra hours, since you are writing Friday, I can give you till seven to send it in."

"Okay," Cathy said tensely. She'd have to read the notes before she decided whether to cancel her appointment with Dr. Martin or not.

Maybe it wouldn't be an enormous rewrite. "Let me get going," Cathy said quickly.

"Sorry about this," Lorraine offered. "But *I* never get to sleep in on Friday."

"That's why you get the big bucks," Cathy countered.

"Yeah, right," Lorraine said grimly as she hung up.

Cathy wasn't surprised by Lorraine's abruptness. Head writing a soap opera was an all-consuming job. There wasn't time for niceties.

She poured another cup of coffee and read the notes. Thank god, they hadn't changed the Dylan/Dana line. That would have been a bummer. Still in her robe, she sat down at her laptop and began.

The next thing she knew was that she was done with her first draft of the scenes, she was starving, and it was one o'clock.

Quickly, she assessed her situation. Rhinebeck was about twenty minutes away. She could grab something to eat, change her clothes, and still get there on time. She couldn't imagine that the appointment would take more than an hour. At worst, she should be home in plenty of time to edit the new scenes.

From what Dr. Martin's assistant had told her, it might be a long time before she could get another appointment. So why not? This could work.

She raced to get dressed, deciding to forgo showering. She threw on shorts, a top, and sandals. Then she quickly made herself an English muffin with peanut butter and jumped in her car.

She was zooming along the normally empty country roads, when suddenly she noticed that the car ahead of her was stopped. Flashing lights. When Cathy finally rushed into Dr. Martin's office, she was fifteen minutes late.

The woman behind the desk greeted her with an almost scolding tone. "Luckily, Dr. Martin is running a little behind schedule. But normally, we run a pretty tight ship here."

"I'm so sorry," Cathy gushed. "There was an accident on Route 199. I had left in plenty of time."

The woman sniffed, "I see." Clearly, she thought that Cathy was just making an excuse. She handed Cathy a clipboard. Cathy really had to go to the bathroom, but figured she better not take the time.

No sooner had she signed the last release form, when the nurse announced, "Dr. Martin is ready to see you now."

The way she pronounced his name, Cathy had the feeling that she was being given an audience with a very important person.

The woman led her down a corridor to a back office where a lively looking man with a twinkle in his eye greeted her. "Hello Cathy, I'm Dan Martin." He thrust out his hand.

Dr. Martin sat her down and asked why she had come to him. "How do you feel?"

"Oh, I feel fine. I just can't stand this flubber around my middle."

Dr. Martin laughed. "Your 'flubber' is very common, often associated with hormone changes and/or stress."

"Stress!" Cathy repeated. "I've just gone through a divorce. My job is very high-pressured. Then, I ran into an accident on the way here. That's why I'm late. So naturally, I'm stressed. Isn't everybody?"

Dr. Martin turned the full focus of his piercing blue eyes on her. He said mildly, "No, everyone isn't stressed. It's your choice to be stressed, or not." Although, his tone of voice was subdued, the impact of his words was not.

Cathy was completely stunned. She had totally expected him to offer her consoling words of sympathy. Everyone else she knew constantly talked about stress.

"I can certainly help you lose the fat," he continued encouragingly. "But my real mission is to offer you a lifestyle change that allows you to be the best you can be—better health, better energy. I'd like to help you manage your stress. I'd like to encourage you to label it something else—a lesson, an adventure, life."

Cathy found herself speechless. This man had a strange hypnotic power, like a guru. No wonder Annie had carried on so about him.

Dr. Martin measured her height and did a complicated computer analysis of her body fat, fluid retention, and general energy level. Finally, he directed her to a scale.

Cathy cringed. She hadn't weighed herself for such a long time. At least she had on relatively light clothes. She took off her sandals and stepped on the scale. Her eyes widened when she saw the number. She was fifteen pounds heavier than the last time she could remember weighing herself. Oh my god. How had that happened?

Feeling sick to her stomach, Cathy muttered defensively, "I do have clothes on, and I do have to go to the bathroom."

Dr. Martin nodded, clearly used to people's reactions to getting weighed. "Even when I subtract two pounds for your clothes and extra water weight, I believe your target weight is about twenty-five pounds lower than you currently weigh."

Cathy's head was spinning. How could that be true. Twenty-five pounds?! Twenty-five pounds was a lot. It was five bags of sugar!

Imagine having five bags of sugar clamped around her middle. No wonder she was uncomfortable.

"Don't look so glum. I already have a pretty good idea of what is going on with you. But I am going to send you a link to a questionnaire that I want you to fill out tonight. Naturally, it is secure and it will go directly to me. Can you do that?"

"I do have to hand in my script. But, after seven o'clock, I can."

"That's fine. Please be honest. I can't help you if you're not. I'm also going to give you a test for a urine sample that I'd like you to use tomorrow morning first thing. Please call me right away."

"But tomorrow is Saturday," Cathy pointed out.

"Yes, I will be expecting your call. In the meantime, I am going to give you an eating plan that concentrates on lots of vegetables, high quality protein, good oils and very limited starches. No bread, potatoes, white rice, pasta. No dairy. Basically, if it's white—it's not right. Heidi, my assistant, will give you some bars and shakes to augment your meals and help manage your hunger. However, first I want you to do a cleanse to reboot your system."

"For the first three to five days, I'd like you to drink only water, sparkling water and herbal tea. I'm going to ask you to drink no coffee, caffeinated tea, or alcohol."

Cathy gulped. This was no Weight Watchers—count your points and have a little of whatever you like. This was boot camp. She wondered if she could give up caffeine.

"Don't you get a headache when you give up coffee?" Cathy asked.

Dr. Martin nodded. "Drink a lot of water. If you need to, take aspirin or ibuprofen after eating. Either tonight or tomorrow, I want you to buy lots and lots of different vegetables. You'll be surprised at how much you will want. For example, you may eat a whole head of broccoli or cauliflower in one sitting."

Cathy's eyes widened. Luckily, she did like vegetables. But a whole head of cauliflower? "Is this what I'm getting into for the long run?"

Dr. Martin laughed. "Absolutely not. I want to clean out your system first, restart your metabolism, then introduce you to an eating philosophy that will provide you with a sleeker, more efficient body."

Dr. Martin looked at his watch. "As soon as you get that script in, please fill out the questionnaire."

Cathy had about a million more questions, but she figured she could ask them tomorrow morning when she called him. She felt a bit light-headed as she stood up.

"Are you okay?" Dr. Martin asked, noticing that she was a little unsteady.

"I'm afraid all I've had today was an English muffin with peanut butter." Cathy scrunched up her face like a guilty child. "I guess that's the last time for a while I'll be having an English muffin."

"Ah," Dr. Martin nodded neutrally. "Since, I suspect you have some blood sugar issues, I am going to suggest that you eat one of the gluco-balance protein bars that Heidi is going to give you right away. That should make you feel much better and drive more alertly. From now on, it's important that you eat properly every three to four hours to keep your blood sugar level stable."

Dr. Martin walked her out to the reception area. Cathy ducked into the rest room. By the time she got to the reception area, Dr. Martin was gone.

Heidi was all business. She handed Cathy a small shopping bag filled with supplies. "Dr. Martin would like you to start with these shakes and bars. The total comes to $92. This should hold you for a week."

A week—$92? Cathy was a little startled by this.

Heidi presented her with a printout. "With the initial $250, the total comes to $342."

$342?! Shaken, she fished out her Visa card.

"Dr. Martin would like to see you next Friday. Is that possible?"

"Yes, the later the better."

"Next week won't be as time-consuming as this week. How about 6:30?"

She would have the full day to finish her script. "That would be perfect."

As Cathy walked to her car, she remembered to pull out one of the bars. Ravenously, she ripped it open and devoured it in several bites.

She looked at her watch. That appointment had taken longer than she had anticipated. She started her car and prayed that the roads would be clear on the way back.

So how was it—meeting the Great and Powerful Oz?

Well, he was pretty earnest and a bit extreme, but something about him was persuasive. I think he really cares about creating better health. (HESITATES) Do you think he was a quack?

Believe it or not, I don't. Annie couldn't say enough about him, right?

Right.

And the testimonials online were glowing, weren't they?

They were.

So either he's got an amazing scam going, or he makes a difference. What do you have to lose?

$342!

Not to mention twenty-five pounds.

Disgusting.

Well, his amazing blue eyes aren't disgusting.

Settle down. He was wearing a wedding band.

Maybe your friends were right. All the good ones are taken.

Stop it.

Feeling good and looking good are priceless. If it works, you're going to thank me.

Are you kidding me? You're taking credit for this too?

If it works, I am.

MEOW

Cathy opened her eyes. She felt a little groggy. She wondered if it was the huge pasta dinner she had consumed the night before. It had been her "last supper."

She remembered the little test tube that Heidi had given her. It had a small amount of clear liquid in it. She went to her bathroom.

"Hello, Dr. Martin, it's me, Cathy. I hope I'm not calling too early."

"Of course not, I've been up for hours. So tell me about the test."

"It turned bright red."

"Just as I suspected."

"What does that mean?"

"It means that your body contains toxins. You need the cleanse. We already talked about your primary food, vegetables. For your protein, I'd like you to have two protein shakes and two protein bars a day. After the cleanse, we will gradually introduce you to the full program. I know it sounds like you can have very little, but I promise, you will not be hungry. Three meals and two snacks a day. Maintaining your blood sugar level is one of the most beneficial things you can do for your system. Have you eaten yet today?"

"No, I was waiting to talk to you."

"Okay. But normally, I'd like you to eat within an hour of getting up. Go have your first shake. Call me if you have any problems or if you're still feeling hungry. I'll see you next Friday."

Cathy had more questions, but she guessed she had all the answers in the packet, and it seemed like Dr. Martin was finished. "Okay. Wish me luck."

"You don't need luck. This works. Just make sure you eat enough." And, with that he hung up.

Cathy opened the large container of shake mix. It was Dutch Chocolate. She mixed the powder with cold water and ice in a shaker. Out came a dark brown concoction. She took a tentative sip. Not bad.

After she finished her shake, she headed to the store. She bought every vegetable she could find—broccoli, green beans, kale, cauliflower, cabbage, zucchini, lettuce, arugula, bok choy, onions and garlic.

At noon, she made herself a gigantic salad. Per the instructions, she dressed it with a drizzle of olive oil and lemon juice. She also ate half a bar.

She was just beginning to feel a tiny headache in the back of her head when she knew what she wanted to do.

She arrived at the cat shelter at 3:30. They were only open till 4:00, but how long could it take to pick a kitten?

Unfortunately, there were two families with children ahead of her. Naturally, the children were considering every possible kitten. Naturally, there were only two volunteers on duty.

It was ten minutes before closing, when one harried volunteer finally got to Cathy. By then, Cathy had identified two kittens that seemed possible and had not been chosen by the children.

"I'm Mary. I'm sorry that you've waited so long. We're usually not so busy. Picking a cat is a serious decision. Cats live to be fifteen to twenty years old. Perhaps you would like to come back tomorrow."

"I'm so sorry, but I can't. I have an idea which kitten I might like."

Clearly, Mary was not pleased with her answer. However, she tried to be pleasant. "All right. Let's give it a go." But first she went over to the door, flipped the lock, and turned over the CLOSED sign.

Cathy had been eyeing a tiny, adorable soft-gray kitten curled up in the corner of her cage. The sign said her name was Cloudy. "I was wondering about Cloudy," she said hopefully.

Mary's face fell. "I'm afraid that Cloudy is not one of our friendlier kittens. But I'll try to get her out for you." She reached into the crate and the tiny kitten squirmed away. Mary finally got ahold of her and pulled her out, but Cloudy looked panicked and tried to crawl up Mary's chest to escape.

Cathy reached out to touch Cloudy, but she could see that Mary was right. There was no point getting a kitten for companionship if the poor thing didn't want to be touched.

Knowing that the clock was ticking, Cathy pointed to a slightly larger beige kitten who was in a crate with a dark grey kitten. The crate was labelled Sandy and Max. "Is that Sandy?" Cathy asked.

"Oh yes," Mary's face lit up with relief. "Sandy is the dearest little thing. And that's her brother, Max. Were you hoping to adopt two kittens?"

Cathy frowned. "No. I have always had one cat at a time," she added. "Do I have to take both of them?"

"Well, no," Mary said reluctantly. "It's just that they get on so well with each other." Mary looked at her watch and reached into the crate. Easily, she scooped out the compliant kitten. She handed her to Cathy. Sandy looked right into Cathy's face with amazing green eyes. Then, she nestled into Cathy's arms and began purring.

It was love at first touch. And then, the significance of Sandy's name took Cathy by surprise. Her mother's nickname in college had been Sandy. It seemed like another sign.

"I don't want to take any more of your time. If it's all right, I would love to adopt Sandy."

Mary seemed to soften at the sight of Sandy in Cathy's arms. "She certainly has taken to you."

As quickly as she could, Cathy filled out all the paperwork. Mary gave her some cat food and a quick briefing about how to feed and handle her. And then they were off.

Cathy hadn't brought a carrying case, so Mary put Sandy in a cardboard box. Luckily, Cathy had Bouncer's old litter box at home.

Cathy started the car. The second the engine engaged, Sandy started mewing frantically. Now what? Cathy looked over. Sandy looked terrified. Bouncer had always been a fantastic traveler, sleeping the whole time they drove. Well, Cathy had no choice. They had to go home.

Forty minutes later, Cathy pulled into her driveway. Her T-shirt was soaking wet. Sandy had literally screamed the whole way home. She had vomited. She had peed. She had pooped. Apparently, Sandy got carsick.

The minute the car stopped Sandy quieted down. Thank god for that.

Gingerly, Cathy picked up the soaked cardboard box, hoping that the bottom of the box would not collapse. She pulled out the old litter box and showed Sandy where it was—not that it was likely that she would need to use it any time soon. Next, Cathy put out a bowl of water and some food. Then she collapsed onto her recliner.

Sitting there, Cathy realized that she didn't feel so hot, either. She remembered that she hadn't eaten since lunch. It had been five hours. With her last ounce of effort, she steamed and sautéed a whole skillet full of vegetables.

Now it was time for Sandy. Although Sandy had done nothing but make noise while Cathy was driving, since they had gotten home Sandy had been quiet as a mouse. Cathy wasn't sure where she was. It looked like Sandy had used her box and had eaten some food. That was good. Cathy finally found her curled up on her mother's afghan in the corner of the living room. Poor thing must be exhausted.

Gently, Cathy picked her up and brought her to her chair. Sandy moved up Cathy's chest and nestled under her chin, like a scarf. "Hey cutie," Cathy murmured. "I'm so sorry about the drive. But I'm really looking forward to having you around." They sat contentedly like that for a long time.

It wasn't until much later that night that Cathy realized it was Saturday night. Cathy hadn't felt alone or restless for one minute. Why had she waited so long to get some company?

PAT II

Pat looked down at her notes approvingly. "You've meditated every day except for one."

"And that day was a bit of a disaster," Cathy confessed.

Pat nodded and smiled knowingly. "That's right, honey."

Pat continued, "You outdid your assignment, not only calling the nutritionist, but getting there and starting on your new body. How do you feel?"

"Okay today. Yesterday was tough."

"However, you did manage to stay on your program even when you went out to a restaurant with Amy yesterday. That is no mean feat. Kudos."

Cathy made a face, thinking of the plate of salad and green vegetables that the kitchen had specially prepared for her. "I survived. My stomach wasn't so grumbly when I woke up today. I think my system is getting used to much less food. If I'm not imagining it, my jeans even feel a little looser."

"Most likely you've dropped some water weight. So how long is this cleanse?"

"Dr. Martin said three to five days. Given how I feel today, I can't see any reason not to go for five days."

"I am so proud of you. And you get extra credit—you've adopted a kitten!"

Cathy made a goofy smile. "Amy thinks I'm crazy. It was the script I had last week. It made me miss my old cat, Bouncer, so much. So suddenly I thought, what's holding me back? I want a kitten!"

"So, you did it."

Cathy beamed like a young mother. "It turns out the shelter had named her Sandy, because of her color. It seemed so fortuitous. Sandy was my mother's nickname. She follows me everywhere. I talk to her. Already, I feel so much less alone."

"It's not surprising, honey. You haven't lived alone for a long, long time. You can never minimize the importance of having physical contact with another living being. I think your mother's spirit is very much with you."

Tears suddenly sprang into Cathy's eyes. "I do sense her presence. I know she didn't really approve of divorce."

"But she would certainly want you to be happy."

"Yes."

"Well, you've made a great start. But cuddling a kitten is no substitute for being held by a man. How did that call to your friend about online dating go?"

"Well, I didn't quite get to *that* homework."

"Something to work on for the next week," Pat said lightly.

Cathy felt a wave of relief. "I will get to it."

"I know you will. When you are ready. Now, let's move on. Time for Dr. Freud." Pat tried to lighten the moment. "So talk to me about sex."

Cathy gulped at the quick transition. Then she blurted out, "I'm afraid that I'm pretty much dead." She made a face. "I simply have no interest—haven't had any for a long time."

Pat smiled. "I doubt that an attractive, healthy woman like you is dead. Perhaps you're in a period of, shall we say, hibernation?"

"But, don't women lose their libido after menopause? It makes biological sense."

Pat gazed at Cathy seriously. "Based on my clients and personal experience, I can tell you that sex often gets better. Making love is largely emotional. Unfortunately, I think you were unhappy for a long time. Naturally, you didn't feel interested."

Cathy was skeptical. She was pretty sure that chapter was over for her.

Pat continued. "In those first twenty years, when things were still good, were you responsive?"

"Oh, yes."

"But you think you're done with sex?"

"I'm afraid I do."

"Okay. I'd like to place a little bet that if you feel good about your body and meet someone new, you will change your tune. The drive for intimacy is one of our strongest drives. Let Mother Nature take her course."

Cathy sighed. "It really is impossible to imagine."

"But imagination is your business."

"I suppose."

"Don't 'I suppose' me. I'm your mother for now, and I'm telling you—just you wait."

Cathy rolled her eyes and laughed. How great to be laughing about sex. It had been such an uncomfortable subject for such a long time. "Yes, Mommy."

NOW OR NEVER

Cathy stared at the phone.

Jeez, what in the world are you waiting for now? Nancy is expecting you.

Could you leave me alone for once?

How can I leave you alone? I am you.

It's hard to believe.

No, it's not. Under that "good girl" facade, is a crazy/sexy/ cool chick. Me. Can you imagine your scripts without me? Dull as dishwater.

(LAUGHS) You may have something there.

So, pick up the damn phone.

Don't swear.

Why not? You love to swear. Don't pretend you don't. You love the reaction you get when that "girl-next-door" innocent drops the F-bomb or some other nasty.

(HAS TO SMILE) It's because of working in television. No one would take me seriously when I first started working at CBS. Those crusty old stagehands and technicians thought I was a pushover until I let a few choice words fly. That got their attention. Then it got to be a habit.

Blah, blah, blah... However, you want to justify it, I know the truth. You love to break the rules. You love to march to your own drummer. You love to make people stop and notice you. And it's all hidden behind that neat, conservative little package, so people don't know what's hit them. Speaking of the package—now that you're done with your cleanse and well on the way to a hot new bod—how about some new clothes, maybe a new hairstyle? Isn't that old hairstyle you've had since you were twenty-two ready for an update? And what about your khaki pants look? You're a hot, artistic, single television writer.

Oh god, don't remind me.

What?! About being single? Single is not an evil word. Divorce is not a death sentence. On the contrary, for the first time in a lot of years you have infinite possibilities available to you. You can recreate yourself however you'd like. You don't have to consult anyone. I think it's damn exciting. Sort of like your freshman year in college. That was such a blast! And if you'd just call Nancy, maybe we'd get to do it again.

(SHAKING HER HEAD, BUT SMILING) Okay, okay. You win.

I always do. But it can be exhausting.

Don't pout. It doesn't become you.

With a smile on her face, Cathy picked up the phone.

"Hey, Nancy, how are you?"

"Matt and I just got back from Paris." Nancy hesitated, then couldn't contain herself. "You just can't believe how much fun it is to travel with your lover. Isn't that the greatest word? After all those years of marriage, I never thought I'd experience romance like this again."

Cathy gulped. "Wow. You sound like you're head over heels."

"Things are really good. But I don't assume anything. It's all so different from thirty years ago. We're both independent adults. Matt and I just make the most of our relationship one day at a time."

"Aren't you afraid of getting hurt?" Cathy asked softly.

"Of course. But the good so outweighs the potential bad. And I do feel like I have perspective. Whatever happens, I still have my career, my children, my home. I'm not a twenty-something girl looking for a man to define me."

"I just can't imagine being with a different man," Cathy whispered. "I can't imagine even meeting someone."

"Isn't that why you called, to talk about the first step—online dating?"

"I decided to go talk to—a counselor. She's encouraging me to go online, says it works."

"It certainly can."

"Wasn't Matt the first guy you went out with?"

"I know, I know, it was a fluke. I went on Match, met Matt, and it turned out he worked in the building next to mine in Manhattan. Talk about coincidence."

"So, is Match what you'd recommend?"

"Match is the only site I've tried, but I know lots of other people who've used other sites."

"So how does it work?"

"Obviously, I'm no expert. I was just on Match a couple of weeks.

But I think the key is your profile. The first thing I'd recommend is to go on Match and look at a bunch of other profiles of men and women. See what appeals to you. See what you hate."

"A profile?" Cathy asked.

"When you sign up for Match you create your profile. It includes at least one photo, preferably a good one of your face, smiling. And I'd recommend a full body shot too. It's sad but true that men are looking for women in good shape, so they don't always trust only a face shot. Of course, it goes both ways. Women are looking for men who are fit too."

"Ugh. That's enough to stop me right there. I've just started seeing a nutritionist. I'd like to do some work on my body before I go public."

"When you're ready, you'll know. It took me months to get up the courage. But it's a really good thing to do some market research first."

"That's what Pat keeps telling me."

"I'm so glad you're talking to someone. I'll tell you something that no one else knows; I worked with a therapist for a year."

Cathy felt a wave of gratitude. It was so good to hear that Nancy had gone through the same steps. She wished she had talked to Nancy a long time ago.

"When you're ready for the photo, I'd recommend asking a photographer friend, or at least someone who's got a good eye. Then take lots of shots in different light so you have choices. So many people post these selfies that they obviously snap as an afterthought and throw online. What's worse, some people take their shot in a mirror. You're in television. You know the importance of image. This is how men are going to form their initial impression of you. You want that impression to be as good as possible. You'll see, there's competition, so you want your photo to stand out."

"The thing is, I'm all too aware of how editing can make a photo look a lot better than the person. I don't want to be a disappointment once they meet me."

"Cathy, this is a lot like college admissions. You've got to get past the first cut. You've got to get them to 'read your file,' or in this case, meet you. So, you want your photo and profile to be dynamite. Then, you have to trust that your personality will win them over, which I'm sure it will. After all, you are a fun, funny, creative person. Who's not going to be interested in you?"

Cathy let out a shaky laugh. "Hey, thanks for that, Nance. But I'm terrified that I'll be so nervous that they'll run as fast as they can."

"I would put quite a bit of money on the fact that they'll be a lot more nervous than you. Most men have been scarred in some way by their experiences."

"Like I have."

"Like we all have."

"Jeez. Then why bother?"

"Because, it's a numbers game. Out of the thousands of men on Match, there are plenty who are like you—attractive, interesting, a little dented by life, but with lots of spunk left in them."

"But you didn't weed through thousands."

"I didn't end up meeting more than one, but I can tell you I reviewed hundreds of profiles and emails before I zeroed in on Matt. And then we just got lucky."

"Do you think lightning can strike twice?" Cathy asked lightly.

"Of course, it can. But I know lots of women who have plugged away online for years. A number of them have eventually found the love of their lives. Some of them have given up. But I think if you search selectively and meet lots of men, your chances are excellent."

"It sounds exhausting."

"It's exhausting and exhilarating. You remember how consuming it was in college—meeting and dating all those boys. Frankly, it's a miracle that we managed to go to class at all. It's not much different now going online. It takes time and effort to review, respond to, and meet men—which is why you need to take time to really polish what you want to say in your profile. Then, be ready to commit a good portion of your time to the process once you post your profile."

"So, what kind of stuff is in the profile?"

"You know. Sort of like beauty pageant questions. But, obviously, you don't want your answers to be overly idealistic or vapid like those rehearsed answers. I'd encourage you to be really honest, in a fun way. Some people are so earnest about finding that 'special someone' that they sound downright scary and desperate. Some even seem angry describing at length who they're looking for, and who they're *not looking for*. That's a real turnoff. Obviously, you'll get the sense of it when you read a bunch of them. But I think humor and interesting detail is the key."

"Would you mind giving me an example of what obviously worked so well for you?"

"Well, I said I was looking for a man who'd sit in the front seat of the roller coaster with me and wouldn't mind when I screamed or squeezed the circulation out of his fingers."

Cathy laughed. "That's cute."

"Cute and true. I have a love/hate relationship with roller coasters.

Lots of guys responded to that comment. I think they liked the fact that they could protect me, and I don't think it hurt that I mentioned holding hands. You don't want to sound trashy. But in general, I would say that men are looking for women who enjoy physical contact. However, if I read one more profile where the guy said he liked to hold hands on the beach, I thought I was going to fall asleep. You'll see. Just find a twist."

Cathy laughed again, feeling a bit more confident that she could do this. "Twist is my middle name."

"So besides writing a charming, playful profile, you need to spend time searching for the men who appeal to you. It's a level playing field. You can and should initiate communication. But I'm not big on winking.

"Winking?"

"It's a no-brainer way to indicate that you are interested in someone. All you have to do is press a button. But I think that you get much more bang for your buck if you write a personal message to the men who appeal to you. I actually wrote to Matt in the first place. Worked like a charm. Men are very flattered by a thoughtful, funny note. Well, for that matter, women are too. You should be great at this."

For the first time, Cathy did feel like this might just work for her. "So, you think it's okay if I hold off losing a little weight and have a great photo taken?"

"Well, I think you look fine already, but you need to feel good. It doesn't matter if you start tomorrow or in a couple of months. Get your head and your body in peak condition. Then, make sure that you have time available. I can promise you the men will be there."

"Nance, I can't tell you how much I appreciate all of this. You have been such a help."

"No problem. Call me anytime if you have any questions. And invite me to the wedding!"

Cathy laughed excitedly, "Not me. You're the one who sounds like she's about to order her dress."

"Hold that thought," Nancy replied.

Cathy was so excited by the call that she sat right down and logged onto Match. She put in some cursory criteria regarding age and location and up came 2,437 matches.

Amazing!

She started going through the men's profiles. There were quite a few guys that she couldn't see herself with at all. But there were also a number of really thoughtful and attractive looking men. Maybe Nancy, Pat, and Amy were right.

HOW MANY?

Cathy arrived at Dr. Martin's office early. She was wearing the lightest summer dress that she owned. She knew she should have, but she had not drunk any water for the last two hours. Psychologically, she needed a big drop on the scale to motivate her to continue. She said a silent prayer that the results would be good.

"Cathy? Dr. Martin is ready for you."

Cathy entered his office. Dr. Martin looked up and smiled at her in his boyish way. "So, how are you doing? How did it go?"

"Well, it was an adjustment. You were right about the vegetables. I couldn't believe I could eat a whole head of cauliflower."

"Vegetables are the key. Were you hungry?"

Cathy thought about this. "No, not really hungry. But sometimes I wasn't completely satisfied."

Dr. Martin nodded. "Well, you were going through withdrawal to an addiction in a way. It takes a while for your body to learn to appreciate a new nutrition language. Well, really, it's an ancient language. Fresh vegetables, fruits, and lean protein are the vocabulary that our bodies were used to for two hundred thousand years. It's only in the last ten thousand years that we introduced grains and processed sugar into our diet. How are you feeling?"

Cathy couldn't wait to get the suspense over and get on the scale. "I had a good week. My work went well. I meditated every day."

Dr. Martin's face lit up. "Oh, you meditate. That's excellent for stress control."

"It's a relatively new practice for me. As far as my energy and sleep go, they seemed about the same."

Dr. Martin frowned slightly. This was clearly not the answer that he was hoping to hear. "My hope was and my experience is that, as your system works more efficiently, you will feel less tired and more energized throughout the day, yet sleep like a baby. So shall we get you on the scale?"

Cathy kicked off her sandals and got on the scale. She found herself closing her eyes.

"Four pounds, that's excellent," Dr. Martin wrote down on his clipboard.

Cathy was devastated. After all that and she had only lost four pounds! Her face obviously showed her reaction.

"Are you disappointed?" he asked, concerned.

"Well, the people I see on those TV shows lose a lot more than four pounds the first week."

"I doubt you've been working out for six hours a day, as they do. But the biggest difference is that they all have at least a hundred pounds to lose. The last twenty pounds are always the hardest. And that's all you have."

He attached electrodes to her fingers and ankles and ran the test.

"Wonderful. Your fat percentage has been reduced by one per cent. Your fluid retention is also down.

Cathy shook her head. "Doesn't that mean that some of that four pounds is just water weight."

"Yes. But that water was being retained because your body was doing everything in its power to dilute the toxins in your system. Once the frontline battle of managing those toxins is under control, your body will set out to remove those unnecessary fat stores."

"My flubber?" Cathy joked.

"Yes, your flubber. Stay on the second stage of the plan. I'll see you next week. Keep up the good work."

Since this visit was covered by her initial expenditure, Cathy emerged from the office with another container of shake mix and more bars. This time it only added up to $80. So far, she had spent $422 and had lost four pounds. That was over $100 per pound! Some bargain.

AN UNEXPECTED DEVELOPMENT

Cathy woke up on Saturday just feeling happy. Sandy pounced on her stomach and crawled up on her chest, purring away madly. Cathy could hardly believe that it had only been a week since she had gotten her. Best of all, she had plans for tonight. A friend from the lake, Maureen, had asked her to go to dinner at the Spiegeltent at Bard College. Cathy wasn't at all sure what it was, but she was delighted to have a new activity to look forward to.

Cathy felt like a child when they pulled up in the parking lot. The Spiegeltent was a fanciful round wooden structure with a canvas tent top trimmed with twinkling lights.

When they entered the tent, it was even better. It had a dance floor, surrounded by a raised tier of tables and booths. There was stained glass, billowing velvet, and mirrors everywhere. Cathy couldn't help thinking that it would make a perfect setting for a romantic sequence for her show. She soon learned that "spiegel" tent meant mirror tent. The college shipped the whole structure from Belgium every year. Entering it was like entering a romantic European cabaret.

"Wow, this is great!" Cathy exclaimed.

"I thought you'd like it," Maureen said, smiling.

As the hostess was showing them to their table she said, "You do know that it's Argentine Tango Night?"

Maureen nodded. "I was told that when I made the reservation."

The hostess continued. "Then you know that we ask you to be finished with your dinner by eight. Thanks so much."

"Argentine Tango Night?" Cathy was really curious. Wasn't tango that sexy dance where the women wore those slinky skirts and the men looked like they would like to ravish them?

Maureen laughed. "I have no idea what it's about. But we have plenty of time to eat."

Cathy's fork stopped half way to her mouth when the group at the table next to theirs arrived. One woman had a tight-fitting black slit dress with lace leggings and sparkling chandelier earrings. The other woman had a red dress with an asymmetrical hem. She wore a shimmering red heart around her neck and dangling heart earrings. The men were primarily dressed in black. All four of them looked sexy and cool.

"Oh, my goodness," she said. "We're not in Kansas anymore."

Maureen laughed. "Who knew that people danced tango up here?"

It turned out that it was not just a few people, it was a lot of people. By eight o'clock the tent was filled with exotic creatures. Cathy found herself dying to catch a glimpse of the dancing.

"I know we're supposed to leave, but do you think we could stay a few minutes and watch the tango?" she asked.

Maureen looked around at the packed room. "Why not? We'll stay until we get kicked out."

Cathy had noticed that the group sitting next to them had all changed their shoes. The women now had on strappy high heels. One man was wearing white shoes with black tips.

Just after eight, a woman with blond hair walked to the center of the circle.

"Good evening, everyone. I am Irena Vasquez. Welcome to our annual tango night at the Bard Spiegeltent. I know you're all dying to dance. So, without further ado, I'd like to invite everyone to come onto the floor for our introductory tango lesson. Please don't be shy. Tango is a street dance that started in Buenos Aires. Anyone can do it."

Almost immediately, people poured onto the floor. Cathy was shocked. There had to be two hundred people.

Maureen poked Cathy. "Go on up there. You know you want to."

Cathy pointed to her flat shoes. "I don't have the right shoes."

Maureen pointed out a few other people wearing regular shoes. "They don't either. Go on."

Cathy was so torn. She was dying to join them. But, at the same time, she felt self-conscious. She loved to dance, but knew nothing about Argentine tango.

"You come too," Cathy urged Maureen.

"No, I have two left feet." Maureen saw that Cathy was hesitating. "I dare you," she teased.

Cathy took a deep breath and accepted the dare. There were now two concentric circles of people ringing the floor. She snuck into a space in the outer circle, hopefully well hidden from the eyes of the cafe hostess.

Irena proceeded to show them how to walk. Her feet slid forward on the ground with her chest slightly forward and very still. She was like a stalking panther.

"Each time one leg moves, the feet 'collect' or pass by each other. Your thighs should be close together, almost rubbing each other. We don't dance tango with our legs apart."

Cathy tried and found herself losing her balance. This walking was hard.

"This is the key to tango. Walking. If you can walk, you can tango."

After some more practice, Irena suggested that they all find a partner. Cathy panicked and decided to go back to the table just as a man with a beard held up his hands and said, "Shall we?"

Cathy had the distinct feeling that this guy was not a beginner. He held out his arms authoritatively. Without thinking, she moved into them. She almost gasped at the sensation.

"Hello, I'm Brad," the man murmured.

"Oh hello, I'm Cathy," she replied nervously.

And with that, the music began and Brad started walking. It turned out that Cathy had to walk backwards to match Brad's forward steps.

"Followers, stretch your leg back before you shift your weight to that foot," Irena called out. "I know that going backwards is more challenging at first. Try to adjust the size of your steps to the size that your leader is taking. Leaders, try to take steps that are comfortable for your follower. You don't want to knock your partner over."

Cathy thought it was weird that the men were "leaders" and the women were "followers." It seemed pretty sexist to her. She wasn't at all sure that she wanted to be a follower.

However, she had no time to think about that now as she struggled to move with Brad. She tried to remember to keep her thighs together, and to pass her extending foot right by the other foot. Unbelievably, the rhythm of the music and the support of Brad's body seemed to fill her with confidence. His right hand circled reassuringly behind her back. His left hand held her right hand softly but firmly. She didn't feel like she would fall over.

"You're doing very well," Brad commented softly.

Cathy felt a flush of excitement. She had to admit that, after the first shock of being in a man's arms—the first man since Bob, it felt pretty good to be held, even if it was just a dance.

The music was so gorgeous, so lush. Violins, accordion, percussion. No wonder people liked tango. Although just gliding along backwards ought to be boring, it wasn't. Brad really seemed to know the music. He moved with the ebb and flow of the melody. Before she knew it, Cathy had lost all awareness of where she was, what she was doing.

And then the music came to an end. Brad seemed to know exactly when it was going to finish. Cathy wasn't at all sure how he did it, but suddenly she was being lowered over his arm into a dip. Oh, my.

Cathy found herself unable to say a word, she was so transported.

"All right, everybody. Now leaders, rotate to the next follower," Irena called out.

"Thank you very much," Brad smiled. "I hope you'll continue with tango."

"Thank you," Cathy finally managed to say, "You were wonderful."

And then Brad was gone, and a young man in his early twenties moved up to her. Cathy wondered if he was one of the Bard students. He looked younger than her sons.

He held up his arms with a friendly grin. "Hey, I'm Eric."

Cathy introduced herself and moved into his arms. What a difference. This boy hardly touched her back. He felt like a jelly fish. He didn't seem to hear the music at all. Therefore, Cathy had no idea when he was going to move next. Jerkily, they made their way around the floor.

This song seemed interminable. Cathy was drenched in sweat when it came to an end.

"Okay, ladies and gentlemen," Irena announced, "I think that's enough for tonight. Even if this was your introduction to Argentine tango, I encourage you to join in the dancing. I also invite you to join me for classes on Wednesday nights at the Rhinecliff Hotel. Beginners are welcome."

"And, now I'd like to introduce Tango de la Luna."

And, with that, the live band on the stage began playing and the floor filled with dancers doing a lot more than walking.

Cathy turned to thank Eric, but he had already run off to join his girlfriend.

Cathy made her way back to Maureen. "We can go now."

Maureen applauded. 'You looked pretty good out there, especially with that guy with the beard."

Cathy laughed self-consciously. "His name was Brad. I think he was sort of a ringer. He actually made me feel like I could dance."

Maureen nodded. "You certainly looked like you were dancing. Nice ending."

Cathy picked up her purse.

"You sure you want to go?" Maureen pressed. "I don't mind staying."

"It was exciting. But that walking was a lot harder than I thought it would be."

"Maybe, you should try those classes in Rhinecliff," Maureen suggested.

"Maybe," Cathy said.

OCTOBER

Cathy slammed her car door and raced along the train tracks to the Rhinecliff Hotel. As usual, she was late.

Oh, bummer. She had forgotten her shoe bag and had to run back to the car. She now had shoes for tango from a special store in Manhattan. They cost $200! The shoes had helped. But shoes were just the first hurdle. Tango was the most demanding, infuriating, and seductive of dances. Tango had no set combinations. The primary job of the follower was to stay prepared to go forward, backward, left, or right. As a result, almost all of the time she felt insecure, uncertain, and apologetic as she stumbled along with various partners. But then, out of the blue, she would dance with a leader who was a lot more experienced than she was and she would be transported to an exalted realm. Just that tiny percentage of bliss seemed to motivate her to continue. It was like a brass ring that seemed almost unattainable. It made the dance even more desirable.

By now she knew from talking to a lot of people that it took years to feel confident dancing tango. And just taking class was not enough. Ultimately, she had to dance a lot of hours with a lot of different partners.

She pushed open the door of the ballroom that they used for their class. Everybody was already in a circle with Irena instructing in the middle. Irena caught her eye.

"Sorry," mouthed Cathy. As quickly as she could, she strapped on her shoes. After three months, the suede had conformed to her feet and was quite comfortable.

"Tonight, we are going to work on close embrace," Irena explained. "I think most of you have heard the expression, *corazon a corazon*. It means 'heart to heart.' In tango, in close embrace the partners connect through their hearts, their chests. It is the movement of the leader's chest that signals to the follower where they are going." Irena demonstrated with Nick, her assistant. "You lean ever so slightly into your partner but at the same time maintain your own balance." Irena demonstrated.

"For this exercise, I'm going to give each couple a piece of paper to hold between your hearts. Try moving through some basic steps without dropping the paper on the floor."

Luckily, there was an extra leader. Cathy went into Phil's arms. She put the paper between them. It didn't take much pressure to hold it in place.

Irena started the music, and Phil took a step forward. Cathy stepped backwards. So far so good. They walked for a while. Then, Phil took a step to the side. The paper dropped.

"Whoops," Cathy giggled. "My fault, I didn't move with you."

Irena had overheard her. "We never need to apologize in tango. We are all learning."

After that song, they rotated, and Cathy moved to Fred, a more experienced dancer. Not surprisingly, Fred kept control. The paper never dropped.

An important attraction of tango was being in such close contact with another person. She knew how important touch was to mental health. Despite the terror she still felt learning this dance—overall, she felt so much better when she came home from tango. It was not surprising that there were so many divorced and single people taking class.

Of course, in the beginning she had been curious about whether any of the men she danced with would turn out to be more than dance partners. But so far, no one seemed promising.

And that is why she was ready to move on to Plan B, depending on what happened at Dr. Martin's office on Friday.

"All right, enough of that. Now, I'd like to work on *boleos.*"

Cathy was very excited. Boleos were the very dramatic move where the follower pivoted quickly and whipped her "working" leg across her supporting leg. It was one of the flashiest moves in tango. Cathy had been dying to learn a boleo for a long time.

Irena demonstrated how the leader begins an *ocho* and then quickly reverses the direction of the ocho. "This is an organic move. Followers—you do not do anything. You let your working leg swing freely."

Cathy was incredulous. Really?

Irena continued, "Let's start with a back boleo."

Cathy counted her lucky stars that she was still dancing with Fred, who knew what he was doing. Deftly, he led her into a back boleo. Cathy found herself "helping" the movement. Irena was watching them.

"Cathy, just relax your leg and let it do what Fred is leading."

Fred led the movement again. This time Cathy forced herself to do nothing. It was so hard to just let go. Shockingly, her foot whipped around behind her and then returned to the other foot.

"Oh wow, that was cool," Cathy exclaimed, amazed that it had worked.

"Very nice," Irena smiled. "It's all just physics."

Cathy had never enjoyed physics so much before. She loved the feeling as her body coiled and then uncoiled, spinning one leg around the other one.

By the time she left, her hair was sticking to her head, she was so sweaty. But she was exhilarated. The drama of the boleo really made her feel like she was finally becoming a tango dancer.

As she walked to her car on this beautiful October evening, she couldn't wipe the smile off her face. And she couldn't get the music out of her head. She found herself trying a quick little boleo. Of course, gravel wasn't the best surface to pivot on. She almost fell down.

Hey, Valentina, watch it!

Oh, take it easy. I'm fine.

Think you're pretty hot stuff, don't you?

You know, I didn't think I could do a boleo, but I'm really pleased with myself.

You could do it 'cause you had a great partner—Fred.

I know he made it possible, but I still had to let go and do it.

(A PAUSE) **You've got a point there. You've been doing a pretty good job of letting go.**

(SURPRISED) Wow. I didn't think I'd ever hear that from you.

You've been letting go in lots of ways. In fact, I think you've let go of quite a few pounds. When are you seeing Martin again?

This Friday. I'm scared.

Oh, don't be ridiculous. Your clothes are falling off. I can't understand why you don't weigh yourself.

I'd rather wait and use his scale.

Suit yourself. But I'll be shocked if you're not near your goal. You're getting to be skin and bones.

Hardly. (ALMOST A WHISPER) But I do think the flubber is almost gone.

Abracadabra! It just disappeared.

Yeah. It was sort of like that. Dr. Martin is a miracle worker.

That was irony, honey. You're the one who has eaten three truckloads of vegetation.

Hmmm. There's some truth to that.

There's always truth to what I say. Frankly, it's amazing that you're not green.

(LAUGHS) You're right.

Good thing, though. Since it's time to get a move on that online dating photo. I'm not sure there'd be too many takers for the "Wicked Witch of the West" look.

Jeez. Do you have to nag me all the time? Can't I just enjoy my little tango triumph tonight without you pressing me for more, more, more?

Look, your birthday is next week. You're not getting any younger.

The men you've met through tango are nice men, but there's no winner. You're looking fantastic. Time to put one little foot in front of the other one again.

You are such a taskmaster.

Honey, if I wasn't, you'd still be back in Ohio teaching second grade, like your Mom.

There's nothing wrong with teaching second grade.

No there isn't. But you were made for bolder things.

A part of me is, I guess.

That's right, the part of you that's me! So, are you going to call Dawn about taking that photo or not?

Pleeeese let me get through Friday.

All right. But I just think going on Match would be a nice birthday present. God knows what other gifts we're going to get.

Thanks for reminding me.

I just want you to be happy.

You know, with tango, Sandy, my job, the kids, and my new friends at the lake—I am happy. What a difference from a year ago.

I'm glad about that. But I think we could be happier.

(OPENS THE DOOR OF THE CAR, CLIMBS IN, AND SLAMS THE DOOR) Enough!

Okay, okay. Don't get your knickers in a twist! Drive safely.

Then leave me in peace.

THE BIGGEST LOSER?

It had been a month since Cathy had seen Dr. Martin.

Dr. Martin took an extra minute to assess her. "You're looking very good, Cathy. It's been awhile."

Cathy smiled, "I'm feeling great."

Dr. Martin nodded. "Just what I wanted to hear." He motioned to the scale.

Today, Cathy had worn her baggy jeans that kept threatening to fall off and a T-shirt. She took off her jacket and shoes and stepped onto the scale.

"Fantastic. Six pounds since last time," Dr. Martin beamed. "I'm not surprised though. You look transformed."

"Wow. I'm shocked. I have to confess that I haven't weighed myself since I was here last time."

"Some people do better when they stop thinking about their weight loss. It's obvious that your body no longer thinks it's going to starve and therefore no longer needs to hold onto its emergency fat."

Cathy couldn't help from smiling. "It does seem like my flubber has just melted away. I feel no rolls when I sit in my car."

Dr. Martin eyed her. "It looks like you could use a new pair of jeans too."

Cathy laughed. "I was waiting."

"If I were you, I would get a pair two sizes smaller. You've already lost nineteen pounds. In my experience, each ten-pound weight loss represents a size. I'm pretty sure you will slim down even a little more."

Cathy was jubilant. Nineteen pounds. That was amazing. She couldn't imagine getting jeans in a size six.

"I'd like to see you again in about two weeks. At that point, I think we'll be adding back a few items to your eating choices. Our next goal is to get you on a stable maintenance program. We don't want you to keep losing weight forever."

"I thought I had six more pounds to lose," Cathy said.

"Well, that was my original estimate. But, based on how you look, I'm not sure you should lose too much more."

Cathy was dismayed. "I sort of wish you hadn't said that. My birthday is next week. I don't want to go crazy and undo everything.

Dr. Martin laughed. "One or two splurges are not going to undo anything. By all means, have some champagne and a small piece of cake for your birthday if you want it. Chances are you won't really want to eat those things. Abstinence from processed sugar seems to diminish the desire to eat it."

"Really?" Cathy said dubiously. "That's hard to believe."

"Don't believe me. You'll see for yourself. And, Happy Birthday! I think you're going to find that your birthday pictures this year are going to look ten years younger than last year."

Cathy sailed out of the office as if she were floating on air. She couldn't care less that she had paid another $220 for her visit and supplies. Transformation like this was priceless. And, after the first week or so, it had really been pretty easy. If she ate what she was supposed to when she was supposed to, she was never hungry.

She was so elated that she knew exactly what she wanted to do.

By some miracle, the tiny boutique department store in Rhinebeck was still open. It was a store that was a throwback to an era when people couldn't drive twenty miles to a giant mall. Terrified that this was all going to backfire on her, she quickly selected three pairs of size six jeans, and just to be safe, three pairs of eights.

She ducked into the dressing room. Hesitantly, she selected one of the eights. They looked tiny. Bracing herself for disappointment, she began to pull them on, not really daring to look. She hadn't worn anything smaller than a ten for a long time. Waiting for the inevitable resistance over her hips, Cathy kept pulling. And then they were all the way up. That had been so easy. She buttoned them. OMG! There was still lots of room in the waistband.

How could that be? With shaking hands, she pulled off the first pair and picked up one of the sixes. This pair was definitely a little tighter. *Good*-tighter. Jeans were not supposed to be loose. After zipping them, she turned around to look at her behind. It looked small and possibly even cute.

She did a squat in the dressing room. No problem. If she lost another couple of pounds, they'd be loose!

For a second, Cathy felt light-headed. She sat on the little chair in the room.

"Are you all right in there?" came a voice. "I'm sorry, but we do close in ten minutes."

Quickly, Cathy tried on the other two pairs of sixes. One of them was a light wash, which she didn't really like. But which one should she pick from the other two?

Are you nuts? What are you waiting for, Foxy Mama? Get them both! You deserve to celebrate. You've lost nineteen pounds! Get that credit card out, the place is closing!

It's ridiculous to spend so much.

So what? You can afford them.

(RUEFULLY) I know I probably can, but I can go tomorrow and get something cheaper at the mall.

Do you feel like going tomorrow?

No. I feel like being impulsive and getting them today.

Well then, live a little! Go crazy! Get two pairs of jeans. We're not talking about two carats at Tiffany's! It's not as if you're exactly breaking the bank living in Dutchess County. Let's see, how much are your tango lessons?

(WITH CHAGRIN) Fifteen dollars.

Oh, man—in that case, you better go to the thrift store for jeans. What is wrong with you? You don't spend a dime on anything other than food and an occasional movie. All you do is write, swim, and dance. When was the last time you bought a pair of jeans? Wasn't the last pair you bought that pathetically worn heap lying in the corner? The pair that has been slipping off your hips for the last few weeks? I'm surprised you haven't gotten arrested for indecency.

When did you get those? Wasn't Ashley in high school? Didn't she encourage you to splurge on those what, eight years ago?

Something like that.

So, put those atrocities on and go pay for the cool, new-size-six you. No, wait! I've got a much better idea. Put on one of the new pairs. The clerk will cut off the tag. Then, throw the antique in the bin. Or maybe you should take it home and burn it! Great idea. Cool, we'll have a little ritual—burning the past. Love it.

(CAN'T HELP SMILING) It might be fun.

We could even throw in a couple of other mementos—some photos, that shawl that Bob's mother gave you ...

Let's not get carried away.

The clerk's voice was just outside the curtain. "I'm sorry. We're closing."

I've gotta go.

Don't forget to call Dawn before the bonfire.

Cathy drove home in a bit of a haze. She really couldn't believe she had *two* pairs of size-six jeans that really fit her. She couldn't remember how long ago it had been since she had worn a six.

She arrived and pulled out her phone, emboldened by her achievement.

"Dawn, it's me, Cathy."

"Cathy, good to hear from you."

"You know how we were talking about you maybe taking some photos of me for my big debut onto online dating?"

"Yes, as an old married lady, it sounds very exciting."

"Well, I was just wondering if by any chance you would have any time this weekend?"

"I'm busy tomorrow. But Sunday afternoon would be good. It would be better to do it towards sunset—the best time to shoot."

"Really, you could do it Sunday? That would be fantastic."

"I'll come to your house."

"Thank you so much."

Cathy hung up and headed for the refrigerator. She poured herself a tiny glass of wine.

Hey, what are you doing?

I'm celebrating.

Martin said you could have wine for your birthday. Today is not your birthday!

Pipe down. This is nonnegotiable. (SHE SITS DOWN AND SANDY COMES BOUNDING ONTO HER LAP)

Don't get too comfortable. We've got a bonfire to build.

There is plenty of time for a bonfire, *if* I decide to do it.

Well, then I think you should go on Match and check out what kind of photos you want to take.

Can't you ever leave me alone?!

Frankly, no. Don't you want to get some ideas about outfits, since you have to go shopping tomorrow?

What?

You can't wear those two-size-too-big rags you have up there in your closet for your big photo shoot. I guess you're going to get

your chance to go to the mall tomorrow, after all! But wasn't it more fun to buy those fabulous jeans today?

(SHAKES HER HEAD DRAMATICALLY) GO AWAY!

Later, alligator...

Cathy stared at the TV. Then, without disturbing her sleeping kitten, she picked up the laptop, balanced it gingerly on the arm of the recliner, and opened it. She typed in: M-a-t-c-h.

THE GOLDEN HOUR

Dawn was going to be here in twenty minutes. Cathy eyed the three dresses that she had laid out on her bed. After doing her research on Friday night, she had gone to T. J. Maxx on Saturday and tried on everything. She had bought three summer dresses on sale.

One of the dresses was a sleeveless black dress with a V-neck trimmed in sequins. It was very comfortable and fun with a touch of bling. After evaluating the Match photos, she had noticed that a number of women had really sexy, somewhat revealing outfits. Cathy didn't have that kind of bombshell body. Secondly, she didn't feel comfortable dressing that suggestively. But this dress showcased her collar bones and arms, which looked pretty good after all the swimming she had done. It was a little black dress with a twist.

The second dress was a simple pink sleeveless dress which skimmed her body. Cathy liked the vibrant color. What's more, it was on sale and a size four! There was no way that she could not buy it when she saw the size. She thought it was flattering against what was left of her summer tan. She figured pink might stand out against the series of little black dresses that so many women seemed to wear on Match.

The third dress was fitted through the bodice with spaghetti straps. It was a turquoise print which again seemed to compliment her coloring. This dress showed the most skin. But Cathy didn't think that it looked too slutty.

Cathy didn't know which one to put on. She was not sure they'd have time for her to wear all three. She figured the first dress she wore was likely to the be the one that ended up on Match.

Sandy was perched on her dresser eyeing the three dresses intently as if she was hoping that one of them was going to move.

Cathy turned to her, "So Sandy, which one do you think I should pick?"

As if on cue, Sandy suddenly leaped onto the bed straight from the dresser and landed on the pink dress. Cathy shrieked because she didn't want Sandy to pull the threads. Sandy immediately jumped off and disappeared in a huff.

"Sorry, baby," Cathy called out remorsefully. "I didn't mean to scare you. But thanks for helping." And with that she slipped on the pink dress.

Dawn arrived with her equipment. She took one look at Cathy and did a double take. "What happened to you?"

"I've been going to this nutritionist. I figured it was time to trim down."

"Well, I almost didn't recognize you. You look fantastic."

Cathy couldn't help beaming. "Thank you so much for doing this for me."

"Anything in the name of love," Dawn joked as she set up on the back deck. "Anyhow, you've been alone up here too long. If this is the way to meet men these days, I say go for it."

"I'm pretty nervous about the whole thing," Cathy explained.

"Well, I give you a lot of credit. If something happened to Dave, I'm pretty sure I'd be alone for the rest of my life. I'd never have the courage."

"I'm not sure I have it, either. But I've got several friends who have really been pestering me to try online dating."

"Nothing ventured, nothing gained," agreed Dawn. "But you do have to be careful. I've heard some pretty weird stories on the news."

"I know. But my friend assures me that your identity is protected, until you decide to reveal it to someone."

"And when is that?" asked Dawn.

"I have no idea. I guess when you decide to trust them."

Dawn took some light readings. "Okay. The sun is going down. Why don't you stand over there? The light looks great. I'm catching some of the colorful foliage in the background which looks fantastic behind your pink dress. Go ahead, smile."

Cathy had observed many photo shoots on her show. But when it came time for her to look into the camera and smile, she felt ridiculous. She tried to change positions to keep her body fluid, but she felt like a complete phony.

Dawn clicked away. "Okay. Now you should be warmed up. Think about a happy time. Try to keep your body relaxed."

Cathy knew that she must look like a complete stiff. She could tell that Dawn was trying to jolly her into a more natural smile. Cathy forced herself to think about the kids when they were little on Christmas morning. But that made her laugh. "Don't open your mouth so much," Dawn called out.

Cathy thought about her mother.

"Well, that was a powerful expression," Dawn commented. "But you almost made me cry. I don't think that's quite what you're looking for."

Cathy scrambled to find a happy thought. Just then, she caught sight of Sandy sitting in the kitchen window, watching her on the deck.

"That's it," Dawn called out jubilantly. Her eye followed Cathy's to the window. "Is that your cat?"

Cathy beamed. "Yes, she's my new best friend, Sandy."

"Maybe, we should bring Sandy out and take a few shots with her."

Cathy thought that was a good idea. Sandy always made her smile. "Should I change my dress while I'm at it?" Cathy asked.

"If you want, but make it quick. The sun is just about to set. Then it will be the golden hour when the light is the most flattering."

Cathy raced upstairs, pulled off the pink dress and pulled on the black. She picked up her brush and lip gloss. Luckily, Sandy followed her upstairs, as she often did, and jumped on the bed. Cathy scooped her up and ran downstairs.

"We don't have a second to waste. That sunset is glinting off the lake and the sequins on your neckline. It's great."

Cathy was having trouble holding Sandy. Sandy was not usually allowed outdoors because there were foxes and coyotes in the area. She was squirming madly in Cathy's arms, trying to get free. Cathy was doing everything she could to avoid getting scratched.

"Okay, Sandy. It's all right," she tried to soothe the cat.

Sandy looked right into Cathy's eyes and then she arched her body suddenly and almost got away.

Cathy couldn't help laughing. "Talk about having a tiger by the tail."

"Look at me," Dawn shouted.

Cathy turned her head to the camera.

"Hold that angle," Dawn commanded.

Cathy tried to keep her eyes on the camera as she held tightly to Sandy's wiggling body. But it was hard.

"Okay. I think Sandy has had enough. Want to take her back in?" Dawn suggested.

Relieved, Cathy took Sandy back inside and rewarded her with some of her favorite treats.

The sky was grey when Cathy came back outside.

"I think that's it," Dawn said as she packed up. "I'll send you copies of everything as soon as I download them into my computer."

"That's great," Cathy was thrilled and terrified about seeing herself.

"Can you stay and have a glass of wine?"

"Sorry, I really can't. I've got to get home to dinner with Dave." She was already halfway out the door.

"Dawn, you have to let me pay you!" Cathy called out firmly.

"Are you kidding?" Dawn replied. "It's the least I can do for a neighbor."

Cathy felt terrible. "That doesn't seem fair. I wouldn't write you a script for nothing."

"Sure, you would."

"At least, promise me you'll let me cook you and Dave dinner."

"Only if you promise to make it a foursome with your new Match man!" Dawn teased.

"How can I make that promise?" Cathy asked.

"Positive thinking," said Dawn confidently. "I'll send you the shots in a couple of hours."

Cathy tried to distract herself by reading the previous week's scripts. But she had to admit that she was on pins and needles waiting for her photos.

Finally, the email came from Dawn. She dreaded opening the attachment. She usually hated photos of herself.

One by one, her heart sank. Although, she had to admit that she looked pretty slim, even in her pink dress, she looked so unbelievably awkward. Her face looked like a smiling mask. No man would ever be interested in her.

She flipped through the shots. There were so many. The backdrop of the trees with the autumn foliage was stunning. The lighting was pretty flattering, but she looked more pathetic in each shot.

What a waste ...

The very last sequence in the pink dress part showed her looking off to the side and smiling. At Sandy. Well, at least she looked human in those shots, although they were mostly in profile. Definitely not her best angle.

Then, came the next batch. Hallelujah! Suddenly, Cathy was holding Sandy and laughing. She looked genuinely happy. It was just like Tyra always said. Her eyes were "smizing." Unfortunately, because Sandy was wiggling so much, all the shots were a little off. Sandy was looking away. Or Cathy's elbow was flying up trying to handle the cat. Or her hair was falling in her face. And then, suddenly, like a miracle, there it was. THE PICTURE! Number 123. Cathy was looking right at the camera with a totally genuine smile. Her chin was tipped down. Her hair was just right. Her earrings were catching the light. Her sequins were shining behind Sandy's head almost giving her a crown. And Sandy was staring right at the camera looking adorable.

Jackpot! If at first you don't succeed—try, try again. Thank god for digital photos. Remember how expensive film used to be? Maybe you should go buy a lotto ticket tonight. Number 123. You are one hot tamale, if I do say so myself.

I know. I can't believe it.

Hey, are those tears in your eyes? You should be ecstatic—on top of the moon!

I am.

You sure have a funny way of showing it. You know, I think you're going to whip the asses of all those other ladies on Match.

It is not a competition.

Get real. Of course, it is. And number 123 is a helluva lot better than any other photo we saw on Match—well, in your age category.

Nice. One hand giveth, and the other taketh away.

Well, let's be real here. Your twenty-something days are over.

You know what else is over. Our conversation.

Not really. Now you've got to write a profile equal to your photo. But that should be a piece of cake.

Not now. I've done enough for one day.

All right, all right. You don't have to get all bitchy. You did good, girlfriend. Keep it up.

Cathy stared at her unfamiliar face and felt like jumping up and down. Who was that? This woman looked happy and fun—and pretty. Maybe someone would want to meet her, after all. Just maybe …

HAPPY BIRTHDAY

Amy had insisted that they celebrate on Cathy's birthday. She understood that most likely she would be the only one staging something special for Cathy this year. They both loved the restaurant Bouley in Tribeca. So Cathy got up early, impulsively dressed in her new black dress, even though it was sleeveless, with a little black jacket and black boots.

She entered the restaurant and, as always, was transported to Paris. From the fine antique furniture, to the tapestry pillows, to the evocative French oil paintings—it was charming and perfect. The crowning touch was the smell of fresh apples. That was David Bouley's trademark—masses of apples tucked everywhere. Cathy took a deep breath. Just the scent was worth the two-hour drive.

Amy blew in, a force of nature as always, a few minutes later. Cathy was just getting up to hug her when Amy stopped in her tracks and let out a shriek. "Oh my god! What happened to you? You've shrunk!"

Cathy had totally forgotten that Amy hadn't seen her for three months. She laughed, embarrassed. "You knew that I was going to a nutritionist," she replied as she hugged Amy. Amy said in her ear, "You've been going to a magician! Did he do your hair too?"

Cathy touched her hair self-consciously. "Let's sit down, and I'll tell you the whole story."

The maître d' led them to Cathy's favorite table. It was in front of a large painting facing the length of the stunning room. She felt like a queen sitting there overlooking her dominion.

"Oh, I love this table," Cathy sighed contentedly. "Thank you."

"That's what friends are for." Amy looked pleased. "Now, let's get some bubbles to soften you up for the interrogation."

"Be gentle," Cathy teased.

A few minutes later they each had a sparkling flute of pink champagne.

Amy raised her glass. "To a new year that will match the new you. That will make it some year!"

Cathy laughed. "Thanks, Amy. I don't know how I would have gotten through the last year without you."

Amy waved her arm, shooing the bad vibes away. "Out with the old, in with the new! It's over. Now, tell me everything."

"I don't know where to start …"

"Start with the hair. When did you do that?"

After three sips of champagne, Cathy was already feeling light-headed. "Well, on Saturday I was shopping for some new dresses for my photo shoot on Sunday. Impulsively, I decided to have my hair reshaped."

Amy held up her hand, "Whoa, whoa, whoa. Photo shoot? New dresses?"

"Well, I felt so elated, after seeing my nutritionist on Friday night and finding out that I had lost nineteen pounds, that I asked a photographer friend at the lake to take my photo."

"Nineteen pounds? That's amazing. I want his name. I want to be you."

"No, you don't. You look great."

"How did you hear about the nutritionist?"

"You know, that workshop I went to at the Omega Institute."

"Oh right, that weird granola-crunching place near you."

"Well, I met a woman who looked great. She gave me his name."

"I saw you that first weekend. Your diet seemed like total deprivation. I was sure you wouldn't last a week."

"It was quite a change. I couldn't drink. I ate vegetables until I was afraid that I was going to grow long ears and twitch my nose."

"Hmmm. No drinking. Maybe, I don't want his name after all." Amy took another sip.

"It actually wasn't so bad after I got started. Not drinking wasn't so much of a problem for me, because I have no social life."

"What about tango?"

"That's true. Tango is pretty social."

"From what you've told me about the way you hold each other, who needs a husband? It's all the hugging without any of the messy stuff. Sounds perfect," Amy teased.

"Anyhow, the good thing about tango is that it takes so much concentration, almost no one drinks when they dance."

Their elegant French server came up at that point to take their order.

The bread cart appeared by their table. Cathy waged a little war with herself. Dr. Martin had told her that a birthday splurge wouldn't hurt her. She hadn't tasted a piece of bread in three months. Her mouth watered for the rosemary bread which she absolutely loved.

She almost trembled when she asked for a tiny slice of it. When she lathered butter on it and placed it on her tongue, it tasted like something sacred, like Holy Communion.

"Well, I think it's amazing that you've managed to lose so much. All the women I know seem to think that weight gain is an inevitable part of aging."

"Look, I know that it's a lot harder to lose and maintain weight when your metabolism isn't what it once was. But Dr. Martin is a tough-love kind of guy. He doesn't think it's impossible. He's been quite inspiring." Cathy took another sip. "And, let's face it, I had some serious motivation to make a change."

Their first course was served. A pristine green salad was set in front of Cathy. A steaming plate of polenta with an egg on it was set in front of Amy.

"So, moving right along. So, photo shoot, hair? Next stop—Match?"

Cathy held up her hand. "I decided to get my photo taken, since I now accept that a photo is an important step. That's as far as I've gotten."

"Did you get a good one?"

Cathy nodded ruefully. "Finally. The 123rd! It wasn't easy. I was a ghastly model. But my brilliant neighbor finally suggested I hold my kitten. That seemed to relax me and my face."

"You're using a photo holding a cat?!" Amy was aghast. "Lots of people hate cats."

"I know. You're one of them."

"I don't hate cats. I just don't particularly like them."

"You're not alone. But I can't help it. It's the best photo. Let's be real, the only usable photo. And, the fact is, I do have a cat. I love cats. So I guess this will eliminate the cat haters, which is probably just as well."

Amy groaned. "And when are you going to take the next step? Nudge, nudge."

Cathy scrunched up her face. "When I get to it." she said firmly. "C'mon now. It's my birthday. Be nice."

"Okay, okay. On that note, your hair looks fantastic."

"You're not just saying that to be nice, are you?"

"You know how hard it is for me to fake being nice. Truly, it looks great. It's not that much different, but it makes you look like you've joined the twenty-first century!"

"My hair was not that bad."

"No, but it was sort of stuck in a time warp."

"I'm so relieved that it's okay. I was pretty impulsive picking this salon in the mall last Saturday and just marching in."

Amy looked almost sick. "You got it cut in upstate New York?! You were really playing with fire."

"It's not that primitive," Cathy protested.

"Most of your neighbors are geese." Amy countered.

Cathy, feeling no pain after two glasses of champagne, laughed. "You should hear them honking every morning. This morning there must have been five hundred of them on the lake on their way south. It's some alarm clock."

Amy winced. "And you left Connecticut for that?"

Two servers arrived with hot plates covered with shining silver domes. With a flourish, they simultaneously set them down and dramatically removed the covers. The smell of the cod wafted up to

Cathy's nose. They dove into the beautiful dishes, talking a mile a minute.

"Two pairs of size-six jeans?!" Amy was incredulous. "You're killing me."

"I know. I almost fainted, myself." Cathy lowered her voice to a confessional level. "Then I had a ritualistic bonfire that night and *burned the old ones!*"

"You have gotten really weird, Cath."

Cathy laughed. "I know. I never know what I'm going to do next. There's this part of me that keeps pushing and pushing."

"And this is a surprise to you?" Amy asked drily. "You're a creative type, with unorthodox thoughts and impulses—like going online with a cat!"

Cathy lowered her voice. "I guess you're right. Sometimes I think I was really playing a part all those years in Connecticut. The way I'm behaving now seems like the real me. It is pretty exhilarating to honor my own impulses. I even think that my scripts have been better."

Amy reached for Cathy's hand and squeezed it. "Well, whatever you're doing, it certainly seems to be agreeing with you. I'm truly so happy for you. I think you could teach me a few things."

"I doubt it." Cathy smiled, hesitated, then plunged in. "Although, if there's any secret to my turnaround, I'd have to say—it's been meditating."

Amy rolled her eyes when Cathy said that. "Oh my god, it just gets better and better. When did you start that?"

"Look, I didn't tell you because I knew you'd react just like you are now. That workshop at Omega changed my life in so many ways. I started meditating. I met the woman who has become my therapist, Pat. I learned about Dr. Martin ..."

Amy interrupted, "I think he was the grand prize."

Cathy continued, "Yes, there's no doubt that he's transformed me physically. But I now think that the most profound outcome of that weekend was inside, not out. I know it seems really strange, but the twenty minutes that I sit still and quiet my mind seem to prime me for good things for the whole day. As soon as I started meditating regularly, everything seemed to improve in my life. I got Sandy. I went to Pat. I discovered tango. I met Dr. Martin."

"You bought new clothes, cut your hair, had a photo shoot! And now you're going online! Soon we'll be double dating!" Amy finished with a flourish.

Cathy laughed. "Whoa, whoa. Let's not jump the gun. The thing that really astounds me is that since I've started meditating, it seems like ideas and possibilities keep appearing in my life. Theo said that meditating opens up the realm of synchronicity. I believe it."

"Synchronicity?" Amy asked dubiously.

"Like what you would call coincidences, possibilities that present themselves and turn out to be amazing—even life-changing—opportunities. He said there are no coincidences in life."

"I'm not sure I believe that."

"I don't think it matters if you believe it or not. The key is to stay open. I think most people trudge along doing the same-old, same-old—not even noticing the opportunities that appear in their lives every day. I know that I did that. I can't imagine my life if I hadn't been assigned the script about two characters on my show going to an animal shelter. Or showing up quite "by accident" at tango night at Bard College. Or stumbling into the workshop at Omega."

Amy held up her hand and placed a small package in front of Cathy. "I'm afraid I got you the wrong gift. I should have gotten you a saffron robe and incense."

Cathy was hurt that she had bared her soul to Amy, and Amy was mocking her. Her face fell.

Amy could see right away what her flippancy had caused. "Hey sweetie, I didn't mean to dash water on you. I'm probably just a little jealous that you look so fabulous and you seem so happy."

Cathy said softly. "I'm just really grateful that I feel so content. My life is full. I'm having fun. I'm learning new things and meeting new people."

"Just don't forget your old friends."

"Are you kidding? You know the song—'Make new friends, but keep the old. One is silver and the other's gold.'" Cathy squeezed Amy's hand.

Cathy got up to use the Ladies Room. She was feeling a little uncomfortable from the rich food already. Her body was clearly not used to it.

No sooner had she slipped back into her seat when a group of servers appeared with a piece of flourless chocolate cake on a beautifully decorated plate with *Bon Anniversaire, Cathy* written on it in very fine writing. There was also a hazelnut souffle.

Tears came to Cathy's eyes. She blew out the candle and made a wish. "You are the best, Ames."

"I 'Ames' to please." Amy was flushed with emotion.

The waiter placed a clean plate in front of Cathy as the cheese cart was rolled next to her. Cathy picked three. The server shook his head and added a fourth. "This is my favorite," he smiled. "It is my birthday gift."

"Thank you," said Cathy, truly touched.

"And now you have to open my gift," Amy said.

Cathy was feeling overwhelmed. "This lunch is more than enough."

"Don't be silly. A birthday is not a birthday without a little package."

Cathy opened the beautiful gold-wrapped gift. "I told you our friendship was gold," she said. Inside was a little box with tissue paper in it. When Cathy unwrapped the tissue, she found a delicate gold brooch of a bird cage with a blue-enameled bird just flying out of the open cage door, wings spread. "Oh, my goodness, where did you ever find this?"

Amy was pleased. "I found it on one of my flea-market junkets. I know you like vintage jewelry, and I thought it was perfect."

"So much better than a saffron robe and incense," Cathy teased. She stared at the tiny bird. "This is exactly how I feel. Like a bird flying free." Cathy immediately pinned it on her black jacket. "I will treasure it always."

It was four o'clock by the time the two of them had picked at the cheese and desserts. All traces of the champagne had worn off after so many hours.

"I'm really going to have to run," Amy said. "As it is, I'm going to have to work till eight to make up for this."

"Of course, I understand." Cathy gave her friend a big hug. "*Thank you, thank you, thank you.*"

"Shall I walk out with you?" Amy asked.

Cathy made a face. "I'm afraid I'm going to have to visit the Ladies again. I have a long ride home."

"Well, at least it's a beautiful restroom. I hope the food wasn't too much for you."

"If it was, it was totally worth it."

Getting out of the city after four wasn't much fun, but she got to the West Side Highway and then crawled her way up to the GW Bridge. After that, it was smooth sailing.

Amy is a good, good girlfriend.

Yes, she is.

Now, you just have to work on a good, good boyfriend. I hope your stomach is not too upset to work on your Match profile tonight.

Oh, c'mon. It's my birthday. I get to do what I want.

I suppose. But don't you think that a birthday is like a New Year's celebration?

(GRUDGINGLY) I suppose so.

So, what better way to kick-off your new year could there be than launching yourself on Match with your hot kitty photo? Meow.

(HAS TO LAUGH) You are incorrigible. Amy was shocked that I was going to use that picture with Sandy. She's terrified that I'm going to turn into a crazy, old, cat lady.

I don't think you look old at all. Crazy? No comment.

You're the one who's crazy.

Maybe. But this has given me an idea. Let's face it, you're a whole new you. Why not rename yourself "Cat" on Match? It's got a lot more zip than "Cathy."

Cat? It's true. Cathy has always seemed like such a white-bread, old-fashioned name. I've never loved my name. I'll think about it.

Will wonders never cease! On that note, I think you should turn on your book. I'm done.

Hey—thanks for everything. Amy made me realize today how much you've spurred me on in life.

I always did like that girl. You're welcome. It's just my job.

THE LAUNCH

On the drive home, all three of her kids called. Ashley sang her the whole happy birthday song. She talked to Michael about his job. Paul told her about his new girlfriend. All three of them were obviously concerned that she was okay and sorry that they couldn't be with her. By the time Cathy pulled into her driveway, she was feeling very loved. The drive from the city had never seemed so short.

After changing her clothes, she checked out the TV but was not excited about the choices. She felt restless. Maybe it was all the extra calories she had consumed. She wished there was tango tonight.

Finally, she grabbed her computer and sat in her recliner. On cue, Sandy bounded onto her lap. Cathy stared at the blank screen of her laptop. She could see her face reflected back at her. She looked tense. Should she, or shouldn't she?

Aw c'mon. How long are you going to stare at your screen? We already discussed this.

I don't think I want to do this.

Then, forget it. Go ahead and watch a movie. Who needs

companionship, romance, adventure? Better to stay curled up alone in front of a screen for the rest of your life. Oops. I'm sorry. You have Sandy. I guess she'll just have to be enough. The thing is, she's very cute but not much of a talker. I'm getting really tired of cracking the whip all the time, anyhow. If you've come as far as you're willing to go, so be it.

Grrrrr .... You are so good at making me feel awful.

I am so good at making you feel good. You thanked me less than an hour ago.

(BEATEN) So I did. (OPENS HER LAPTOP, TYPES IN MATCH. COM) Are you ever going to leave me alone?

When I think you've done all that you can, I will.

That's going to be *never!*

If you say so.

Cathy looked at the time. It was early. She should be able knock off this profile and still have time for Netflix. The first page asked for her name, email address and birthday. Boldly, Cathy typed in *Cat* for her first name. Cathy had done some reading and knew that men tended to look for younger women. Impulsively, she subtracted a few years from the year she was born. They didn't have anyone checking these things, did they? What difference did a number make? Her photo would tell the story. Absently, she wondered if men cheated about their age too. They probably did.

Oh god. Now she had to come up with a username. She was so sick at having to come up with a username for every account that she set up. It needed to be intriguing, revealing, but not too suggestive. She thought about something to do with cats, since her picture had

Sandy it it. *CatandMouse?* Definitely too suggestive. *Catsplay?* No way. *CatintheHat?* She had always loved that Dr. Seuss book, but it made no sense. Cathy put her laptop down and paced around her living room.

An orange light was just creeping over the hill. Cathy realized what it was—a huge orange harvest moon was rising in the sky. The moonrise.

She went back to her computer. She tapped in *Moonrise* for her username. Of course, it was already taken. At first, she felt completely thwarted. Then, she realized that she could add a number. She tried *Moonrise16*, the date of her birthday. Bingo!

Right away, she was asked a million multiple choice questions about whom she was looking for—his hair color, eye color, body type, height. She thought about it. She didn't care about hair or eye color. For body type, she clicked on *Slender, Athletic and Toned,* and *About Average.*

The next section was Education. She checked the last three choices: *Undergraduate Degree, Graduate Degree, and PhD.* She didn't care about the languages he spoke other than English.

For Ethnicity and Religion, she checked *No Preference.*

Hmmm... The next section was Relationship Status. The choices were *Never Married, Widower, Currently Separated,* and *Divorced.* Although, she figured she would have more in common with someone who had been married, she decided to click them all, except *Currently Separated.* It seemed like a bad idea to get involved with someone who wasn't through the whole mess yet. Once was enough for her.

Then, there was the question about him having children. Cathy decided to click *No Preference.* To be truthful, she thought they would have more in common if he did have children. But, again, she wanted to be as inclusive as possible.

This was taking a lot longer than Cathy had thought it would. The fact is, she had never thought about these issues before.

The next part was the hardest so far. It was Salary Range. Cathy stared and stared at the categories that ranged from less than $25,000 to over $150,000. Again, she wanted to cast a wide net. She checked *No Preference.*

The drinking and smoking questions were a little easier. Naturally, she didn't want an alcoholic. But, the most extreme option Match gave was *Regularly.* She wondered how that was different from *Social Drinker.* She would have to say that most of the people she knew drank *Regularly.* She checked *No Preference.* For smoking, she did not hesitate to click on *No Way,* and for the first time checked *Deal Breaker* at the top. Just the smell of smoke gave her a headache.

That seemed to be the last question about the man she was look-ing for. Now it was time to answer the same questions about her. When she got to body type, she paused. Up until a couple of months ago, she would have answered *About Average.* But she figured, after buying a size four, she could now truthfully answer *Slender.*

She thought that the next question about profession would be easy. But out of the list of twenty-one categories, there was no option for *Writer.* She finally decided that *Artistic/Creative/Performance* was the closest she could get.

And then—the famous salary question for her. Cathy was sur-prised that talk of money was included in the questionnaire at all.

She stared at the choices. Then she quickly checked *No Answer.* Just because they asked the question didn't mean she had to answer it.

For drinking, she had already decided that she would check *Social Drinker.*

Cathy clicked and clicked through page after page and wondered when these questions were ever going to end. No wonder kids liked apps where they just swiped through photos. Who needed all this?

Finally, she got to a blue box where she could actually write her own words.

What are some of your favorite local hot spots?

There were so many possible answers. Quickly, Cathy decided to write the first thing that came to her.

I like anyplace that has dancing, especially Argentine tango. I also love sitting with a great cup of latte, reading the paper, and chatting with whomever I meet. Preferably by the water. I love the Ice House in Poughkeepsie right on the Hudson River. I also enjoy grabbing a beer at hole-in-the-wall bars and shooting the breeze. There's a pattern, isn't there? Yes, I do love to talk to people.

Cathy reread her paragraph. She nodded. She thought she had managed to communicate a little bit about who she was instead of just listing a bunch of places.

Cathy moved to the next page. Oh, yay. Another blue box.

Share a few of your favorite things. Movies, Music, TV shows, etc.

Again, Cathy just dove in.

Raindrops on roses and whiskers on kittens, bright copper kettles and warm woolen mittens …. Okay, okay—someone else got to those first—but I do love musicals. The Sound of Music might be a little on the sappy side for me, but West Side Story never fails to bring me to tears. For movies?

I really liked Avatar and the Lord of the Rings series. I am a TV writer who happens to love TV. Good thing, huh? Of course, I watch the soap I write for—also prime time soaps, sports, crime dramas, Masterpiece Theater, and (horror of horrors) even reality shows. I pretty much watch everything. I guess I'm a TV omnivore. But—lest you are backing away in intellectual repulsion, I have to assure you that I do also read. About two books a week.

Cathy reviewed her response. Funny, flippant, and totally true. Moving on.

Tell us something you recently read.

Cathy figured she had to make up for her mindless TV watching by coming up with an impressive array of titles. Thank god she was in a book club. She listed a mix of classic and contemporary books including Updike, Austen, and Nabokov. But she didn't mention the chick-lit that she also loved. She hoped she wasn't pandering to the intellectual snobs. But she didn't want to seem vapid.

She moved to the next page. Here was a big box.

Write about you and your match. This is a short description of who you are and who you are looking for.

What in the world should Cathy say? Clearly, this was the moment of truth in this profile. She started typing slowly.

To tell you the truth, I'm not completely sure who I am. Like all of us, I think I play different roles. If you've read my previous answers, you can tell that I'm a writer who is pretty active. I swim every day and feel like I'm reborn every time I come out of the water. I love the arts—almost all of them—from highbrow to lowbrow. I love to talk and laugh with people. I find conversation is the greatest sport and spend way too much time talking on the phone. Texting still doesn't do it for me. I love cooking and eating interesting food. As I mentioned before, Argentine tango is my new addiction. It's the most infuriating and intoxicating dance.

As far as "you" goes—I have to admit that first and foremost I'm looking for a playmate. Now, don't get all excited. I use this term in the most innocent way. I'm looking for that "kid" down the street who comes when I call after dinner to join in a quick game of kickball or monopoly. (Oh, right— monopoly is never quick.) If you can make me laugh, share a nice meal, talk, and listen—I will be very happy. If you can dance Argentine tango, I think I may have died and gone to heaven. But, truly, I don't expect that.

Cathy scrunched up her face as she reread this answer. She realized that her playmate answer was dangerous. She was afraid that men would only think of one association—sex. That was the last thing she was looking for. She just wanted someone to have fun with on Saturday night. She scrutinized what she had written again. All the tips about Match advised you to be honest. She had tried.

It was getting really late now, close to midnight. How had that happened? The truth was time consuming. She quickly proceeded to the next page and managed to download Photo #123 without too much trouble. Then, she picked another full body shot standing down on the dock during the sunset. That would have to do for now.

She selected a subscription for three months. That should be long enough to figure out if this process worked for her. And, then it was time to hit the SUBMIT button. She could almost hear the fanfare. This was it. She was doing it.

Match thanked her and informed her that her photos had to be approved by their team before they were posted.

Cathy felt a wave of relief. She suddenly felt absolutely exhausted. She couldn't spend another second overthinking what in the world she had done. She wondered if anyone would find her when her photos were approved, whenever that would be.

She glanced at her phone and noticed that she had a text. She hadn't heard it come in.

It was from Bob.

Happy Birthday, Cath. Sorry it's so late. I remembered in the nick of time. Big meeting tonight. Hope you had a good day.

Bob

Cathy just stared at the message. He could have written that birthday greeting to anyone. How ironic. The man she had lived with for all those years—the father of her children—and here she was, posting her online profile.

A tear snuck down her cheek.

Then, she noticed some activity on her computer. She suddenly had three new emails. Three messages from Match! Already? Had her photos been approved already?

She opened them up.

Tonythetiger wrote: You looking for a playmate? I'm ggggrrreat!

Madman wrote: Looks like you're new to Match. Nice profile.

Sharksoup sent her a wink.

Cathy had to smile. Well, she had obviously managed to post her profile. And she wasn't the only one still up at midnight. She was going to have to rethink that playmate thing, but—tomorrow.

She flipped her computer closed.

Happy Birthday, Cat! Who knows what's going to happen next!

THE DELUGE

Cathy was really disoriented when she woke up the next morning. It took her a minute to remember that she had played hooky from writing yesterday because of her birthday. She groaned and jumped out of bed. She had to get cracking on her script.

She checked her computer for any emails from Lorraine and almost fainted. She had email after email from Match. She had completely forgotten that she had posted her profile last night. She clicked on the first few. *Hey, beautiful—Nice smile—Love to talk to you—Here's my number...*

Cathy felt dizzy. What was all this? Never in a million years had she expected this kind of response. She was incredibly curious about who had written her. But not now. She had to work on her script.

By sheer force of will, Cathy made herself return to her script and immerse herself in the world of Smithfield. She struggled with the baby shower that she was writing for Mindy. She tried to focus on the sparks flying between Dana and Dylan. But the whole time, she was distracted by the sparks that were flying in her direction.

She wrapped up her writing in the late afternoon. Everything she had written today had been a struggle. None of it had flowed. She hoped to god it wouldn't read as badly as it had felt when she was writing. Thank goodness she still had tomorrow for polishing.

She got herself a snack and a cup of tea and settled onto her recliner. She clicked open her email and practically catapulted from the chair. She had to have forty messages from Match! A lot more had come in during the day.

She had already decided that the only polite thing to do was to answer every email. However, before she started responding she wanted to get a sense of what the pool was like. Imagine that. A pool of men. Boy, her Connecticut friends had really been wrong.

She clicked and read and clicked and smiled. Admittedly, most of the messages were obvious pickup lines, superficial and kind of silly, like she might have gotten thirty years ago in a bar. They called her *beautiful, pretty, a stunner, eye candy, great smile, hot.* In her heart of hearts, Cathy knew that they were all bullshit. Still, the last time Cathy had received this kind of flattery was when she was a freshman in college. How could it be that a mother of three grown children could feel like the belle of the ball?

Cathy found that her heart was pounding. Yikes. This was fun. After breezing through the whole collection, she could distinguish between the ones that were just a mass mailing, and the ones who seemed to be specifically interested in her. She had already ruled out Winks. Nancy was right. What kind of interest did it show when a man simply clicked the Wink button and expected her to respond? How hard was it to write a little note?

Cathy was shocked that a number of them were from men under thirty. What was that about? Were those guys looking for a sugar momma? Think again. She was also shocked at how many of them misspelled words. She tried to remind herself that all these compliments meant nothing, but she couldn't help noticing that a lot of them commented on her smile. She knew that she had been right, and that Amy had been wrong. Holding Sandy had been a good thing, even though some men might not like cats. Cathy knew that she had not had such a radiant smile captured in a photo for a long time.

About ten of them were appealing and well written. Cathy knew that this kind of note took time. She appreciated the effort. The first one signed Ed was a rather overweight man from Florida. Oh dear. He seemed lovely and articulate, but listed himself as *About Average* in Body Type. Hmmm .... He was carrying more than a few extra pounds. She felt guilty for reacting that way. But let's face it, virtually every man who had written to her had commented on her appearance. Wasn't she, too, allowed to evaluate men on their looks?

Cathy noticed that most of the men who sent her a long personal note signed their first name at the end of the note. Maybe that's how this game was played. First you used your username. Many of the usernames were revealing. *Golfcrazy, ProudGeek, TravelMad, etc.* Then, you signed your first name at the end of your first message. Cathy was worried about protecting her identity. However, she finally decided that revealing her first name wouldn't be that risky.

After going through the profiles, there were five interesting men who appeared to have potential.

All of this "editing" had taken two hours. Nancy wasn't kidding about how time consuming this could be.

First off, she picked HudsonLover. He had an open, youthful, clean-shaven face. He lived in Kingston. His message read:

GET OUT OF JAIL FREE

Hey, Moonrise,

Were you watching it last night? It was awesome.

It was a pleasure to read your profile. I also used to love Monopoly, made my killing with the red and yellow properties. What were your favorites? I figured the best thing I could offer you was a "Get out of Jail Free" card. That always used to come in handy.

I wish I could also offer you "a slice of heaven," but Argentine tango has not transformed my life—yet. There's always time.

My cat's name is YoYo, 'cause he jumped around as a kitten. What's yours?

Frank

Cathy had to smile as she read the note. She liked the fact that he was clever and funny. He seemed to have a basically positive attitude.

Cathy had already discovered that a lot of the messages that she had received were from men who seemed to have a chip on their shoulder. *Don't bother contacting me if your picture is five or more years old—I value honesty—Don't answer if you're not serious—I'm looking for an independent woman, not someone who is needy—etc., etc.*

Nancy was right. Obviously, a lot of men felt burned. She wondered how that had happened. She felt a little guilty about what she had listed for her own age. If she actually met someone who she was interested in, she'd tell them the truth right away once they met. She had noticed that most of the men who made these comments were not exactly fabulous physical specimens. It still bugged her that men

felt entitled to someone younger. Didn't men know that on the average women outlived men by four years?

Back to Frank—he had a cat with a cute name! She read his profile carefully. He listed himself as Single, *not* Divorced or a Widower.
She wondered if he had ever been married. He didn't refer to his
occupation at all. She thought that was unusual. The men she knew
seemed to define themselves by their work.

If she kept reading and thinking, she'd never get anything done
tonight. She took a deep breath and started to write.

Dear HudsonLover/aka Frank,

*I have to start off with a full confession. You are the first man online
that I have ever responded to. Yes, I am a virgin. So please be kind if I do
this badly.*

*Yes, I did watch the moon rise last night. Cool that we were watching
together/apart. Imagine that.*

*So, HudsonLover, do you have a Hudson view from your home? I actu-
ally live on a lake. It's smaller than the mighty Hudson but still shimmers
in the moonlight. Do you like to swim?*

Not to worry about Argentine tango. It has a very rarified following.

Love your cat's name. Mine is named Sandy, an homage to my mother.

*We do have one potential glitch, though. I also made my mark with
the red and yellow properties. I have to admit, I can become a bit ruthless
playing Monopoly. Perhaps, we'll have to skip that game.*

*So, as you must have gathered from my profile, I am a writer. I do love
the written word. Yours were very fun. What do you do?*

Cathy hesitated before she signed her name. Her new persona. Her new life?

Cat

She had written the whole thing in a blur, not stopping to edit. She read it back and cringed. She remembered that double-entendres had been fun back in the day. But you had to walk a fine line so they didn't become crude. She was hesitant about the *virgin* line, but figured it was sort of funny. She wondered if the *game* line was too suggestive. But she had this overwhelming feeling that that was exactly what they were both doing—playing a game. After all, it wasn't called *the game of love* for nothing.

Some of the men's profiles she had read had openly scolded the reader about *not playing games*. But Cathy thought those men were dead wrong. Life, and especially love, should be playful. Not deceitful, but playful. Again, she felt a pang regarding her age "spin." Oh well, it was too late now. She was not about to go back and change her profile. She'd just have to live with the consequences. With her heart bursting out of her chest, she hit SEND.

OMG! Be still my heart. You actually did it. You sent an online dating message! Congrats, Girlfriend! How do you feel? Should I call 911?

Maybe. I have no idea what I'm doing.

Oh, stop it. You've taken to this like a duck takes to water. What was that "playmate" and "virgin" business?

Those words just slipped out of me.

Exactly. Just like I've been telling you—you were always good at this. You love to flirt.

I guess I sort of do. It's fun.

No false modesty. You're a pro. I suppose it's not surprising after all the banter you've written on the soaps. Do you believe how many messages you've received in the first twenty-four hours?

It is totally amazing.

I have to admit that I'm surprised, myself. You look pretty good for your age, but I wouldn't consider you a knockout. However, if I do say so myself, that picture is damn good, cat or no cat. Who knew how many old single guys would be sniffing around looking for a good time? Well, I suppose we have no idea if they're really single ...

Thanks a lot.

You know the pitfalls. Apparently, a lot of married men mess around online. You just have to keep your antennae up. But you're a smart girl. You'll figure it out.

I'm not sure how. Pretty much all my friends have warned me about the men. That they're all married or players. Married men are not for me. But, I'm not sure I care if they're players. I'm not looking for a commitment. I would just like to have some fun.

(SINGING) **Girls just wanna have fun ...**

Please stop.

Hey, heads up! Looks like you've gotten a bunch more new messages since you've been flirting with Frank, the "Hudson Lover". Woo-hoo!

(LOOKS AT THE SCREEN) Oh dear, you're right. I think just being online attracts more activity. How am I ever going to answer all of these?

Better get crackin'. There are worse problems. You could have been a bust.

I'm not sure that would have been worse.

Sure, it would. You'd feel like a total reject. As it is, you're Cinderella at the Online Ball—and I'm your Fairy Godmother!

(SNORTS) Right.

Aren't you the consciousness-exploring one who went to Omega and learned about synchronicity? The universe is sending you a big message. You're meant to get out there and mix it up. I'm making myself scarce so you can concentrate. Break a leg!

Suddenly, Cathy's head went silent. She couldn't help smiling as she clicked on the new messages. More of the same. *Stunning—Cute—Can't believe your age ....* It was hard to imagine, but these hollow compliments were already getting boring.

She forced herself to concentrate and whipped off personal responses to Henry, Ben, and D.

Then she began to plow through all the ones she had eliminated.

A part of her was dying to write the naked truth: *Why is your face covered in grey fuzz?—What are you hiding?—I'm sorry, but your picture is lousy, and you're not an Average Build, unless Average Build is undeniably overweight.—I am a writer and I really can't handle all of your spelling and grammatical errors.—You are thirty years younger than I am. I am not interested in being a Sugar Momma or a Cougar.*

But she knew she couldn't. She understood how hard it was to expose yourself like this, even online. There was no need to be mean-spirited, even if it was truthful. Her mother had always said, "If you can't say something nice, don't say anything at all." She wanted to answer everybody. She had to remember the kind of things she used to say thirty years ago.

"*Thanks so much for your kind words. I'm afraid you're really too young for me, but good luck!*"

"*Thank you for writing to me. But I'm really looking for someone who lives a lot closer.*"

And finally, when she couldn't figure out what else to say, she wrote "*Thanks so much for taking an interest in me. The fact is, I'm a bit overwhelmed right now. I'll get back to you when I can.*" She knew that this reply was probably not true. But, wouldn't most men get the message?

It was 12:30 a.m. by the time Cathy finished with her initial list. Just as she was signing off, an email from Frank popped up. She couldn't believe it. Already?

This was all going too fast. She was sorely tempted to open his email. Then, some part of her had more sense. There was no way he could expect her to still be up. His email could wait until tomorrow morning.

TOSS AND TURN

Cathy woke up exhausted. Her night had been filled with unsettling dreams about losing her family. The grief that she thought she was done with had welled up again. More than any other changes she had initiated so far, becoming a single woman on the open market was terrifying. How would her children feel? She wondered if she was still harboring the hope that somehow, far down the road, she and Bob could find their way back to each other? That they could be a family again. Sometimes she was such a ridiculous soap-opera-writing romantic.

Then she got ahold of herself. That old family paradigm was over. Bob had started a new life. She was pretty sure that her grown children wanted her to be happy. Pat, Amy, and Nancy had all encouraged her to try this. So far, it was going pretty well. Even if it was terrifying.

Right. Cathy shook her head and climbed out of bed. She muttered her mother's often repeated words, "The only thing you can count on in life is change." She had better get going. She had to submit her script today.

She did a quick meditation, then coffee. Time to check her email. Didn't these guys sleep? There were at least ten new messages. She had thought that going on Match might be like a game of tennis, but it was more like a manic game of ping pong with thirty balls coming at her at once. The good thing was—there was nothing from Lorraine. But there was that email from Frank. She knew herself well enough to know that she would never be able to concentrate on her script if she didn't take a look.

Cat,

I will stifle my immediate urge to Meow. I know, I know. A stupid joke.

Thanks for writing me back so soon. It was especially thrilling from a "virgin"—LOL. I'm not exactly an old hand at this myself, but your note belied your experience.

It's late, so I'll make this brief.

No, I don't have a view of the Hudson from my home, more's the pity. However, I grew up here and have always loved the river.

I can swim, but don't do it regularly. I mostly work out at the gym. I also hike and fish.

Sandy? Your mother? If I'm reading between the lines correctly, it's possible that you may have lost her. My mother is still alive, but my father passed away several years ago. It's amazing how we can be so old, or should I say 'mature,' and yet miss their presence so much.

What do I do? That is a long story. My degree is in anthropology, but it's been a long time since I've used it. Perhaps not the most practical degree. I think this tale would be best in person. What do you think about a cup of coffee?

I promise I won't bring a Monopoly board, although I think 'The War of Red and Yellow' might be fun.

Frank

Winning! He sounds like a fun, sensitive guy. I liked that part about his father.

Yes, he does. I wonder what he's like in person.

There's only one way to find out.

It seems so fast.

Well, having a cup of coffee is a pretty risky thing. After all, you are a virgin. Better line up your chaperone first.

Okay, okay. I get it. Nothing ventured, nothing gained.

You are such a good student. But you better fix Mindy's shower scenes first. They stink.

Why are you always right?

That's my job. T.S.

Despite her ragged night, Cathy cut right through the jumble she had written yesterday. She found herself laughing out loud as she wrote the complicated dynamics of the girl gathering. In contrast to yesterday, when she had felt overwhelmed and distracted by all those messages, today she felt like a high school girl anticipating her first date. She felt all the excitement and vitality of feeling young, feeling like anything could happen.

In a matter of hours, she had one of the best scripts she had ever written. If this one didn't get submitted for an Emmy, what would?

Suddenly, her heart was beating fast again. This was ridiculous. She signed onto Match.

Dear Frank,
It was fun reading your note.

Yes, you are a good between-the-lines reader. My mother died two years ago. I still miss her terribly.

It's taking all my courage to say this, but okay, let's meet for coffee. Where? When?

I'm sure you probably have plans for the weekend, but I have submitted my script for the week and am pretty free until I start a new one on Monday.

Cat

She hit send before she could think.

Jeez. You sounded pathetic. "I'm pretty free this weekend ...." I thought you remembered how it works with guys. Playing a little hard to get is a good thing.

I didn't think. I don't want to play games.

Weren't you the one carrying on about life being a game yesterday?

I guess.

Stop being scared! He sounds like a nice guy. He's not going to eat you. Not in the middle of a coffee shop. I think you need to get some exercise and clear your head—then tackle the two million emails you have to answer. And don't answer Frank right away—like you're sitting by the computer waiting. By the way, the shower scenes are really good.

I know. I'm good.

That's more like it!

Cathy got up from her computer. She did feel like she had been glued to it for the last thirty-six hours. Getting some exercise was a great idea.

She decided to take a walk around the lake. She grabbed a fleece and her earphones and headed out.

Forty-five minutes later, she was back. It was already getting dark. It was Friday night. She wondered if she had blown it by being too eager with Frank. She opened up her email. Apparently not.

Dear Cat,

Shall we seize the day? I have some errands to run tomorrow over by you. Do you know Good and Plenty on Route 44? (BTW, I have always liked Good and Plenties) How does two o'clock sound?

The middle of a Saturday afternoon doesn't sound too scary, does it?

Even for a virgin ...

Sorry, I couldn't resist.

Frank

Cathy had to shake her head. She had forgotten how funny men could be. They got a titillating image in their head and there was no getting rid of it.

She knew that she was supposed to wait and play it cool. But, forget it, she was excited.

Dear Frank,

Two sounds great. Good and Plenty it is. (BTW, I like them too.)

Oh, I think I look pretty much like my picture. It was taken only a few weeks ago. However, I will not be holding a cat, just being one.

Cat

Humming to herself, Cathy went to the kitchen to figure out what to have for dinner. What fun to have something to look forward to tomorrow. She couldn't help feeling excited, optimistic. Frank was very funny. An anthropologist, huh?

The more she looked in her refrigerator, the more she couldn't bear the idea of eating anything in there. She knew that she should stay home and deal with all her mail on Match. However, now that she had her first meeting with Frank, it was going to be hard to concentrate.

Making an executive decision, she decided to run down the road for dinner and be back in plenty of time to catch up on Match.

When Cathy walked back into her house two hours later, she was a little embarrassed at her behavior. She had acted like a teenager, sitting at the bar of her local restaurant chatting up everyone with her story of her first online date. She had gotten lots of advice, and her head was swimming.

Impulsively, she picked up her phone and dialed.

"Cathy?"

"Amy! I can't believe I got ahold of you. You busy?"

"You seem to have forgotten. I'm an old married woman. Ed isn't even home yet. I'm on my third glass of wine."

"Perfect. Guess what?"

"You have a date!"

"How did you guess?"

"'Cause you sound like a cat who swallowed a canary."

Cathy couldn't help giggling. "You must be psychic."

"Why, 'cause I guessed about the date? I'm not so out of it that I can't recognize that giggle."

"Well that, and the fact that I'm using 'Cat' for my online name."

"Are you kidding me? Isn't that a little cutesy?"

"I don't know. All I know is, contrary to your advice, I used my cat photo, and it seems to be a big hit."

"What do you mean, big hit? When did you post your profile? Are you holding out on me?"

"Whoa, whoa. After I got home from the city, I was all charged up and ended up doing my profile. It was probably all those calories from our sinful lunch. I thought it would take maybe an hour to write the profile. It took me four!"

"I'm surprised. Isn't this the kind of stuff you do for a living?"

"All I can say is—it was pretty daunting to figure out what to say about myself and to identify who I'm looking for. I posted the whole thing around midnight. Match tells you that they are going to review your content and photos and that there will be a delay before the whole thing is approved."

"How long did that take?"

"That's the kicker. Right after I posted my profile, I got this anemic birthday email from Bob. By the time I had read it, I already had three responses."

"Wow. Three is pretty good. Were they any good?"

"Not really."

"What does that mean?"

"Well, they were kind of generic. But, when I woke up the next morning, I opened my email to find about forty messages. They had all come in while I was sleeping."

"Are you kidding me? Even with that cat picture?"

"Even with the cat."

"*Who knew?!*"

"I know it's hard for you to believe, but lots of people like cats. Obviously, I've read a lot of the messages at this point. The majority of them are one-liners, sort of like the pickup lines we used to get at bars."

"What kind of lines?"

Cathy was a little embarrassed. "You know. *You have a great smile. You're cute, etc.*"

"I don't think I ever got those."

"Sure, you did. We all did."

"Well, maybe I did back then, when I was cute. But you got them *now*? At your age?!"

"Thanks for rubbing it in. But, yes. Isn't it amazing? You can't imagine how it feels!"

Amy responded dryly, "No, I can't."

"Well, anyhow, what I'm trying to tell you is that, although the majority of these messages are pretty empty and frankly not that believable, there are a handful that are really great. The ones that are really exciting are several paragraphs long, referring to specific things that I said in my profile."

"What kind of things do they mention from your profile?"

Cathy should have known that legal-eagle Amy would want specifics. Inwardly, she groaned at the stuff she had written. Frantically, she searched her mind for the least damning detail. She obviously wasn't going to mention the "playmate" thing. "Well, I said that I loved dancing and was recently into Argentine tango."

Amy groaned. "Jeez, Cathy. Do you have a death wish, or what? Cats everywhere and Argentine tango? What man dances Argentine tango?"

"Look, it seems to be a good conversation starter. I think part of the trick, if you will, is to paint a picture of a fun, sexy life. Most men think tango is a hot, sensual dance. So, even if they don't do it, they think it's sort of cool that I do."

"Oh, now I get it. You got so many hits because they think you're a slut."

"Thank you very much," Cathy said coldly, afraid of the very same thing.

"Oh, stop it, Cathy—or should I say, Cat?"

"If you're going to make fun of me, let's just hang up now," Cathy said, suddenly feeling perilously close to tears. "You're the one who nagged and nagged me to go online."

Cathy heard Amy sucking in a big breath. "You're absolutely right. I did. Please forgive me. It's that green-eyed monster talking. I absolutely hate it when women treat each other like this. I am just insanely jealous that you're being treated like a prom queen. Jeez! Forty responses?! I always wanted to be the prom queen. Anyone taking one look at your girl-next-door wholesomeness would know that you're not a slut. Plus, with your incredible weight loss, you look ten years younger. I'm just sitting here with my third glass of wine, feeling like a has-been and a bitch."

Cathy softened. "You could never be a bitch, Amy. You've had my back for as long as I can remember."

"Thank you. You're a better man than I, Gunga Din."

"Nancy gave me some great advice. She told me that most people tend to write the same stuff. She told me to include interesting details and to be honest. Tango is a real passion of mine right now. Another thing that seemed to work for me was mentioning Monopoly."

"Monopoly?!"

"I wrote that I loved to play Monopoly when I was a kid."

"Cats, Argentine tango and Monopoly. I get it. You're the cute, quirky one."

"Maybe." Cathy had to agree with Amy's analysis.

"Well, more power to you. But, let's get back to business. You started out by saying that you have a date tomorrow! Tell Mommy everything."

Cathy briefly filled Amy in on what she knew about Frank. "We're meeting at two for coffee."

"Two in the afternoon? Some hot date!"

"It's a perfect first run for me. But actually, I think maybe this is how people generally start, very low-key. That's the thing. It's really just a chance to meet, not a date. For that reason, I have no idea how to dress."

"In keeping with your *cute and quirky but somewhat-sexy* brand, shouldn't you wear a casual but somewhat-sexy outfit? Something that shows your legs? You have great ones, by the way."

"Okay, now you're becoming obsequious. I talked to a bunch of people at a local restaurant here, and a couple of men said not to get too dressed up. They said that's a big mistake that women make."

"Then, tight jeans and a cute top it is. Maybe boots."

"Just what I was thinking. I think that's the first thing we've agreed on in this conversation," Cathy said, smiling.

"How long does this coffee *meeting* last?"

"I guess, as long as it takes to drink a coffee. Forty-five minutes? An hour?"

"What if you instantly hate him when you sit down?"

"Amy, I can't ever remember instantly hating anyone. Well, there was that one obnoxious VP at the network. However, I'm wondering how to politely exit if it isn't working. A trick I read on the internet said to have a friend call you during the meeting. You can use that as an excuse to leave."

"Oh, cool. Shall I call you at two-fifteen?" Amy replied eagerly.

"Be nice. I think that's too soon. How about two-thirty?"

"Two-thirty it is."

"And just in case we're getting along famously, I may just ignore your call. So don't be upset if I don't answer."

"Oh, man. That's a bummer. How can I live vicariously through you if you don't answer?"

"I'll call you as soon as I can when I leave."

"Promise?"

"Promise."

VIRGIN RUN

What a night. Cathy knew that she shouldn't put all her eggs in one basket. But she had been so distracted by thoughts of Frank and how charming he seemed that she couldn't make herself focus on the rest of the emails she had to answer. Lurking in the back of her mind she thought, why bother if Frank's the one?

Cathy knew this was ridiculous. Even if it had worked that way for Nancy. She knew that even if she did like Frank, everyone said that you had to have a rebound relationship first. That first one was never *The One*.

She had gone to bed early in the hope of answering all those other guys in the morning. Cathy couldn't believe it when she signed onto Match on Saturday morning and a whole set of new messages had come in. What had she gotten herself into? She could almost hear the pounding of countless fists on her front door. She smiled wryly. Amy was a fool to be jealous of her. This was really too much.

On top of it, Henry, Chris, Ben, and "D" had all written her back. As quickly as she could, she responded briefly to all of them. She apologized for not writing longer notes because she had a busy weekend. She promised to write more later. What harm could it do to let them think that she was a social butterfly?

Then she scrolled through her other messages. A couple of the guys she had rejected the first night had written argumentative or even nasty notes back. *Hey, Moonrise, age is just a number. Give me a chance. What's wrong with youth? I've gotta be better than some old guy.*

That's a pretty lame excuse. I don't live close enough? I get it. You're not interested.

Oh sure, you're going to get back to me. I'm not holding my breath.

Cathy resolved right there and then to be more careful. Maybe it didn't pay to respond to everyone. There was no easy way to reject someone. In a bar, you could flash a smile and soften the blow. But in writing, the words alone seemed harsh.

She realized that two hours had melted away as she had tried to get through her messages. It was already noon. It would take about fifteen minutes for her to get to Good and Plenty. She didn't want to be the first to arrive. But she didn't want to be late, either.

In her new jeans, a somewhat form-fitting red top, and cow-boy boots, Cathy drove by Good and Plenty ten minutes early. She wished that she knew what car Frank drove. She drove past, turned around, and headed back.

At two o'clock on the dot, she parked her car. It was another warm October day. As she arrived, she noticed a man in a tweed jacket with a scarf wrapped around his neck sitting at an outside table reading the paper. He looked very intellectual. Like an anthropologist. She was pretty sure that he hadn't been there before. That must be him,

PFM

waiting for her. She licked her lips, got out of the car and headed over to him with a smile on her face.

"Frank? Glad you didn't bring the Monopoly game." As soon as she blurted out these words, she regretted it. This man looked nothing like Frank's picture.

At the same time, the man jerked his head up. "I'm sorry, I'm not Frank," he said as he checked her out. "But I wish I were."

Cathy wished she could vanish into thin air. How could this have happened? There were so few people here and she had messed it up. "Oh, sorry. I was supposed to meet someone here."

The man smiled, curious. "A blind date?"

Cathy felt her face matching the color of her top. "Something like that." All she wanted to do was run back to her car. Speechless, she pushed open the door of the coffee shop.

"If he's a no show, come back," the man called after her.

Inside, there were two women and a man wearing a leather jacket and jeans. The man looked like he was trying not to laugh. He had obviously been watching her and instantly jumped up. He held out his hand. "Cat?"

Cathy was so discombobulated that she didn't recognize her new name. She froze and then her brain kicked in. "Right. Frank, hi."

"I thought that was you. You do look like your picture. But then you went up to that man outside, so I thought I must be wrong."

Cathy flopped down in the chair opposite him. "No, I goofed it up. I told you—"

Frank smiled pleasantly finishing her sentence. "I know. You're a—" He lowered his voice. "You're—*inexperienced*."

Cathy had to laugh.

178

"What can I get you?" Frank asked. "Coffee? Tea? Water?"

"An herbal tea would be great. But I can get it." She tried to get up, but he started to the counter.

"I got it."

Cathy had made up her mind that she would pay for herself the first time. This wasn't like old-fashioned traditional dating where the guy asks the girl out. But she realized that there were still traditional roles to play. She couldn't emasculate Frank by insisting on paying. In any case, she didn't think she would be indebted to him because of a cup of tea.

Frank moved to the counter. She couldn't help checking him out now that he wasn't right in front of her. He looked like his photo. But a little heavier, a little older. He wasn't great looking. But he wasn't bad looking. His leather jacket was ancient.

By the time he returned with her tea, Cathy had collected herself. She was ready with questions about him, his life. "Thanks," she smiled. "So, tell me about yourself. Tell me about being an anthropologist."

Frank smiled wryly. "That was a long time ago. I worked all over the world—Tahiti, Europe, Chile. But then I came back home to help my mother when my father suddenly died. Somehow, I've never left."

Hmmm, Cathy thought. That was odd. Most of the men Cathy had known in Connecticut were driven. Their careers were their lives. Frank sounded a little wistful.

"Actually," he continued before she said anything. "You're the one with the fascinating job. My mother loves your show, by the way. How do you think up all that crazy stuff?"

Okay, Cathy thought. I got this. Soap opera question number one.

Pretty much everyone she met asked the same thing. She launched into her well-rehearsed response. "Every day, the news reports on way more outrageous stories than we tell. It's just that our stories happen to the same group of twenty-five people. So, it seems far-fetched. The cool thing is, we get to create a new show every weekday of the year. That's like one hundred and twenty feature films. So, you can imagine that some of the stuff we air isn't Emmy-quality. But daytime soaps have pioneered many contemporary issues. Personally, I think I was better prepared for my divorce because of the situations I had explored in my scripts throughout the years. Writing those scenes that I hadn't yet lived was sort of like a rehearsal for life."

Cathy held up her hand, "Hey, sorry. I get on my soap box sometimes."

Frank laughed. "Seems a good place for a soap writer."

Cathy laughed too, just as her phone rang. Oh my, that had to be Amy.

"Do you need to get that?" Frank asked.

Cathy made her decision. "No, I'll call whoever it is back." She reached into her purse and silenced her phone.

Cathy felt comfortable chatting with Frank. Before she knew it, she went for the topic that she was most interested in. "So, you've never been married?"

Frank made a face. "It's not because I'm against marriage, or any-thing. I've had one long-term live-in relationship. But we ended up going our separate ways after eight years. Somehow, the opportunity didn't arise again."

Cathy sensed that this was a sensitive subject for him. "So, no children?"

He laughed wryly. "I'm old-fashioned enough to have wanted children within a marriage." He looked her in the eyes. "I have five nieces and nephews. I love them very much. I would have loved a couple of my own. It wasn't meant to be, I guess."

Again, Cathy picked up that wistfulness in him.

"But *you* have children," he commented brightly. "Tell me about them."

Her favorite topic. Happily, Cathy launched into a description of her beloved kids. Frank was a great audience. He seemed to lap up all the details. When Cathy got a glimpse of her watch it was three o'clock.

Frank caught her glance. "Do you have to go?"

"Actually, I should get going," Cathy felt incredibly awkward. Next time, she would have a specific plan about where she was going next.

This was obviously an awkward moment for Frank too. Purposely, he looked her in the eye. "I really enjoyed talking to you. Do you like Thai food?"

Not quite understanding what was happening, Cathy answered reflexively. "Yes, I do."

"There's a great place in Red Hook. I'd love to take you there."

Oh god. This was all happening so fast. Cathy had assumed that, to ask her out again, he would wait until they were both home. But their conversation had been easy. She couldn't think what else to say. "Sounds great," she said brightly.

Quickly, he got up as if he had accomplished his mission. "I'll be in touch."

That sounded like a kiss-off line if ever she had heard one. Didn't she remember from her twenties that guys would say that and never be heard from again?

They walked together to the parking lot. Frank followed her to her car. Cathy's palms were sweating. Was he going to hug her, kiss her? But, instead, he just opened her car door for her.

Cathy slid in automatically. Frank closed the door. She started the car and rolled down the window. "Thanks very much!" she said. He leaned in and spoke to her softly. "So, you're not a virgin anymore," he observed with a smile. "Wasn't too bad, was it?" And without waiting for an answer, he stepped back and waved his hand.

Her head whirling, Cathy waved back and pulled away.

Don't you ever use that word, virgin, again! Talk about a fixation!

I know, can you believe it? You'd think *he* was the virgin. He said that he had been in a long-term relationship.

But when was that? My guess is that he's been single, really "celibate-single," not "player-single," for a long time.

I guess I have to be careful about the way I talk. On the soaps we talk about sex and romance all the time. It never occurred to me that virgin would be such a loaded word. It's used all the time in other contexts, *virgin run, Virgin Airlines*—heck, even *virgin bloody mary*!

You don't have to explain. I know what you mean.

Right. He seemed very nice, though. Really considerate and funny.

Reality check! Nice guy, but no cigar. What in the world does he do?

This is the Hudson Valley. Everyone's not type A. Look, I'm relieved. The conversation flowed.

Oh, c'mon. I already told you, you can talk to a rock. Look, it was a good first step. But I'm thinking there should be some ZING!

Zing? I haven't had zing for years.

He never even touched you! I get that he didn't want to come on too strong. But, wasn't the point of meeting to take a step farther? I was hoping for a little physical contact. He could so easily have touched your hand at the table. I thought, when he leaned into your car window, he was very sexy. I was waiting for a big smackeroo. But then, NOTHING!

I know. As much as I was nervous about that part, I did sort of want him to make a move.

I was waiting with baited breath. And what was the deal about Mommy and Daddy? The man is not a baby. I'm afraid this is a case of arrested development.

You've got me. He does act like life has passed him by.

He reminded me of a lost puppy. Endearing, cute, but clueless.

(LAUGHS) Puppies can be trained.

Are you kidding me? You want to train a puppy? You're a cat person. And you told him you'd go out with him!

I thought he was nice. There was no reason to say no. One dinner can't be so bad.

Don't be stupid. You can always be unavailable when he contacts you.

He probably won't contact me, anyhow. You know what "I'll be in touch" means.

In his case, it means a wagging tail and a wet tongue hanging out. On second thought, I take back the wet tongue part. If only. I'm afraid that Frankie is looking for a nice bowl of kibble and a home.

We'll see.

Thank goodness you have tango tonight. I'm all for the close embrace. Those Argentinians have it right.

Cathy jumped when her ringtone sounded through her car speaker. "Hello?"

Amy's voice came screeching through. "Are you okay? Have you been abducted by the anthropologist? Or did you just have a quickie in the parking lot?"

Cathy couldn't help laughing out loud. Mostly from the relief of surviving the last hour. "Ames, you're the one who should be the soap writer! What an imagination."

"Okay, okay—spill the beans. How was it? How was he?"

So Cathy launched into a full description.

"So, what's the bottom line?"

"I don't know. It was fine. He was nice looking. Nice."

"Nice? Fine? What kind of boring words are those? What was your chemistry like?"

"Chemistry?" Cathy was baffled.

"Jeez, Cath—*you're* the soap writer. Do I have to spell it out? Did you feel any tingle being near him? Did you want to touch him? Did you like his smell? Did your heart beat faster? Did you find yourself smiling for no reason?"

"Wow, Ames. You're good at this. We did laugh a lot."

"Laughing is good. Anything more?"

Cathy hesitates. "Not really, I guess."

"Obviously not, or you would have mentioned that first. Sounds like today was a good, functional icebreaker. No axe-murderer. No heartthrob."

"I've told you before. My heart-throbbing days are over."

"Forgive me, but you are the smartest and dumbest person I may have ever met. They are not over."

"I wish I could believe that. I do have one more thing to confess."

"Cough it up."

"I did sort of agree to have Thai food with him sometime. But he'll probably never follow through."

"Well, he sounds innocuous enough. You'll undoubtedly live to talk about a meal with him. He'll be good practice. You do need to get your sea legs back."

"Amy, that is so cruel. He's a human being, not a practice run."

"Enough with the bleeding heart. Dating is a cutthroat business. Either it's right or not. It's nobody's fault. You'll learn."

"I'm not so sure."

"Look, you're going to go home and dig through your Match mail. According to my calculations, you've got about ten more interesting men waiting in the wings. And how about being proactive on your own? Didn't Nancy advise you to search the available men who interest you instead of just waiting for them to contact you first? It's a two-way street on Match. This is a brave new world, darling."

"I do want to do that. I just haven't had time because of all the men who have contacted me."

"So, what are you doing tonight?"

"Actually, I'm going dancing."

"With whom?"

"By myself. It's my first *milonga*."

"What?"

"My first tango dance. They're called milongas."

Amy sighs. "What a day. First date. First mi-longa. Your life is about five hundred per cent more exciting than mine. We're going to the Smiths for the thousandth time. I'm sure she'll make her Mediterranean chicken."

"You love the Smiths."

"I do. But it would be fun to do something new."

"Be careful what you wish for ..." Cathy said softly.

When Cathy got home, she checked her email. At the top of her list was an email from Frank.

Hey Cat,

I had a great time today.

Are you free on Wednesday for Thai?

Frank

Told you! Get out your mop for the drool. Puppies can be messy.

FIRST MILONGA

Well, that was a bust—I thought Tango was supposed to be fun. I don't remember being such a wallflower since the seventh grade.

It was pretty awful. I really thought I'd be better than that after months of lessons. But, none of the steps that I do in class seemed to work in the middle of actual dancing. I almost fell over trying to do a boleo.

And what was with that obnoxious dude, Vincent? Who did he think he was criticizing everything you did as if he was your teacher?

I think he's just like that.

Well, I think it's bullshit. I swear, if one more man told you to relax your arm, I was going to slap him.

(AMUSED) I'm afraid that's not tango etiquette. The problem is, I get so nervous before I start dancing, that I'm really tense. It must be like holding a board. I can't blame them.

Well, you certainly do sweat like a pig. What's with that?

Gee, thanks for pointing that out. You do get really close to each other, but I think I'm so scared and trying so hard to concentrate that I pop out in a sweat.

Not the sexiest thing. And you still like this dance?

I know it's really crazy when, ninety-five percent of the night, I felt like crying. But that one *tanda* with Brad somehow made it worthwhile. He is so gentle and yet so secure in his lead. And he never criticizes anything I do. Dancing with him, I get a glimmer of what it could be like. And there's something absolutely irresistible about that possibility. That glimpse of tango heaven. I've heard other women say it's a little like falling in love.

But, how long is it going to take? I'm not sure I have the patience for all this.

You don't have the patience for much.

True. Thank god you do. We're a good team.

It's not like we have any choice in the matter.

Speaking of falling in love—it's not that late. I wonder what will be awaiting you on your Match dance card!

No one's going to write on a Saturday night. Anyhow, I'm pooped. I need some time off.

But, wouldn't it make your bruised ego feel a whole helluva lot better to read some mash notes from your online suitors? Think about it.

Cathy let herself into her house. As quickly as she could, she changed out of her black sequined dress. She knew it was weird, but she had a feeling that some of her clothes were more "lucky" than others. She had purposely worn the black dress that she had worn in photo number 123, the shot that seemed to work so well on Match. Unfortunately, that luck hadn't held for tango.

Sliding into her recliner with a plate of leftovers, Cathy felt herself sinking into one of her old Saturday night funks. She knew that it was ridiculous to feel this way. She had successfully had her first Match meeting. She had gotten asked out to dinner. She had attended her first milonga.

But it had been hard to walk into the dance by herself. When someone had finally taken pity on her and asked her to dance, she was a mess. She had been so tense that she had stumbled all over the place. All in all, she wondered if she would ever try tango again.

She glanced at her laptop on the coffee table in front of her. Maybe, she should try to get a little boost from her Match mail after all. In any case, she should answer Frank.

She clicked open her Match account. As she suspected, she hadn't gotten a lot more hits since she had looked earlier today.

She decided to write back to Frank.

It was very nice to meet you too, once I finally found you. Wednesday sounds great. Any time after 7:00. Just let me know when and where.

Well, that was something. Her second date. That should make her feel a little better.

She clicked on a few new messages. More silly stuff. Then, she noticed that Henry had written her back from this morning.

Cat,
I'm sorry to be responding to you so late.

Cathy checked the time of his email. He had actually written to her at 10:00 p.m. Maybe, his night had been a bust too.

I am up in Millbrook. Been riding all day—actually, fox hunting.

I know it's a little presumptuous, because we haven't communicated all that much. But I'm going back to the city on Monday and I wondered if by any chance you might be free for a drink at the Millbrook Golf and Tennis Club Sunday (tomorrow) night?

I figure, seize the day! How about you? Up for an adventure?

Henry

Cathy had to smile. Well, Henry sounded pretty different from Frank. The Millbrook Hunt? He didn't sound like a lost puppy. He sounded a lot more like the men she knew from Connecticut.

Impulsively, she typed.

Why not?

What time?

Cat

MASTER OF THE UNIVERSE

Fickle October pulled one of its tricks overnight. The temperature dropped twenty degrees. What was she going to wear?

Cathy stared at her closet. She needed to get some new smaller fall clothes. All she could think of was that Henry had been out hunting yesterday. She unearthed an old black skirt. With her red top, knee high boots and a little, black, fitted jacket from ages ago, she thought she looked pretty "Tally ho."

She had to laugh at herself. She had framed the saying "All the world's a stage, and all the men and women merely players," when she was in high school. She thought that Shakespeare had it exactly right. Each day was like a new little play. And somehow, she always felt compelled to wear the right costume, whatever it was. She guessed that it was no surprise that she had ended up in television.

Although she often carried a large, inexpensive, colorful purse, she unearthed a Chanel bag from the top of her closet. She knew the club game. Good shoes and good bags were a must.

All clean, scented, and dressed—Cathy headed out the door. It was fun to spend so much time primping and getting ready. She couldn't help remembering all those years when she was always racing to deal with the kids, her job, the house. She stepped into the garage and discovered it was really freezing. She ran back inside and grabbed the first thing she found, one of those lighter-than-air puffy down coats. She hadn't worn it since last April.

She pulled up in the circular driveway of the club. There was valet parking. That was unusual in Dutchess County. Feeling a little like a queen, she stepped out of her car and handed it over. She consciously pulled her shoulders back, put a smile on her face, and licked her lips. She opened the door and climbed the steps into the lounge area.

She looked around and spotted a man who looked like he might have participated in a hunt. He had on khaki pants, a navy blazer, and a pink tie. His hair was neatly parted, and he was clean shaven. But Cathy wasn't about to make the mistake she had made yesterday. She hesitated and glanced his way. He looked up from the *Wall Street Journal* he was reading.

Cathy couldn't miss the split-second sweep his eye made down her body. If she wasn't mistaken, his face hardened a little. But then, artfully, a disarming smile appeared on his face. "Cat?"

Thank goodness. She smiled back in relief and moved toward him. "Yes. Henry, I presume."

He held out his hand which she took. Then, reflexively, he gently pulled her toward him and gave her an air kiss on the cheek. "Thank you for dropping everything and meeting me tonight."

"I always like an adventure," Cathy replied a little flirtatiously.

Once again, she couldn't believe how this stuff just slipped out of her.

"May I take your coat," he asked smoothly.

Cathy turned so he could slip it off her back. "Thank you." She turned back to see him eyeing her again. This time his face looked quite different.

"What?" she asked.

"Sorry. I always forget how deceiving those down coats can be. It made you look twice your size. Not to be boorish, but a lot of women exaggerate a bit about their body type. I can see that you didn't. You are lovely. And, you look exactly like your photo."

Cathy wasn't sure whether to be flattered or irritated. Now she understood what his first look had meant. He had thought that she was fat. Clearly, that would have been unacceptable.

He hung up her coat and put his arm imperceptibly behind her back. "I had thought that we would have a drink at the bar, but I find that I am starving. Shall we go into the dining room and have a bite to eat? Do you have time?"

Cathy felt herself split into two people. On the one hand, she was attracted to Henry's confidence, polished grooming, and accomplished manner. But on the other hand, she was well aware that he would never have mentioned having something to eat if she hadn't "passed the test." There was a part of her that gave him credit for having such a neat system. It was all so artfully orchestrated. But she wondered whether, had she been physically unacceptable, he would suddenly find an excuse that forced him to leave early.

While all that was buzzing through her head, she found herself replying. "I could eat something, I suppose." Two could play at this game. She could counter coolness with coolness. She made a mental note to remember how he operated for her scripts. He was good.

With a little smile he nodded and escorted her into the dining room. The hostess walked them up to a corner table with a reserved sign on it. She removed the sign and said, "Enjoy your meal."

Cathy couldn't help wondering how many times Henry had used this maneuver. Obviously, the table was reserved for him if he should choose to use it. She also noted that the hostess didn't address him by his full name. She wondered if that was part of her instructions, so that Cat wouldn't learn his last name until he wanted her to.

Henry ordered a dry martini. She ordered a glass of white wine. Henry asked a few questions about her. Cathy countered with some questions about him. She learned that he had a place in Millbrook, but that he worked in the city, even though he listed himself on Match as living in Millbrook.

His first martini disappeared quickly and was seamlessly replaced with a fresh one. Cathy noticed that Henry seemed to quite enjoy talking about himself. She gathered that he was very successful in business.

After the second martini, she asked him about yesterday's hunt.

"It was a perfect day."

"Have you always ridden?"

"I didn't grow up riding. But I got interested in it when I was in my twenties. I met my wife riding," he added.

Cathy's ears perked up. "Oh, how long have you been divorced?"

Henry's mouth formed a wry smile. "The first time, or the second?"

"If you don't mind, I'd love to hear about both marriages. After all, I'm a soap opera writer. Always looking for material," she added flippantly.

"Oh dear. Then I am going to have to be careful."

"Don't be silly. You would never recognize anything from what you say today. It's just that love is so complicated and so endlessly interesting. It's a story that never gets old. You tell me yours; I'll tell you mine," she teased.

They both ordered the sole special. Cathy could see that Henry was very aware of his trim waistline. He didn't touch the bread basket.

With a third glistening martini in front of him, Henry looked her in the eyes. "Well, I guess that the "soap opera" part of my life is that my first and second marriages were to the same woman."

Cathy's eyes widened. "Interesting. I must admit I am hardly shocked. We have one character on my show who's been married to the same man four times."

For the first time, Henry seemed to let his guard down, put his head back, and laughed heartily. "I should have gone out with a soap writer before. All my friends think that I was a complete fool."

"I sincerely doubt that you were or are a fool," Cathy said softly. "It sounds like you loved her very much."

Henry sighed. His last bit of veneer seemed to melt away. "I did. It all started with those damn horses. I thought she was a goddess when I met her. Aphrodite on horseback."

"So, what happened?"

Henry stared at his glass. "She was Aphrodite all right. Stunning. Electrifying. She loved all the beautiful things in life, including herself."

"Did you have children?"

"Yes, I have two grown sons." Cathy was surprised that he didn't ask her about her children at this point. But he was so absorbed in his own reflections that she seemed to have disappeared.

"So, what happened? What made you get divorced, then remarried?"

"After about ten years, I realized that she was a beauty, all right. But as far as a companion—as someone to talk to in the dark of the night—I hate to say this, but she just didn't offer very much. My career was at a very precarious point. I was under a tremendous amount of stress. I realized that I needed something more. I got out that time without too much damage."

Cathy waited, wondering if she should ask another question. But Henry seemed to be on a roll now.

"The problem was, she was just so damn irresistible to me. And, of course, we had the boys. So, naturally, I did see her in the course of things. I managed to navigate this critical transition at work and ended up coming out on top. I realize this now in hindsight, but coincidentally she seemed to discover a newfound interest in me. Before I knew it, I was proposing again. After a barely respectable amount of time, I was served with divorced papers. She took me to the cleaners the second time."

Cathy had to admit that she was privately shocked that this suave, controlling man was revealing how bitter he was. She was also surprised that he was obviously more upset about losing his money and getting hoodwinked than losing his marriage. "Oh, I'm sorry," she murmured weakly.

By now, they were done with their dinners. He reached across the table and covered her hand with his. "You are very easy to talk to. And very easy to look at."

Cathy wasn't sure why, but this comment made her squirm. Especially in light of the Aphrodite story. Naturally, she wanted to feel attractive. But she didn't want that to be the bottom line. Was the whole dating thing still the same as in their twenties? Was it still mostly about how you looked?

"Would you like coffee?"

Cathy felt herself wanting to leave. "You know, I can't drink coffee this late. Even decaf. I think I'd better get going. Driving at night in the country is pretty tricky."

He got up and pulled out her chair. Obviously, since it was his club, there was no point in her offering to pay. The evening would just be billed to him.

He walked her to the door and settled her into her coat. He took both of her hands. "Thank you so much for joining me tonight. I had a lovely time. In the interest of full disclosure, I do have to tell you that I have just started seeing someone who lives in the city. I have no idea where the relationship is going. But, I'm not the type of man who plays the field for long."

Cathy was flustered. What in the world was he telling her? Was he gently blowing her off? She hadn't been at all sure that she would have wanted to see him again before he said that. Now, she felt a little disappointed. "I know what you mean. We'll see what tomorrow brings, won't we?" she responded enigmatically. "Thank you so much for dinner."

He reached down and gave her that practiced kiss on her cheek. Her car instantly appeared at the front door.

Cathy slid into her car and pulled away without a backward glance. She was surprised at how off balance she felt. She felt like she had been manipulated from the minute she had walked into the club.

You too, huh? I feel like the lady who's just been sawed in half in the box. Talk about an illusionist. Now you see him, now you don't. He deserved Aphrodite. He's just pissed that she beat him at his own game. Good for her!

I think you're being a little harsh.

You do? What about that obnoxious comment about the down coat? What an asshole!

It is pretty scary how important looks are to men. I understand that the male brain is wired to pick an attractive, healthy woman to bear his children. But we're way past that stage.

Honey, I don't think the male brain is any different at fifty than it is at twenty.

Maybe not, but I feel like I'm looking for something different.

Do you? In your heart of hearts, aren't you looking for a Master of the Universe? Well, kiddo, Henry is the Chairman of the Board! Can you believe how he liked to talk about himself? Blah, blah, blah. Then there were the three martinis. Imagine what he does at home when he doesn't have to drive? Not to mention that final bomb. Oh, I'm such a loyal, true-blue guy that if my new relationship in Manhattan works out, you might not hear from me. What was he waiting for—his purple heart—the applause machine?

Can't you say anything encouraging? You said Frank was a loser. Now Henry is full of himself. At least he held my hand.

True. But, what about a kiss? All that continental cheek-kissing stuff! It's been a long time, baby.

I hate to admit that I agree with you. I'm pretty curious about how it would feel to kiss someone other than Bob. But I suppose the Millbrook Golf and Tennis Club is not the place. I wonder how long it's going to take?

The problem is, life is not a soap opera. You want to wave your wand and meet your soul mate in one try. That's how you would have written it, wouldn't you?

Maybe.

Well, life isn't quite so neat. The good thing is, you've got dozens more possibilities stacked up over the Match runway. Get the air traffic control tower to wave in the next one.

I know I should be excited about that. But, I'm already tired. This whole process is exhausting.

You're tired because you've jumped off the cliff. You're free-flying. The adrenalin rush is too much. For the first time in about thirty years, you've had dates with two strange men on the same weekend. I'm really proud of you. Go to bed and see how you feel in the morning. You know that's what your mother would have said. Everything looks different in the morning. You've only just begun.

I hate it when you quote Mom. I can't believe that I have dinner with Frank on Wednesday.

Practice, practice, practice. If at first you don't succeed—try, try again.

Yeah, yeah. Got it. I don't think online dating is for me.

I doubt that's the explanation, since you seem to be the Goddess of Match. But, it's certainly possible you won't find The One.

Thanks a lot.

It wasn't that late when Cathy got home. She was very tired, but she was also restless. She knew she shouldn't, but she couldn't help peeking at her mail. *ChrisMD* had written her again. She hadn't answered him the first time.

Just checking in again. I've been on call all weekend. I'd love to get a chance to chat with you. Here is my number. I'll be home Monday and Tuesday night. Or, send me your number, and I'll call you.

Cathy felt the back of her neck prickling. Those words were all too familiar. On call. She didn't think she was ready for another physician yet. She was not sure that she ever would be.

The whole phone calling thing also opened a can of worms. Although, she had gone straight to meeting Frank and Henry without speaking to them on the phone, she could imagine that it would be useful to speak to someone before you met, so it wouldn't be such a blind date. But she was uncomfortable about giving out her number. On the other hand, it would be weirder for her to cold call him.

She wasn't going to decide what to do right now. She read another message from *BurntUmber*. It turned out that "D" was an artist named Donald.

Moonrise,

How do you feel about becoming my muse? Seems pretty appropriate for a moon girl.

No, this is not just a sketchy artist pickup line. Your mention of Monopoly inspired me. I unearthed an old set lurking in my barn. The next thing you know, I incorporated some of the cards and playing pieces into a new multimedia work. I'm really excited about it.

I'd love to show it to you.

Donald

How much fun was that? An artist was sure a lot different than the doctors, lawyers, and stock brokers that she had known in Connecticut. He had to be a lot less pompous than Henry. Her Monopoly reference was really paying off. Who knew? Impulsively, she wrote him back.

BurntUmber,

I'm terribly flattered. I must confess that I've always dreamed of becoming a muse.

To be truthful, I'd love to see your piece. Not sure about your barn, though. Is your piece portable?

Cat

Suddenly, Cathy felt much better. Suddenly, she felt like she was flying again.

She headed up to bed with a much lighter heart, imagining herself as Aphrodite

LITTLE RED RIDING HOOD

"Oh honey. I wish I had a gold star for your forehead. Your birthday, going online and two dates since I saw you last week?! Be still, my heart."

Cathy had to laugh. "It was pretty amazing."

"When it's time, it's time," Pat chuckled. She leaned in conspiratorially. "So how did it feel?"

"Well, both dates went pretty well, I think," Cathy admitted modestly.

"I'm sure you dazzled them both," Pat added enthusiastically.

"I'm not sure I'm quite in the *Bewitched* category yet. But conversation flowed easily."

"So how did you like them?"

"It's weird. They're complete opposites. Frank is very low-key. He was trained as an anthropologist, but he doesn't seem to do that now. I'm not sure what he does for a living. He's never been married."

Pat scrunched up her face. "I sense some red flags."

"And the other man?"

"Henry was just the opposite. Totally controlling. We met at his club in Millbrook. He loved to talk about himself and all his accomplishments. He also had three martinis in an hour."

"Oh, a Master of the Universe?"

"You got it."

"Well, it's not surprising that neither of them was the perfect match for you. It takes some time to find the right person. How did you feel about being near them? Did they wake up the dead?" Pat flashed her a minxish smile.

"No, not really. Frank didn't touch me. Henry held my hand and air-kissed me."

"And?"

"Nothing. Well, Henry's hand was dry and cool. It felt nice to be touched. But I have to admit, I get more excited being held in tango."

"How is the tango going?"

Cathy groaned. "Well, I was humiliated at a milonga last Saturday. You can't imagine how awful it was to feel like a preteen lined up on the side wall of a ballroom hoping that some 'boy' would ask me to dance. I don't even have acne."

Pat laughed. "You most certainly do not. Can't you ask a man to dance?"

"It's crazy. It seems to be the Argentinian etiquette. The man asks the woman. I was so desperate that I might have done it anyhow, but I'm such a rank beginner that I was only confident asking the people from my class. For some reason, those men always seemed to be busy dancing with someone else."

"Well, I have to admit that I know very little about Argentine tango. But I am very impressed that you have stuck with it this far. I wonder if it isn't 'breaking the ice' for you a little in terms of physical intimacy. The couples I have seen look very intense. It certainly looks a lot to me like making love to music."

Cathy beamed. "There is something very powerful about the connection that can happen between two dancers. So far, it's only happened to me a few times."

"Aha! Just as I suspected. I'm not calling in the undertaker yet. You just haven't met the right guy. It's only a matter of time."

"I wonder. It's true that I've had a lot of hits on Match. But now that I'm learning to read between the lines, I'm a little discouraged about the kind of men who have written to me. Many of them seem rather petulant."

"I have heard that some women, especially the attractive ones, make a habit of getting free meals by meeting a lot of guys that they're not serious about at all."

"For that very reason I've decided on a policy to pay my way the first time. It only seems fair." Cathy made a face. "'Course, it hasn't worked out like that so far. Frank insisted on paying for my cup of tea. It seemed like a point of pride for him. And Henry invited me to *his club*."

"Have you been proactive at all about writing to the men who appeal to you? Men are conditioned to be the aggressor. But I think they are tickled when a woman approaches them."

"I haven't had time yet. When I do, I think the key is to be funny and clever. You can't sound desperate."

"That's the human condition, isn't it, honey? We are all suspicious of anyone who wants us too much."

"It's why we go to such ridiculous lengths to create so many obstacles on the soaps. Somehow, love can't be too easy, or it's not worth it."

"Well, I think you've had a banner week. Didn't I tell you that you were a prize?"

"You've been a great cheerleader from the beginning, Pat. I can't thank you enough. In fact, you've been exactly like my mother. Well, maybe not exactly—I'm not sure I would have discussed sex with my mother."

"I'm your mother with a twist," Pat teased. "I'm your mother who gives you homework."

Cathy sighed. "Now what?"

"I know you'll get to it sooner or later. But while your Match iron is hot, I'd really like you to initiate communication with some men on Match who haven't written to you first. Go for it."

"Between my script, Thai dinner with Frank, and countless polite rejections—I'll get right on it," Cathy replied sarcastically.

"Good girl." Pat nodded, ignoring her attitude.

As tantalizing as it was, Cathy refused to let herself glance at Match after she got home from Pat's. If she wasn't careful, Match was going to take over her life. The whole time she was working on her new script, Match was like a siren calling to her.

Eight new messages had popped up. She felt a little shot of adrenalin. She had to admit, part of this process was definitely a high. Her eye caught a new message from BurntUmber. Quickly, she tapped it.

Are you afraid of coming to my barn to look at my sketches, little girl, asked the Big Bad Wolf?

LOL. I don't blame you.

As a matter of fact, the piece would easily fit in my truck. Or, I could actually take a photo of it and send it to you if you would give me the privilege of your email address. Although a photo would certainly not do it justice, since it's three dimensional. OR, we could talk and get to know each other a little more before we do anything rash in a barn or anywhere else.

If you would be so inclined, send me your number.
TBBW

Cathy found herself laughing. TBBW—*The Big Bad Wolf*. He had gotten it entirely right. A woman of the world, and all she could imagine were his long fangs gleaming in the shadow of his barn. She thought maybe she would send him her personal email address. Her address had nothing to do with her name. She wondered if that was safe.

But Donald's request that they talk on the phone reminded her of *ChrisMD*. She was reminded that Chris had asked her to call him. She scrolled back to his last message. He wanted her to call him on Monday or Tuesday night. She had never even answered him.

It was Monday night. Cathy knew that it wasn't fair, but something about Chris's terse little note reminded her so much of Bob. She knew they didn't mean to be, but doctors just seemed arrogant. They expected to give an order and have it followed. She reread Chris's profile. He certainly seemed like a thoughtful and articulate man. But he wasn't entertaining, like Donald.

Donald seemed so amusing that she was inclined to write him

right now, ask him for his number and call him. She could always block her number when she phoned.

Quickly, she typed a response to Chris.

Sorry not to get back to you sooner. I'm just running off to class. I'll try you on Tuesday night. 8-ish?

No sooner had she sent it than she wondered why she had lied. She wasn't going to any class tonight. But somehow she didn't want to say that she just didn't feel up to talking—to him. Oh, who cared.

Then she zipped off a note to Donald.

Dear Wolfie,
"Anything rash in a barn?"
My face is as red as my riding hood.
Those sorts of thoughts NEVER crossed my mind.
However, I might consider hearing your voice, or should I say growl, if you sent me your number.
I've never talked to a wolf before.
LRRH

Feeling like her car had just tipped over the crest of a roller coaster, Cathy hit send.

Cathy was a little surprised that she hadn't heard from Henry. She had figured that she'd at least get a polite lovely-to-meet-you note. But, the Master of the Hunt must be busy with his other prey.

All right. Time to go *hunting*, herself. Since she had signed up, Match had sent her a new group of matches every day. Supposedly, the Match algorithm figured out who was good for you. So far, Cathy hadn't even had time to check them. She clicked on the first one. Ugh. This guy was a match? *No thank you.* She went through the next five. For two of them she clicked: *Maybe.*

She was thinking that she really should set up her own search when she clicked on the last match. A dashing man in a tuxedo popped up. Nice. There was nothing more flattering on a man than a tuxedo. After all the scruffy beards and bikers, this "James Bond" was quite a change. She opened his profile. *GottaDance.*

Cathy's heart skipped a beat. He danced? Quickly, she read through his details. He was divorced. Children. He liked to hike, bike, and *dance*! She wondered what kind of dancing. Probably not tango. And then there was the final item. He worked in Medical/Veterinary. Oh, no. Not another doctor. What was it with her? Was she an MD-magnet?

Just as she was mulling over what to do, a new message pinged through. It was *BurntUmber.* Now, she had his phone number. Without waiting another nanosecond, she blocked her phone number and dialed.

The phone rang and rang. Cathy was upset. Wasn't he there? Then, finally on the sixth ring, "Hello?" His voice sounded curt and impatient.

Cathy was taken aback. "Wolfie?" she squeaked. What in the world was wrong with her voice?

"Red?" This time his voice sounded much more friendly. "I never answer unidentified calls. I thought you were a telemarketer."

"Oh sorry. I'm really not that good at all this yet. All the books say to block your number. You're supposed to protect your identity."

Cathy grinned as she listened to a deep, frustrated growl on the phone. Donald continued with a gravelly voice. "But my dear, I am only your old grannie with a little cold."

"But Grandma, what big eyes you have." Cathy teased.

"Big eyes, big ears, big nose…" Donald let his words trail off suggestively.

Cathy felt her face burn. Now what had she gotten herself into? "Okay, okay. I'm just coming off a twenty-five-year marriage. I'm out of practice."

Donald let out a huge laugh. "I thought you were a soap writer. Isn't this sort of dialogue your bread and butter?" For the first time, Cathy heard his real voice. It was deep and warm.

"We actually have pretty strict standards on all our scripts. Anyhow, it's harder when it's me and not a character talking."

"I get it. Twenty-five years? Mazel tov. I only made it fourteen. But you know how unstable artists can be."

"Actually, I have no clue what artists are like. My world has mostly been the suit-and-tie guys—stockbrokers, lawyers, doctors."

"Poor bastards," Donald remarked. "Which flavor is your ex?"

Cathy had to laugh. Donald was really clever and bold. She liked that he was going right to the heart of the matter. "Actually, he's a cardiologist."

"A man dedicated to matters of the heart. You don't have to answer this, but what happened?"

Cathy sighed. "I guess he was just better at fixing other people's hearts than tending to mine."

"Relationships. Can't live without them. Can't live with them."

"How about your marriage?"

"I told you I was an unstable artist. You're not wrong to worry about the Big Bad Wolf. I was a bad boy. Probably still am."

"Is it possible I'm not your first muse?" Cathy flirted.

"I'm pleading the Fifth. The fact is, I find beauty irresistible—in all forms. I'm a little older and wiser now, but if you're looking for a diamond ring, I'm probably not *your* wolf."

"The last thing I'm looking for is a diamond," Cathy said fervently. "Been there, done that. I went on Match hoping for a playmate. Some fun. New activities. The fact is, I hate sitting at home on Saturday night." Cathy couldn't believe she had just blurted all this out.

"Gosh, this is sounding better and better. Playing is my specialty. Now when are you going to see what you inspired? I understand about the barn reluctance. But, do you ever get near Woodstock?"

"As a matter of fact, there's a tango night at some restaurant there on Thursday nights."

"Oh, that's right. The Tango Queen."

"Hardly. I've just started. I'm having a love-hate relationship with the dance. It is the most frustrating and fascinating activity I've ever attempted."

"Sounds perfect for being fresh off a twenty-five-year marriage. Time to grow some new wings."

Cathy laughed delightedly. This guy had it exactly right.

"So, are you going this Thursday?" Donald asked pointedly.

"I'm not sure. I've got plans on Wednesday night. It'll depend on how my script is coming. It's due Friday."

"Ah. Big date on Wednesday, huh?" Donald guessed unerringly.

"I'm going out to dinner with a friend," Cathy responded primly.

Donald laughed again. "So, this is the thing. I like you, Red. I think we should meet. And since I'm a flexible non-suit-and-tie kind of guy who totally understands the creative process, you can call me at the last minute on Thursday. If it's a go, I'll get out the turpentine, clean the paint off my hands, change my T-shirt, toss my Monopoly-piece in the truck, and meet you before or after tango. Or during, if you wouldn't mind me watching. Maybe, I could even do some sketching."

Cathy didn't know what to think. Could she have her fourth date in a week? Why the heck not? She couldn't afford to lose her job. But if her script was in good shape, she was a free agent. She had thoroughly enjoyed talking to Donald. Wasn't it time for her to live a little? "It's a deal."

"Cool. I'll be thinking positive thoughts. Write like a demon."

"Not sure my show would appreciate that," Cathy laughed. "We're not into witchcraft, either."

"Oh, and one more thing, Cat. I completely respect your desire for privacy. But I'd like you to check me out if you'd like. My name is Donald Lancaster. Feel free to Google me. I want you to know that I'm a real person. And you can see some of my work."

Cathy felt the force of his personality. "Okay. Lancaster. Like Burt?"

"That's right. Just think of me and *From Here to Eternity*. I'll be looking forward to Thursday. Sweet dreams, Red." And with that, he hung up.

Cathy just sat there for a moment holding the phone. What had just hit her? This man was a force to be reckoned with. She found herself suddenly very excited. She had felt like she could tell him almost anything. Henry might be a Master of the Universe, but Donald seemed like the Master of Fun.

She poured herself another glass of wine and tried to remember what she had been doing when she called him. Oh, that's right. *GottaDance*.

Feeling more sassy and bold than she had felt in years, Cathy decided to do her homework. She clicked on *GottaDance's* profile and started typing.

Dear 007,

The great gods of Match have offered you to me as a potential match. They seem to think that we have something in common. They are definitely right about one thing. I love to dance. It seems you do too. I have recently taken up Argentine tango. What kind of dancing do you do?

BTW, I have to confess that I'm a sucker for the James Bond look. Why don't men wear tuxedos all the time? If we do meet, would you mind wearing it?

Moonrise

THE MERRY-GO-ROUND

Cathy was pleased that her writing had flowed so easily today. She thought that having the motivation to go to Woodstock on Thursday was helping her.

She checked into Match. Not much happening. She found that she was a little disappointed that *GottaDance* hadn't responded to her. So much for men being flattered by the tables being turned.

She looked at the clock. Time for *ChrisMD*. Okay, here goes.

"Hello?" The voice on the other end of the phone was a little husky.

"Chris, this is Cat, from Match."

"Oh, Cat, how do you do? Thank you for calling me. What class did you take last night?" He sounded very old-fashioned. She could just picture him in a crisp white jacket, stethoscope, and bow tie.

Cathy hesitated. What was he talking about? Then, she remembered her excuse for not calling last night. She had to give him credit for paying attention. "Oh, I take—a dance class." Might as well get close to the truth. "How are you tonight?"

"To be honest, I'm a little weary. I had a busy weekend on call."

A little weary? How old was Chris? "What kind of a physician are you?"

"Actually, I'm an orthopedic surgeon. It was a big football weekend. Always a lot of bad breaks."

"I imagine. It's tough when your life is not your own. My ex is a physician too."

"Then, you know what it's like. I'm surprised you actually called me."

Cathy appreciated his dry humor. "Me too. I'm not going to lie. I had some misgivings."

"No doubt. We're a tough breed to live with. Well, you must be under a lot of pressure too. A soap opera writer. I don't think I've ever run across someone like you."

"We don't break our bones too much sitting at the computer. Maybe a little carpal tunnel."

Chris laughed. "You're funny."

"Well, I am in the entertainment business."

"How nice. I could certainly use some entertaining."

"Why is that?"

"How about we meet in person and I'll tell you my deep, dark story."

"Oh my. That's the most irresistible thing you could say to me. I love deep, dark stories."

"You're in Dutchess County, right? I'm in Westchester. By any chance would you be free for lunch on Saturday? I know a cute, little Italian place right on the Taconic sort of between us. I'm not on call this weekend."

"I do know the place." Cathy hesitated, then followed her instinct. "I've been wanting to go there. But please don't bring your stethoscope."

"That I can promise."

They hung up after making specific plans. Cathy took a deep breath. OMG! Saturday would be her fifth meeting/date in a week. This was ridiculous. She had been so sure that she couldn't handle another doctor. But against her better judgment, she had liked Chris, even if he did sound a little like a fuddy-duddy. She wondered if he was really the age that he said he was. There must be men who lied about their age too.

She had a clear, mental picture of a lean man with thinning hair and glasses. Or was she imagining her childhood GP? Then, she looked up his Match photo. It was a very shadowy picture. Well, she'd find out soon enough.

What is the deal? Are you trying to get into the Guinness Book of Records with the most Match dates in a week? How are you ever going to keep track of all of them?

I thought this is what you wanted. To go for it!

I do, but don't you think this is a little crazy? You've got Frank tomorrow night—then you're chomping at the bit to meet Donald on Thursday. Now, "Dr. Welby" on Saturday.

Look, I'm just trying to go with the flow.

Flow? This is more like a gusher!

Nancy told me that momentum was important. Once the ball gets rolling, it's important to follow up. Otherwise, the men will just move on.

This isn't a ball, it's a bloody boulder threatening to crush everything in its path.

Let's not get overly dramatic. Theo encouraged us to be open to what the universe brings. At the moment, this is what I'm getting.

Well, you better copy all of their profiles and make a folder. Then,

you can make notes every time you talk to one of them, or see them. Unless you're a genius, which I know you're not, it's going to be impossible to keep track of what you've said to whom.

After keeping track of twenty-five characters on the show, I think I can keep track of four men.

As long as you stick with the truth, you're probably okay.

I always tell the truth.

Right. How old did you say you were? And, what about that dance class last night?

Okay, okay. But those aren't important details.

Your age isn't important? By the way, when are you going to tell Frank your real age? I thought that's what you had decided. You'd tell them the truth once you met.

I'll tell him tomorrow.

I'll hold you to that. And by the way, why don't you prepare an excuse for not seeing him again. Frankly, Donald and Chris seem like much better prospects.

I will. It's just that Frank seems like such a nice guy. I already feel sentimental about him. He's my first.

Stop being a simpering fool. Nice is not enough. You've known that since you were thirteen. Find out what the heck he does for a living. And get him to touch you! It's time for the chemistry lab.

Got it.

Cathy stared at Frank's mouth. A little pad thai noodle had fallen onto his chin. He was wearing a blue oxford shirt with the sleeves rolled up. Always a nice look. And, of course, the ubiquitous jeans. Unfortunately, there was a small stain on the pocket of his shirt, which was partially untucked. He looked like a little boy who had dressed himself. He looked like a little boy who needed a mommy.

Their conversation was easy, as it had been last time. Cathy told him about her house on the lake. "What about you? Where do you live?"

Frank squirmed in his chair. "Actually, the owner of the cottage I was renting took her place back this past summer. So for the moment I'm living at my mother's place. She's in Arizona already."

Cathy tried not to be surprised. "So you don't own your own place?" The minute she said it, Cathy was embarrassed that she had been so blunt.

Frank didn't seem insulted. "My mother has always said that there's no reason to waste the money." He dabbed his mouth with his napkin and finally wiped the noodle off his chin.

"So, tell me about your anthropology travels."

Frank's face lit up. "It was the greatest period of my life. I traveled all over the world. That's when I fell in love with Thai food. And I met—Diana."

Cathy's soap sense told her that this is where the heart of Frank's story lay. "Diana? Was she your long-term relationship?"

Frank set down his chopsticks. He seemed to suddenly have lost his appetite. "Yes."

Cathy waited for him to tell her more. But Frank was silent. "What happened?" she encouraged. She didn't want to be insensitive, but it had been years ago.

"I thought we were going to be together forever. She seemed to love my life. And then, suddenly, she didn't. Right after she left me, my father died. I was in pretty bad shape. So, I came home to help my mom. I'm still here." He shrugged his shoulders.

Cathy's heart sank. "So you never got back to anthropology?"

"For a long time I couldn't face being on the road without her. Then, after all that time, I had fallen out of the loop. You know, it's publish-or-perish in a field like that."

"So you've ended up working for your father's accounting firm?" Cathy prompted him.

"Yes. But, I'm not a CPA. So I'm sort of a second-class citizen."

Oh god. This was getting worse and worse. Did this guy feel good about anything in his life? "I'm surprised that you never went back to school. Surely, you weren't too old."

"I never wanted to be an accountant. Naturally, that was my father's dream for me. But I wasn't like him. I can't stand numbers." Frank made a wry face. "So that's my own little soap opera."

Cathy's heart was breaking from the pure pathos of Frank's sad story. Impulsively, she took his hand. "Hey, we all have soap operas. That's why they've been on the air for so long. Life is messy. Unexpected things happen. It's up to us to pick ourselves up and move on. If you could wave a wand and become whomever you'd like to be, who would that be?" Cathy asked.

"I sometimes think I'd like to go back to the South Pacific."

"Well, I think anything is possible. I'm sure you could go back, even if you had to start at a lower position."

"No." Frank was definite. "It's been over twenty years. The indigenous people that I studied are virtually gone."

No. What a disgusting word, Cathy thought. *No* stopped everything.

They finished their meal, and Frank paid the bill. Cathy felt really guilty, sensing that Frank didn't have a lot of money. But what could she do? He had asked her out.

He walked her to her car. On an impulse, Cathy leaned over and kissed him on the lips.

Frank seemed surprised. "I had a great time tonight, Cat. I hope we can see each other again. For a virgin you seem pretty wise. I haven't talked about some of that stuff for ages. If you use any of my material, just do me a favor and change my name."

Cathy laughed with delight. The charming, self-deprecating Frank was back. Too bad he was just a cover. She hesitated and then decided that now was the time. She took a deep breath.

"Frank, I've been meaning to tell you something. When I went on Match, I had been told by my girlfriends that men always looked for younger women. I don't know why exactly, but I fudged my age a little. I'm actually four years older than I listed."

Frank hardly blinked. "Cool. Then we're just the same age."

Cathy knew that she should let this go, but she was curious. "So you're not upset? A lot of men seem to be paranoid about being lied to."

Frank laughed. "You look exactly like your picture. And you look great. I think that's what most men care about."

"Well, my photo was taken just over a week ago."

"That may be a first. I would guess some of the women I've met had photos that were over ten years old."

"Thank you, Frank." She got into her car, waved at him and drove off, keeping a smile on her face.

Well, you dodged a bullet with the age thing.

I'm just glad I was right. What difference do a couple of years make at our age?

Well, it's all moot, anyhow. I hope you learned your lesson with Frank. Case closed.

Actually, I feel really sad for him. He was a few hours out of my life. I learned a lot.

What a mess. What happened to him? Hard to believe that one relationship derailed him.

I think it was more complicated than that. It was the combination of Diana leaving and the father's death.

Well, thank god you finally managed to touch him. At least, the night wasn't a total waste. He sure wasn't going to make any moves. What did you think?

Don't be cute with me. You know what I thought. Nothing. Just like the song from *A Chorus Line*, "I felt nothing."

Agreed. Then there was the noodle on his chin ...

(CAN'T HELP LAUGHING) I know.

At least you didn't agree to see him again. How did it feel to kiss someone other than Bob on the lips?

It was pretty scary, but I did it.

Sort of like riding a bicycle, don't you think?

Not exactly. It felt like a pretty foreign action.

You'll get used to it. Maybe with Donald tomorrow?

I'm not sure I have the stomach for all this.

Forget it, sweetheart. You have jumped off the diving board. The video is not going to reverse. Enjoy the flight.

Cathy had felt completely wiped out when she left Frank. But when she got home, she got a second wind. She had to admit—it was fun to be part of all this drama, instead of just writing it.

She clicked open her Match account. There was a message from *BurntUmber.*

Hey Red,

Hope your date was a bust. Also hope your script is in great shape.

My sketch pad and charcoal are ready. Always wanted to sketch a Tango Queen.

Waiting with bated breath—rather difficult for a Wolf.

TBBW

WOLFIE

Cathy couldn't believe that her last scene was done by one o'clock. She made herself a late lunch and then called Donald. She was feeling a little giddy when he answered the phone.

"Hello."

"Who's afraid of the big bad wolf, the big bad wolf, the big bad wolf?" Cathy even surprised herself when she opened her mouth and started singing the old Disney song.

Donald let out a huge belly laugh. "I recognize the euphoria. Can I assume that you were a creative genius today?"

"It takes one to know one," Cathy retorted.

"So, what time shall I meet you?"

"The class starts at seven at the New World Restaurant. Why don't you come by at about eight?"

"Sounds like a plan. Hey, thanks for giving me so much notice. I've still got hours before I need to get the turpentine out."

"Happy painting."

Cathy used the next few hours to straighten her house and get ready. She found herself whistling in anticipation. She wore a red and black skirt that she had just bought at a consignment shop with a handkerchief hemline and a red camisole top. Red and black were the classic tango colors. Her outfit was totally different from her old suburban mommy clothes.

As she drove to Woodstock she couldn't deny how excited she felt about meeting Donald. She had googled him, as he had suggested. He was quite an established artist—with work exhibited in a number of small museums and public buildings.

The class was held in the back room of the restaurant. Before she knew it, Cathy was completely absorbed trying to learn an *ocho cortado*. After every song, the teacher had the leaders rotate. So Cathy danced with all seven men. She had to concentrate furiously because each different leader made the same step feel completely different. But, if she did say so herself, she had improved a lot since the summer. Now, if only she could translate the steps she learned in class to a milonga. It was so much easier when she knew what was coming next.

The teacher, Marco, moved through all the couples giving them pointers. Cathy tried not to tense up when he moved over to her. Her partner led her through the steps.

"Very nice," Marco said after watching their feet.

Cathy felt elated. After her disaster last Saturday when everyone seemed to criticize her, it felt so good to have someone say that she was doing something right. She beamed.

"Thank you very much, everyone. Good class. Now, I will play music for your dancing enjoyment," Marco announced, marking the end of the class.

Cathy had been so transported, she had completely lost track of the time. Suddenly, it all came to her in a flash. Donald was meeting her here. She looked around for her purse and started to head out to the bar. That's when she saw him.

Tucked in a dark corner behind a piano, a lanky man with a greying pony-tail was sitting with a sketch pad in his lap. He leered at her devilishly and moved toward her. "Little Red Riding Hood, I presume."

All Cathy could think of was Ichabod Crane. He towered over her, but looked like he might not weigh all that much more than her. She tried to cover her surprise, and plastered on a big smile. "Wolfie!"

With no hesitation, Donald swept his wiry arm behind her and pulled her in for a hug and a dramatic twirl. "Hey, this was a blast. I did some great sketches of you."

"How long have you been here?"

"Awhile," Donald answered, flipping through several pages of his pad. "I can see why you like this. What a trip. Maybe I'll take up tango myself."

Donald took her hand and led her off the floor. "Shall we get a drink? We can toast to you being my muse."

Cathy followed him out to the bar. They both ordered a beer. Almost immediately, Donald flipped open his pad.

"You're really good." Cathy couldn't believe how he had caught her expression and movement with only a few lines. Her asymmetrical skirt twirled out. Her feet were graceful and pointed.

"I aim to please my muse," he flirted. He tore the best drawing out of his pad and signed it. "For you."

"Oh, my gosh. Thank you." After her disappointed reaction to his appearance, Cathy could feel herself being seduced by his disarming manner again. "Thank you for coming here. How far is it for you?"

"I'm about thirty minutes away. I live on a mountain in a house I built entirely myself. It's just me and the birds. And the bears, of course. It's a fantastic place to work. No distractions."

A chill went up Cathy's spine. She knew that she had left Connecticut to live a different kind of life. But, up a mountain with only the birds and the bears? Then, she realized she was jumping way ahead of herself. She wasn't moving in with him, just yet.

"Speaking of work, are you ready to view the Monopoly master-piece? I parked the truck under the light, so you could see it."

Without waiting for her answer, he took her hand and led her out of the restaurant. As soon as they rounded the side of the building, he pointed out the full moon. Cathy shivered from the cold night. "My muses," he whispered. "La Luna and you." He leaned down and kissed her ever so gently on the lips.

Cathy was startled. But, that's all he did, barely brushed her lips.

Then, he pulled away, flipped open the back of his truck, hopped in, and helped her up onto the back.

He flipped a tarp off of a big canvas that was at least five by three feet. Donald had used all the bright colors of the Monopoly proper-ties to create a maze. Several property cards were built into a little house. Cathy spotted the dog, the shoe and the top hat playing pieces embedded in the paint. "This is lots of fun," Cathy commented. "It makes me smile."

Donald looked pleased. "I think it's a great metaphor for life, and I have you to thank for the inspiration." With that, he pulled her into his arms and began kissing her again.

Cathy couldn't believe that she was standing in the back of a pick-up truck next to an unusual piece of art that she had somehow helped inspire kissing a pony-tailed man under the moonlight after being sketched in a tango class. Never in a million years did she ever picture something like this happening to her. What would her Connecticut friends think? She had to call Amy ASAP.

Then, she realized that Donald was still nibbling away on her lips.

What is it with this guy?

Go away! Not now.

Why doesn't he just open up and stick his tongue in your mouth?

You're disgusting.

You know you want that.

That's not the point. Go away.

Cathy shook her head. What was wrong with her?

Donald pulled back, obviously misinterpreting her movement. "Sorry, I got a little carried away."

Cathy couldn't figure out why she wasn't carried away. She couldn't have invented a more unusual or romantic situation.

Obviously, very sensitive to her signals, Donald jumped off the truck, put his hands around her waist and guided her down. They walked back to the bar.

Cathy was so confused. What had happened? They sat at the bar, and she tried to make conversation. But something had changed.

"I love your piece."

"Me too." That seemed enough encouragement for Donald to regale her with endless stories about his work.

Cathy could not suppress a yawn.

"Oh dear, I'm boring you to death," Donald observed.

"Not at all. I guess I'm just a little tired after a day of writing and class. Tango takes a lot of concentration. And I do have an hour drive home."

"Of course, you do," he agreed solicitously. They paid their bill. This time, Cathy managed to pay for her own beer.

Donald walked her out to her car. "Hey, this was a hoot." He leaned down and this time surprised her with an open-mouthed kiss. His tongue went deep.

"Hmmm..." he murmured. "You're quite delicious. I'm finding you irresistible."

Cathy pulled back. "Thanks for the sketch. I love it." Artfully, she slid into her car.

"I wish you would come back to my place," he leaned into her open window with a confident smile as his fingers trailed up her arm.

"I've got to submit my script tomorrow. I'm sorry." Very slowly, Cathy started moving, and Donald pulled back from the window.

"I'll call you!" He waved.

And with that, Cathy was gone.

Oh, man. How could I have been so wrong? That tongue down the throat thing was not a good idea at all!

It was all I could do not to gag.

What happened?

I have no idea.

I think this is the problem with online dating.

What's that?

Chemistry.

Chemistry?

Exactly what Amy was talking about. The right chemistry.

I don't remember this kind of problem in my twenties.

In our twenties, you met almost everyone you ever dated in person, in a bar, at a party, at work. So the animal part of you knew that you liked the animal part of them before you even talked to them. With this online stuff, you don't get to figure that out until you meet them. You knew the minute you laid eyes on that scarecrow.

Guilty as charged. I don't understand it. He's so funny and clever and creative. He sketched me! That was such a heady experience. It was so romantic.

And then you stood in his truck under the full moon, and it didn't work.

You're right. It was worse than with Frank. With Frank, I felt nothing. With Donald, I couldn't stand the way he kissed me. It was either too little or too much. I told you, I'm dead.

You aren't dead. He didn't taste good. He didn't turn you on. Me, neither.

Of course, not you either, you idiot. I just didn't think this would be so complicated. I really wanted to like him. I did like him. He is so funny, the Big Bad Wolf. He had all the right moves. Actually, his moves were better than I could have imagined.

Love is complicated, ducky. That's why you make the big bucks.

Well, that is one thing. I have some great new material to use.

Back to the drawing board ...

(GROANS) Oh please, don't talk about drawing. How am I going to let Donald down when he calls.

You'll think of something.

I have to tell Amy.

You do that. She won't be so jealous when she hears this story. Or maybe she will.

DOCTOR, DOCTOR

Thank goodness Cathy had Friday night to recover. She poured herself a big glass of white wine. She needed it. Then she started writing in her journal to try to make sense of everything.

Amy had been going to bed when Cathy had called the night before. They had made a date to talk tonight. The phone rang.

"Ames!" Cathy said delightedly.

"How's the dating wonder?"

"Not so wonderful," Cathy confessed. "This is so hard. There's something wrong with everyone, which I'm sure means that there's something wrong with me."

"Of course, there's something wrong with everyone, including you. Ever heard the expression, 'No one is perfect'? Jeez. You've been at it for one week. How many dates have you had so far?"

"Well, they're not really dates. But I've sort of been out four times. And I'm supposed to meet some doctor tomorrow."

"Four times! That's amazing."

"I was already half in love with the artist I met last night, Donald. He was so funny, so outrageous when we emailed and talked. He even sketched me dancing. But when I met him, I wasn't attracted to him at all. He reminded me of Ichabod Crane."

"Who?"

"From *The Legend of Sleepy Hollow,* a tall, skinny beanpole with a stringy gray ponytail."

"I told you that the choices up in the boonies were going to be limited."

"Look, I went out with a Master-of-the-Universe hunt club type on Sunday. Just like all the men we know in Connecticut. He was obnoxious. I really need a change. There must be some other men in the world. Something between a know-it-all and a lost puppy."

"Yup, skinny artists with ponytails."

"Nancy met Matt on her first date! What's wrong with me?"

"Nancy was an exception. At the risk of repeating myself, you've been at it for one week!"

"It's that chemistry thing. I'm an idiot. We write about it on the soaps all the time. We create couples who hate each other but have explosive chemistry. We know that certain actors click on screen when they 'have chemistry.' I just didn't think about how it would apply to me."

"You are correct. You are an idiot. Why do you think I'm still married even when I sit home alone every Friday night? Because Ed and I still have chemistry, even if we never talk."

"Oh Ames. I'm sorry."

"Don't be. It's my choice. But, back to you. How about being a little patient? I'm sure there is someone out there who will get your juices flowing again."

"Patient. What's that? I'm getting more and more convinced that I was right in the first place. It's over for me. No more butterflies."

"Have you kissed any of these guys?"

"I'm sorry to say, I have. Two of them. Frank was an absolute blank page. Shockingly, the hot artist actually kind of repulsed me. That's the part that has me so discouraged. I liked him in every way. Except for that way."

"The most important part. Honor your reaction. You may learn to love someone over time. But if the chemistry isn't there. It's never going to be. That's why everyone talks about chemistry. It's a bloody mystery."

"I'm beginning to get it now. How could I have been so ignorant?"

"I have no idea. Honestly, it's a greater mystery that you've been able to write all those scenes all these years."

"I truly think I understand chemistry. It's just that, when I dated in college, all the guys I was involved with seemed to—turn me on just fine. I wouldn't have gone out with anyone that I didn't think was cute. I think that's a problem with this online business. You get to know the men and like them without knowing what the chemistry is going to be like. Then, when you meet them and there's nothing, it's even more disappointing."

"So, are you actually meeting a doctor tomorrow? I thought you had sworn off them."

"I had. I have. I'm flying by the seat of my pants. For some reason, this guy said all the right things. He sympathized with me for being married to a physician. Oh, and then he promised to tell me his deep, dark story. I couldn't resist."

"Deep dark story?' What do you think that's about?"

"Oh, some relationship trauma—probably his divorce."

"You want a guy with that kind of baggage?"

"I'm beginning to realize that we all have baggage at this age."

"You know, last Friday your life sounded so exciting, it really bummed me out. This Friday, you're putting me in a great mood," Amy said contentedly.

Cathy pulled her car into the parking lot right off the Taconic. The green, red and white striped awning read *Trattoria Italia*. She had worn her Connecticut clothes today. Her new expensive jeans, a tucked-in oxford shirt with the collar popped, good black boots and a black blazer. Actually, she felt exceedingly boring. She felt like the PTA president. She wished she had worn her new crazy tango skirt. But she hadn't had the courage to dress like that for a Westchester doctor. What a hypocrite.

Her heart was pounding as she walked through the parking lot. A silver Jaguar convertible had MD license plates. Could be him. Nice car.

Why was this part so awkward? Probably, because the first time she had made such a fool of herself. She walked through the doors looking for a thin, older man, possibly with a bow tie. She scanned the tables. The only single man was a tall, handsome, athletic looking man with a nice head of dark hair. Couldn't be him. That man looked barely fifty. He looked nothing like the shadowy photo of *ChrisMD*.

Maybe, Chris was in the restroom. She drifted to the bar. As she moved, the athletic man got up and came towards her. "Cat?"

Cathy was startled. "Yes?"

"I'm Chris," the man said warmly as he took her hand in greeting and covered it with his other hand. His hands were large and warm. Cathy felt a pulse of something surge through her. "You look exactly like your photo," he said as he squeezed her hand.

Cathy had to tip her head way up to search his face. "You look nothing like yours." What was wrong with her? Why did she always let every thought just blurt out of her mouth?

Chris let out a big laugh. "Guilty as charged. That's all part of the story. Please, come with me." Deftly, he led her over to his table. "I've ordered a bottle of wine. I hope you'll join me."

"I don't like to drink when I'm driving."

"I don't think one glass will impair you. Have some antipasto. Drink lots of water. I have a feeling that we might be here awhile. Anyhow, I'm hoping that we will."

Cathy had that niggling feeling of being artfully manipulated again. But at the same time, she was intrigued by him.

Chris poured her a small glass and raised his. "Cheers. Thank you so much for coming to meet me." He seemed genuinely appreciative.

Now much closer to his eye level, Cathy stared at his face as she raised her glass to her lips. The man was drop-dead gorgeous. He had piercing blue eyes. He reminded her of a blue-eyed Cary Grant. "So, whose picture is that on Match?"

"The photo is of a friend. I don't mean to be evasive. And I absolutely promise to tell you the whole story, but before I do, could we just chat a bit and get to know each other? What do you have to lose except a couple of hours? The food is supposed to be good here. It's a beautiful late October day. And, despite the fact that football games are going on at every high school in the area, I am not responsible for any of the injuries. That is worth celebrating, at least for me."

He turned his mesmerizing eyes towards her. Cathy felt her knees weaken a little. She wondered if she was getting scammed. She wondered if he would be asking her for a check in a little while. It seemed unlikely if that was his Jag. But she found that she didn't really care and prayed that she could keep her wits about her if it happened.

"So, please tell me your story first. Are you from New York? Somehow, I suspect you're not. Tell me about your favorite toy as a child. Tell me about your first kiss. Tell me how you got into television. Tell me about your children. I'd really like to hear it all. I loved your profile. I've been very excited to meet you since we talked on Tuesday."

Oh my. This man had charisma. The power of his eyes made the rest of the room disappear. For a second, Cathy had a flash of being with him in bed. She took a deep breath. "I grew up in the Midwest." Then, she began talking about her favorite toy, a red suitcase—how she loved packing and unpacking it and how she had once tried to run away. About her first kiss in a summer theater production when she was thirteen. About her journey into television. About her kids. Every topic opened up endless anecdotes about her parents, her older brother, her childhood friends, her marriage, her dreams.

Chris was a master at this. He let her talk, asking her fascinating questions that spurred her on at all the right times. It was a very intoxicating feeling—having someone really listen to her. She loved the way his eyes crinkled up when he laughed. She found herself wishing that he would hold her hand again.

After what seemed like forever, Cathy noticed that Chris's plate of

Veal Marsala was completely finished, while her Chicken Scallopini was barely touched. She held up her hand laughing. "Oh wow. Are you sure you're an orthopedic surgeon and not a psychiatrist? I feel like I should leave $150 on the table for this session. On second thought, after seeing your car, your fee is probably higher."

Chris laughed. "I love hearing about you. Especially how you threw the Monopoly money all over the lawn when you got mad. You weren't kidding about conversation being your favorite sport. I think you could win a gold medal."

"So, your turn. What's your favorite sport?"

Chris took a sip. "Well, I was a football player. Ironic, huh? I grew up in Nebraska, had a pretty good shot at a college scholarship, but then had a career ending injury in high school. I was really devastated. Football had been my life. You know what they say, *when one door closes*. Funny how life works. That's how I came to be an orthopedic surgeon. I wanted to be able to fix what had happened to me."

Chris went on to talk about going to University of Nebraska undergrad, then Harvard Medical School. He talked about his two kids. Cathy learned that Chris was fifty-eight, although that was impossible to believe.

"So, tell me about your marriage. You know my story," Cathy prompted.

"I met my wife when I was in med school. She was in law school. We were both driven Type A's. It's a miracle that we didn't kill each other. But somehow it worked."

"When did you get divorced?"

Chris took her hand. His eyes bored into hers. "That's the thing. We didn't. We aren't."

Cathy felt a rush of anger and yanked her hand away. She stood up and threw her napkin on the table. "What?!"

Chris took her hand again and somehow managed to pull her back down into her chair. "Please don't run off. I told you I had a deep, dark story. My wife, Marcy, developed early dementia when she was fifty. It progressed very quickly. She's been in a home for the last three years. Some days, she doesn't even know me. Some days are better. I will never divorce her, for my kids' sake and because I love her very much. But I am as alone, as single, as I have ever been. You said in your profile that you were looking for a playmate. I am completely sincere in saying that I am very interested in you. You are attractive, smart, funny, and full of energy. You love to dance. I would love to learn to dance. I am looking for a little fun in my life in whatever form it is offered to me. There are no sexual strings attached."

"I am trying to be discreet on Match. I don't want my kids to be embarrassed, although they want me to be happy. Lots of my patients know that I am married. They don't all know about Marcy's disease. That's why I'm using another photo."

"It's one thing to use another photo. After all, you must know that you are way better looking than your friend. But you list yourself as divorced," Cathy said accusingly.

"I tried being honest. But you can't imagine the type of woman who was interested in me when I said I was married. I changed my listing to *Divorced,* and promised myself that I would never get involved with anyone before I told them the whole truth."

Cathy felt her face burning at her own subterfuge. "It seems like small potatoes after your story, but I promised myself the same thing regarding my age. The fact is, I lied by four years."

Chris laughed. "It does make me feel a little better to hear that you weren't completely honest either."

Cathy sighed. "I'm terribly sorry about your wife."

"Look, I don't want your pity. I take care of patients every year who will never walk again, or worse yet, will be vegetables for the rest of their lives. I have had a great life. I believe that someone will come into my life who will understand what I can give and what I can't. If it's not you, I totally understand. You are a lovely, entertaining, and enticing woman with the whole world in front of you. If you're interested, let me know. Otherwise, please chalk this up as a Match experience."

"I knew there was something too good to be true about you. When we sat down, I had visions of you trying to scam me for money."

Chris laughed again. "That's funny."

"Although it didn't quite add up when I saw the Jag in the parking lot."

Chris paid the tab and walked her out. "Just think about it."

They were silent until they got to Cathy's car. She turned to him. "Thank you for a fascinating experience. It was not the deep, dark story I expected."

"What did you expect?"

"Affairs, betrayal, that kind of thing."

"Your everyday soap stuff."

"Right."

With no hesitation, Chris leaned down and kissed her on the lips. Time disappeared before she forced herself to pull away. Her lips were burning as she darted into her car. She willed herself not to look back at him.

She was barely a mile down the Taconic when she dialed Amy.

"That was a long lunch! What was the deep, dark story?"

"Not what I thought. He's not divorced. His wife has dementia."

Amy exploded. "Are you kidding me? And he lured you under false pretenses!"

"I know. I know. My head is reeling. The ridiculous thing is, I really sort of understand his predicament."

"You're not thinking of seeing him again, are you?" Amy sounded very stern. "Don't you dare sell yourself short. I will not let yourself fall in love with a dead end."

"Aaarrrghhhh!" Cathy let out a primal scream in her car. "That's the problem. I'm afraid that could happen. The thing is, ironically, I felt something! You may be right. Maybe, I'm not dead!"

Amy shrieked into her phone. "You did? Fantastic! So, there was chemistry?"

"Ames, the man is a Greek god. But, it wasn't just his looks. He was smart, kind, funny. When he turned his blazing blue eyes on me, I was a goner."

"Oh my god. Do you think you feel like this because you know he is unavailable?"

"I wish, but I don't think so. I was attracted to him the minute I saw him. It wasn't until much later that I learned about his situation. I feel like crying."

"God, it is frustrating."

"Frustrating? I feel like smashing something."

"But you really should be rejoicing. In one week, you've met some-one who excites you!"

"But I can't have him. Well, I suppose I could. Maybe, I should get him out of my system. It's been such a long time."

"Look, you're a big girl. I can't stop you from doing whatever you want. But a romp in the hay with the man of your dreams who can-not be yours can only lead to heartache. You don't want a part-time involvement. It's not enough."

"Oh, Amy, I really don't know what I want. I thought I could meet a man to do things with, who is nice and smart and someone I'd like to kiss."

"And you have. Chris was only the fourth man you met. One in four. Those are great odds. Just keep at it for a little while longer and you're sure to find someone who fits the bill and is actually available. You should feel ecstatic."

Cathy walked into her house in the late afternoon. It was already getting dark. She hated this time of the year. It was so depressing that the light disappeared earlier and earlier every day. In a week, daylight savings would end.

She flopped down in her recliner. She was too honest with herself to pretend that it was the light that was getting to her. It was Chris. Impulsively, she googled orthopedic surgeons–Westchester. The third name and photo that popped up was Chris Henderson. Bingo.

For the next hour she read all about his amazing work. He got stellar reviews from his patients. She saw photos of him and Marcy from fundraisers that dated back a number of years. Marcy was a stunning brunette. Tall, slim. The look in Chris's eyes when he looked at Marcy made Cathy cringe. Chris looked at Marcy as if she illuminated his life.

For a split second, Cathy wondered if Chris had lied to her about the status of his marriage. Maybe, his story was all a big ruse. But then she found some photos taken when Chris had received a big award last year. He was flanked only by his children. There was no Marcy in sight. Cathy knew that Marcy would have been there if she could have been.

Her heart broke for Chris. She wanted to scream. She knew deep down that she couldn't see him. She would have liked to be his friend. But Amy was right. Being his friend would not be enough.

Angrily, she signed onto her Match account. What was the point? Her eye scanned down the one-liners. The same nonsense. *How did I miss you?—Cute smile—Meow.* And then her eye stopped. She had finally received a message from *GottaDance.*

Hey. I see that you wrote me a couple of days ago. Sorry for not respond-ing sooner. I don't check my Match mail much anymore. But, thank you for writing. Hearing from you made my day.

Yes, I do love to dance. Took up ballroom dancing after my divorce. Now, I'm an addict. In fact, I'm about to run off to a swing dance right now, so I can't write much.

But, if you'll take a rain check, I'll pour my guts out tomorrow.

One disclosure. I haven't had the courage to tackle Argentine tango yet.

007

In an instant, Cathy felt so much better. Thoughts of Chris and poor Marcy just melted away. *GottaDance* sounded charming. Plus, he had specifically referred to his divorce. Unless he was very clever and devious, Cathy suspected that he was telling the truth. She didn't think she could face another Chris situation. Cathy wished that he had signed his first name. But he had obviously taken a fancy to her *007*.

She clicked on his profile. He wasn't as handsome as Chris, but he had a nice head of hair and a youthful look. She read over his details. She almost groaned. She had totally forgotten that he listed his work as *Medical Professional*.

She debated about writing back to him, even though he had said he would write tomorrow. Then, she made her decision. If she felt like writing to him, why not?

007,

Glad you surfaced from your top-secret mission. Were you on a submarine caper? A helicopter-chase? Jet skiing in the Bahamas with a 22? I was beginning to worry about your safety. Undoubtedly a waste of time, since you're 007.

Nice that you're getting a chance to let off some steam at swing tonight. Even nicer that you haven't tackled Argentine tango, "yet." That little word is so hopeful. Perhaps, I can offer some encouragement in that department.

In the meantime, I am off for my own fix at a milonga in Hudson tonight.

Looking forward to hearing your story. Nothing like a good session of true confessions.

Cat

Cathy finished typing the last word and hopped up, suddenly full of energy. If *007* could go out dancing tonight, so could she. She hadn't thought that she had any interest in dancing tonight after the Chris disaster. She hadn't thought she had the courage to face another milonga after last week. But the only way she was going to get better was if she danced. Something that her mother use to say echoed in her mind: *If at first you don't succeed—try, try again.* She ran up the stairs.

She didn't have much time to get ready.

DANCING ON AIR

How the hell did that happen tonight?

I have no idea. If I could tell you, I would.

I simply don't understand how you could go from being a pathetic wallflower, to being the Belle of the Ball. It's only been one week!

I know, I know. It's crazy. It seems like that's the way tango is. You never know how it's going to go. It's a roller coaster. Maybe that's part of the fascination. It's sort of like gambling. Are you going to come away with keys to a Ferrari or will you have to pawn your watch to pay for a cab?

Well, I think one of the keys was bumping into that bearded guy right away.

I agree. Brad. He may, in fact, be the reason that I pursued tango at all.

Oh, come off it, you slut. You know it's all that touching and hugging that appeals to you. Sometimes, I think that it's a miracle that people keep their clothes on at all. Did you see that woman in the aqua dress? Talk about making love to music.

(LAUGHS) I'm not denying that. Physical contact is important. There's been too little of that in my life since I got divorced.

Amen.

It was like the answer to my prayer that Brad happened to sit down next to me to put his shoes on.

The answer to your prayer was that he took a good look at your legs. They have held up pretty well. He moved up from them to your face.

It was just such a miracle that he asked me to dance right away, before I had a chance to get all tense and feel like a loser wallflower.

Honey, you danced way better than a loser wallflower. I sort of felt like you were flying.

Wasn't that the best? He's so good. I really didn't have to do much, except to remember to wait and let him do the work.

Well, whatever he did, it seemed to set the tone. The minute you finished with one partner another man was waiting for you. Hard to believe.

I'm afraid some of the other leaders were a little disappointed, though. I didn't dance as well with all of them.

That's because they're not as good as Brad.

I know that, and you know that. But, I'm not sure they do.

The challenge of this whole tango thing is that you can't get good until you dance with good leaders. And most good leaders can't be bothered dragging some off-balance beginner around. So I'm not sure how you ever improve. Frankly, I have no idea why you're pursuing this whole thing in the first place. I think you're screwed. Although, there's always the slut-factor.

The slut-factor?

Yes. Case in point, "aqua dress." Did you notice how that dress clung to her? Did you notice her cleavage? As I recall, she never stopped dancing. I think you better invest in some more provocative

clothing. That should get you some more dances. And frankly, I think you'll love flaunting your new hot bod.

I suppose, the Connecticut matron look is probably not the ticket.

For anything.

Point taken.

Now, how about a little peek at Match?

I'm a little matched out.

Ah c'mon.

Please don't whine.

You're the one with the wine!

Ha, ha.

Cathy stared at the computer. She wondered if she was becoming addicted to Match.

Uh-oh. There was another boy wonder. *Hey mama what you doin tongiht?* Cathy cringed. What was this illiterate twenty-four-year-old thinking? She deleted his message.

And then, her face lit up. *Gotta Dance* had written her an hour ago. She certainly wasn't expecting to hear from him tonight.

Hey Twinkletoes,

I got home a little early. A slow night. How was your gig? What's it called again—a milonga? You'll have to explain the tango lingo to me.

I was just sitting here thinking it might be nice to talk. I've been preparing my life story for you.

I'll probably be up till midnight, if you feel so inclined.

Here is my number.

Tim

His name was Tim. Cathy just sat staring at his message. She felt so buoyant from her night of tango that she knew she would be in good form.

She reached for the phone. Then something stopped her. She clicked on Reply.

Swingin' Tim,

I did just get home and am feeling a little rambunctious. I'm pretty sure you get the same high when you dance. Isn't it a great drug?

I feel funny about calling you so late, but you're welcome to call me. I must confess that I'm quite a night owl. I'm sitting here with a glass of wine and sore feet. Imagine dancing in high heels? What is wrong with women?

Tag—you're it.

Twinkletoes

For the first time, she added her phone number and hit send. She organized her thoughts about what she'd like to know about him. The first question was his occupation.

Almost immediately, her phone trilled with the tango ringtone that Paul had downloaded for her. Pleased, she answered it after the first ring. "Hello, is this the Dancing Doc?"

Tim laughed a throaty chuckle, obviously surprised by her greeting. "It is. So, is this the Dancing Cat?"

Cathy giggled. "So, you *are* a doctor," she mused. "I knew it. What is it with me and doctors?"

"Ah, do I sense that your ex is a doctor?"

"Guilty as charged."

"Well, if it's any consolation, I am a PhD—not an MD. I am a Doctor of Physical Therapy. By the way, I could do wonders for those tango feet of yours. And yes, you're absolutely correct. High heels are the invention of the devil, but they do keep me in business."

"Are you for real? You're a dancer *and* a physical therapist? Be still, my heart."

"I hope not. At least, not until we get to meet. So, how was tango tonight?"

"Actually, it was fantastic. And, I have you to thank for it."

"Me?"

"I wasn't planning on going until you wrote that you were off to your swing dance. Somehow, you inspired me to get up out of my recliner and go. The tango gods were with me tonight. I had a great time."

"It's hard for me to believe that you ever have a bad time."

"Trust me, tango is a very fickle mistress. Last Saturday was a nightmare."

"Well, you're welcome. I'm afraid the swing gods were not quite as kind to me. It was slim pickings tonight."

"Well then, you'll just have to take up tango," Cathy quipped.

"I might be persuaded."

"I can be very persuasive," Cathy flirted openly, wondering why she was acting like this. How much wine had she had?

"Sounds promising," Tim responded warmly.

Cathy decided she better put on the brakes. "So, Dr. 007, tell me about yourself."

Tim gave her a thumbnail of his life. Born in Chicago. Played baseball growing up. Went to school in Boston."

Thinking of Chris, Cathy asked, "Did you decide to become a physical therapist because of a sports injury?"

"No, not really. I've always been fascinated with the human body. You're probably going to think this is odd. But I like the feeling of being able to touch people to help them, to heal them."

A shiver went up Cathy's spine. "Healing hands."

"Something like that. But, I'm not a weirdo or anything." Tim seemed to feel uncomfortable. "What about you? Is your mission to help people through soap operas?"

"Are you mocking me?"

"Not really." Tim hesitated. "Well, maybe a little."

"If you must know, although I got into soaps simply because it was the best job I could find in television, I actually do think we help our viewers by dramatizing some of the more difficult moments in life. I know that I have definitely benefited from having explored some challenging situations in my writing before I had to live them. Sort of like an emotional rehearsal."

"Too bad we're not facetiming. I would have liked to have seen your face when you said that. If it's not too personal, what kind of situations?"

"Well, my divorce for one thing."

"How long were you married?"

"Twenty-five years. How about you?"

"Twenty-three."

"You have children, right?"

"I have two sons, twenty and eighteen."

"Oh, so you're still in the thick of college tuition."

"That's right. You are talking to an impoverished PT. So if you're looking for a gold mine, you better keep looking."

"Actually, I'm not looking for anything," Cathy volunteered spontaneously.

"What?" Tim sounded confused.

"I got into this Match thing because all my friends and my counselor insisted that I should. As I said in my profile, I'd like a playmate. After all, I was part of a duo for years. I'm trying to be open." Cathy was not at all sure why she was spilling her guts to this man, but she was.

"Fair enough. I've been divorced for three years. Sounds like you're still a newbie."

"I've only been official since last winter."

"Oh my gosh. You are a baby bird barely out of the nest. How are those wings working?"

Cathy had to laugh. That's exactly how she felt. "Flying is still a challenge, especially when there's any wind," she kidded.

"Well, if you're 'trying to be open,' how about meeting me tomorrow? I think this conversation deserves to be continued, and I must admit my eyelids are beginning to flutter."

"Must be the stimulating repartee."

"Seriously, why don't I drive up to wherever you live. We can have coffee or lunch."

Cathy's mind was racing. Could she really meet with Match Man number five in the space of nine days?! Wasn't that totally crazy? Didn't she need some time to digest what had happened?

On the other hand, this Tim guy was really easy to talk to. He had made her laugh. And he seemed to be truly divorced.

"Why not?" she surprised herself.

"Beautiful and bold," he teased.

"I hate to have you drive all the way up here just to see me," Cathy commented. "Why don't we meet in the middle?"

"Aren't you pretty close to Red Hook and Rhinebeck?" Tim asked.

"Yes."

"Well, I have a proposal. No, don't get all excited, I'm not getting down on bended knee or anything. There's this vintage diner in Red Hook that I've always wanted to go to. Do you know it by any chance?"

"I have passed it, but I've never eaten there."

"Even better. What do you think about meeting there?"

"I could do that."

"What time?"

"Well, I'm going to need my beauty sleep. Not before one o'clock."

"One it is. Afterwards, I thought I might hike up to a fire tower that overlooks the Hudson just outside of Rhinebeck. If you begged me real pretty, I might let you join me. So, bring some hiking shoes if you think that's a possibility."

"I'm not much on begging. But anything is possible. I've learned that."

"Cool. Then I'll see you tomorrow," Tim said.

"Oh, there's one more thing."

"Why does that phrase always make me nervous?"

"I was serious about hoping you would wear your tuxedo. It would be easier to recognize you. I've had some problems with that."

Tim burst out laughing. "Oh, rats. I just took it to the dry cleaners. See you tomorrow, Cat."

Cathy clicked off her phone, smiling from ear to ear. She was getting better at this.

LETHAL WEAPON

When Cathy opened her eyes the next morning, it all came back to her. The whole crazy week: Frank, Henry, Donald, Chris—and now Tim. She groaned. She rolled over and almost screamed when she looked at her clock. It was after ten. How in the world had she slept so late?

The night of tango had taken its toll. Her feet were still throbbing. And the side of her left leg ached, not to mention her back. It didn't help that she had been so wired after talking to Tim that she hadn't fallen asleep until 2:00 a.m.

She dragged herself out of bed and made some coffee. Why in the world had she agreed to meet Tim today? As entertaining as their conversation had been, she realized that she should be taking a day off from her Match madness, cleaning her house, and doing her laundry. She also had breakdowns to read. There definitely could be too much of a good thing.

She seriously thought about contacting Tim to postpone their meeting. She clicked on her Match account. As if he had read her mind, there was a message from Tim written two hours earlier.

Hope you're not having second thoughts. It's a beautiful day, and I'm really looking forward to meeting you. Also, the PT in me is wondering how your poor tango feet are feeling. See how compassionate I am.

As I mentioned last night, in addition to a good cup of coffee, a tasty omelet, a vintage diner, and a fire tower, I can offer you a mean foot rub. No strings attached. I hate to see anyone suffer.

Dancing Doc

Maybe it was the coffee that was starting to percolate in her brain. Or maybe it was his irresistible offer. Her feet were killing her. In any case, she didn't have the courage to cancel, when he seemed so excited. The fact is, she really did want to meet him. Anyhow, he was right. It would be a crime to stay in the house all day. Alone.

She had enough time to meditate before she had to get ready. She closed her eyes, tried to clear her mind, and concentrated on her breathing. It was not so easy. Flashes of the previous week kept popping into her head—walking up to the wrong man at Good and Plenty, the look on Henry's face when he took off her down coat, the noodle on Frank's chin, standing on the truck bed under the moonlight kissing Donald, Chris's blue eyes staring at her as he told her that he wasn't divorced. How was it possible that all that had happened in one week? One by one, she let those images go and drifted off.

Wearing jeans, sneakers, a T-shirt, and a bright pink fleece, she walked into the diner. She looked around the old railroad car. The bar stools were the classic twirly chrome ones with black seats. She looked to the left. Every booth was packed with three or four people. She looked to the right. At the very end, sitting by himself was a boyish-looking man in a tuxedo jacket, crisp white shirt, bow tie and jeans—reading the paper. As if he sensed her presence, he looked up and waved.

Cathy couldn't help giggling as she moved down to his booth. "I thought you said your tux was at the dry cleaners."

"I lied," he confessed with an impish grin. He stood up as she slid into the booth. He was tall and fit. He had light brown hair that was nicely cut and neatly parted. A faint male scent drifted towards her from his side of the booth. He smelled delicious.

He motioned to the orange juice that was sitting at her place. "I ordered juice for you—shaken, not stirred."

Oh my. This guy was good. "Thanks, James," she played along seductively.

"My pleasure, Cat" he smiled. He appraised her openly. "You look just like your picture."

"So, I've been told."

"Ah, so I'm not your first."

"No comment."

He laughed with delight. "I liked the sparkle in your eyes in your photo, but I thought it might just be the lighting," he commented as his eyes met hers. "It wasn't."

Cathy gulped. This man had all the lines. Slightly flustered, she looked at her menu. "Have you decided?"

"Yup. I'm a mushroom and swiss omelet man. They're supposed to be good here. And, home fries, of course."

Suddenly, Cathy felt a little dizzy and not hungry at all. "That sounds great. Make it two."

"Coffee?"

"Well, if you're prepared for me to lift off after I drink it, yes."

"Get ready for take-off. Perfect for the fire tower." Casually, he held up two long fingers. Almost instantly, a smiling young woman appeared with a pot of coffee.

"I think we're ready to order," Tim said, smiling. "Thanks for being so patient, Jordan. I told you she'd come." He gave their order and leaned back. He just seemed so comfortable in his own skin. This was no lost puppy.

Cathy was impressed at how charming he was with the server, calling the cute redheaded girl by name. "So, you and Jordan are fast friends already?"

"Well, if you must know, I was a bit early. I didn't want to be late. The place is obviously hopping, so I felt a little guilty taking a booth. I told Jordan our story. She was very sympathetic."

"Our story?"

"You know, the Match thing. Young people are charmed and a little surprised that old people can still get excited about meeting someone new. I think they think that when you get older it's all over. Probably from watching their parents," he chuckled.

Cathy was surprised that Tim was basically telling her that he had told Jordan that he was excited. Before she could stop herself, she murmured. "I sort of thought that myself."

Tim looked at her quizzically and spoke softly. "Give me your hands." He reached out and held his hands out to her.

His voice was calm and authoritative without being bossy. It was clear that Tim made these requests all day long fully expecting that his patients would comply. Without thinking, she placed her hands in his. A jolt of energy flowed down her spine. What the hell was that? His hands were large and warm and pulsing with strength even though he was holding her ever so gently. How could she feel so comforted and aroused at the same time?

He looked at her hands and then at her very earnestly. "Some people understand the world through their eyes, some their ears, for me it's my hands. I hope you don't still think it's all over?" His brown eyes seemed to reach into her soul.

Cathy forced herself to look him in the eye. "Maybe not." What in the world was happening here? She could feel her heart beating. Her fingers tingling. Something melting at the very core of her being.

Just then, Jordan bustled up with their steaming plates of omelets. Cathy reluctantly retracted her hands, feeling like the railroad car they were sitting in had just run over her.

But Tim seemed to take whatever was happening in stride. He was all business, salting his potatoes and diving into his omelet. "Don't let it get cold," he admonished. He took a big bite. "Wow. This is good. I'm starving."

Cathy sat there paralyzed. She stared at the generous portion of eggs and potatoes and couldn't imagine being able to swallow one bite. She played with the salt and ketchup, trying to look busy.

What was happening to her? She finally forced a smile on her face and looked at him. She tried not to stare at his hands. She had to get the ball into his court, but she couldn't even swing her racket. "So, tell me about your boys," she finally mustered. If the man was worth anything, this subject should occupy him for quite a while.

The strategy worked. He obviously loved his boys very much. With very little prompting, Tim told her everything about Ken and

John. On autopilot, Cathy nodded and pushed the food around on her plate.

"Of course, they're both at college now. But in the summer, when we can, we love to go camping. They were both Eagle Scouts," he added proudly.

"Do you like to camp?" he asked.

"Well, I went to girl scout camp when I was a kid. We had cabins. But I've never really done the whole pitch-your-tent-anywhere thing—although I enjoy living close to nature so much now that I suspect I might like it. Except for the bathroom situation."

Tim chuckled. "Yeah. Somehow, that category is a lot simpler for the male of the species. We won that design category, didn't we?"

"I think you won quite a few," Cathy commented dryly.

Tim looked very thoughtful. "I'm not sure about that. Being a student of the human body, I have to confess that I never stop marveling at the female version. What a complex masterpiece. A design that produces and sustains life. A design that is so beautiful and alluring. A design that survives longer and yet is so much more sensitive to almost everything. The only thing we males really have going for us is strength. I am convinced that we were developed to be the drones. No question, you ladies are the queens."

Cathy's head was spinning. When had she ever heard a man wax so enthusiastically and comprehensively about women? "How is it that your marriage ended? You sound like one man in a million." she blurted out.

Tim gave her a wry smile. "Thanks. I wish. But apparently, I drove my ex-wife crazy. She found somebody else who didn't."

"Oh, I'm sorry."

"Ancient history. I'm sure it's for the best. But, since we're on the topic, how about you? What's your sordid story?"

"Kind of lackluster. We just grew apart. As a soap writer, I wish I had a more dramatic tale."

"No, you don't." Tim's grin disappeared as he turned his head away.

In that moment, Cathy glimpsed a flash of vulnerability and pain that almost made her wince.

"So, what do you think about splitting this pop stand?" Completely transformed, Tim turned back to her with a smile and a wink. He looked at her plate. "Would you like that wrapped up?"

"Thanks. I guess I wasn't that hungry. It'll make an easy Sunday dinner reheated."

Again, Tim raised his hand and Jordan materialized with the check. Cathy wondered if Jordan was transfixed by Tim. She wouldn't be surprised if she was.

"I'd really like to pay my half," Cathy said. "I like the idea that this online dating thing is a level playing field. Equal."

"Ah now, you're just trying to protect my fragile finances. I should have never complained about the tuition." He stared at the check. "Even I can afford thirty dollars. And I did suggest this see-and-be-seen place."

Cathy laughed and pulled out fifteen dollars. "The diner is great. I'm so glad I finally got inside. But I'm the one who contacted you in the first place. Please."

With a wink, Tim nodded his head. "So be it. To the brave new world. Now, how about that fire tower? Enough caffeine for a climb?"

Cathy followed Tim in her car for the short drive to Ferncliff

Forest outside of Rhinebeck. It was a spectacular sixty-degree day. Tim ditched his tux jacket and bow tie.

Cathy felt herself almost hypnotized by his lean, muscled fore-arms with a light sprinkling of hair. There was nothing better than a crisp white shirt with rolled up sleeves on a man.

"You ready?"

Cathy had to shake herself out of her reverie. What in the world was wrong with her? "Aren't you bringing a jacket?" she stammered.

"There's not a cloud in the sky. I don't think I'll need one. But I do have this." And with that, he slipped a small backpack onto his back.

"Good for you. You are prepared."

"I told you that my sons are Eagle Scouts. I've learned a lot along the way."

As casually as breathing, he reached for her hand. "This way, I think."

With his hand encircling hers, Cathy found that she almost couldn't breathe. Her hand felt supercharged. She couldn't under-stand what was going on. This wasn't just good chemistry. It was a nuclear reaction.

Desperately, she tried to hang onto some semblance of sanity. But the sun was dancing through the tangle of rainbow-colored leaves, the wind was ruffling her hair, and all Cathy wanted to do was put her arms around his waist. She had wondered yesterday when she had felt something with Chris. But now, definitely, she had to con-clude that everyone else had been right. She had been dead wrong. She was very much alive.

Tim chatted away as if everything was completely normal for him. He asked about her childhood, her schooling, her kids. Cathy had to force herself to answer in complete sentences. Her head was splitting from the effort.

After a little while, they approached a wooden bench. "Why don't we sit down for a second. I have a question to ask you."

For some reason, Cathy was startled. Now what?

He pulled out two bottles of water and handed her one. Then, he turned intently to her. "I've resisted so far, but how are those tango feet of yours? I know it was probably pushing things to ask you on a hike today."

Cathy had an impulse to laugh. For a split second, she had thought he was going to ask her something kinky. "They're still protesting."

"Let Dr. Hunter see," he said lightly as he effortlessly flipped her feet onto his lap and pulled off her shoes.

Before Cathy could protest, his hands, his incredible hands, were touching her feet. For a split second she worried that her socks were sweaty, her feet smelly. Then, almost immediately, she realized that she didn't care. She closed her eyes, feeling the pure bliss of being outside on this glorious day with the sunlight caressing her face and his unbelievable hands caressing her feet. "Oh. That's amazing," she finally managed to form intelligible words.

"I told you that high heels were my bread and butter. You can't imagine the stress they put on the metatarsal bones."

Cathy wanted to say something, but she found she had been reduced to a puddle. Instead, she just sat there with her feet in his lap wondering what she had done to deserve this.

After an eternity, after a blink of time, Tim gently patted her feet and handed her back her sneakers.

Cathy groaned. "You don't really expect me to walk now, do you?"

"I certainly do. That was all prepayment for the steps we're going to have to climb shortly. We're almost at the tower, I think."

"You are a cruel man," Cathy teased, wanting ever so much to kiss him.

"C'mon, c'mon. It's going to be worth it." He pulled her up. For a moment they were nose to nose, and then Tim turned up the hill.

In a few minutes they were at the old metal fire tower.

Cathy stared up at the "Erector Set" structure climbing into the sky. "Do you think it's safe?"

Just then a young couple came skipping down the endless steps. They were grinning from ear to ear. "Awesome view. No one's up there right now. Hurry!"

"Looks like they managed fine. You go first. I'll be right behind you," Tim directed confidently.

The endless metal steps zigzagged inside the exterior shape of the structure. Cathy stopped counting after fifty. She stopped looking down after the first two levels. There were seven!

At first, she was very self-conscious about the view that Tim must have following her on the narrow steps. Then, she forgot all about him and just concentrated on putting one foot in front of another.

Miraculously, she arrived in the small enclosed room at the top of the structure. Tim was right behind her.

"Oh my god." She looked across an ocean of blazing leaves at the Hudson River and the Catskills. Tim moved next to her and slipped his arm around her waist. It seemed like the most natural thing in the world. Right then and there, Cathy knew that she couldn't wait another second. She turned her head toward him. Tim didn't hesitate. Their lips touched.

His kiss was soft but definite. There was no tentative nibbling. Just a delicious connection. Within seconds, her lips parted, and their tongues danced like the sun. It was all so easy. Why had Cathy worried so much?

Tim sighed and touched her face. "I've been wanting to do that all day."

"Me too," Cat confessed.

Her admission triggered a very different energy from Tim. He leaned down and crushed her mouth with his. His hands burned through the back of her fleece. Cathy felt like she was being consumed. All she wanted to do was rip off her clothes.

One of his hands moved around to her front and slipped under her fleece. It stopped right over her heart and rested there. It was the most loving, affirming, comforting feeling Cathy had ever known. She wanted it to stay there forever.

She found herself sinking down to her knees. Tim followed her. Cathy found herself kissing him with more variations than she had ever imagined. She was burning up. She started unzipping her jacket. Why not? Her insides were on fire. She was a grown woman.

Tim pulled back enough to look at her. "I really don't think ..." his voice was hoarse with the effort of restraint.

Cathy couldn't stop herself. She didn't even want to try. She pulled him back for a deep kiss. That's when they heard the creaking of the steps.

This time Tim stood up, pulling her up with him. "To be continued," he whispered.

Cathy felt like she had been awakened abruptly from a glorious dream. She looked around and vaguely remembered where she was. How had this happened? Unsteadily, she zipped up her jacket and ran her fingers through her hair, trying to tame the tangle it had become in Tim's fingers.

"You look beautiful," he commented. He took her hand again just as the next group emerged onto the top. "Have fun," he said, smiling at them as he headed to the steps.

Cathy couldn't believe that he could talk so casually. She tried to take a step and found that her legs were weak. How in the world was she going to get down? "Just a second," she begged Tim. She stood at the railing—trying to breathe, trying to calm herself. She imagined that he must think she was desperate for love, the way she had acted.

Tim put his hand around her waist. "My legs are shaking too. Must be the height," he joked. "I'll go in front of you this time. You'll be fine."

Tim's shared vulnerability and quiet assurance seemed to stabilize Cathy. Carefully, slowly, they climbed down.

They got to the bottom and looked back up. "I always knew that I wanted to climb this fire tower. But I had no idea the experience would be quite so powerful," he murmured softly.

Cathy's mind was racing. What was happening? This was all going too fast.

They climbed down the hill without saying much. Tim seemed to be lost in thought too.

They got to their side-by-side cars. Tim turned to her. "Thank you for a fantastic day. I wish we could go grab a beer or something, but I have to get back for dinner with John."

Cathy felt disappointed and relieved. She didn't want to leave him. And she was terrified to stay. "Oh, that's okay. I have a ton to do at home. Have a lovely dinner." She looked up at him, waiting for him to ask when he could see her again, certain that he would. Suddenly, the old traditions fell into place. She found herself unable to suggest anything about getting together again. It was too important.

He said nothing, but took her hands and gave her a light kiss. "You are a puzzle," he murmured.

It was all Cathy could do not to crush him in another kiss. But instead, he opened her car door for her, and she got in.

Cathy wished that she could sit there for a minute to collect herself. But clearly, Tim was a gentleman and was going to wait until she pulled her car out. With tremendous will power she forced herself to back up. She pulled out onto the road. Tim was right behind her.

She had to breathe. At the first opportunity she blinked her lights, waved goodbye, and turned into a store parking lot. Thankfully, he beeped his horn and drove on.

She pulled into an empty corner of the lot and collapsed onto her steering wheel. What in the world had happened to her? She had been bewitched by those hands from the moment he had touched her at the diner. Then, the foot massage. Then, the top of the tower.

Well that was quite a performance. Talk about releasing your inner bad girl!

I have no idea what just happened. With the other four guys, I was thinking and evaluating what was going on the whole time. I felt in control. With Tim, I just lost my head.

No kidding. And then he called you a puzzle.

I feel like a puzzle, like a jigsaw puzzle in about a million pieces.

I don't think he was talking about that. I think he was referring to the fact that one minute you confessed that you thought "it was all over" and the next minute you had knocked him to the floor of the tower and were about to rip your clothes off. Even I am a little confused. But, grateful. That was fun. Talk about repressed desire.

Stop torturing me. It was those hands. They're a lethal weapon.

It was a lot more than those hands. You were a goner from the minute you smelled him. The fact is, we're all just animals.

Do you think I scared him off? Do you think he'll call me? On the soaps this would be a death knell. No romance that starts this well has any legs.

This is not a soap. He seems like a good guy. He did say, "To be continued." I can't imagine that you scared him off. He's a big boy. I'm not sure if you're the kind of girl that he's hoping to take home to Mom, though.

Well, that's okay then. I have no desire to be taken home to Mom.

What do you have a desire for? You ready to rock and roll?

Honestly, I have no idea. It's been so long. All I know is that whatever happened up there in the tower was powerful. Maybe it was just the unbelievable setting.

I don't think so. As far as I could tell, the same thing could have happened at the diner. I think what we've got here is unbelievable chemistry. Winning!

I think you're right. I guess that's what all the fuss is about.

Yup. Pretty much.

What do I do now?

Take a cold shower? Wait? Call him later tonight and set up a follow-up, a more private follow-up? You have options, girlfriend.

I think I've gone as far as I can go as the initiator. I'm going to have to just wait. Do you think he liked me?

Oh, stop it! False modesty isn't like you. He clearly felt that first jolt too, when he held your hands at the diner. He's the one who wanted to massage your smelly feet. After you kissed him, he said that he'd been wanting to do that all day. And then he just about inhaled you with that second round of making out. Not to mention that hand-over-your-heart trick.

Wasn't that unbelievable? I don't think any man has ever done anything like that to me before.

I have to admit, it was a good move. But you haven't been with that many men—and most of them were decades ago. That's what this whole online thing is about. To learn. To experiment. If today was any indication, it's gonna be a lot of fun. Yee-haw! My only word of advice is, play a little hard to get. Everyone likes a challenge.

Okay. Point taken. I'll wait.

Good girl. Now put your car into reverse and go home. You need to concentrate!

THE WAITING GAME

The minute Cathy got home she checked her phone. There was a polite message from Chris thanking her for lunch and asking her to think about his proposal. Frank had written wondering how she was doing. Donald had sent her a suggestive little sketch of two people intertwined on the back of a truck under the moon.

A part of Cathy couldn't help feeling pleased that all of the men except Henry seemed to have liked her. Apparently, she was doing something right. However, having met Tim, she found she really didn't care.

But there was nothing from him. She had fantasized that he had been so smitten that he had stopped on the road and sent her a little text. But, of course, he hadn't. He was out to dinner with his son.

Or was he? Suddenly, paranoia bubbled up in Cathy. Maybe, he just wanted to get away from her ASAP. Maybe, she would never see him again.

Would you please quit it! Stop obsessing about Tim. You had a fantastic day. C'mon, you're the airy-fairy one. Be grateful for your

exciting day. Let go of your expectations. If it's meant to be, it will work out. Now go make yourself something to eat and read your breakdowns. Don't look at that phone again tonight!

With every ounce of willpower she could muster, Cat turned away from her phone and warmed up her omelet. Unfortunately, just looking at the omelet transported her back to the diner staring across the table at Tim's dancing eyes.

Oh god. She had it bad. Maybe she should call Amy. But she felt too fragile to even talk about today. She was afraid to jinx it. Like a bubble— if she got too close, it might burst. With determination she picked up her first breakdown.

Thank god it was an engrossing week on the show. They were writing November sweeps, an important period for TV ratings.

Three hours later she had finished them. Every day was a block-buster. She wondered which day she would be assigned.

Cathy headed to the basement to move a load into the dryer. When she came upstairs she heard that funny little ping. It was her phone. Someone had sent her a text. Probably one of the kids.

She picked up her phone. It was a number. Not a name. Not one of the kids. Not someone from her contact list. Who was it? She clicked on the text, fully expecting some marketing nonsense.

Roses are red,
Towers are steel,
Today was a wonder.
Was it true? Was it real?
007

Cathy's face burned. Tim had written her a poem, a love poem. From the sound of it, he was just as shaken as she was. Thank god she wasn't just imagining the fireworks.

She read it again and again with a big grin plastered on her face. It was so simple, so sweet. Like those valentines they used to write to each other in grade school. She immediately wanted to send off a reply.

It was pretty late. They had talked about how he got up early to run before he went to his office. Maybe she should wait a little while until she was sure he had gone to bed. If he knew she was up, he might even call her. She didn't think she could handle that right now. She needed to make sense of her thoughts, her feelings.

Her mother had always advised her to sleep on any big decision. She decided to go upstairs and take a bubble bath. Maybe that would relax her. Maybe that would give her clarity.

She lit a candle, climbed into the lavender scented water, and piled the bubbles over her body. Her body. Suddenly, she was so aware of the body that she had ignored for so long. She lay there in awe of her body—glistening skin peaking through the bubbles—the health of it, the life of it. After today, she knew it was just as responsive as it had been all those years ago. It was an amazing affirmation. It was a miracle.

She realized in a flash that she was a new person. She was no longer boring, steadfast Cathy—Connecticut matron, mother of three. She really was Cat—a lively, unpredictable, funny, creative writer and tango dancer. Like a cat, she could do exactly what she pleased.

She said a brief prayer of gratitude for the seemingly random steps that had led her to meeting Dr. Martin and losing her flubber, for toning her body in her daily swims, for creating a new look for herself, for feeling like a whole new person.

Then, she closed her eyes and sank back into the tub. Suddenly, she had the overwhelming sensation of Tim's hand resting on her heart. She felt her heart—her guarded, wary, bruised heart—burst open.

To think that the final step in having this all come about was online dating! Cat found herself giggling. Regardless of what happened with Tim, she was going to have to send Amy, Nancy, and Pat flowers.

She returned downstairs with a clear head. She picked up her phone, found Tim's text and started typing.

Although it seemed like a dream, it wasn't. I had the omelet for dinner to prove it!

Bet you didn't know that cats like eggs.

Meow.

C

Cat went up to bed with a spring in her step. She felt exactly right about the tone of her response. She slipped into bed, confident that she would sleep like a baby.

BRAVE NEW WORLD

Cat woke up feeling more rested than she had for ages. She had an unbelievable pinch-me feeling. Never in a million years had she thought that she could feel like this less than a year after her divorce. Somehow, she just knew that whatever happened, she was on a fantastic path.

She made her coffee and calmly checked her messages.

Good Morning! I've already seen two patients. It was very difficult to concentrate. When I was working on one of them all I could see in my mind's eye were your enticing feet and legs. I just wanted to run my hand up, up, up …

What have you done to me?

T

Cat caught her breath. She had never received any message like this before.

My goodness, Doc. Control yourself. You don't want to be accused of anything untoward.

Don't you love that word? So Victorian.

xoxo

C

Feeling more youthful than she had felt in a long time, Cat collected herself and headed off to see Pat.

Pat stood up from her chair and applauded. Then she hugged Cat. "I knew it. You are too vibrant and loving to be dormant for the rest of your life."

Cat laughed joyously. "I have to say, I feel like a new person. I am so grateful. Last night, in the tub I felt like my heart just cracked open."

"How wonderful, honey. I'd say your heart has had a rough time. It needed to be cocooned, protected. Now the butterfly is ready to emerge. I'm not surprised that it's happened with someone that you chose."

"I really don't know how to act with him. A part of me just wants to jump into this with two feet. A part of me doesn't want to scare him or me by moving too fast. My friend, Nancy, told me about her Thirty Hour Rule. She believes that with online dating, you should get to know someone on the phone or in person for thirty hours before you sleep with them."

Pat burst out laughing. "I certainly don't disagree that it's a good idea to feel really comfortable with a person before you take that step. The fact is, sex is powerful stuff. You need to feel safe and willing to become extremely vulnerable. But there are no rules in human interactions."

"I already feel ripped open. I couldn't believe how I didn't care what happened up in that tower."

Pat smiled delightedly. "My best advice to you is, trust yourself. If it feels right, go for it. You're a smart, responsible, loving woman. Heavens, you certainly haven't led a wanton life. You have never been unfaithful to anyone. As you told me the first day, you're a good girl. I think it's time to be a little less 'good' by other people's standards, and a lot more good for yourself. You've done a great job of raising your kids and taking care of your parents. Now, it's time for *you*."

"If I'm really honest with myself, I think I just want to get 'it' over. I'm not sure I even know what to do."

"It's totally natural to feel anxious about someone different after all these years. But, let me ask you one thing. How was kissing someone else? You've tried out a couple of people this week. Did you feel awkward? Uncomfortable?"

"Well, as I told you, I didn't really like kissing Donald."

"But, did you feel like you didn't know what to do?"

"No, it seemed pretty natural. I guess you never really forget."

Pat smiled triumphantly. "Exactly. Well, guess what? That's what making love is going to be like too. You're not exactly a virgin."

Cat looked doubtful. "But I didn't have to take my clothes off to kiss Donald."

Pat held up her hand and referred to her notes. "Whoa, whoa. Didn't you just tell me that you felt like ripping off your clothes in the fire tower with Tim? And, didn't you tell me how you felt about your body last night?"

"Yes."

"So, what's the problem?"

"That all just happened organically. I didn't have to make a decision."

"You don't have to make a decision about this next step with Tim either. Just let it happen."

"Is that realistic? Isn't it going to be obvious what's coming next if he invites me to his place or vice versa? Isn't just going there making a decision in advance?"

Pat shook her head. "Even if you go to his place, or vice versa, you are still in control. You can change your mind if it doesn't feel right, even at the last minute. The only thing you have to do is tuck a condom in your purse."

"Are you kidding? I'm not going to get pregnant."

"This is not about pregnancy. It's your responsibility to protect yourself. The last thing you want is to contract a disease. When and if you make love without protection, I'd certainly advise that you both be tested."

Cat wrinkled up her nose. "That is so weird. Of course, I have no disease. I've only ever been with Bob all these years."

"And what about Bob? Can you be 100% sure that he never experimented? On any of those professional trips? With staff at the hospital? Aren't hospitals supposed to be hotbeds of affairs? Why take a chance."

Cat laughed. "Okay, okay. You're right. It is a brave new world. None of us used condoms back in the day, except for birth control."

"Back in the day is over."

Cat held up her hand. "Got it. Thanks, Mom."

"You're welcome. So where do things stand with Tim?"

Cat flushed. Since they were talking so intimately, she confessed,

"Well, he sent me this text this morning. It was pretty suggestive. I think it was my first experience with *sexting*."

"How did it make you feel?"

"Excited. In fact, ever since yesterday I feel like my hormones are raging."

"Wonderful. They probably are, after the enforced hiatus they've been on. I don't think there's anything wrong with sexting. You're consenting adults. Of course, there's good taste in everything."

Cat looked horrified. "Are you kidding me? This text was just words, actually quite Victorian."

Pat looked as pleased as a cat who had just consumed a bowl of cream. "How lovely. Nothing like enacting a Harlequin romance. He sounds perfect."

"He's a doctor. What is it with me and doctors?"

"Well, for one thing most doctors are smart, compassionate, and caring—not a bad combination for a lover. If he happens to be good looking too, you've won the lottery."

"Well, if you put it like that …"

"There are always two sides to everything. Doctors are also used to having the last word. But you've come a long way from that young, uncertain woman who married Bob. You know they are just human beings, not superheros."

"I would hope so."

Pat looked at her watch. "Well, I can't wait for next week's install-ment. I am so proud of you, the progress you've made." Pat got up from her chair and hugged Cat again. "Just trust yourself. The real you inside of you knows what to do."

Sure enough, when Cat walked out to her car, there was another text from Tim.

I told you that my hands see the world. No matter who I touch today, all I can "see" is your heart beating. For the life of me, I can't imagine why I didn't sneak under your T-shirt. I am dying to feel your skin, your breasts …

My goodness. How was Cat going to drive home now? She too wished he had touched her skin. Her legs were shaking. She had to get ahold of herself. She had to start her script when she got home.

More than anything, she wanted to respond to him. But, what would she say? "I wish you had."

Instead, she took several deep breaths and put classical music on. She hoped Bach would work.

Wow, you are a train wreck, girlfriend.

Thanks for telling me something I didn't know.

I think Bach is a good choice, but wouldn't a book be better? You need words to distract you.

I need a cold shower.

True. Can't wait to see how your script turns out. Lorraine better be ready for heat.

LITTLE LIES

Cat thought she was losing her mind. Every time she looked at her phone there was another text.

I didn't tell you about my dream last night. We were up in the fire tower at midnight. The moonlight made your skin glow. This time no one interrupted us. My hands saw the world. My mouth tasted heaven. It was pure bliss.

I think we should sneak up there some night.

T

Shaken, not stirred. That's how I feel. Is it possible you feel the same way?

James

Are you a screamer, or a moaner? I suspect the former.

How is your script coming? Any ideas for us?

However, despite these torrid texts, Monday night came and went, and Tim did not call. He sent her a text very late.

Horrendous day. Early day tomorrow. Sleep tight. Dream of me.
xoxo
T

Cat felt like she was dangling on the edge of a cliff. Why couldn't he find a moment to call? She found the texting very frustrating. Maybe he was just a player. Maybe he got his kicks maintaining a whole stable of titillated women.

Of course, she had googled him. Dr. Tim Hunter, PT. He appeared to be exactly who he said he was. His Facebook page was mostly him and the boys. He certainly didn't have photos of himself with a bunch of women. But then, if he was really a player, would he?

She had only known him since Saturday night. Two and a half days. She felt like she had known him forever. She was desperate to see him again. Yet although he was constantly alluding to seeing her, being with her, he had not suggested anything specific.

And it wasn't only the sexting. He had written her descriptive little glimpses of his life, his work. He had sent her pictures of the view from his office. He had sent her funny shots of his dog, Bones.

She, in turn, had sent him a photo of the sunset over her lake. And Sandy, of course.

She went to bed feeling incredibly restless. She tried not to think about Tim, but she tossed and turned feeling like a hooked fish thrashing on the end of a line.

She woke up exhausted, but with the clear conviction that he had to make the next move.

He continued to text her all day. She finally silenced her phone while she was writing. The random pings were driving her crazy. He might have breaks between patients, but writing wasn't like that. Once she was focused on her script, she had to stay immersed.

At her lunch break and at the end of the day, she responded casually to his texts. In all his texts, there wasn't one mention of them getting together again.

Thank goodness she had tango class that night. She couldn't wait to escape. She ate an early dinner and sent Tim a text.

Off to tango. Hope you're not working too late.
C

When she walked back into her house, her cell phone immediately started buzzing in her purse. She had forgotten that she had muted it in class.

She fished her phone out. Finally. It appeared he had tried to call her a couple of times already.

"Hello" she said coolly.

"How was tango?"

"Good. We worked on close embrace."

"That sounds like fun."

"Actually, it's super hard to dance when you're so close together."

"Must be difficult not to get your feet all tangled up."

"Yes, that's the trick. It's the opposite of ballroom. In tango, you need to be heart to heart with your feet slightly angled away from each other. Like a teepee."

"Hmm. That would be hard for me."

"It's hard for everybody."

"That must be why you like it."

Cat smiled. He was astute. "I think that's part of it." He said nothing. She sensed that he was hesitating and had the urge to fill the silence. But she forced herself to wait.

"How was your day? How did the writing go?" he finally asked politely.

Cat wanted to answer that she had been driven crazy by his non-stop texts, but instead she answered. "Pretty well." There was more silence. What was going on? Why were they suddenly so awkward?

"Cat, could I ask you a question?"

Cat's heart started to pound. What was going on? He sounded funny. "Of course."

"You mentioned something about when you were in college. It's been bothering me. When did you graduate?"

Cat gulped. So that was it. She should never have lied about her age. She had obviously said something in their conversation that had indicated that she was really a little older. She took a deep breath and told him the truth. "All my friends told me to post my age as younger. They said that everyone did. I must admit it didn't seem like a big deal at the time. Now, I'm sorry that I did. For what it's worth, my photo was just taken a couple of weeks ago."

There was a long pause as he digested this fact. "I feel a little funny about this, but I googled you when I learned your name. The fact is, I don't really care if you're a couple of years older than I am. But I do want to be able to trust you."

Cat laughed nervously. "I know. The whole Match thing seems like a game, until it isn't anymore. I had intended to tell you as soon as I met you, but somehow, I never got around to it." She couldn't confess that she had been so undone by his very presence that she couldn't think straight. "I believe I am a pretty trustworthy person. But I guess you'll have to figure that out for yourself."

"Well, I did read about all of your other accomplishments, winning an Emmy, your college accolades, etc. You're a pretty impressive person."

"Not really. I also googled you. No surprises there."

"Yes, it's quite a world. Everybody researching everyone else. Well, it's good to hear your voice. I've been thinking about you."

Surely, now he was going to suggest they get together.

But Tim said nothing.

Cat was beside herself. What in the world were all those messages about? She wanted to say something, but found that she couldn't make the words come out.

"Well, I'm glad I caught you. Sleep well," Tim said.

He was signing off. Cat sighed. "You too."

And with a click, he was gone.

Cat sat there with her head spinning. How could that voice be the same man who had written her all those texts? A part of her was chagrinned that she had jeopardized her relationship with her "little lie." And a part of her was irritated that he had felt the right to call her on the carpet like that.

Suddenly, Cat was able to let the whole mess slide off her

shoulders. If there was something special between them, it would work out. If not, so be it. She wasn't going to act like a heartbroken teen.

The old song lyrics, "Got along without you before I met you, Gonna get along without you now," popped into her brain. She headed up to bed.

No wonder the soaps had survived for so long. Life was a soap opera.

THE GAVOTTE

She woke up on Wednesday with a clear head. After forty-eight hours of not seeing him her hormones finally seemed to have calmed down. The fire tower was becoming a memory. Thank goodness.

She checked her messages when she had her coffee. Tim was at it again.

FYI, I had a dream in which we were dancing tango. Close embrace. Very close embrace. I think I'm going to have to learn tango. Will you teach me? T

Cat didn't quite know what to make of this text. His stiff, serious tone had vanished overnight. But she had no time to analyze his metamorphosis, she had to work on her script.

She wrote back quickly:

I'm in no position to teach anyone tango. However, it would be great if you took it up. I think you'd be very good. C

She thought this message was a good balance of being discouraging and encouraging. Plus, a little flattering. He'd have to make of it what he would.

She didn't check her phone again until lunch.

Are you around this evening? Eight-ish? Love to talk to you.

Now what? Cat couldn't even let herself imagine that he was going to ask her out.

Yup. No dancing tonight. Just home where the hearth is. In fact, it might be cool enough to have a fire.

Her phone rang, just after eight.

"Hey there, Tango Dancer. Did you build a fire?"

"As a matter of fact, I did. My first of the season."

"I'm jealous. I love fires."

"It's one of the best features of my house."

"Hey, I just want to cut to the chase. I want to apologize for last night. I think I went off the deep end a little this week. Sunday was—well, it was really something. I haven't been able to stop thinking about you. It seemed that every word we spoke kept replaying in my head. And then, when I realized that something didn't add up in terms of when you were in college and your age, I got a little crazy. The fact of the matter is, I do have some trust issues. I had no right to act like such a heavy last night. You're right. Lots of people 'spin' their profiles a little. Heck, I'm a doctor. I know perfectly well how difficult it is to get the truth from my patients."

Cat felt herself softening. She knew that he was special, that their chemistry was special. She just waited for him to ask her out.

"Anyhow, I just wish I was there next to you in front of the fire."

What in the world did that mean? Suddenly, Cat couldn't stand it anymore. "Well, why don't you come up here and see my lake, then? What about this weekend?" There she had done it, just what she had vowed not to do.

"Oh, man. I wish I could, but I have to go to Boston this weekend for a conference. I've been trying to figure out when I could see you again all week."

There was a part of Cat that wondered if Tim was telling the truth. If he had been wondering so much, why hadn't he brought it up? "Are you sure you're not married or something?"

Tim broke into a hearty laugh. "I may be a lot of things, but I am not married. I am very much single."

"Then, how about dinner next week? I'll cook."

Tim groaned. "There is absolutely nothing I would like better than a home-cooked meal, but you live about an hour from me. I am slammed next week because of the conference. Could I take a rain check on your cooking and very unchivalrously ask you to come to me for dinner? I promise I can offer you something better than an omelet. I know it's a lot of driving, but I would so very much like to see you again."

Well, it was about time. "I'm usually finished writing around 5:30. How would Wednesday work? I could probably get there by 7:30."

"That would be fantastic. Could you meet me at my house and then we'll go out?"

Cat gulped. She wasn't sure that it was good form to go to a man's house right off the bat. At the same time, Cat couldn't deny that she was dying to see his place. You could tell so much about someone from their home.

"Sure, why not?" she responded boldly.

"Great. Now I think I can get through the conference with Wednesday to look forward to."

"Me too. Hump Day." The minute she said this she wanted to bite her tongue. Oh god, she didn't mean to suggest anything.

"Right," he laughed. "I'll send you my address."

Cat ended the call and immediately dialed another number.

"Hello?"

"Nancy, it's Cat, Cathy. I think I need your advice."

"What's up, Cath. You sound rattled."

"I am," Cat confessed. Her whole Match saga burst out of her. "You didn't prepare me for this."

Nancy answered ruefully. "I didn't prepare you, because I didn't have the same experience. Not by a long shot. You must have a helluva photo."

"Oh, who knows. It's probably the time of year, or something. But, what do I do about next Wednesday? I told him I'd go to his house."

Cat could almost see Nancy pursing her lips. "Well, I certainly wouldn't have agreed to that so soon, but you must feel all right about him or you wouldn't have either."

"He seems like a very nice, responsible, compassionate doctor. The thing is, I want to see him again to see if the chemistry I felt is for real." Cat could hear herself almost whining.

"Chemistry? I did tell you about the Thirty Hour Rule, didn't I? Don't be hasty."

"I spent four hours with him on Sunday. Since then he's texted me constantly about all kinds of stuff. I've talked to him on the phone twice. I feel like I know him pretty well. Of course, I've googled him."

"Look, Cathy, you're a big girl. Just make sure you have your phone and call me if anything is suspicious."

Cat felt like weeping with relief. Even prudish Nancy seemed to be giving her the green light.

"Thanks, Nancy. I really appreciate all your advice."

"I'm just happy that you actually followed it. Isn't it nice to be out there again?"

"It's pretty confusing. But, pretty thrilling too." Cat confessed. "How is everything with Matt?"

"Never better," Nancy giggled. "I hope this Tim guy is as wonderful. I'm looking forward to that double date."

Maybe we'll go to the malt shop, Cat thought wickedly.

HUMP DAY

Cat parked opposite Tim's charming house in an older neighborhood in Beacon, New York. It was an old farmhouse with a wrap-around porch. She turned off her lights and took a deep breath. Her heart was pounding. Her hands were sweaty.

So, should I call you a "lady of the night"? Making a house call?

C'mon. Give me a break. You know how this came about. What happened that day in the fire tower has haunted me. I've been walking around like a powder keg ever since then.

To be fair, his sext messages haven't exactly extinguished the fire.

No kidding. I needed to see him again to get him out of my system.

I'm not sure I believe that. I think you want him in your system.

Don't be crude. I already feel a little like a whore.

I wonder why, since he snapped his fingers and you are appearing at his door.

That's not how it happened. His conference was just bad timing. Anyhow, he drove up to me the first time. It's my turn.

Okay. You have a point. But, seriously, do you think you'll ever make it to dinner? Do you want to?

Of course, I do.

But even more, you want to kiss him, don't you? Don't lie to me. There's no point. I just want to hear you admit it.

Yes, I guess so. I can't help wondering if last Sunday was a fluke. It's just that I haven't felt like this in such a long time.

So alive. I know. It's been exciting. Well, as Nancy said, you're a big girl. Assuming he's not a criminal, I agree with her and Pat.

Stop it! He's not a criminal. You know perfectly well that he's a well-established Doctor of Physical Therapy. His practice is booming. Tons of people put themselves in his hands every day.

Just like you want to.

Is that so wrong?

Wonder what else he has up his sleeve?

(REACHES FOR THE DOOR HANDLE RESOLUTELY) Fasten your seatbelt, we're about to find out.

Godspeed, girlfriend.

Feeling more vulnerable than she had when she was thirteen years old and meeting Joe Caputo behind the barn at summer camp, Cat pressed the front doorbell. Instantly, the door flew open. Tim stood there in mid-motion pulling off his tie.

Cat was dumbstruck. He was wearing a grey suit and white shirt—and looking ever so professional, ever so irresistible.

"I just walked in the back door. Haven't had a minute to change. I am so sorry. I had absolutely planned to be here an hour ago. But

I had a last-minute walk-in patient in serious pain. I had to help," Tim explained apologetically.

"I understand," she mumbled. She should. She had been married to a doctor for twenty-five years.

"Thanks." He reached down to her in a fluid motion and brushed her lips with his. "By the way, you look great."

Cat didn't think her casual outfit of a short skirt and boots was any match for his.

"How about I get you a glass of wine while I run upstairs and change? Gotta get the doctor gear off."

"Sure." What in the world was wrong with her? She was monosyllabic. She followed him into the kitchen. Deftly, he poured two glasses of wine and clinked her glass with his. "I really appreciate you coming here. I'll be down in five minutes." And with that, he bounded up the old-fashioned staircase.

Cat was left in a daze. She wandered through the quaint house. It looked like most of the furniture was well-used, undoubtedly cast-offs from his former family home. He had a well-worn leather recliner and an old sectional in the living room in front of a flat-screen TV. The TV looked like the newest acquisition in the house.

She sat down on the edge of the gigantic sofa, which dwarfed the modest living room. There was some mail and professional journals scattered on the coffee table, along with an empty beer bottle and some napkins. It looked like he ate at the coffee table. Not exactly a neat freak.

She heard noise from upstairs and realized that he was taking a shower. She was shocked at her reaction. She wanted to run upstairs and join him.

However, she restrained herself. That wasn't the plan for tonight.

She looked around for something to distract herself. There were small framed photos on a corner table. As expected, there were several photos of Ken and John at different ages. There was one shot of Tim with the two boys in scout uniforms in the woods. There was no evidence of his ex-wife.

She wandered back to the couch and sat down again. She took another sip of wine and marveled that she was sitting in a strange man's house. To think that she just went on Match two weeks ago. She heard footsteps, and a pink-faced Tim in jeans, a clean shirt, and jacket appeared and slid next to her on the couch.

Immediately, Cat was almost overwhelmed by the smell of him. It was some alchemy of soap, shampoo, deodorant, and maybe shaving cream. Had he quickly shaved? The animal part of Cat was totally enthralled. He was like a magnet. She couldn't stop herself. She found herself leaning toward him, closing her eyes. She tried not to sigh out loud when his lips settled on hers. Oh my. That felt so right.

Tim gently placed his hand on her face, softly framing it. Her face immediately tingled. Unconsciously, their mouths opened. Cat totally lost track of time and place.

As one, they finally parted, almost panting.

"So, I wasn't imagining it, was I?" he whispered.

"No. Neither was I." Cat couldn't believe that those words just slipped out of her. So much for playing hard to get.

Tim groaned softly and pulled her back onto his shoulder. His strong arm encircled her. Cat felt totally protected, safe, whole. She hadn't had a feeling like this in so long.

After another timeless period of exploration, Tim gently took her hand and stood up. She rose with him. Her legs were so shaky that she had to hang onto him.

"If we don't go now, we're never going to go. And, I want to do this right. It's important to me. Plus, I skipped lunch and I'm starving." He tried to finish with a joke, but Cat could hear the huskiness in his voice.

Cat knew he was right. There was no need to rush anything. But she couldn't deny the voracious desire that had welled up inside of her. She felt so vulnerable.

She took a deep breath. "So where are you taking me? Do I have to climb any steps?"

Fifteen minutes later, they were ensconced at a window table at The Roundhouse staring at a hypnotic waterfall cascading into a dramatic creek.

"Oh my," Cat said in awe. "What an amazing place!"

Tim smiled. "I thought you'd like it. This building was originally a textile factory two hundred years ago using the hydropower from the waterfall. Now, it's a restaurant and a hotel."

"It is fantastic." Cat looked straight down from their table at the white water which was swirling by the round brick building. She took his hand. "Pretty good, Doc. First a vintage railroad car, then a fire tower with a view of the Hudson, and now an old factory with a waterfall window seat. Thank you."

"You're welcome. A special person deserves special places."

Cat found herself choked up. Could this really be happening to her? Seriously, this was better than any script she could have concocted.

The server came up to them. Cat wasn't sure if she could have another glass of wine and still drive home. "What do you think, Doc?"

"Well, it's still pretty early. And, you're about to eat. I think you'll be fine." He hesitated and smiled coyly. "Of course, you don't have to drive home."

Cat flushed. She knew that she had been fishing for that very invitation. But when it was offered, she felt even more confused. "It's true, I could always sleep on the couch." She tried to banter and keep it light.

"Right," he said sarcastically, looking straight at her.

Cat ordered the salmon and Tim ordered the steak. He continued to hold her hand while they waited for their food. They chatted effortlessly, but Cat had no clue at all about what was being said. She was so distracted by the electricity short-circuiting her brain from his fingertips.

Somehow, her food disappeared from her plate, so she must have eaten. Apparently, she had kept up her end of the conversation, although she had a feeling that Tim had talked quite a bit.

Finally, the check was paid and they left the restaurant. Tim guided her to the wrought iron railing over the turbulent stream. A crescent moon adorned the sky. He turned her to him and let out a little sigh as she went into his arms. She tipped her head up and immediately his mouth captured hers. The sweet and powerful connection went on forever. His tongue, lips, and teeth were as skillful as his hands.

"I'm not sure we can go out to eat in public like that again," he finally whispered. "It was torture sitting there only holding your hand when I wanted so much more."

Cat felt like her head was going to explode. She looked up at him with stars in her eyes. All she could manage was, "I know."

And with that, Tim led her to his car. They drove home in silence. Words were beside the point right now.

Tim led her into his living room. Cat expected him to lead her straight upstairs. But he immediately pulled off her coat, dropped it on the floor and navigated her to the couch. Before she knew it, he was on top of her, kissing her madly.

Cat was so transported. Sensations that she hadn't felt for so long coursed through her body. The symphony of their kisses ranged from pianissimo to fortissimo. At times she felt like she was being consumed. At times she felt like she was sipping the sweetest nectar of the gods. Very quickly, she lost track of which part was hers and which was his. Their mouths were one.

Without any awareness of it happening, his hand slid under her top. Oh, dear god. The warmth of that incredible hand. Her bra was unhooked. She gasped. Her breasts were being celebrated. Cat couldn't ever remember anything ever feeling so good. Every time his fingertips brushed over her nipples, she almost arched off the couch.

Cat wasn't sure how much longer she could stand this. She felt like she was burning up. And then he had pushed her top up and his mouth was on her breasts. Cat ascended to an even higher plain. Desire shot through her body. But Tim was in his own world—licking, nipping, creating sensations in Cat that stunned her.

Now every vestige of time had vanished. Cat had no idea if it was October or May. She had no recollection of where she was, who she was, what she might have to do next. There was no next. There was just now.

She did know what she wanted now, though. She tried to sit up. Tim looked up at her. "Let's go upstairs," she urged.

Tim sat back. He looked at his watch and then smiled with regret. "It's almost midnight."

Had they really been on the couch all that time? How was that possible?

"Of course, I meant it when I said you could stay over. But I do have a pretty early day tomorrow, and when we go upstairs, I want to be able to relish every minute. I truly believe the better we get to know each other, the better it will be."

"How could it be any better?"

Tim laughed. "True. But I want the most out of our journey, out of you. You are very new to all of this. Let's take our time. The anticipation will only make it more delicious."

"If it doesn't kill me."

"Abstinence is a powerful aphrodisiac."

"Whatever you say, Dr. Hunter." Feeling like a cold bucket of water had just been splashed over her, Cat stiffly redid her bra and straightened her clothes. Then, she stood up and looked for her purse.

Tim looked surprised. "I don't want you to go."

Cat said simply, "I don't think I can stay and—wait. Anyhow, I'm somewhat of a night owl. I can sleep late tomorrow. I'd rather drive home now. There won't be any traffic."

Tim looked very confused now. "I hate to have you driving home in the dark."

"Look, I drive home this late from tango all the time. I'll be fine."

Tim clearly didn't know what to say, how to persuade Cat not to go. Up until now, he had been in charge. But this was not how he had envisioned things. Cat could tell that he wasn't used to being countermanded. Well, for whatever reason, she was trusting her instinct, and it was telling her to go.

She kissed him warmly. "Good night. Thank you so much for dinner, for everything."

Tim raked his fingers through his hair. For the first time, he looked unsure of himself. "All right, if you have to go. But I'll only let you if you promise me first that you'll see me this weekend."

"Sure, why not?" Cat said lightly, and with that she was out the door.

Tim pulled her back to him and kissed her intensely. "Please call me when you get home. I will fall right back to sleep."

Cat couldn't remember the last time someone had cared so much about her safety. "It's really not necessary. But, okay."

With every ounce of willpower that she could muster, she walked on her trembling legs to her car. She slid in, started it and pulled away from the curb as smoothly and quickly as she could manage. She knew that Tim would be watching until she pulled away.

She traveled down the block until she was out of sight of his house, and then she pulled over. There was no question that she was rocked to her very core.

What the hell are you doing pulling over on the side of the road? Waiting to be mugged? Why in the world did you leave? Jeez. What a performance.

I know, I know. I just had to get out of there.

Why on earth?

I don't really know. Everything seemed so great. I've never been like that in my life—so forward, so wanton. I couldn't believe it when I basically begged him to go upstairs. And then, he said no. I felt rejected.

Look, this is not college. He can't just blow off his classes tomorrow 'cause he's so wiped out. He's a mature man with responsibilities. Frankly, I think he is the real thing. He cares for you. He knows you are just back in the saddle. He wants you to trot before you gallop.

Since when are you the big equestrian?

You know what I mean. Didn't you write that very phrase in one of your scripts a couple of months ago?

Maybe.

Of course, you did. Where do you think I got it from? Your hormones are just raging. When they calm down, you'll understand.

That's the truth. I can't believe we spent two hours making out.

It was sort of like high school, wasn't it? But you only got to second base!

(LAUGHS) Pretty crazy, wasn't it? Sort of like going back in time. But it was fantastic. I guess we have it right on the soaps. Sexual tension is the key.

He's right. It'll be much better when neither of you have to get up for work. He's not a "WHAM BAM, THANK YOU MA'AM" kind of guy.

I'm not sure that's better for me. I think it would have been much better if it had just happened spontaneously. Now, I'll have the next few days to worry.

I have no idea what you're worrying about. The man just touches you and you become a brain-dead, quivering mass of nerve endings. You don't have to think at all. Just let it happen. He knows what he's doing.

I am pretty pathetic, aren't I?

I just think you've hit the motherlode in the chemistry department.

It does seem like that, doesn't it?

Sure a lot different from Frank, Henry, Donald, and Chris. Well, maybe not Chris. There were some sparks there.

But lots of baggage too.

Other than his trust issue, Tim seems like a good guy.

Yes, he does. You know, you've made me feel a lot better. Thank you.

Always here to help.

Just then Cat's phone rang. She looked at the incoming call. Of course, it was Tim. Now what? Had he had second thoughts? She stared at the phone deciding whether to answer it, or not. But she finally decided he would be terribly worried if she didn't.

"Hey, did I forget something?"

"No. I just wanted to make sure you got out of Beacon okay. Where are you?"

Quickly, Cat computed where she might be if she had been driving ever since she left him. "I'm on the Taconic," she fudged.

"You made good time."

Cat realized she had overestimated her progress. "I just got onto it."

"How's the driving?"

"Fine. There's almost no traffic."

"Well, just watch out for the deer. It's rutting season, and sometimes they jump right out onto the road."

"Oh, great. Thanks for that, Doc."

"I really wish you had stayed. I don't feel good about this at all."

For a split second, Cat felt like telling him that she was actually right down the block. But then she realized that she couldn't. It would be really awkward to go back. "Don't worry, Doc. I'll be fine. I'm listening to Sinatra. "Come Dance with Me." He'll keep me awake."

"All right, then. I better get off so I don't distract you from your driving. But please call me when you get home."

"If you insist."

Cat sailed home. Maybe Tim had been right. Maybe they did need to take this one step at a time. It felt right to be going home, to be able to savor what had just happened.

She dialed his number when she walked into her house.

"You okay?" he answered groggily.

"More than okay," she responded. "No deer, no traffic, no problem."

"I'm relieved. Sleep tight. Now I will too."

Cat had to smile. "Night."

She ended the call and sat back in her recliner. She closed her eyes and could feel his lips on hers.

Suddenly, she picked up her phone again and typed.

Roses are red,
Moonlight is white,
My mouth is still burning,
What a fantastic night.
xoxo
C

As soon as she typed this, Cat started to second guess herself. But then she thought—trust yourself—and hit SEND.

COME DANCE WITH ME

Cat was shocked when she woke up. She had totally overslept. At first, she panicked. Then she calmed down. She reminded herself that her script was virtually done.

She got her coffee and absentmindedly checked her phone. Nothing from Tim.

Then she noticed an email from Lorraine.

CALL ME!

Oh god. Barely awake, Cat immediately called Lorraine, only to find out that there was a total change to one of her storylines. One third of her script had to be rewritten. She had only a day and a half to do it.

Cat gulped down her coffee and started reading the changes Lorraine had sent her. This was going to take her all day.

Tim was suddenly a faint memory as Cat immersed herself in the new Dylan and Dana storyline. The network had decided that the week didn't have enough pop for the last week of sweeps. So, since Cat was writing the Friday episode, she now would have to have Dylan build to a proposal at the end of the show.

Cat knew how important this storyline was, since Dana and Dylan were the hottest new couple on the show. Lorraine had asked her to pull out all the stops. So Cat wracked her brain for the most imaginative and romantic situation that she could think of. Not surprisingly, she found herself developing a sequence where Dylan takes Dana up a fire tower. Art reflecting life?

She ran the idea by Lorraine who thought that it was brilliant. "Go for it."

Cat was so transported as she was writing the scenes that she totally lost track of time. Lorraine had asked Cat to send her whatever she had at the end of the day. At six, Cat sent the first draft of the six scenes.

It was only then that she remembered to check her messages. How weird. There didn't seem to be any from Tim. She hastily checked her email. Cat's heart beat wildly. Nothing. Apparently, her hasty retreat last night combined with her goofy poem had sent him running. Cat felt deflated. Well, maybe she could write romance, but apparently, she couldn't live it.

She was just putting together some dinner when her phone rang. She rushed to answer it, heart thudding. Maybe, it was Tim.

It was Lorraine. "Holy cow—you are a miracle worker! I'm going to give you last minute changes more often. This new material is the best stuff you've ever written. I'm so turned on my husband is not going to know what hit him tonight. The network is going to be eating out of our hands after this. Not only is the situation on the fire tower fantastic, the material is so real. In a way, I hate to spoil those damn executives like this. They're going to think they can pull a stunt like this every week."

Cat had to smile. It ought to be real. She had lived it a week ago. "Thanks, Lorraine. The idea just came to me."

"Right." Lorraine knew her pretty well. "That, or your life has experienced a major turnaround that you haven't told me about. I have to say, your work—especially your romance—has been crackling the last couple of weeks. That's why I assigned you Friday. You can submit your script an hour later since you had this last-minute rewrite."

"I don't think I'll need the extra time. But, thanks."

"No. Thank *you*. I can't wait till lay-out next week coming off your wonderful new material. You've given me all kinds of ideas."

Cat hung up feeling pretty proud of herself. Well, at least one good thing had come out of her escapade with Tim.

Cat felt a lot better after eating her dinner in front of the TV. She was sick of checking her phone for something from Tim. He had mentioned the weekend last night, but talk is cheap. The weekend starts tomorrow! Clearly, he wasn't planning anything. She was absorbed in her favorite crime drama when the phone rang. It was almost ten o'clock. Could be one of the kids. They often called pretty late.

She answered without looking at who it was. "Hello."

"Hey, voodoo woman."

Cat felt like a bolt of lightning had shot through her. It was Tim. "Hey." She warned herself not to be too eager. After all, he had not written her a word all day after she had made a fool of herself.

"I am so sorry for not writing. The whole day's been a blur. I loved your poem so much I couldn't fall asleep—not to mention that my mouth was on fire. Then I overslept. I've had one emergency after another all day. I am only now coming up for air."

Cat wasn't completely convinced. Surely, he could have managed some answer to her text last night. "I had a crazy day too. Found out I had to rewrite one third of my script this morning."

"I'm afraid that midweek dates are a challenge. I hope you survived."

"As a matter of fact, the new material came out pretty well," she replied coolly. Cat wasn't about to tell him that he was her inspiration.

"Anyhow, I had an idea for this weekend. I think it was something you said last night. How would you like to go dancing on Saturday?"

Cat couldn't keep her heart from lurching. "But you don't tango."

"No, but I'm not too bad at ballroom. Have you done ballroom at all?"

"A little bit here and there. But I've never really taken classes."

"Somehow, I just have this feeling that we'll be fine. We both love to dance. I am an expert at bodies, after all," he added suggestively. "So far, I think our bodies work together very well."

Cat's face was flaming. "If you can lead, I can probably follow the basic stuff. But don't expect anything fancy."

"The basics are fine with me. Frankly, just holding you in my arms will be good enough. After last night, I really want this weekend to be special. Have you ever been to the Rainbow Room?"

"Years ago, before they closed it down."

"Well, it's reopened. They have a big band playing on Saturday. I was hoping that we could have dinner and dance, and then I thought maybe I'd get a hotel room, so we don't have to drive home. If it's any extra enticement, we could go all out, and I could wear my tux."

Cat was totally blown away. "Are you kidding? Just like Fred and Ginger. It sounds like a movie."

"Since my place is on the way, I thought maybe you could drive to me and we could drive into the city together."

"Sounds good. But only if we practice dancing at your house first. I don't want to make a fool of myself at the Rainbow Room."

"Great idea. But I seriously can't imagine you making a fool of yourself anywhere. After Argentine tango, foxtrot and swing are going to be a piece of cake for you."

"We'll see," Cat kidded.

Tim's tone grew serious. "And look. I don't want you to feel any pressure. If you want to drive home, we can. I just thought that a hotel room would make it so much easier. Then we wouldn't have to worry about having some champagne."

Cat hesitated and then said softly, "I think you're right."

"Cool. I'll make all the arrangements. See you on Saturday."

Cat set down her phone and screamed. How could her whole life flip around in two minutes? Not only was Tim not done with her— even on a day when he had gone crazy—but he had also come up with the evening of a lifetime.

Cat's thoughts were whirling. What was she going to wear? How was she going to concentrate on polishing her script tomorrow? Was she going to make a fool of herself dancing in front of all those people? How awkward was the hotel room going to be? Was she ready for any of this?

Cat clicked off the TV. She closed her eyes and took a deep breath. She had to accept that whatever was supposed to happen was going to happen. All she could do was go along for the ride and savor every moment.

She snatched up her phone and called Amy. After five rings, Amy answered. Cat couldn't keep the shrill excitement out of her voice, "Ames, you are not going to believe what just happened!"

CINDERELLA

Cat had crazy dreams. Her brain was at full tilt. She woke up with a brainstorm. Didn't she have a red, chiffon, strapless, ankle-length dress? She had worn it to the club years ago for Valentine's Day and then had never worn it again. She said a silent prayer that she hadn't given it away. She jumped out of bed and started searching. In the last closet, she found it buried way in the back. She pulled off her nightshirt and slid it over her head. Now, the tricky part. Could she zip it? A boned strapless dress was totally unforgiving.

Almost dislocating her shoulder, she managed to get the zipper up. It felt pretty good. With her heart in her mouth, she walked to her full-length mirror and almost shrieked. Amazing. She twirled around. It looked perfect. She must have put on all that weight after she had worn this dress. Thank god it had been in a plastic bag all these years.

Dancing around in her bare feet with her bed hair sticking out at all angles, she felt like Cinderella.

With that problem solved, she headed for coffee and her script.

Her phone pinged several times during the day as Tim sent various messages and old photos of the Rainbow Room. She couldn't help glancing at them. She found herself humming and smiling as she worked. Who cared what tomorrow evening would be like? This anticipation was priceless.

Feeling higher than a kite, Cat submitted her script. She didn't even need the extra hour.

A half hour later, she got a text from Lorraine. "Great work. Thank you so much. I owe you."

Cat thought about having a quiet night, but she felt restless. She didn't feel like cooking. Anyhow, she had one errand to run.

She drove to one of her favorite little restaurants in Rhinebeck, sat at the bar, and ordered the chicken with roasted vegetables. Before she could help herself, she was telling the woman next to her about her big date at the Rainbow Room.

"Congrats, honey. Sounds like you hit the jackpot. Hope it goes well."

Cat didn't tell her about the hotel room part. She was still pretty nervous about that.

Afterwards, she headed to the drug store. It was late and it was empty. Perfect. No chance of running into anyone she knew. After several tries she found the right aisle. She stared at the boxes and boxes of condoms, her face burning. There were so many kinds. She had never bought any before. But Pat was right. She needed to take responsibility for herself.

Cat finally chose a box of ten. Trying to pretend she was invisible, she grabbed bottles of her regular shampoo and conditioner and headed to the counter. She stacked the shampoo and conditioner on the counter with the small box hidden behind them. Luckily, the female clerk was talking to another clerk next to her behind the counter. Absent-mindedly, she swiped the bar code on each item and stuck them in a bag.

Clutching her bag, Cat headed to her car. She had done it!

At home, she pulled out an overnight bag and tucked in her toiletry case, a night shirt, some jeans and a sweater. And her little box.

On Saturday afternoon, Cat gave Sandy some extra food and fresh water, and headed for her car.

"See you tomorrow, Sweetie," she cooed to the cat.

She wore her red dress and jewelry with comfortable shoes. They were going to check in at the hotel, first. But Cat had decided that changing in the room with Tim was just too much. She would feel like a school girl ducking into the bathroom to change. And the alternative was mind-boggling. It was one thing to take her clothes off, but something else entirely to stand there putting them on. She preferred appearing for the "prom" all dressed up.

She was so excited and nervous that her hands kept slipping off the steering wheel. She couldn't handle this. The big night of dancing *and* what was going to come after. But it was too late. The die was cast. Tim had stressed over and over that he didn't want her to feel any pressure. The hotel room was merely a convenience. As if she believed that. If the whole thing was a bust, she could sleep on the floor.

She had done that before. She tried to remember some of her crazy, pre-marriage nights. She remembered a college night that she had spent in a hotel bathroom with another girl, eating crackers they had scavenged from a room service tray left in the hall, while their dates were passed out in the room. She had survived that. In an effort to create a more buoyant atmosphere, she played her Sinatra CD. Almost immediately, his warm, playful voice transported her. This was such an adventure. That was the thing about adventures. They had to be a little risky to be fun.

As *Ol' Blue Eyes* was singing "Come Dance with Me" her mind immediately flashed to the foxtrot and swing videos she had watched last night.

Hey there, cutes,
Put on your dancin' boots,
And come dance with me ....

The goofy lyrics couldn't help make Cat smile. She listened to the rhythm and thought, slow, slow—quick-quick. It was a foxtrot.

Cat tapped the beat of the dance as Frank kept singing. Then, he came to the best line of the song:

'Cause what is dancing, but makin' love set to music, playin'....

Cat gulped. Well, Cat certainly understood that tango was like that. Apparently, foxtrot was too. She would know soon enough.

Holding her bag, Cat rang Tim's doorbell. After a beat, he opened the door. His face broke out in a grin, he took her bag, put his arm around her, and kissed her thoroughly. He looked delighted. "You made it."

He was wearing his tux shirt. It was blindingly white. He looked magnificent.

Cat found herself taking in a sharp breath. She had to hold it together. "James Bond, I presume," she tried to sound flippant.

Deftly, he slid her coat off her shoulders. He let out a sharp wolf whistle. "Hmmm. I thought your name was Cat. But, perhaps, it's Pussy Galore."

Cat laughed at the Bond reference. "No, just Cat."

"I'd offer you a glass of wine, but let's save that for later. Are you ready for your lesson?"

Cat held up her hands. "Let's do it."

Tim put on a dance CD that he had gotten from his Fred Astaire classes. He had pushed his furniture to the sides of the room. "Shall we start with the foxtrot?" He started the music, slid his right arm firmly behind her back, and took her right hand in his left.

The shock of the touch of his hand almost knocked Cat over. What was wrong with her? Using all her will power, she stayed upright. With no apparent effort, Tim started moving her. Slow, slow—quick-quick.

"Hey, you're a ringer," Tim accused her.

"Not really. But I did watch some videos last night."

"Well, you're as light as a feather. We are going to wow them at the Rainbow Room."

Cat laughed delightedly.

They spent the next half hour working on the foxtrot, swing, waltz and rumba. She had watched swing the night before. Waltz was, of course, *one*-two-three. Cat didn't know anything about rumba. But it was pretty slow and easy. And, very sexy. With a similar beat to foxtrot.

The music came to an end as Tim twirled and then dipped her into his arms. Cat was inches from his face. He leaned down and kissed her, then twirled her out and clapped his hands. "Bravo. You are fantastic. What a good idea I had."

FRED AND GINGER

Their drive to the city was actually fun. They chattered away like old friends, both excited as kids about their big outing. It was as if they were playing dress up.

Tim pulled up to a hotel at 11th Avenue and 48th Street. It was called Kimpton Ink 48.

"That's a funny name for a hotel," Cat commented.

"Actually, the 'Ink' is because this building use to house an old printing company, and it's on 48th."

"How do you find all these places?"

"A patient told me about it. It's just crosstown from Rockefeller Center. I thought it would be easier to park here and take a cab to the Rainbow Room."

The valet took their car, and they strolled into the lobby. An attractive young woman immediately approached them with a tray. "Would you like a glass of wine? It's our welcome hour," she explained to them.

What a gracious touch. Cat couldn't ever remember a hotel offering wine at check-in before. She and Tim both took one. Cat sipped hers as Tim checked in.

When they got on the elevator, for some reason they were the only ones. The doors closed. Tim looked at her and clinked her glass. "To a lovely evening with a lovely lady," he said. "I know it will be." Then, he leaned down and solemnly kissed her, sealing the toast.

Cat felt her knees give in. Could there be a more romantic situation than to be alone on an elevator with a man—a dashing, kind, thoughtful man in a tuxedo? It was all Cat could do not to press the stop button and attack him.

Somehow, she restrained herself. They arrived on the ninth floor. Tim led her down the beautifully decorated hallway. He paused in front of their room. Then, with a flourish, he opened the door. "*Ta-da.*"

All of Manhattan shone like Tiffany jewels through the floor-to-ceiling windows.

Cat was drawn like a moth to the incredible view. "How breathtaking."

Tim came up behind her and gently put his arm around her waist. "I chose the city view instead of the Hudson view. I hope that's okay. I thought that this view was more special for us. We get to see the Hudson all the time."

Cat turned around to face him. She was so moved by his incredible thoughtfulness, she felt her eyes fill. "Thank you so much—for all of this. I am a soap opera writer and you have outdone even my most outrageous fantasies."

Tim laughed and kissed her again. "What is life for, but to grab for the gusto?"

Cat put her glass down and circled his neck with her arms. She kissed him, seriously. Tim groaned and pulled her over to the king-sized bed. For minutes they were lost in wonder. Then, with great effort, Tim pulled away and stood up. Cat could see how aroused he was.

"Look, Miss Galore. We must be on our way." Tim spoke with a terrible English accent.

Then, he plopped down next to her, gently tracing her collar bone. "Unless, you don't want to …"

Cat hesitated. So far, everything Tim had planned had been perfect. She stood up suddenly, anything to break the allure of the bed. She also adopted a British accent. "You're terribly right, James. So far, everything has been brilliant. What's next?"

Tim went to his overnight bag and brought out a small clear box. He presented it to her with a flourish.

Cat couldn't believe it. It was a dewy white gardenia wrist corsage. "A corsage? Are you kidding me? How did you know? I have felt like I was going to the prom for the last two days."

Tim laughed. "Actually, I was looking at a lot of the old photos from the Rainbow Room in the Thirties. Many of the women wore corsages. My mother always liked gardenias. And, of course, I knew it would go with any color dress you wore."

Cat couldn't help giggling with delight as she slipped the corsage over her wrist. "You are just full of surprises."

Tim picked up her black pashmina. "All right, are you ready, Ms. Galore?"

Thankfully, this time there were other people in the elevator. They got to the lobby just holding hands. But that was actually no relief for Cat. She couldn't decide if his hands or his lips were more electrifying.

In the lobby, Cat started to head for the street. Gently, Tim guided her over to another elevator.

Cat looked at him quizzically. "Did you forget something?"

"No," Tim smiled enigmatically. "We have another stop here."

A lot of people joined them in the elevator this time. They headed up, up, up. Everyone got out when it stopped. Cat took a few steps and then stopped in amazement. The top of the hotel was a roof bar completely open on all sides to the twinkling lights of Manhattan.

"Wow," Cat gasped.

"My patient was a great source of information. She said we shouldn't miss the fantastic view up here. This rooftop bar is called The Press Room."

Confidently, Tim led her through the main bar to a side area where there was a series of couches. As if fated, there was one empty couch.

"You sit tight. I'll be right back."

Cat sat on the trendy off-white couch with lots of cool, young people and took a deep breath. A little over two weeks ago, she had been a recovering divorcée—a suburban matron trying to find her way. Now, here she was—on top of the world.

Tim returned with two sparkling flutes of pink champagne. Tiny blush bubbles floated to the top of each elegant glass. Tim clinked hers for the second time that night.

"To grabbing for the gusto!" Tim said.

"To Match.com!" Cat countered. They laughed and each took a sip.

Tim put his right arm around her and held her hand with his left one. It was all she could do not to purr.

Cat couldn't help thinking that, among all the beautiful people sitting in this glorious place, she and Tim looked darn good. Well, Tim looked amazing in his tux. And she thought her strapless red dress was pretty splashy too. Not to mention her wrist corsage. She noticed that a number of the other people were looking at them and smiling.

Cat turned her face to Tim and kissed him. She couldn't believe her behavior. She didn't know if the wine and champagne had gone straight to her head, or whether her pent-up desires were running wild—or whether she just really, really liked this man. When had she ever done anything like this before? Never.

They sat there snuggled together—kissing, sipping, and people-watching while the lights of New York City danced all around them.

Eventually, Tim looked at his watch and groaned. "I think it's time to move on. The music calls us."

Just the mention of music sent a little zap of apprehension through Cat. She prayed that she would not make a fool of herself. "I could stay here all night."

Tim looked at her solemnly. "We could, you know."

This man really knew how to handle her. The more he tried to please her, the more she wanted to please him. "Skip the Rainbow Room? No way."

Outside, the bellhop hailed them a cab. Within seconds, Cat was nestled in the back seat next to Tim. He held her close. Unerringly, their lips found each other's again. Before she knew it, they were being dropped off at Rockefeller Center.

Another elevator. This time to the sixty-fifth floor. The elevator doors to the elegant art deco space parted, and Cat was immediately transported to another time, another place. They were shown to their table on an elevated tier just above the dance floor. It was the perfect vantage point to watch the dancers and still have a feeling of privacy.

"Oh my gosh, I forgot that the floor rotated," Cat exclaimed as she watched the parquet dance floor slowly turning.

"You know, I've never been here before," admitted Tim. "It's going to be an experience to dance on that."

A beautifully printed menu sat on each of their plates. The impeccably dressed waiter came up and asked them if they'd like a drink.

"I better have sparkling water for now," Cat declared with a smile. If she had one more drop to drink, there would be no hope of dancing.

"We'll order a bottle of champagne a little later," Tim agreed smoothly.

The band began to play. Cat wondered if anyone would dance. Immediately, several couples moved onto the floor. Cat noticed that many of the men were also wearing black tie. The women wore an array of fun, sparkling, long and short dresses.

Tim got up and held out his hand, "Shall we?"

Oh god. It was now or never. Her heart was pounding so loudly, Cat thought it was going to drown out the drummer. She forced what she hoped was a smile. It would be so terrible to ruin this perfect evening on the dance floor. "Let's do it."

They walked down to the floor. Cat stepped onto it gingerly. But the rotation was so slow that she didn't feel it moving at all. How cool. The big band was playing Glenn Miller's "In the Mood." Tim took her hand and whispered into her ear. "It's swing. You look beautiful. You'll be fine. Just follow me."

He took her hands and began moving side to side to the beat of the music. Then, subtly, he began to shift her right, left and back. Cat concentrated. Triple step—triple step—rock step. Before she had even repeated the combination a few times, they were moving together seamlessly, and Cat wasn't thinking anymore.

By the middle of the song, Tim was twirling her. During the first exhilarating spin, Cat let out a squeal, and Tim laughed out loud. She felt like she had when she was about four—twirling and twirling in the middle of her living room in her favorite tutu. And now, here she was—all grown up, doing the same thing. Her red dress was amazing. The full skirt flowed all around her.

"In the Mood" ended and Cat stood there clapping and clapping— for the band, for Tim, for her triumph on the dance floor.

Tim leaned down to her ear. "See, I told you that you'd be great— that we'd be great."

Cat couldn't remember the last time she had felt so high. Adrenalin was coursing through her system. "It's because of you."

"It's because of us," he whispered.

The music started again. Tim winked at her. "Foxtrot."

Cat's heart thumped again. But Tim confidently took her into his arms and set off. They glided around the rotating floor. Cat's long dress swished around her ankles. It was pure bliss.

When the song came to an end, Cat felt like she had just appeared in a Hollywood movie—the big band music, the floor to ceiling windows showcasing Manhattan, the rotating floor, the slowly changing color of the ceiling lighting. Talk about a fairy tale.

The music changed again. Cat recognized the song from her Sinatra collection, "It was a Very Good Year." It was a slow, poignant testimony to time and change. This time Tim pulled her into his arms in a tight hold. This time there was no special step to follow. Subtly, they rocked back and forth to the haunting music. Cat's cheek was right next to Tim's. She felt as protected as an infant. She felt as aroused as a woman. She was absolutely melting. She had never felt so alive.

Out of the blue, she realized that tears were trickling down her cheeks. Emotion that she couldn't contain came flowing out—for the life she used to lead, for the life she was embarking on, for the joy and sadness of it all.

The song came to an end, and Tim pulled back. He saw her face and was surprised. Ever so tenderly, he brushed away the tears on her face. "Are you okay?" he asked with concern.

"I'm wonderful," Cat sighed, her eyes still shining. "It was a very good year," she whispered.

Without saying anything more, Tim led her back to their table clutching her hand as if she was the most precious being in the universe.

Cat excused herself to go to the ladies' room to check her face and to collect herself. She stared at herself in the lightbulb-rimmed mirror. She looked emotionally ravaged, but at the same time, transformed. She understood that her life would never be the same after tonight. She knew that it was a very good thing.

With her head held high, she walked back to the table. Tim stood up when she arrived. He searched her face, and his face broke into a huge smile. "Wow. You look radiant."

Cat took his hand. "I think a big block of ice dissolved in me tonight. And I have you to thank for that. Thank you, thank you."

He picked up her hand and kissed it tenderly. His brown eyes met hers. "It was my pleasure. It is my pleasure."

The waiter came up and poured them each a glass from the bottle that Tim had ordered while Cat was away from the table.

Cat said, "I better be careful with this. I don't want to stumble on the dance floor."

"Why don't you nibble on a roll until our food comes?" Tim suggested. "You'll be fine once you've eaten."

Cat stared at the delectable basket of bread, rolls, and breadsticks in the gorgeously starched white napkin. She hadn't really touched any bread since she had met Dr. Martin, except for her birthday. But tonight was out of the ordinary. It felt like all the rules were being broken. She selected an amazing-smelling olive roll.

The waiter asked if they were ready to order.

"If I may be so bold," Tim replied, "I think the Oysters Rockefeller are a must, given where we are. And then, how about a Beef Wellington for Two?"

Cat nodded. "Sounds perfect to me."

While they waited for their food, there was more dancing. At each new song Cat felt herself loosening up. At each dance, Cat found herself feeling more and more excited by this man with the amazing hands. Sinatra certainly got it right with *"What is dancing, but making love set to music ...."*

Cat tried valiantly to enjoy every bite of her delicious dinner. But she couldn't deny that she was incredibly distracted.

They danced and danced. Cat felt like a princess doing a stately waltz, a forties starlet gliding through a foxtrot. Cat wasn't sure she had ever twirled so much. She imagined herself spinning as they went round-and-round on the rotating floor. Circles within circles within circles.

The band took a break after the third set. It was almost midnight. Tim took her hand. "I love being here and feeling like Fred and Ginger. But I think I'd love to go back to our view even more. What do you think?"

Cat found herself unable to speak. She nodded and picked up her bag.

In the cab, neither spoke. The atmosphere was so charged, it seemed almost unbearable.

But, somehow, Tim was opening their room door and there was the Chrysler Building with its orange lights.

The whole night had been such exquisite torture. There was no question what Cat wanted now. She dropped her purse and pashmina on the floor, wrapped her arms around Tim's neck and devoured his mouth. Tim ripped off his jacket, scooped her up and carried her to the bed.

Tim's strong, warm hands stroked her arms, her back. His lips entertained themselves on her ears and her neck. Cat undid his bow tie. Then Tim's hand slipped down the front of her strapless dress. Oh my god. That felt so good.

Cat tugged off Tim's suspenders. Almost frantically, she struggled with his shirt. She needed to feel his skin.

Coming to her aid, Tim undid his remaining studs and shrugged off his shirt. Then, in a seamless motion, he unzipped the back of her dress. It slid off. There she was—naked, exposed, with only her lace panties on. A part of Cat couldn't believe it. She was lying there with a man she had only known for two weeks, a completely different man than the one she had lived with for twenty-five years. What was most unbelievable was that it all felt wonderful, effortless, amazing. She wasn't embarrassed or awkward. The whole evening had been foreplay. Tim had been so right. Anticipation was amazing stuff.

He pulled her into his arms and she felt the wonder of his hard chest against hers, his skin against hers. They kissed more heatedly now, unable to consume each other fast enough. Then, Tim took her hand and pulled her up. "Come shower with me," he whispered.

Shower with him? Cat was startled. But she was beyond resisting anything he suggested. Never letting go of her hand, Tim gently led her into the sparkling marble bathroom. Masterfully, he lowered her underwear. He waited until she did the same for him. They stepped in and water splashed over every part of them. Tim enfolded her in his arms and kissed her passionately.

Then, Tim picked up the soap and lovingly massaged her entire body lingering in her most sensitive places. It was a sacred ritual. Cat stifled her urge to scream. Then he handed her the soap and she did the same for him. Never in her life had Cat done anything like this.

Just as Cat thought that they were going to finish what they had started right there, Tim turned off the water. He led her out of the shower, lovingly toweled her off and carried her back to the bed.

Cat was a giant tangle of screaming nerve endings now. Gone was any sense of modesty or reserve. "Please, Tim. Please," she whispered.

Tim looked her deeply in the eyes. "If you're sure."

"I'm sure," she breathed.

"I want this to be right for you."

"Please."

Tim reached for a small foil package that was in his night table drawer. Very distantly Cat wondered when he had put it there. She had totally forgotten about her box.

And with that, Tim moved on top and entered her. As if she was having an out of body experience, Cat heard herself gasp. Then tears came to her eyes for the third time that night. It felt so right. She had forgotten what a wonderful feeling it was to be connected in that way. Her body throbbed with joy.

Hours later, Cat woke up. It was still dark. The Chrysler Building was still shining, a beacon of their lovemaking. Cat sat up a little and looked down at Tim's tranquil face—his firm jawline, his delicious lips. Then her glance traveled around the room, that wonderful room, and she hugged the sheet around her. What an incredible night. She was so relieved to have gotten past this hurdle. At the same time, she was chagrinned that it hadn't been a hurdle at all. Pat had been absolutely right. Her body had not forgotten.

It was a miracle how fantastic she felt. After all the drinking, all the dancing, all the lovemaking, she felt energized and clear-headed. Maybe, it was because she felt so supremely happy. Some pretty crazy and powerful hormones must be flooding her system, neutralizing the negative effects of the alcohol and the fatigue she should be experiencing.

WOWSER!!! I couldn't have waited a second more!

Cat was startled as that familiar voice popped into her head. Surely, he had heard it too. But Tim was sleeping like a baby with an almost imperceptible grin on his face.

It really was easy, like breathing.

Easy?! That's all you can say? 'S wonderful! 'S marvelous!—whatever Cole Porter would say.

My body just knew what to do.

Instead of patting your recently transformed, but admittedly lovely, body on the back—how about giving some credit to Tim? He played you like a fiddle—outdid even your outrageous fantasy life, titillated you all night, but never pushed you. No wonder it was easy. You were desperate. He even dragged you into the shower. Talk about fantastic foreplay. I know that feeling clean was one of the many concerns you had about being intimate with someone new again.

It's true. He was great, inspired.

How many women hit the pot of gold like you did on Match? I think you won the lottery on your first try.

I have been out with five guys.

Whoop-de-do. You have met five guys. Let's face it. Tim is your first.

So, are you saying that I should stop looking?

You are an idiot sometimes. I'm saying that I think that you should be one hundred percent in the moment and savor every second. Wait and see. But it wouldn't surprise me if you've already found the winner.

Really? That's the last thing I expected from you. I figured you'd be warning me about the danger of rebound relationships.

Stop jumping ahead of yourself. You have had one night, not a relationship—rebound or not.

I'm just wondering if this has all been too good to be true.

I swear I might just give up. If you're bound and determined to worry about every little thing, be my guest. But my advice is to snuggle down next to that hot dude next to you in bed and count your blessings.

Got it.

One more thing …

What?

You are not dead yet.

Cat slid down under the sheet and curled her body into Tim's. Immediately, his arm reflexively wrapped around her. In seconds, Cat was asleep.

TAKE TWO

When Cat's eyes fluttered open, she had no idea where she was. Then, she realized that she was nestled up against Tim's chest and he was looking down at her.

"Hey, Ginger," he said softly as he pushed a tendril of her hair away from her eyes.

"Hey, Fred," she replied with a sleepy grin.

He leaned down and brushed her lips. "You look beautiful when you're sleeping."

Cat's eyes opened wider. Was he mocking her? But then she saw the look in his eyes. Maybe, she had traveled to an alternate plane of existence. But it truly seemed like he thought she looked beautiful. How could a woman with crow's feet and three grown children look beautiful first thing in the morning? She sat up and caught her reflection in a mirror in the room.

Amazing. She did look pretty good, if she did say so herself. Her hair was all tousled but sexy-looking. Her skin was clear and glowing. Her lips were pink and chapped from all that delectable kissing. And she looked so unbelievably happy. A certain unselfconscious, radiant smile filled her face. Forget plastic surgery. The key to looking good, looking young, was obviously something else.

Tim's voice was husky. "I planned on surprising you with a room service breakfast. But, since I've been watching you as you slept, I've had a better idea." He slid down under the covers next to her. His hands seemed to be everywhere.

Oh my god. It was as if she had died and gone to heaven. Suddenly her body was wide awake and responding in full gear.

"Can you wait?" Tim asked.

Cat groaned. "I can certainly wait for breakfast. But that's about all." Under the covers, she looked down the length of his lean, muscled body. It was very obvious that he didn't want to wait, either.

Without any hesitation, Cat moved on top of him. "My turn," she laughed.

A part of Cat floated away from herself and watched this naked woman on top of this man.

What a wanton hussy!

Yup. I am a wanton hussy, and proud of it. Go figure.

Cat smiled lusciously as her hair brushed onto Tim's face. She started nipping, licking, and kissing and continued down, down, down.

It almost broke Cat's heart to walk out of the room. Well, if truth be told, walking wasn't that easy. She was clearly out of practice. Wearing jeans and carrying the red dress on a hanger, Cat wondered if she would ever have a night like that again. Who cared?

The drive home was idyllic. They chatted companionably about the other dancers they had seen at the Rainbow Room. Cat thought the whole evening was as good as a Broadway show.

"Did you believe that dip the lady with the green dress did?" Cat asked. "Her hair actually brushed the floor."

"Maybe we should take some ballroom classes and spiff up our routine," Tim suggested. "Then, we could show off too."

There was a part of Cat that wondered if these were just easy words to say on the morning after, or if Tim was really serious. "Why not? I'll sign up for ballroom, if you try tango."

"It's a deal," Tim said, smiling.

They slipped into a comfortable silence. Tim put on some music. Whenever possible, his hand rested gently on her thigh. Cat closed her eyes and just enjoyed the feeling of the weight of his hand. She couldn't believe she had gone so long without being touched like that. She had always thought that she was a person who appreciated words and ideas. But now she was getting an entirely different glimpse of herself.

Sooner than she wanted, they arrived at Tim's house in Beacon. He shifted her bag to her car. "Would you like a bite to eat?"

Cat laughed. "Are you kidding? That breakfast was huge. I won't need to eat till dinner."

"I wish we could spend the whole day together. But John is coming over to watch the football game. You know, our tradition."

Cat vaguely wondered why he wasn't asking her to join them. "Of course, I understand. I've got a bunch to read and catch up on. Anyhow, I'm pretty beat. You gave me a workout."

Tim wrapped his arms around her and almost squeezed her to death. "I think I'm going to buy Match stock," he whispered sexily.

"I wonder if they need any more investors in the Rainbow Room?" Cat countered. "Thank you so much for the evening of my life."

Tim groaned and bent down. His lips branded hers. Her legs felt like Jello. A searing desire ripped through her core, again. If she didn't pull herself together, she was going to embarrass herself right there in the middle of the street.

"Are you sure you don't need a little massage? You must have some sore muscles after last night. I'll give you the family and friends discount."

Cat smiled teasingly up at him. "Football, football—remember, football."

"I hate football," Tim swore. "Remember? I'm a baseball player."

Cat used every ounce of her willpower to pull away. "No, you don't. Your son is important. Go take a cold shower." She laughed as she got into her car.

For the third time since she had met Tim, she found herself in her car attempting to drive with her senses reeling. She said a silent prayer that she wouldn't kill anyone. Miraculously, she managed to put the car in drive and ease forward.

Tim stood on the street waving like a maniac. Why didn't he go back into his house? This time Cat couldn't pull into her favorite spot at the end of the block. She figured that she had to turn the corner so he couldn't see her anymore. She turned right. Turning left was too much of a challenge.

Shakily, she pulled her car over. She tried to calm herself. She had an overwhelming desire to talk to someone else. She dialed her car phone.

"Cathy?"

"You can call me Cat, now," Cat didn't try to keep the excitement out of her voice.

"Uh-oh. Meow." Amy said knowingly. "I am so happy for you. I told you."

Suddenly, Cat grew very serious. "Yes, you did. I'm never doubting you again."

"I doubt that. Now, tell me everything, every last detail. Well, maybe not every detail," she laughed. "How was your dress? Did you do okay on the dance floor? Were there any awkward moments?"

"I swear, Amy, I'm still not sure if it was all a dream. My dress was perfect—so much fun to twirl around in. It was pretty dressy, but it fit right in because lots of people wear black tie and sequins at the Rainbow Room. Tim even got me a corsage."

"A corsage? Are you kidding me?"

"I know. Can you imagine? Apparently, he had been looking at photos of the Rainbow Room in the thirties."

"Am I going to be your matron of honor?"

Cat continued, "Stop it, Ame. Tim is a really good dancer and he made everything easy. Our room was amazing, with a view of the Chrysler Building. Probably the glasses of champagne helped, but it was so much fun, and I didn't think too much."

Amy interrupted, "Well, that is a miracle."

"I know. Everything just flowed."

"Halleluiah!" Amy almost shouted. "Now, I might have to scratch your eyes out because I'm so jealous."

"I wouldn't be satisfied, if you didn't feel like that," Cat teased.

Suddenly, Amy's voice grew serious. "You know, I'm really proud of you. With a little prodding you've taken some risks, and I think they've paid off."

Cat couldn't contain herself. "They sure did. Twice!"

"Twice?! Now, you're just being obnoxious."

Cat chortled, "You're right. I am. Sorry."

"No, you're not."

"You're right. I'm not."

THE CANDY STORE

Cat vowed to light a candle at church when she opened the door to her kitchen. How she had managed to drive up the Taconic she would never know. She mused that it was just as dangerous to drive after sex as it was after drinking.

You would think she was a sheltered virgin whose world had just been turned upside down by her first carnal experience. She reminded herself that she was not Little Red Riding Hood who had just discovered her first wolf.

But the fact was, she was "shaken, not stirred." That phrase suddenly popped into Cat's head. She lugged her overnight bag and red dress upstairs and dumped them in the middle of her bedroom.

She looked around her room. It seemed totally unfamiliar. Everything was different. Then she thought about it. No, it was the same. She was different.

She knew that she had tons to do—unpack, read her breakdowns, talk to the kids, get ready for the upcoming week. But all she wanted to do was lie down and close her eyes. She felt so vulnerable. She took a calming breath.

Her mind gravitated to Tim. He had obviously been hurt at the end of his marriage. Cat had no idea who or what he was looking for. For all she knew, he never wanted to be deeply involved again. Well, for that matter, she had no idea if she wanted that either. For the tenth time that day, she cautioned herself not to let her emotions run away with her. But it was hard.

She headed downstairs in her robe, fully expecting a text or email. She checked her phone. Nothing.

Stop it! Time to change gear. Think about something else. Make yourself some dinner. Read your breakdowns.

You're right, of course. I'm getting crazy.

That's right, sweetheart. Let go and accept whatever happens. Either Tim is the love of your life, or not. Time will tell. And I sincerely hope you'll give it time. Lots of time. Frankly, you're not ready in any way, shape, or form for monogamy. It's time to fly, taste the wine, smell the roses—blah, blah, blah. You've bumbled into the candy store. Don't stop with the first Milky Way.

You're mixing your metaphors.

I'm not the writer. You are.

Hmmm. I'm not so sure about that.

No comment. Get to work.

Cat opened her email and started printing her breakdowns. She couldn't help notice that there were a bunch of new Match emails. Ten of them were just winks. But there were a few written messages. While she was waiting for the printer, she found herself opening a couple of them.

hey, pretty kitty …

A thirty-nine-year-old with a ripped T-shirt fuzzily leered at her from his profile picture. Cat erased that one immediately.

i wud like to meet you. coffee?
hogwild

A heavy-set man stood proudly in front of his bike. A motorcycle and spelling errors! Cat shuddered and hit delete.

Maybe Tim really was the holy grail. Cat was about to stop reading when she spotted a message from *CloudNine*. That was a fun name.

A clean-cut man with gleaming teeth dressed in what looked like a uniform smiled at her. Nice.

Dear Moonrise,

I see that you've been on Match for a couple of weeks. Sorry I missed your debut. But hopefully, the mad flurry that seems to greet every attractive woman who goes on Match has died down a bit.

If perchance you don't have a diamond on your finger already, which I imagine is all too likely given your photo and profile, I'd like to throw my hat into the ring. For what it's worth, it's a pilot's hat. The reason I missed your big entrance on Match is that I have just returned from a couple of weeks in Rome. Yes, I am senior enough to get the good routes to Europe. And yes, "Senior" is a euphemism for old.

Okay, I have just pulled out all the stops for you, shamelessly trying to impress you with the possibility of seeing the world. But it's true, my job gives me a fair amount of free time and travel, I'd like to think that I

*clean up pretty well and I have some interesting experiences to talk about.
I also like to yammer about the wonders of the world. There are so many.
It sounds like you enjoy pondering the mysteries of the universe too.*

So, maybe we can talk. I'd like that.

Craig,

aka CloudNine

P.S.—I will be on it, if I hear from you.

Cat found herself smiling. Craig was insightful, playful, self-deprecating, and flattering. Clever of him to imply she was an attractive woman on Match, without resorting to the obvious stuff. His writing was fluid. He even used the word, euphemism. His spelling was perfect. And best of all, he wasn't a doctor!

Cat was shocked at how, in a matter of seconds, all of her angst about Tim suddenly shrank into perspective. She knew it was crazy to respond to Craig right after her amazing night with Tim, but for some reason she wanted to. She felt like he had appeared on her horizon for a reason. If she was really honest with herself, she knew that she was scared to death by last night. What if it didn't work out with Tim? What was the chance that it would?

Feeling tremendously impulsive, Cat clicked on the Reply box.

Captain Craig,

Up, up and away …

*I enjoyed your note. I can assure you that there's no diamond on my
finger. After a twenty-five-year marriage, that doesn't seem like an obvious next step to me. In any case, if the situation ever were to arise in the
far distant future, I think I might prefer a sapphire.*

What about you? It appears you are also divorced. What are your stats? How long were you married? When were you divorced? Children?

I hope this doesn't seem too nosy. I am always fascinated by people's stories. (Being a writer is a good excuse to pry, anyhow.)

Rome? Very tantalizing. FYI, I have never been. It is on the top of my list.

Yes, talking sounds like fun. Why don't you send me your number?

Cat

Cat hit the send button without hesitating. It was like jumping off a cliff each time she sent a message to a new person. She had to admit that she got a thrill each time. Who knew what might happen? So far, this little click of her finger had gotten her kissed—on the back of a truck, up a fire tower, in public at a rooftop bar, on the rotating dance floor of the Rainbow Room—and of course, at the hotel. Now that she thought about it, she had gotten kissed a lot.

Maybe they should call it, Kiss.com.

MONDAY, MONDAY

Cat woke up and immediately checked her phone for messages. She smiled when she saw that Tim had written.

I could have danced all night. Why did we have to stop? It was pure torture watching football and thinking of you.

Busy day. Call you tonight.

Fred

For the life of her, Cat couldn't understand why she had gotten so paranoid last night about Tim not contacting her right away. In the bright light of the morning, she realized that she had just had a little relationship-panic-attack. She had forgotten how getting involved made you a bit nuts.

She winced when she saw that Craig had already written back to her.

Sapphires it is. I always did think that diamonds were a little cliché. Tiffany, okay? Or do you prefer Cartier?

What a coincidence. I'm also in the quarter-of-a century marriage

club. Four children, 21–28. Divorced five years. I don't think you're being
nosy. That's required info. But you didn't tell me about your children.
   Rome is a slam dunk. I'm there three times a month. La Dolce Vita.
   But maybe we should talk before we pick our departure date.
   I'll be home from the gym around eight. Any time after that …
   I am on Cloud Nine. C

Cat stared at Craig's number. Well, she didn't have to call him.
She reread his note. He was a clever man. She couldn't deny that the
idea of Rome was enticing. But she was getting way, way ahead of
herself.

She smiled as she wrote Tim a quick response. Then, she thought
about tonight. Was she enough of a juggler to manage both men?

Cat wished that she had her usual Monday appointment with Pat.
Unfortunately, Pat was away. However, she had encouraged Cat to
keep in touch via email.

She starting typing.

Re: Riding a bicycle. You were right. Now I'd like some advice on
juggling.

Cat had been afraid that all of this interpersonal intrigue would
distract her from working on her script but found that her own personal activity seemed to energize her point of view. Today, her words
were flying.

Which reminded her of Craig. Thank goodness, she had told him
that she would call him. He had said he wouldn't be home till eight.
Hopefully, Tim would call her before then.

Pat responded to her immediately.

Fantastic.

Just remember, this is your time to fly, your time to honor whatever you want to do. Ignore that "good girl" voice. She crushes her own desires to try to please other people and makes herself miserable. Please yourself!

You have not made any sacred vow to anyone, including Tim. You are a free agent. You have worked very hard to become one.

If you feel like flirting with the pilot, go for it. If you feel like impulsively flying to Rome, I say, "Bravissimo!" If you feel like a roll in the hay with Tim the night before you leave, why not? Just use protection. STD's are no fun.

See you next Monday.

Pat

Cat laughed out loud when she read Pat's note. She couldn't believe how lucky she had been to find her.

Cat started to get a little nervous at around eight o'clock. Tim still hadn't called. Craig would probably be waiting for her call. Maybe she should keep her life simple and concentrate on one person at a time. She was pretty sure that Tim wouldn't be pleased to hear that she was flirting with other men.

Then she got a little irritated with herself. She had only known Tim for a couple of weeks. Surely, just because they had slept together once didn't mean she had taken a vow of fidelity. What was wrong with her, feeling guilty about her every move?

She realized that she was tying herself into knots trying to figure everything out. Sitting here waiting and waiting. Waiting for Tim to call. Waiting to call Craig.

That was it. She didn't want to wait anymore. But she also didn't want Tim to call when she was on the phone with Craig.

Quickly, she texted Tim.

Just jumping in the shower. I'll be out in twenty minutes. Talk after then.

Ginger

Cat felt a twinge of guilt. Why had she resorted to that little lie? Just because Tim had said he would call, she didn't have to be sitting by the phone. Oh well, too late.

Without hesitating, she dialed Craig's number.

"Hello?" A well-modulated, soothing, male voice answered the phone after one ring. She could just imagine him on the loudspeaker of a jumbo jet. They must train them to talk like that.

"Is this the Captain speaking?" Cat asked.

"Yes, it is. We are approaching 32,000 feet. You can see the moon-rise out the aircraft's right side. It is especially beautiful tonight."

Cat had to laugh. "Oh, that's a good one. Are you sure you're not the soap opera writer?"

"Sometimes, I think I'd be a good one. I'm not sure you'd believe some of the drama I've witnessed."

"Try me."

Without missing a beat, Craig told her a bizarre tale about a baby pig who was smuggled aboard in a carry-on. He told her about an adopted son and biological mother who discovered their connection while seated next to each other on his plane. Then he told her about the couple who had just met on his flight and asked him to marry them.

Craig was a terrific storyteller.

"Wow. I had no idea flying was so exciting."

"An airplane is part fantasy, part prison, part pressure cooker, part mental asylum. You trap a couple of hundred people in close quarters together for a number of hours, anything can happen. Then, throw in a little physical jeopardy—like bad weather, mechanical difficulties, or medical emergencies—and just watch the fun."

"And through it all, you are the voice of tranquility."

"That's why they pay me the big bucks," he joked.

"I'm impressed."

"Excellent. That was my hope. So, tell me about yourself. Your children."

Cat started to describe her children when another call beeped through. Oh, man. It was Tim. Was twenty minutes up already?

Craig seemed to notice her pause. "Do you have another call?"

Cat responded without missing a beat. "It's Ashley. I'll call her back." Another little lie.

"Oh, your daughter. Go ahead call her back. I know how it is when a kid wants you. You can call me back."

Whoa. This was getting too complicated for Cat. "I never have any idea how long her calls will last. Why don't we finish up for now?"

"No problem. But I've very much enjoyed talking to you. How about we finish up in person? I'm off to Rome again on Sunday but mostly free until then. Any chance of meeting this week?"

Cat's head felt like it was going to explode. "I'm not sure about my schedule this week. My script is due on Friday. I am supposed to meet my friend Amy one night. Can I check with her and get back to you?" Why-oh-why was she building in all these details that she'd have to keep track of? She reminded herself that less was more.

"Absolutely. You can text me your availability anytime. Or call."

Cat hung up and quickly dialed Tim.

"Hey there," he said. "I did try to call you."

"I know. Ashley called with an emergency."

"Oh? Is everything okay?"

Of course, he would ask. "That's right. You don't have a daughter. Emergency means the usual boyfriend problems."

"You know what they say, 'Love makes the world go 'round.' I understand that all too well, because my head has been spinning." Tim lowered his voice to a barely audible intensity. "I never had a night like last Saturday in my life. I can't wait to see you again."

Cat's heart started pounding. She took a deep breath and attempted to talk. "Me too. I thought maybe you could come out to the lake this weekend. It's supposed to be cool. We could build a fire."

Tim groaned. "I would absolutely love that. But, I can't. I have to go to Ken's parents' weekend. He's a senior and it's his last one. He's performing in his a capella group."

Cat felt totally deflated, but she tried to cover. "Oh, that's too bad. But I'm sure you'll have fun." She couldn't help wondering if his ex-wife would also be there. Most likely.

"I'd really like a rain check."

"Of course," Cat agreed as she was thinking—if I'm not in Rome.

"I spent all day trying to figure out how to see you this week. But my schedule is insane. I want to be full of life when I get to see you again. The fact is, the weekend took it out of me. I was dragging around all day."

How did he think she felt? She couldn't even walk. She knew that she would do almost anything to see him again. But she guessed that sitting and writing all day wasn't nearly as draining as handling patients.

Suddenly, she felt somewhat rejected and a little discouraged. "You know, I promised Ashley I'd call her back."

"That's fine. I'm pretty beat. I'll call you tomorrow."

"Okay. Bye." Cat's voice trailed off. What a disappointing ending to what should have been a fantastic conversation.

She clicked her phone off.

Jeez, talk about something that the cat dragged in. You are pathetic.

I just thought he'd be dying to see me. But apparently, he has other priorities.

Get a grip, girlfriend. Despite the fact that you have had conjugal relations, you are a recent entry into his world. Apparently, he is not prepared to drop his considerable professional and family responsibilities to make you the center of his life just yet. Maybe next week.

Very funny.

Look, dollface, neither of you are spring chickens. Neither of you are the clean slates you were when you dated last, back in the dark ages when your hormones were raging and all you had to do was cut your nine o'clock class.

I suppose. It's just that I thought what happened last Saturday was really special.

Yeah, yeah. The sun, the moon, and the stars moved for you.

It seemed like they did for him too.

I think they did. But it was your first "first time" in three decades. He's been divorced for a couple of years. It's possible that he has a little more perspective about the sun, moon, and stars than you do. Anyhow, he's a man. They put one leg into their pants at a time.

Point taken.

Get those stars out of your eyes. Deal with reality.

Reality is what scares me. It's obvious that he's very close to his sons. It seems clear that they take a lot of his focus.

And don't you like that about him? That he's a caring father? The fact is, those boys will grow up soon enough. The older one is a senior.

Of course. It just seems like he doesn't even care about me.

Bullshit. It seems like his plate is very full. My advice is load up your plate too. As I recall, there's a very sexy-sounding pilot who is hoping to see you this week. Well, guess what. The coast is clear.

I can't just call him back tonight

Why the hell not?

THE JUGGLER

Although, Craig lived in New Jersey, he generously volunteered to drive over the Hudson River to Cold Spring on Friday. She told him she would try to finish early before it was dark so they could see the river.

Tim called Cat on Wednesday night. "Hey, I've got great news. It turns out there's no need for me to be at the parents' weekend on Friday night. My son isn't performing until Saturday evening. In fact, he wants to do something with his friends on Friday night. I just need to get there in time for the football game on Saturday. So, I can see you on Friday night. Since I'm heading up north anyhow, I could stay at your house if you don't mind me getting up early."

Cat felt like throwing up. She had never imagined in a million years that this would happen. Her mind was racing. What should she do? Either she had a moral center, or not. The fact is, as much as she believed that kids were important, something about Tim changing his plans because his son suddenly wanted to hang with his friends on Friday night bugged her. "Oh, I can't believe it," she moaned reflexively.

"What? Did you make plans for Friday?" Tim sounded just a little accusatory. "Do you have tango?"

Cat fervently prayed that she had more time to come up with an explanation. But she didn't. She took a deep breath. "The thing is, Amy invited me to come to Connecticut for the night. Her husband is away. We've been trying to plan a girls' night for forever. I think she got tickets to some concert too. What a bummer." The entire time that Cat was fabricating her little story the voice inside of her was screaming.

Stop it, stop talking! Less is more. You're going to hang yourself on the details.

"Oh, I see," Tim said coolly. "I guess you can't reschedule your big night."

"Hey, I'm really sorry. But Amy's husband is almost never away on the weekends. How about we plan for you to come to the lake the following week? You know what they say, 'absence makes the heart grow fonder.'" Then she tried to laugh to lighten the moment.

"It's just that I'm so disappointed. I realize that I'm the problem here, not you. Of course, you have to honor your commitment to Amy. I'm just a little frustrated with my son. My kids think that they can just click their fingers and make me jump. As much as I love my son, I would give anything not to have to go this weekend."

Jeez. Cat just about melted right off the chair she was sitting on. This was the sensitive man who had totally disarmed her. If Tim had approached her like that from the beginning, if he hadn't just assumed that she would be waiting for him, she might have changed her date with Craig.

"I wish you had mentioned your plans last Saturday," she added regretfully.

"I don't think my feet ever touched the ground last weekend. I could barely remember my name, much less my son's schedule."

Cat laughed. "For someone whose feet never touched the ground, you danced a mean foxtrot."

"So did you. I think you're a dance prodigy."

Nothing that Tim could say would have made her feel more flattered. "Thank you, Doc. It's going to be a long week, but I'm sure you'll have fun with your son. After all, these moments with him are precious." Suddenly, Cat found herself being able to say all the right things.

Tim groaned. "I know, I know. Things have been rough since the divorce. It was really hard on both of them. I'm sure I've gone overboard trying to make everything as supportive as possible since then."

"Do they know why you got divorced?"

Tim hesitated a long time. "No, not really. As betrayed as I felt, I didn't think there was any point in ruining their image of their mother."

Cat was blown away. Talk about taking the high road. She wondered if she would have been able to do that. "So, what did you tell the boys about why you got divorced?"

Tim sighed. "Well, it was some mumbo jumbo about growing apart and me being tied up in my work."

"So they blamed you?"

"Well, at first, maybe a little. But when Madeline got involved with another man so quickly, I think they became a little more savvy."

"Kids don't miss much."

"That's true. I just wish I weren't always so busy."

Cat couldn't resist. "Me too. I don't mean to complain."

"You have every right to complain. Even our 'school night' date almost put me over the edge. Unfortunately, I have a lot of responsibility. I'm really not dying to be sued for malpractice."

"Yeah, all *I* risk if I become brain-dead on a work day is getting snide notes from the head writer or, I suppose, eventually getting fired. However, in the creative world most people understand that you can't be Shakespeare every day. Except for Shakespeare."

Tim laughed. "My work has a tendency to take over. I think that was one of the things that drove Madeline away. I'm trying to work on that."

"Look, I'm the novice in this new world of grown-up dating, but I think we're doing pretty well so far. There's no rush."

"Is that the kind of wisdom you dole out in your scripts?"

"Depends on who's talking. If our matriarch, Barbara, is advising one of her flock, it's certainly possible."

"No wonder you've won an Emmy," Tim kidded.

"Actually, when I'm writing someone like Barbara, I just channel my mother. She was the Queen of Common Sense."

"You were lucky."

"Yes, I was."

There was a poignant silence on the phone as they shared this moment. Cat felt closer to Tim than she had ever felt, even when she had been in his arms.

"Okay. I better get to bed. I hope you have a great time with Amy."

"Thank you."

Cat clicked off the phone and let out her breath.

Meryl Streep move over. The Oscar goes to Cat.

Lay off. I feel guilty enough.

I have to tell you, honeybun, I was plenty impressed by that performance. One piece of advice though, when you're creating a little story, don't keep embroidering the details. You didn't need to mention Amy's husband going away, you didn't need to mention tickets to a concert. Now, you better check and see which one you're going to attend.

I just thought I needed to make it difficult to change the date.

You didn't owe Tim any explanation, except the answer to his question which was, "Yes, I made other plans." He was the one who couldn't be bothered to tell you about his son's weekend. He was the one who changed his mind and announced that he was coming to see you after all. He is not your husband. He does not own you. You had a right to schedule something else. All you needed to express was regret if you felt it.

You know I was sorry. I would never have made plans with Craig if Tim had been available.

Well, I think that everything works out as it's supposed to. Craig seems like a great guy.

You just said that about Tim last weekend.

Well, it's true. Who knew you'd meet two good guys. You're on a roll. Who knows how many more good men are around?

Despite what my friends told me.

We've already established that your old married friends know nothing. Online dating has opened up the world. Twenty years ago, you never would have found these choices. Now, they're at your fingertips—frankly pounding down your "e-door." So, take advantage of the time you live in. You need to be open to every experience right now. How bad could it be to jet around the world at a moment's notice? Honestly, you're such a hypocrite.

What are you talking about?

"There's no rush." Didn't I just hear you giving that sagacious advice to Tim as if you meant it. The next minute, I feel like you're ready to hang his class ring around your neck. How about a happy medium? You have no idea about Tim. Let's face it, no one's perfect. It's obvious that he's got some trust issues from his marriage. He seems a little overboard about his sons. And unfortunately, it also seems like he could be a workaholic.

Boy, when you put it that way ...

But he also orchestrated the most fantastic date ever, puts the female body on a pedestal, and didn't tell his sons about his wife's affair.

I am so confused.

That's correct. You are confused. You are in a fact-finding, experience-gathering freefall right now. Listen to Pat. Trust your gut. We'll find our way.

I hope so.

In the meantime, I expect we're going to have a helluva time.

EXPLORING

Two nights later, Cat met Craig in Cold Spring. As if sent by Central Casting, he was a formidable-looking man who held himself with military bearing, even though he was dressed in jeans and a bomber jacket. Immediately, Cat felt like she could trust him with her life.

They took a sunset stroll down by the Hudson River. Very confidently, Craig tucked her hand into his large one. Cat couldn't help noticing that she felt a surge of warmth, but she did not feel as if she had been struck with a cattle prod like she always felt with Tim. As she had suspected, their conversation never lagged. She loved hearing about his four grown children who were all over the country. She was pleased to hear that he was still very friendly with his ex-wife.

Cat learned that Craig was into fly fishing and tennis. "What do you think about dancing?" she asked.

"Well, I haven't had lessons, although I've always liked to hit the dance floor."

'Oh, that's great." That was a big point in his favor. So many men simply hated dancing at all.

"I'm really curious about your interest in Argentine tango, though," he said. "I've been to Buenos Aires, and frankly some of the tango I've seen should be X-rated."

"Well, if you're serious, I think you should take some classes and see what you think."

"Sounds like a plan. I've watched couples tango in Rome at one of the piazzas that I often pass."

As always, talk of Rome made Cat's heart flutter. She couldn't stop herself from flashing to a fantasy of them intertwined doing the tango in front of the Colosseum.

It was very dark when they finished dinner.

"I know it's late, but I was wondering if you could handle another little walk by the river. I hate to end this evening." Craig said.

Cat shivered. "I'd love to," she agreed.

This time Craig put his arm around her and pulled her close to him as they walked. The heat from his body felt wonderful. "It's very weird, but I feel like I've known you forever. I can't remember ever having an easier time talking with anyone."

"I'm sure you say that to all the girls," Cat teased.

"No, I don't," Craig said seriously as he looked down at her. She could see the intensity in his eyes. He looked very much like he was about to kiss her, then he started walking again.

They ended up in front of a charming raised Gazebo at the center of the riverfront. Craig led her up onto the round wooden floor. "So, I think I should get my first tango lesson."

"Here?" Cat asked, totally surprised.

"Yup. Right here. Can you imagine a better place?" Craig

countered. "We've got a private, wooden dance floor, the moon, and the river. Now if we just had some music."

Cat thought about her Colosseum fantasy. "Well, as it happens, I think I can do something about that." She pressed a few buttons on her phone and tango music began to play.

Craig laughed. He held out his arms. "Let's go, Teach."

Cat was such a novice herself that she felt ridiculous trying to teach Craig anything, but she was able to show him the basic hold.

They tried walking and Cat was impressed at how relaxed and graceful Craig was. He seemed surprisingly comfortable in his body.

"Okay, Teach. Shall we dance?" Craig pressed.

Cat selected a slow-paced tango and they began. Craig clearly had a good sense of musicality. They rotated their way around the Gazebo.

When the song ended, Craig continued to hold her close. "I don't want to rush things, but I can't help myself." And with that, he leaned down and placed his lips very tenderly on hers.

An image of Tim suddenly flashed in her head.

Craig immediately felt her stagger. "You okay?" he asked, holding her up.

"I think I better sit down for a minute."

He guided her to one of the benches on the side of the gazebo.

Cat smiled apologetically. "Sorry, I just felt a little dizzy. I think I'm just a little overwhelmed by all of this." In her head, she knew she was talking about everything that had happened to her in the last few weeks.

Craig accepted her comment seriously. "You're not the only one feeling a little overwhelmed. I think I should let you go home. I don't want this evening to end, but I do want you to get home safely."

"I think when I'm away from the moon, the tango music, and your arms—I'll be fine."

Craig chuckled. "I want you to promise to pull over if you feel even the least bit strange and call me. Maybe, I should escort you home."

"Now, don't get all captain-ish on me. I'm fine. I'm sure you understand how daunting it is that a life can change so much so quickly. A year ago, none of tonight would ever have happened."

"Well, I'm glad it did."

"Me too."

Carefully, they kissed again. Cat felt like Craig was holding her like a piece of spun sugar.

He walked her to her car and begged her to text him when she arrived safely. Somehow, she managed to drive off.

As soon as she was in her car alone, she felt her sanity return.

When she got home forty-five minutes later, she dialed her phone.

"Are you home safe and sound?"

"Yes, thank you."

"Thanks for a very special evening and my first tango lesson."

"Thank you. Have a good trip to Rome."

"I will. I'll be in touch. Sleep tight. Arrivederci!"

It was only when she hung up that she noticed that Tim had texted her.

Give my love to Amy. Have a great girls' night! I'm sure you will. Off to bed in preparation for my early start.

Fred

FALLING IN LOVE

"So, this is the thing, Ames. I feel foolish even admitting to my ruse, but on the crazy chance that somehow Tim will stumble upon you, I want you to know that I told him that you and I were having a girls' night last night."

Cat went on to explain the whole situation.

"Not to worry. I've got your back. Consider it a night of 'Girls Gone Wild.' Serves him right for assuming that you were waiting on pins and needles for him. It does sound like his sons could be a problem."

"I actually think the fact that he's so busy at work could be an even bigger issue. I'd like to have someone I can do things with most weekends. So far, he's only been available half the time."

"So, tell me about the pilot. Can you imagine hopping on a plane anytime you want? I bet he gets to fly first class too." Amy sounded truly thrilled. What is he like? Cute, smart?"

"He's a hunk, just what you would expect for a pilot. Charming smile, gleaming teeth, impeccable grooming. But he's got a lot of depth. Great talker."

"Sounds like you have your hands full."

"It sounds like it, but the fact is I'll be alone for the rest of the weekend. Although I am thinking of going to tango tonight."

Amy sighed. "Just like my life. Choosing between a pilot and a doctor with a little tango woven in between."

Cat snorted at Amy's sarcasm.

"I'll be lucky if I get a movie on Netflix tonight," Amy added. "But it sure is fun hearing about your adventures."

For some reason, Cat was in rare form at the milonga on Saturday night. She wore a new polka-dotted dress with a fitted bodice and twirly skirt. The confidence that she had felt last night dancing with Craig in the gazebo seemed to carry over. From the minute she walked into the art gallery in Kingston where the milonga was being held, she knew that she had "it" tonight. Whatever that was.

Her regular classmates all asked her to dance. But, even more astonishing, a number of men whom she had never danced with before asked her to dance. Normally, she was very tense when she danced with a new man. But tonight she didn't have any major stumbles in the first two tandas she danced with new men. She couldn't believe it. Maybe, she was actually getting the hang of this crazy obsession.

She had just slipped into a chair on the side of the gallery hoping to take a little break when a debonair man appeared in front of her holding out his hand. He was tall and thin. She had watched him dancing before and knew that he was very good. She also knew that it wasn't good etiquette to decline an invitation unless you were really exhausted. She smiled, put her hand in his and stood up. He led her to an empty spot on the floor.

The music started. He smoothly slipped his hand behind her back. She put her arm around his shoulder. He raised her right hand and he waited. Cat knew by now that this part of the ritual was an almost sacred moment when two people eased into each other's arms. Each of them became familiar with the size, muscle tension, even the smell of the other person. They connected.

Then, he placed her weight on the foot he wanted, and finally, when the music was right, glided to the left. Closing her eyes to enhance her focus on his body's subtle movements, Cat flowed with him. The song was a classic tango song—haunting, sensual. Cat almost sighed as she realized how effortlessly he communicated where they were going. It was such a relief to realize that all she had to do was surrender to his lead. On top of that, the way he moved to the music, prolonging some movements over a couple of beats, accenting others with short quick steps, was absolutely in sync with the way Cat was hearing the music.

Cat had come to realize that people do not hear music the same way. She had also learned that it was absolute torture to try to move to music with someone who was hearing it in a completely different way. In those cases, Cat sometimes had to try to shut out the music altogether and just try to move when her partner did.

Cat was extremely grateful that this leader did not try anything too fancy for their first song. The music ended and he seamlessly brought her to a stop on the last note. Cat couldn't keep herself from smiling up at him in delight.

"I'm Sid," he introduced himself, smiling back at her.

"I'm Cat," she returned.

There was not a lot of talking in tango, and that's all they had time for, as the second song of the tanda began. The second song was another slow classic tango melody. For this song, Sid began to introduce a bit more complexity into his choreography. Now, very much enjoying her "ride," Cat felt herself following along without even thinking. She felt completely balanced and supported. She knew that she could trust him implicitly.

The second song ended and they looked at each other.

"How long have you been dancing?" Sid asked.

Cat was embarrassed. "About four months." She felt almost apologetic knowing how little that was in the tango world.

"You're doing beautifully," Sid murmured encouragingly.

Cat felt like she had just won an Emmy. She was glowing from ear to ear, when the third and last song of the tanda began. Cat didn't know too many songs yet, but she did recognize this one, "Oblivion." She had it on one of the CDs that she played in the car. She loved the emotional, heart-wrenching song. She was thrilled that she was getting to dance to it with someone who was so good.

The music began. Cat closed her eyes and totally relaxed into Sid's embrace. And then some metaphysical alchemy happened. Cat knew that Sid was actually making the decisions, but somehow she felt like they were moving as one. Every little hesitation in the notes, every pause was perfectly mirrored by their sensuous feet. Every thought flew out of her head, and she felt like she was floating along effortlessly on an exultant sea.

And then, she found herself being slowly lowered, lowered. She and Sid were in a very deep lunge. The last note was played.

It took Cat a couple of seconds to come out of her reverie and stand up. How had she gotten into that position? Her heart pounded as if she had just been forced to wake up from a beautiful dream.

"Oh my," Cat whispered, looking up at Sid.

"That was lots of fun. Thank you," Sid grinned casually as he escorted her back to her chair. And then he was gone.

Cat sat there. Numb. What had just happened? And then, she knew. She had just experienced what she had heard the more experienced followers talk about. The beauty of the music and the power of the connection had worked their spell. Cat had just "fallen in love" for the duration of the song. Two minutes of pure oblivion where nothing else mattered. And then it was over. And life continued until the next fix. No wonder people became addicted to Argentine tango.

SURPRISE!

Cat wasn't sure if it was her date with Craig or her tango awakening with Sid, but she found that she was totally wiped out on Sunday. And that was fine. She didn't have anything that she had to do other than read her breakdowns. She didn't bother to shower and spent the day puttering around her house in her most comfortable grey sweats. Cat never could figure out why grey sweats, the most unflattering color, were always the softest.

It was already getting dark when her phone rang. It was Craig.

"Hey there. I couldn't cross the ocean without saying goodbye."

"What a nice surprise," Cat smiled.

"I had a great time on Friday night. Especially, the tango lesson."

"Me too. That was fun. Don't be surprised if you see a scene like that on my show. The gazebo, the moon—pretty heady stuff."

Craig's voice grew husky. "Yes, it was. I'll be back late on Wednesday."

Cat's doorbell rang and she interrupted him. "Oh, I'm sorry, someone's at my door."

"Are you expecting someone?"

"Nope. Probably just one of my neighbors needing a cup of sugar or something."

"Do they still do that?"

"Up here they do."

"How nice. Well, they're paging me too. I better get going."

Cat walked to the door with the phone at her ear. "Safe trip."

"I intend it to be. Ciao, bella."

Still holding the phone, Cat pushed her reading glasses on the top of her dirty hair and flung open the door. Then she felt like slamming it closed.

"Surprise!" Tim looked delighted with himself.

Cat was horrified. She couldn't handle this. Hastily, she checked that she had really hung up on Craig.

Tim pulled a brown bag out from behind his back. It had a strong smell of sesame and ginger. "I brought dinner."

Cat took it from him. Chinese food.

"May I come in?" Finally, Tim seemed to get that Cat might not be ecstatic to see him.

"I suppose," Cat tried to be gracious. She looked down at her ancient grey stained sweats. They were no match for her red strapless dress. "If I can quote Mary Tyler Moore without dating myself, 'I usually look so much better than this.'"

Tim threw his arms around her and kissed her thoroughly. "You look adorable. Like a teenager scrambling to finish her homework on Sunday night."

Cat was slightly mollified. It never hurt to be compared to a teenager. "What are you doing here? Why didn't you call?"

Tim took the bag from her and set it on a hall table. He wrapped his arms around her. "I kept thinking about you all weekend. As I was driving back, I couldn't stand it one more second. Suddenly, I was at your house."

"With a bag of Chinese food," Cat added dryly.

"Well, I was hungry, and I figured you might be too." His mouth dipped to hers again, consuming it.

Cat found that his proximity was having its usual effect. "Shall I get some plates?"

"Only if we can eat in bed," he replied suggestively.

"The thing is, I'm really not hungry at all."

"Well, I am. But, not for Chinese food." And, with that, he scooped her up and started up the stairs.

Cat couldn't help laughing. "I haven't even showered today."

"That's easily remedied. I'm especially good at showers."

"I remember."

Tim was true to his word. The good thing about her sweats were that, they were so old and stretched out, they came off easily.

Cat had never imagined that the first man in her bed after Bob would be like this—her weekend clothes strewn all over the place and the last rays of the afternoon light filtering through the open curtains. But it didn't matter at all. From the minute they were skin to skin, it was all a blur.

Their night in Manhattan had been orchestrated and executed perfectly. But this tumble into her king-sized bed was crazy and spontaneous and fabulous. There was no anticipation. No script. Just throbbing desire.

Already, on only their second weekend, Tim seemed familiar.

She knew him. His smell. His touch. The feel of his skin. How could that be?

And clearly, he knew her. Those incredible hands triggered responses in her that she had no idea she possessed.

She tried not to scream, but she couldn't help it. And then she stopped worrying and did exactly as she pleased.

She had no idea how much time had passed when she opened her eyes. She was on Tim's shoulder. They had obviously fallen asleep. Carefully, she snuck downstairs and heated the Chinese food.

"Hey, sleepy head," she kissed Tim's cheek. "You hungry?"

Tim's eyes flicked open and he smiled a lazy, sexy smile. "Actually, much less than I was before."

They propped up the pillows and dug in.

"So how was the concert?" Tim asked with his mouth half full.

"Concert?" Cat was in the middle of a bite of General Tso's Chicken. "With Amy?"

Cat almost choked. In the heat of their spontaneous combustion, she had forgotten her whole alibi.

"Well, as it turns out, Amy and I were having such a good time talking, we decided to blow it off."

"Were the tickets expensive?"

"I'm really not sure. But it was worth it. How was your weekend with Ken?" Cat eagerly shifted the topic.

"They lost the game, but my son's performance was amazing." Suddenly, Tim hopped out of bed. "I almost forgot. I have something for you." Completely comfortable without a stitch of clothing on, he trotted downstairs and returned quickly. He handed her a small bag.

"What's this?"

"Just a little momento."

Cat opened the bag. She pulled out a rather small pair of purple panties complete with a college crest. Her face immediately matched the underwear.

"I saw them at the store and just had to get them for you."

"I hope you were alone."

"Actually, Ken helped me pick them out," he said matter-of-factly. "What?!"

"Just kidding. I had a few minutes alone to shop earlier today."

Cat couldn't help feeling a little thrill. The man had bought her panties. How sexy was that? "Well, thank you. Can't wait to wear them."

"You don't have to. I'm fine with commando too," he said with a wink.

Again, Cat's face flared. Commando?

Tim crawled down to the end of the bed and unearthed her foot from under the sheet. He lifted it up. "How are we doing?" he asked, as he looked at her. "Any tango this weekend?"

"I got home from Amy's yesterday and went to tango last night," she confessed.

"Just as I suspected. Good thing Dr. Hunter makes house calls." And with that, he began expertly massaging her feet. As Cat slipped away, her last cogent thought was *how is it that I am in bed on a Sunday evening? Instead of watching 60 Minutes, I am getting the most orgasmic foot massage from a man who just thoroughly made love to me and brought Chinese food, to boot.*

SPINNING PLATES

Amy was clearly aghast. "You were on the phone with the pilot, who was just leaving for Rome, and your doorbell rang and Fred Astaire unexpectedly arrived—*at the lake*? You're making this up, aren't you? Just to make me feel bad."

"No, I swear, the whole thing has gotten out of control. Craig is returning from Rome tomorrow and Tim has already planned the whole weekend for us. I don't know what to do.

"Who do you want to see more?"

"Well, things are much further along with Tim. But I'm pretty intrigued with Craig. I'd like to see them both. How can I manage that? *Can* I manage that? Have I turned into a slut?"

"Duh. Tim has asked you first this time. It won't kill Craig to get his act together sooner, or to see you during the week."

"I suppose that's right. Tim has already decided that weeknight dates are no good for him."

"So, you've got your answer. The doc is Mr. Weekend when he's not with his sons. The pilot is Mr. Weekday when he's not in Rome."

And very soon that's how it seemed to work out. Cat found herself talking to both men many nights. If she wasn't out with Craig, he usually called on the early side. Tim always called later, after a full day of work.

"So how are you doing juggling Tim and Craig?" Pat asked in their next session.

"So far so good. Luckily, Craig's trips to Rome have mostly been over the weekend. When we see each other on weekdays we usually meet between his house and mine. We've had so much fun. We've gone mini-golfing, bowling and go-carting."

"I'm so happy for you, honey."

"It's pretty amazing. I haven't had this much attention in years. I have to admit, I feel like a kid."

"Well, you look like one too."

"Oh, c'mon. You're making me blush."

"A mother is allowed to say these things. Even a surrogate mother."

Cat felt her heart fill with love for this woman who had fortuitously appeared in her life. "You have been the answer to my prayers. I'm not sure where I would be if I hadn't met you."

"You would be fine. But it seems pretty clear to me that we were supposed to meet. Back to Craig. So you haven't been to either of your houses, yet? No bedroom-time?"

"No. He's invited me to come to his house in New Jersey a couple of times, but it never made sense on a weeknight. I do have to get up and write the next day."

"How do you feel about not getting more intimate with him?"

Cat hesitated. "I'm a little relieved."

"Relieved? So you don't feel like sleeping with him?"

"I don't know. I like him very much. We talk a mile a minute. He makes me laugh. But when I kiss him, it's nice—but I don't turn into the maniac I am with Tim."

"So your chemistry with Tim is a lot more powerful."

"Yes. Then sometimes I think—since Tim was the first one, and since I had been so sure that it was all over for me—maybe what I feel with him is all that repressed desire. Maybe Tim was just in the right place at the right time."

Pat looked her squarely in the eye. "Really? And after the first time with Tim, after all your latent need was satisfied, has your response diminished?"

Cat looked away. Her voice dropped to a whisper. "No, it has only gotten stronger."

"So, are you the one steering Craig away from more intimacy?"

"I don't know. Maybe. Probably, yes. I love getting to know two men. What's more, I have to confess that I haven't stopped looking on Match. It's so much fun to be in the middle of this social merry-go-round that I really don't want to stop. It's an ego trip, I'm sure. I never thought that I could be desirable at this stage. But at the same time, there's something in me that doesn't feel like it's right to sleep with more than one man."

"Are you kidding me? After all those years of marital monogamy, don't you feel the right to be free?"

"I know it's ridiculous. Intellectually, I believe that I have a right to do exactly what I want. But emotionally, I still feel like I'd be a bad girl to sleep with more than one man."

"You would feel guilty?"

"I think I would feel guilty because I think that Tim would be upset.

I feel like something has changed in the thirty years since I last dated. It seems like being single now means not being involved with anyone. But as soon as you sleep with someone, you have to be monogamous until you move on. Thus, the concept of serial monogamy."

"Despite the fact that there has been no discussion about it between you and Tim."

"I feel like it is an unwritten rule."

"Hogwash. You're the one making up all these rules. You are a free woman who can do what she pleases, as long as you're not hurting anyone else. You and Tim are both consenting adults. I know I'm like a broken record telling you to trust yourself. I can only assume that if you are not sleeping with Craig, it is because some part of you really doesn't want to. However, I think the more experience you get at this point, the better. Now is the time to fly."

Cat had a lot to think about driving home.

So, did "Mommy" make you feel better?

What do you mean?

Honestly, this innocent act of yours is getting pretty old. I know how guilty you feel about dating both Tim and Craig. I just don't get why. Clearly, Pat doesn't either. You are a grown woman, a free agent. You've just dipped your toe into the dating world for the first time in thirty years. Surely, you're allowed to splash around a little.

It's just that I think that Tim would be so hurt if he thought I was seeing someone else. It kills me every time I'm not completely honest with him.

Well, this is a no brainer. Must I spell it out for you? You have two

choices. Stop seeing Craig, which in my opinion is really premature and foolish. Or, ta-da—tell Tim the truth!

The thing is, the whole point of going on Match was to figure out who I am and what kind of man I might like. I like Craig, enormously. I really don't want to stop seeing him.

Or the possibility of going to Rome.

Stop it. It's not that.

So ...

So?

Don't make me scream. You used to be a quick study. What has happened to you?

So I have to tell Tim the truth.

Bullseye! Now, why did that have to be so difficult?

Because I'm scared ...

Of what?

I'm scared that he'll stop seeing me.

The man who orchestrated the Fred and Ginger dream date? The man who appeared at your house on a Sunday night because he couldn't stand not seeing you? The man who makes the earth move every time he touches you? You think he's going to be scared away by some simple competition? You think he won't understand your situation, your needs?

I think he's a pretty black and white guy. Especially after what happened with his ex-wife. He's all in. I think he just assumes that I am too.

You know what they say. Never assume. I think he's an intelligent, empathic man. I don't necessarily agree that you have to tell him, but I think not being completely honest with him is eating you up. And since I care about you first and foremost, I think you need

to tell him exactly how you feel. The fact is, you don't want a guy who controls you, do you?

(SHUDDERS) Oh god, of course not, when you put it like that.

So ...

So I'll tell him soon.

When?

TO TELL THE TRUTH

Cat took a deep breath as she walked up Tim's front steps. Before she could ring the doorbell, the door flew open and Tim pulled her inside for a passionate kiss. His powerful arms encircled her. His ever so gentle hands cradled her face. All thoughts of Craig disappeared from her consciousness.

Sometime later, they sat on his couch having a glass of wine, talking and laughing and sharing their stories of their week.

"You said Ashley sent you a picture of her new boyfriend."

"Yes, she's in seventh heaven."

"Can I see?"

Cat pulled out her phone and flipped to the photo. She handed her phone to Tim.

"He looks pretty serious," Tim commented.

"He is. Ashley says he's a genius. A math major."

Casually, Tim starting flipping through her photos. "Do you have any more?"

Not looking at what he was doing, Cat answered. "I don't think so. She just sent that one." Then, she looked at Tim's face. He was suddenly not grinning.

"I didn't know you liked go-carts," he commented flatly.

Cat's stomach dropped. Craig. Why hadn't she deleted the photo? Tim was intently studying the photo. "This was taken a week ago." He turned to her and pointedly handed Cat her phone. "Who is he?"

Ah, the moment of truth. For a split second Cat thought about making up a story. A cousin? A neighbor? But she knew in her heart of hearts that it was time for full disclosure.

"His name is Craig."

"Craig? And who is he?"

"He's a man I met on Match. He's a pilot," she added flatly.

"A pilot? So, you're seeing other men?"

"C'mon now, Tim. You know perfectly well that, after a twenty-five-year marriage, I went on Match a month ago. I met you after the first week."

"And the two of us almost spontaneously combusted in the fire tower."

"True." Cat was relieved that he could make a joke. Maybe, this wouldn't be so bad.

"But you went go-carting with Craig a week ago?"

"I did."

"As I recall, you told me you were doing tango. You lied to me."

Cat hated being put on the defensive. "That's true. How would you have felt if I had told you the truth?"

"I would have been furious."

"Right." Cat was desperately trying to figure out what to say. "Look,

Tim, you know how much I love being with you. But you have to understand. I've just been let out of my cage."

Looking like a caged tiger himself, Tim suddenly bolted off the couch and started pacing the room. He was obviously trying to get control of himself. "Of course, I understand the feeling. It's just that I thought that we had something special." He turned back to her fiercely. "I know we do."

Cat got up and took Tim's hands to force him to look at her. "I think we have something amazing. But you're the first man I've been with since I was married. I have no basis of comparison for anything."

Tim spoke intensely. "Well, I've been gathering information for three years. I know that what we have is something very much out of the ordinary."

"I'm not disagreeing with you. But you need to let me find that out for myself. I need time. You must remember what it was like."

Tim turned away and replied hoarsely. "I remember what it was like when my wife lied to me."

Of course. That was the crux of it. That was the reason that Cat had been feeling so guilty. She went to Tim, put her arms around him and turned him around to face her. "I know we should have talked about it. In many ways, I wish I had met you much later. It would have been so much easier," she added.

Tim's eyes bored into hers. She could see that he was struggling. Then the words finally slipped out. "Are you sleeping with Craig?"

"I'm not sure you have a right to ask that. As far as I know, we have made no commitment to be exclusive. Nor would I agree to at this point, in any case."

Tim turned away. "You're right. Of course. I'm being a prick."

Cat had to laugh. She had never heard Tim talk like that. "No, you're not. Our timing is just a little off. But I don't think it's insurmountable if you can just be a little patient."

Tim rubbed his hand over his contorted face. "I'm not sure that I can stand the thought of you being with someone else. You are right. I don't want to know. But mostly, I can't stand the thought of you lying to me!"

Cat couldn't stand his pain. She put her arms around him. "I agree completely. So please don't ask."

Tim nodded. Cat could see thoughts whirling around in his head wildly. "You're right about everything. I will give you all the time you need. I have no choice. But what's good for the goose is good for the gander," he added reluctantly.

"What does that mean?"

"It means that we are agreeing that we are not in an exclusive relationship."

Cat had to admit that his words took her by surprise.

"That's only fair, isn't it?" Tim asked pointedly.

Cat gulped. "Absolutely."

"Let's shake on it," he suggested.

The minute she put his hand into his, he pulled her into an intense kiss. "As far as I'm concerned, however, tonight you are mine."

It seemed that their conversation had opened the floodgates. Tim pulled off her jacket and unzipped her jeans. Frantically, she ripped open the buttons on his shirt.

They never even made it upstairs. Who knew that such a difficult discussion would provoke such heightened lovemaking? Cat had no idea it could get this good. Apparently, a little competition was heady stuff.

Vaguely, she hoped that no one could see into the dark living room or hear her sounds of delight.

DARK DAYS OF NOVEMBER

Cat's lips were bruised after that weekend in Beacon. Tim couldn't keep his hands off her. Her body was so totally spent that she could barely drag herself home. When she walked back into her house on Sunday night carrying Sandy in her carrying case, it was all she could do to make it into the kitchen.

She had just crashed on her couch after changing her clothes when her phone rang. It was Craig.

"Hey Cat, how are you? I'm at JFK, I just got in from Rome."

"Welcome back. How was it?" Cat struggled to sound upbeat.

"The weather was beautiful. Much better than here."

"Well, it is November."

"You sound tired."

That was one way of putting it. "I'm feeling a little—under the weather."

"Oh, that's too bad. I was hoping to see you tomorrow or Tuesday."

"If you don't mind, let's talk tomorrow and see how I feel."

"Sure thing. My shuttle is here. I better go."

Cat hung up. Well, she had bought herself a little time. The fact was, she seriously wondered whether she wanted to see Craig again.

She made herself some dinner and watched some television. Then she decided to catch up on her emails. Out of habit, she found herself clicking on the Match site. Low and behold, right at the top of the screen were a series of photos of men who were *New on Match*. Guess who was right in the middle? Complete with his tuxedo—007, Tim!

He must have put his profile back on Match as soon as she left his house. Looking at it made her feel sick to her stomach. She knew that she was being unreasonable, but she didn't want him to meet other women. He had been divorced for three years. He had already done all his research. He had as good as told her that he knew that she was the one. But here he was, bigger than life on Match.

Cat knew she was too tired to think clearly. But she felt very hurt.

"Hey, Ames, you busy?"

"Nope. Just another boring Sunday night. Ed is watching football. I was sorting my coupons."

"Your coupons? You, Ms. High-Powered Attorney, saves coupons?"

"Yes, I do. I learned from my mother. It's very relaxing. And fun. You have no idea how satisfying it is to save on the groceries I would buy anyhow. What's up? Is this another Dear Abby call?"

"Sort of. I'm sorry. This must be getting so tedious for you."

"Are you kidding? I'm getting to live out all the drama of a new divorcée without any of the heartache. I can't tell you how much fun your online dating stories have been. I've had the best watercooler stories in the office."

Cat winced at the thought of this. "I hope you changed my name."

"Of course, your identity is safe with me. So, I sense some problem. Did Tim find out you weren't with me that weekend?"

"Not exactly, he was looking at pictures on my phone and found a photo of me with Craig last week when we went go-carting. Of course, the date was on the photo."

"That wasn't very careful of you."

"I know."

"Methinks you may have had a Freudian slip. Maybe, you wanted him to know."

"I was going to talk to him."

"So, did he get all territorial and hurt?"

"Yes, initially. Then, I pleaded my case. I need to test the waters, etc., etc. He seemed to understand, and I thought everything was going to be okay."

"But?"

"But then, he announced that what was good for the goose was good for the gander."

"A bit old-fashioned, but immanently fair."

"Agreed. And then he turned into a wild Casanova."

"Oh, here we go. I'm not sure I can handle those details."

"Anyhow, suffice it to say, I hardly got out of bed all weekend."

Amy sighed deeply. "Those men. They can't escape that warrior hardwiring. Nothing excites them like a little competition. That's why marital monogamy is such a bummer. As soon as there's no threat, they retreat into their caves to watch football."

"I'm afraid you may be right. But the point of the story is ..."

"OMG. You haven't gotten to the point yet?"

"The point is, I crawled home tonight, barely able to walk."

"Stop, stop. You're being cruel."

"And, guess who is already back on Match?"

"So I take it, he actually had gone off of it after he started seeing you."

"Yes."

"Well, that's quite a testimony."

"I guess it is."

"You don't sound too happy."

"I'm not. I felt sick when I saw his profile online."

"Ah. The plot thickens. So, you can dish it out, but you can't take it."

"I know. The thing is, he's been divorced and playing the field for three years. I've only been online for a month. I need to know what's out there. It doesn't seem fair."

Amy snorted. "It's not fair for him to be online when you are? Good thing you're not a judge."

"I know, I know. I'm being a selfish, pathetic, possessive bitch."

"I wouldn't go that far. I would say that you may be finding out that you care more than you thought."

"So, what do I do?"

"You follow your heart. You continue to see Craig until you don't want to anymore."

"But what if Tim meets someone else?"

"Life's a gamble. But gambling is exciting, isn't it?"

Cat sighs. "I guess."

"On another topic. What are you doing for Thanksgiving? I've been worried about you, your first Thanksgiving after the big D."

"I really don't know. The kids have all conveniently been invited to friends this year. I don't think any of them could face the holiday with our newly deconstructed family."

"More like they couldn't face Bob's new babe."

"Hmmm. I didn't think of that."

"So, are you going to celebrate with Tim—or Craig?"

"I must admit, I'd love to meet Tim's sons and it would be fun to have Thanksgiving with them. But so far, he hasn't invited me to meet them. I doubt if I'll get an invitation after today."

"True. I would think it's a big deal to introduce your kids to someone you're dating."

"I'm sure you're right."

"So, what about your brother?"

"No, he's going away."

"Goodie, that leaves us. Ed and the kids would love to have you join us. And, of course, my mother adores you. She has asked me several times what you're doing."

Cat felt tears come to her eyes. "Oh, it would be so nice to be with your family. I must admit I was trying not to freak out about what I was going to do."

Amy's voice grew stern. "I just assumed that if you didn't have other plans, you would ask me. You know, I'm always here for you."

"Thank you, from the bottom of my heart."

THE HOLIDAYS

Cat was expecting Tim to act a lot differently after their conversation. But life continued much the same. 'Don't ask, don't tell' seemed to be his guiding principal. However, when she was with him he couldn't seem to get enough of her.

Craig continued to ask her out during the week. So everything was easy and uncomplicated until one afternoon when the phone rang.

"Ciao, bella!"

"Craig, what are you doing calling? You're in Rome."

"That's right, I am. I wish you were here with me."

"Oh, me too," Cat agreed lightly.

"So I was just thinking that Thanksgiving is next week."

Cat's heart started to pound. Was he going to ask her to join him?

"Since I'm going away for the week to be with my kids, I was hoping you might be free to come to my place on Saturday. I thought I'd wow you with my cooking."

Cat gulped. Tim had not talked to her about any plans for Saturday yet. She realized this was now or never. "Not only can you fly a jet to Rome, birth a passenger's baby, and deal with a panic attack—you can cook. Unbelievable."

"I'm a man of many talents," he kidded, "and incredible modesty. Seriously, I am bringing back some black truffles. I thought I'd make a drop-dead dish I learned here. I also have some fabulous wine."

"How can I refuse? It sounds like a meal of a lifetime."

Craig laughed, pleased. He obviously had not been certain of her reaction. "Fantastic."

"What shall I bring?" Cat offered.

"Just yourself."

Cat was silent. There was no mention of staying over. But she figured that was implied.

Craig seemed to read her mind. "For your information, I have a very nice guest room. We've only known each other for a few weeks. Let's see what happens ..."

Cat took a deep breath. "Sounds great."

Her conversation with Tim the next night was a bit different.

"Hey, Cat. It's me."

"How was your day, Doc?"

"Fine. A patient told me about this great movie he had just seen. You up for seeing it Saturday night?"

Here it was. "Any chance we could see it on Friday, or Sunday?"

"You're busy?"

"Yes."

When Cat didn't offer any details, there was a pregnant pause. "Oh. Got it. Let me see what my schedule looks like on Friday." The tension was palpable in his voice.

"Hey, Tim, what are you doing for Thanksgiving?" Cat asked suddenly, deciding to go for broke.

"The boys are coming to my sister's for an early dinner. They're going to their mother's later in the day."

"Oh, I'd love to meet them sometime. I was even thinking of inviting all of you to my house." Her comment hung in the air.

"Aren't you getting together with your kids?"

Cat tried to keep her voice light. "No, as a matter of fact, none of them are coming home for Thanksgiving. I think they're a little reluctant to face the new family paradigm."

"Oh, that's too bad." Tim's voice softened. "So, what are you doing?"

"Amy invited me to join them."

"Well, that'll be okay, won't it?"

"I guess." Cat couldn't help sounding wistful.

Tim hesitated and then said slowly, "You can't have it both ways, Cat."

"I know. I'm still figuring things out."

"It takes time."

"Right."

"I'll get back to you about this weekend."

"Okay." Cat hung up the phone, feeling sick to her stomach. Then she felt mad. Why did she feel like a bad girl who was getting punished?

On Saturday she packed an overnight bag. Before it got dark she drove to Craig's house. Her GPS took her to a modern development of trendy townhouses around a beautiful golf course with a lake.

Not bad. The man lives in style.

It's very nice.

That was really enthusiastic. Don't go getting cold feet now.

I just am not sure what I'm doing here.

You are OTF.

What in the world?

You are Out There Flapping—which is just what a bird that has been recently let out of her cage should be doing. You certainly should not be immediately flying into a new cage!

Tim is not a new cage.

We've been through all this before. Tim is great. But you need to experience a lot more.

I just don't know if I want to sleep with Craig.

Well, you know my opinion. Sex is not the end of the world. You don't have to march right down the aisle afterwards. You can just have fun. No strings. However, you are a big girl. Craig has already offered you the guest room. I'm pretty sure you can finesse your way out of doing the dirty deed if it doesn't feel right. How many of those scenes have you written in your career, anyhow?

More than I can count.

Exactly. I remember the time at the motel that the fire alarm went off—and the time that bird flew into the window—and the time Marsha couldn't stop hiccuping and they ended up at the emergency room.

Stop, stop. I get it.

Or you could just be honest and tell him you're not ready. I know you can handle that.

I suppose I can.

Do me a favor?

Don't I always?

(IGNORES HER) **Just savor the moment. Enjoy the amazing situation you are in, getting courted by two terrific men, and trust that your instincts are right on.**

(SUDDENLY SUSPICIOUS) Are my instincts—you?

No comment. Here's the house. Break a leg!

Taking a deep breath, Cat pulled up in front of Craig's house. Because they weren't playing mini-golf or go-carting, Cat had decided to wear a wrap dress with boots. Craig opened the door, took her coat, and let out a wolf whistle.

"I'm going to have to cook for you more often. You look sensational." Then he leaned in and kissed her.

Cat curtsied. "Thank you, kind sir. I thought I better dress for the occasion. It's not often that a man cooks truffles for me. Well, the truth is, it's never happened before."

Craig laughed with delight. "I thought you were the right person for this treat. My kids would be useless."

An extraordinary scent was coming from the kitchen. "Oh my, I think I've died and gone to heaven," Cat sighed.

Craig showed her around the two-story townhouse, which was military neat. It had top-of-the-line leather furniture and two great mid-century chairs. A gas fire was glowing in the elegant stone fireplace. Craig poured her a generous goblet of red wine and settled her into the buttery couch. There was a decadent slab of cheese on an Italian ceramic platter on the coffee table.

"Let me guess. Customs looks the other way when you return from Italy."

"Pretty much," Craig grinned like a proud six-year-old who had gotten away with something as he slid next to her on the couch.

Cat couldn't help feeling incredibly relaxed as she enjoyed the sensory delights that surrounded her—the delicious aroma, the mesmerizing fire, the seductive opera recording, the incredible cheese, the out-of-this-world wine, and the warmth and vitality of the man next to her. Their conversation flowed as easily as the wine.

Cat had absolutely no idea how much time had passed when Craig finally got up and offered her his hand. "I think I better cook, before I forget how." He leaned down and placed a kiss on her neck.

They went into the kitchen, where Craig topped off their glasses. Cat was feeling a little unsteady on her feet and settled onto a stool at the gleaming quartz island while Craig whipped up the truffle pasta dish.

In what seemed like no time at all, Craig dished up two plates of steaming pasta with veal cutlets. They carried them into the small dining room where the table was set with a red-checked tablecloth topped with a dripping candle in a chianti bottle. There was also a bud vase with one perfect red rose.

"Are you sure you've never worked on the soaps?" Cat quipped.

"Nope. I've just spent considerable time in Italy," he kidded. With that, he picked up and kissed her hand. *Buon appetito!*

And with that, he dove into his pasta with gusto. Cat did the same.

She closed her eyes and sighed with guilty pleasure as the incredible taste filled her mouth. "Oh my god. This is unbelievable."

Craig nodded. "If I do say so myself, it is. Can't you just picture the rolling hills of Tuscany?"

"And hear the snuffling of the pigs?" Cat added.

"I think they mostly use dogs these days."

"Pigs are so much more interesting," Cat commented.

And with that, they launched into a high-spirited conversation about pigs. It turned out that Craig grew up in Vermont and knew quite a bit about pigs. Then, of course, there was the pig on his flight.

Cat laughed until her sides hurt. She had no idea how much time had passed when she realized that she had eaten every bite on her plate.

Craig looked at her plate pointedly. "Would you like some more?"

"I would love some, but I'm afraid that I am totally stuffed. By the way, the veal was also delicious."

"Thank you. I figured you always liked some protein." Deftly, he cleared their plates and topped off their wine glasses. Smoothly, he moved them back in front of the fireplace.

Now, the music was soft jazz. Gently, Craig put his arm around her. Without thinking, she put her hand on his thigh and her head relaxed against his shoulder. It was such a lovely feeling to be resting against his chest. Why had she ever thought she was done with this? Before she could answer herself, he was kissing her, and she was kissing him back. She tried to gather her wits about her. Is this what she wanted? But her head was too fuzzy.

Minutes melted. Hours dissolved. Somehow, her wrap dress was a little unwrapped.

Always the Captain of the Ship, Craig led her upstairs. Cat followed his lead, floating on a sensory sea. There was no hesitation, no doubt. Craig was in charge—masterful, confident. The take-off was heady. The landing was sublime.

P F M

Cat woke up a few hours later, entwined in Craig's arms. Carefully, she disentangled herself and tiptoed to the bathroom. She still felt a little light-headed. She drank a glass of water and crept back to bed.

So?

So it was great. I feel very appreciated, very alive.

And, a little drunk?

A little. I was nervous.

The man knows what he's doing.

For sure. With everything. The truffle pasta, the music, the cheese. But …

But?

But, some corner of my brain kept thinking of Tim.

I'm aware. You were awfully quiet.

388

BLACK FRIDAY

Cat's eyes fluttered open. Weak November light filtered into her room. Gradually, she came to consciousness. It was Friday. Black Friday. A perfect name for today. Yesterday she had driven to Amy and Ed's house in Connecticut. It was a lovely, festive dinner. Cat knew and loved everyone at the table. She talked and laughed and ate her whole dinner with a smile on her face and an empty feeling in the pit of her stomach.

It was all wrong. For the first time in thirty years, she had sat at the Thanksgiving table with no family. No Bob, no Paul, no Michael, no Ashley. No mother, no father, no brother. She was totally surprised at her reaction. It was just one day. One silly holiday. Why was she so upset?

She yanked off the covers and jumped out of bed. She had no time to wallow. Thanksgiving or no Thanksgiving, she had a script to submit today. The show must go on.

She made coffee and absently checked her email. Nothing from Lorraine. Oh, cool. There was one from Craig including a shot of him and his four kids. Good-looking kids. Not surprising. Craig was definitely the square-jawed, super-hero type.

P F M

Happy Thanksgiving! Miss you. C

She scrolled down. All three of her kids had sent her cute notes. She could tell this year had been hard on them too. And then her eye caught an email sent this morning at six.

Happy Thanksgiving, Ginger. Thought of you the whole meal yesterday. Are you hitting the malls today?
Fred

Cat ripped off a response.

Hardly. Although some lazy docs get the day off, we soap writers have our noses to the grindstone. It's Friday, shopping or no shopping, and my script is due at five o'clock, as usual. G

She hit send and retrieved her script. She had worked like a fiend late on Wednesday. Her script was done. All she had to do was edit it. Good. Maybe she would have time for a little shopping after all.

Her script was airing the week before Christmas. As she read it she had a brainstorm that would improve her Dylan and Dana storyline. It took some time to rewrite, but she was pleased with the result. Then she polished the rest of the festive script. Several hours later—her mind filled with nutcrackers, Christmas trees, and mistletoe—she had totally forgotten that yesterday was Thanksgiving. She was in the thick of the Christmas season. That was one of the weird things about writing a soap. She was always ahead of the real calendar by a couple of weeks.

She was just about to submit her script when she heard jingle bells outside her door. Who in the world was that?

As she walked to her front door, she heard a jolly, "Ho, ho, ho."

Curiously she opened the door to Tim wearing a Santa hat and shaking jingle bells like a mad man. Confidently, he stepped in and gave her a bear hug. "Brrrr. I thought you were never coming."

"Santa, I think you're a little mixed up. It's only Thanksgiving, not Christmas," Cat teased.

"Santa couldn't wait. Have you been naughty or nice, little girl?"

"Santa, I'm afraid you know that better than anyone," Cat flirted back.

"Oh, that's right," Tim said as he leaned down and crushed her mouth with his.

"What are you doing here?" Cat said as she came up for air.

"I came for a Christmas surprise, but I don't want to interrupt your writing."

"Amazingly, my script is finished. I was just about to send it in."

"Ho, ho, ho," Tim bellowed. "A Christmas miracle! Well, send it in, lassie, and we'll be off."

"Lassie?" Cat couldn't help laughing.

Tim peered outside. "We don't have much light left. Hit that button, grab a warm coat and gloves, and let's go."

"Where are we going?" Cat asked breathlessly as she slid into the seat of Tim's SUV.

"A Christmas adventure," Tim answered mysteriously. "I do have one question, though. Does Santa need to bring the sleigh back at any specific time? For tango—or any other plans?" he asked carefully.

"No, Santa. I have no 'other plans' for tonight. What did you have in mind?" Cat appreciated the he was not assuming anything about her social life.

"Well, you do understand that Santa is always concerned about naughtiness."

"I see."

"But before we deal with that, Santa thought that dinner in Rhinebeck might be nice."

Delighted by the turn of events, Cat settled back in her seat like a child. "Dinner is always nice, Santa."

They arrived at a farm about fifteen minutes from her house with the last rays of the setting sun glimmering behind the trees.

"We better hurry, my little elf," Tim said, as he plopped an elf hat on her head.

"What are you up to?" This was not Rhinebeck.

"We're cutting down Christmas trees, of course," Tim answered as he pulled out a saw from the back of his car.

"I've always wanted to do that," Cat laughed delightedly.

"I know. You told me that on one of our first dates. There's nothing better than a fresh-cut tree."

They made their way to the Fraser Fir section of the farm. A few stragglers were dragging their conquests to the baling barn. Tim looked at his watch. "I think we have about five minutes to make a decision."

Cat shrieked. "Are you kidding me? I've never picked a tree in less than an hour. Ashley and I make it a sacred tradition to consider every possible choice."

"Good thing Ashley is not here," Tim grinned happily. "On your mark, get set, go! I bet I'll find a better one than you!" he challenged as he set off at a run.

Giddily, Cat ran in the opposite direction to a tree that looked pretty good. The backside wasn't perfect, but it would be all right against her French doors. It seemed to be about the right height. Tim circled around and ended up with one nearby hers. In another ten minutes, Tim had sawed down both trees.

"Whew. That was a world's record," Cat exclaimed.

"I had no doubt that we could do it," Tim teased. "Where there's a will, there's a way."

It was nearly dark as they dragged them to the barn.

"I can't remember ever having so much fun picking a tree, Santa," Cat smiled.

"I promised you a Christmas miracle, my pretty little elf," Tim replied.

Cat stopped. "Thank you," she whispered as she reached up to give Tim a big kiss.

Cat's head was spinning when they reached the tiny French Bistro in Rhinebeck. It looked quite chic. "I can't go in there. I'm not well-dressed enough."

Tim popped her elf hat back on her head. "How long have you been living up here?"

"Full time since January."

"This is Dutchess County, not Connecticut. We'll be perfectly fine. In fact, we'll probably be the celebrities of this place in our holiday hats." And with that, he straightened his Santa hat, took her hand, and led her into the restaurant.

The hostess's face lit up when they entered, and she showed them to the best table by the window.

Then they were presented with a complimentary Candy Cane Cosmo in recognition of their holiday spirit. The drink was rosy liquid in a martini glass with a small candy cane curled over the edge.

They raised their glasses and clinked. "You were right," Cat beamed. She took a sip. "I love cosmos."

"They're no fools. They put us right in the window with our hats and cocktails, and look how many other people have stopped, looked at us and come in since we've been here. However, I'm not much on cosmos and I'm driving, so why don't you plan on drinking both of them. I think I'll order a beer."

"Santa, are you trying to get your elf a little tipsy?" Cat teased.

Tim leered. "Santa works in mysterious ways."

As difficult and unsettling as Thanksgiving had been, Cat had more fun on Black Friday than she had ever had before. Her two drinks certainly made her feel very jolly. But it wasn't just the alcohol. Tim was so playful—like a little kid. On their way home in the car, they sang "Santa Claus is Coming to Town" and "Jingle Bells" at the top of their lungs. Cat rang the jingle bells while Tim was driving. When they ran out of steam, Tim put on a radio station that was already playing Christmas music.

"I'm going to be sick of all these songs in a couple of weeks. But today, I'm loving them," sighed Cat.

They held hands most of the way back to her house.

"Why don't you get your stand and put it where you want it," Tim suggested when they got back to the lake.

Cat rummaged around in the basement and found her stand. By

the time she had put it in front of her French doors, Tim had flipped her tree off the top of the car, made a fresh cut on the bottom, brought it into her living room, and put it onto her stand.

He held it while she decided if it was straight or not. In a couple of easy adjustments, it was done.

"I can't believe it's only eight o'clock," Cat was amazed at how smoothly everything had gone. She could remember so many years of struggling with the tree, bickering over how to get it into the stand, endlessly adjusting it to get it straight, and then having it crash down in the living room after all. "I'm impressed, Fred. You can dance and deal with Christmas trees."

"It's all that time with the boy scouts."

Tim sat on the couch and admired the tree. "Pretty nice, Ginger. But I think mine is better."

"Them thar's fightin' words," Cat bantered. "Yours is too fat. I like my trees slim and elegant."

Tim shook his head. "Uh-oh, I think we've got a serious red flag. I hate those skinny little Charlie Brown trees."

Cat was mock-offended. "This is not a Charlie Brown tree. You'll see, when I get it decorated. Aren't you going to need help to set up yours? It's a bruiser."

"The boys are coming over tomorrow. We're going to have our annual football, beer, and baubles celebration."

Mention of his sons always made Cat quiet. She wanted so much to meet them.

"So, what shall we do next, my little elf? Shall we tackle the lights?" He leaned over, kissed her neck, and snuck his hand under her fleece. "Or something else?"

Instantly, Cat felt a jolt of electricity seer through her. "Something else," she replied huskily as she led him upstairs.

Tim flopped down on the bed. Cat disappeared into the bathroom. She reappeared in the bedroom and lay down next to him. "I'm a little chilled. I think we should take a bath together."

"Sounds good to me," Tim mumbled as he rolled on top of her and began nibbling her neck. "Then we better take off our clothes."

Cat barely managed to shut off the water before it overflowed. Laughing, always laughing, Cat climbed into the tub between Tim's legs and leaned against his chest. Immediately, his wondrous hands found their way all over her body. It never seemed like Tim was even conscious of what he was doing. It was all completely instinctive.

No time at all passed before Cat nearly levitated out of the water. "*Oh* my god, Tim," she gasped.

"I think we better get out if we don't want to flood your house."

Tim lovingly toweled her off. Cat responded in kind with a few special kisses.

Tim groaned, scooped her up, and carried her back to bed.

"The day after Thanksgiving has never been so fun," Cat sighed, appreciating Tim's hard body.

"Santa was pretty sure that you were a naughty girl," Tim sighed happily.

"The truth is, Santa, you bring out the naughtiness in me."

"The truth is, Santa knows that naughtiness can be very nice." Tim disappeared under the sheet. "Let me show you."

PARTY TIME

Something about the Christmas spirit seemed to heighten everything between Cat and Tim. After the most amazing night, Santa's Christmas miracles continued. On Saturday, Tim helped her put the lights on the tree, and every string actually worked. Cat thought that was the first time it had ever happened.

Then, reluctantly, Tim headed home to his boys.

Cat spent the rest of the weekend leisurely decorating her tree. Saturday night, there was a milonga for dancers who were desperate to dance after a long weekend of family events. Cat wore a new, slit, tango skirt and had a great time.

Craig called her on Sunday night. "I've missed you so much." He sounded very serious. "I can't wait to see you again."

"I'm sure it was wonderful to see your kids," Cat responded. "They're all so attractive."

"I always love seeing them. But I realized that I don't want to be 'single dad' for the next holiday gathering. I want a lovely woman at my side, and I have a good idea who that woman should be."

Cat immediately panicked. It sounded like a switch had flipped in

Craig. He had grown so intense since their evening at his house. Was it because they had slept together? Cat felt like his reaction was a role reversal. Wasn't that the reaction that the woman was supposed to have? For the life of her, Cat couldn't think of what to say.

Craig didn't seem to notice her silence. "Unfortunately, I'm off to Rome again this week. But I wanted to ask you to my company Christmas party. It's at the Empire State Building. It should be fun."

Cat had just been thinking that, somehow, she was going to have to slow Craig down, when he asked her to the party. "The Empire State Building? So is King Kong going to be there?" she quipped.

"I wouldn't be surprised. Management usually goes all out for this party. I'll send you all the details. You could come to my house first and we could drive in. Or we could meet in the city."

Craig just seemed to assume that she would come with him, and Cat found herself going along with him. "I have to write that day. I better meet you in the city. I can work on the train."

Cat's heart was thumping as she got out of the cab at the Empire State Building. True to his word, Craig was waiting in the lobby for her. His face lit up when he saw her, twinkling in her silver dress. He dashed towards her and pulled her into a big hug. He looked totally fabulous in a dark suit and tie.

As if she were a precious object, Craig guided her onto the elevator. They arrived on the eightieth floor where a lavish party was set-up. There was a spectacular ice sculpture of a jet plane as the centerpiece of a champagne fountain. Cat and Craig filled their glasses.

"I want you to meet some people," Craig said eagerly as he led her across the room to the CEO of his airline.

Cat spent the next hour talking to an endless series of pilots and airline executives. The one thing they all had in common was they all really seemed to love what they did. They were all passionate about flying.

Cat noticed that Craig had an irrepressible smile on his face. He kept his arm possessively around her shoulders. She definitely had the impression that he was proud to introduce her to his colleagues. Everyone, as always, was fascinated to hear about her work on the soaps.

Finally, Craig extricated them from the throng and whispered in her ear. "Let's fill our glasses and go up to the observation deck."

Cat had no idea that they could. "I'd love to."

They took the elevator up to the eighty-sixth floor. Cat walked out onto the legendary deck. "Oh, my goodness," she sighed as she looked out over the galaxy of lights. "I've never been here before. I feel like Fay Wray."

Craig laughed. "Then, I guess I'm King Kong." Immediately, he started to beat his chest.

"No, no," Cat laughed. "King Kong dies."

"Oh right, I forgot."

"I thought King Kong's death was one of the most tragic endings I've ever seen in a movie. It absolutely broke my heart. He loved her so much."

"You are a romantic, aren't you?" It was cool outside. Craig took off his jacket and put it protectively around her shoulders. Then, he guided her to a private corner of the deck, leaned down, and kissed her ever so lovingly.

"Thank you so much for coming with me tonight," he sighed. "You charmed everyone."

Cat was embarrassed. "Oh, I bet you say that to all the girls," she bantered to lighten the moment.

Craig's face suddenly grew more serious. "No, I don't." He pulled a small wrapped box out of his pocket. "I wanted to give you your Christmas present a little early."

Cat was startled. "But I don't have anything for you."

"Why would you? You'll see why I wanted you to open it tonight. What better place could there be?" he insisted.

Cat stared at the small box with a thudding heart. It couldn't be, could it? She had no clue what was going on. Surely, he wasn't giving her a ring. That would be ridiculous.

With shaking fingers, she unwrapped the gift. She felt a little better when she could see that it wasn't a hinged jewelry box. It was just a small cardboard box. Holding her breath, she pulled off the top. Nestled in some tissue paper was a tiny model of the Colosseum. She let out her breath in a whoosh. "Oh, you brought this back for me from Rome. It's adorable."

"Yes, I did. But, it's a symbol."

"Oh?"

"I'm not sure what your holiday plans are, but I was hoping that I could whisk you off to Rome, for at least part of it. Of course, I have flexibility. But I thought toasting in the New Year in Rome with you would be wonderful."

Cat's heart stopped. What in the world was happening? She must be living in The Twilight Zone. Or caught in a soap opera matrix. Was she really standing on the deck of the Empire State Building with this gorgeous man asking her to go to Rome with him?

Craig's eyes were glued to her face. She could only imagine what he was seeing. A thousand emotions must have flickered across it.

Isn't this what she wanted? To savor the endless possibilities that were in the world? To swoop and soar around her empty cage?

She looked away from Craig's intense face over the sea of lights to collect her thoughts. A mosaic of images flashed through her head—Tim's face inches from hers in the fire tower, Craig running up to her tonight in the lobby, Tim's profile as he massaged her feet that first day, Craig's expression as he concentrated on tango in the gazebo, Tim sitting in the diner in his tuxedo, Craig's steamy brow as he cooked the truffle pasta, Tim twirling her on the Rainbow Room floor, Craig presenting her with Rome in the palm of her hand .... What a montage. Each image was like a postcard. Yet, for one set of memories, her whole nervous system was ignited. For the other set, she felt detached, like she was watching herself star in an incredible movie.

Turning back to Craig with glistening eyes, she solemnly held the little box in front of her. "I have never had a grander gift in a more fantastic setting, but I can't accept it." And with that, she gently placed the box back into his pocket.

Powerful man that he was, Craig didn't look away. "There's someone else, isn't there?"

Cat nodded. "You know I'm at the beginning of this new chapter of my life. Every day since I went online, I have learned something about myself. You have been a major part of my experience. Every minute that I have spent with you has been so easy, so entertaining. I don't want you to think I have just been stringing you along. I honestly haven't known how I felt. But when you offered me Rome, the most incredible gift that I have ever been given, in that moment I knew that I couldn't accept it. It wouldn't be fair to you."

A fleeting look of pain and anger crossed Craig's face. Then, dignified and composed captain that he was, he gave her a wry smile. "I guess I am King Kong, after all."

Cat felt like a knife had been stuck in her. "Oh please, don't say that. I never wanted to hurt you."

"I know. But, that's the nature of getting close to someone, isn't it? Running the risk of getting hurt?"

Cat found herself impulsively putting her arms around Craig and hugging him tightly.

After a moment, he pulled away. "Don't worry. I'm a big boy. If I can handle a stowaway pig and emergency landings with two hundred people's lives depending on me, I imagine I'll survive. And for what it's worth, I respect you for turning down the Rome junket if your heart is not in it. Plenty of other women would have enjoyed the spoils and then run."

"I couldn't," Cat whispered, knowing that Amy and Pat were going to think she was crazy.

"So, shall I put you back on the train, or do you want to go downstairs and eat, drink, and be merry?"

"I'm fine with the merriment part, if you are. I have no desire to curtail our evening. Just because I don't feel I can go to Rome, doesn't mean that I wouldn't like to dance the night away. We're here. Let's seize the day."

Craig laughed and took her hand. "It's a deal."

What a bummer!

Oh great. It's not like I don't feel bad enough. Now, I have to listen to you.

Would you stop jumping to conclusions.

Well, spit it out.

I think you have balls. Not many women would pass up that offer.

I wanted to say yes. So much. But, I couldn't.

Of course, you couldn't. Craig is a great guy. But I want to throw those coins in the fountain with Santa Tim. I think we should do Rome right—if we ever get there.

Really? You think I made the right decision.

Unfortunately, I do. It just sucks that we're not going to Rome.

PFM

A week later Cat found herself walking into Rockefeller Center holding Tim's arm. Of course, they had to stop and pay homage to the gigantic tree.

"Can you believe we're back here again?" asked Cat, gazing up at the magnificent Manhattan tradition.

"It is amazing. Hey, you skate, don't you?" asked Tim, staring at the ice-skating rink located right under the tree.

"Yes, I do. Although I haven't in a while," Cat said.

"We have to do that—soon," Tim declared.

"That would be great," Cat agreed happily. "But now we better get upstairs for my big party."

"How did you manage to get your show to hold their Christmas party at the Rainbow Room? And Black Tie! It must be costing a fortune."

"Well, I wish I had any influence at all. But, it's a coincidence. This year is a big anniversary for the show. I guess they combined our normal holiday party budget with the extra money for the anniversary. Remember, we're talking about the entertainment world here—not healthcare. Whatever publicity we get will be worth a fortune in ratings."

"I'm pretty nervous about seeing all the celebrities," Tim confessed. "As you just pointed out, I don't operate in this glamorous show-biz world."

"I promise you, they're all just flesh and blood. Just look at them and imagine how their feet are killing them and how you could help them." Cat teased. "That should humanize them for you. Maybe you could set up a little station in the corner and massage their feet in return for an autograph. The *PT of the Stars*! I can just see you in *People Magazine*. I imagine the line would be out the door."

Tim laughed. "That does help."

They got off the elevator on the sixty-fifth floor. Tim helped Cat off with her coat and realized that she was wearing the same strapless red dress that she had worn on their big night. "I'm really glad you wore that dress," he commented huskily as he leaned down to kiss her neck. "The only problem is, I remember all too well how easy it is to take off."

"Hey, take it easy, 007," she protested. "I've got to be able to stand up for the next few hours, and my legs are already feeling kind of rubbery."

"All right, all right, I'll behave," Tim agreed. "For a while,' he added mischievously.

Cat reached up and straightened Tim's bow tie, took his arm, and sailed into the sea of beautiful people. The minute they stepped into the magnificent room flashes went off.

Tim smiled in surprise. He leaned down to whisper in her ear. "You were being modest before. You must be a big deal!"

"No, I promise you I'm not. I'm an invisible face behind the scenes. I think it's you who's creating the sensation. The photographers are not sure who you are, but you look so damn distinguished and hot that they think you might be someone important."

Tim laughed delightedly. "Me? You've got to be kidding. I'm just a little upstate-New York physical therapist."

"They don't know that. Let's give them something to shoot." And with that, she leaned up on her toes, rapped her arms around his neck and kissed him with fervor. Again, the flashes exploded.

Tim emerged from the kiss looking a little dazed. "Whoa there. Now who's the one with rubbery legs?"

Cat realized that she was so proud to have Tim at her side. "Let's go get a drink."

They were on their way to the bar when a stunningly beautiful twenty-something blond with flawless skin, who was poured into a gold dress that left virtually nothing to the imagination, came up to Cat. Cat glanced at Tim, who looked like he was gulping hard and trying to keep his eyes on the young woman's face. The blond smiled engagingly and said, "I don't think we've ever met, but I had to find you tonight to thank you for the killer scenes you've written for me and Ben. The animal shelter scenes almost broke my heart. And, those scenes in the fire tower were so hot that we practically ignited the whole studio the day we shot them."

Cat turned to Tim who had obviously not missed the reference to the fire tower scenes. "Tim, this is Hannah who plays the role of Dana on the show. Hannah, this is my friend, Tim." Then, she turned back to Hannah and squeezed her hand. "Thank you so much, Hannah. I guess we're a mutual admiration society then, because I think that you and Ben are doing a fantastic job. I have had so much fun writing your stuff. I love what you do with it. The audience loves you too. You've created a romance that's very unique, which isn't easy to do on a soap."

The starlet flushed at Cat's obviously genuine tribute. "Thank you. You've made my night. This job is my first big role. I just pinch myself every day that I get paid to do what I love. Plus," she leaned closer to Cat. "Ben and I have pretty awesome chemistry—which helps."

"You certainly do," Cat agreed, as a photographer came over to pull the stunning starlet away for some special shots.

"Whew," Tim shook his head. "Talk about being with the beautiful people."

Cat laughed. "I forget how unreal-looking everyone is. That's what the soaps are like. Life, but better. Most of the actors are unbelievably attractive to begin with, and then it doesn't hurt that they've been styled within an inch of their lives for tonight."

"Well, she certainly is a fan of yours," he added. "And, I couldn't help noticing a reference to scenes in a fire tower. Wonder where you got that idea?"

Trying not to blush, Cat handed Tim a glass of wine. "A writer has to use what she knows. Anyhow, I should probably be giving you a cut of my pay. My head writer has never raved about my material as much as since I met you."

"Good to know." Tim clinked her glass with a grin. "I'll drink to that."

At that moment, a not particularly glamorous woman with salt and pepper curly hair came up to them. Cat grinned, "Speaking of the devil."

The woman let out a snort, "The devil?"

Before she could continue, Cat said smoothly, "Lorraine, this is my friend, Dr. Tim Hunter. Tim, this is Lorraine Beldon, my beloved head writer."

Lorraine took a long swig of her cocktail. "Which is it, the devil or your beloved? Make up your mind."

Cat bantered back. "You know perfectly well, it's both."

"Can't argue with you there," Lorraine agreed good-naturedly. Then she turned her laser focus back to Tim. "So, you're *the* Dr. Tim Hunter. I've been wanting to meet you. I think you might have to become a consultant to the writing team."

Tim looked at a loss for words. Cat jumped in. "Take it easy, Lorraine. Don't scare the man."

Lorraine eyed him closely. "I suspect this one doesn't scare all that easily. All I have to say is, from what I know, it sounds like you're a man who understands romance. It's not that easy to romance a soap writer."

Tim laughed. "You're right. But I try."

Cat held up her hand. "All right. That's enough, Lorraine. Don't you have some network execs to schmooze?"

"Don't I always have some network execs to schmooze? What a silly question." Lorraine started to turn away, and then turned back to Tim. "Can't wait to see you dance, 007. I've heard good things." And with that, she gave him a wink and walked off.

"Sorry, about that," Cat said, embarrassed. "Lorraine is a character."

"Definitely no need to apologize. I think I'm going to have to start watching your show."

Cat and Tim made the rounds of the party. Tim was easy and charming as he chatted with everyone. When they learned that he was a Physical Therapist, their questions were endless. Cat realized that she hadn't been wrong to suggest that he could have set up a booth.

The music started playing, and for the second time Cat and Tim twirled their way around the rotating floor. Clearly, everyone was impressed with their ballroom dancing. When Cat returned from a visit to the Ladies Room, she found Tim waltzing with Hannah.

Hannah gave him a peck on the cheek when he dipped her at the end.

"Should I be jealous?" Cat teased.

"Despite the gold dress, she's a very nice girl. From Ohio. She played Belle in *Beauty and the Beast* in high school, so she knew how to waltz. She asked me to dance. What could I say?"

"Now your photo could really end up in *People*," Cat commented. "Hope your patients can handle their famous 'Dancing Doc.'"

It was late when Tim and Cat finally said their goodbyes and headed for the elevator.

"How tired are you?" asked Tim as he led her out of Rockefeller Center.

"Well, if you want to know the truth …"

"Absolutely."

"I'm totally energized from the party. I feel like I could dance all night. I've been to lots of soap holiday parties, and this was the most fun, bar none. It's because of you."

"Well, I think that everyone loves and admires you and your work very much. But I'm happy to take the credit," Tim grinned slyly. "So if you're not going to turn into a pumpkin anytime soon, I have an idea."

"Uh-oh. What kind of an idea?"

"You said you could dance all night. How about skate all night?" He motioned to the skating rink under the tree.

Cat giggled. "We're all dressed up."

"So?" Tim rolled his eyes. "Wouldn't that be cool? You have a nice warm coat. There's no time like the present. I dare you!"

Cat couldn't believe what she was saying, but his dare was infectious. "You're on."

Fifteen minutes later, they were holding hands and trying to remember how to skate. Cat's red dress twirled around her ankles. Tim looked like a leading man in his tux.

Cat almost took a nose dive into the railing. "I used to be so good at this when I was in middle school," she moaned.

"It's like riding a bike," Tim assured her. "Just give it a few laps."

Cat couldn't help thinking about all the things that she had tried in the last year that were like "riding a bike." She took a deep breath and pressed on.

Sure enough, after a couple of circles around the rink she found herself skating with the music and even being able to appreciate the tree. The full moon appeared to be perched on the top of the tree. "Oh look," she gasped.

Tim spun around and caught her in his arms. "What?"

"Look at the moon. It's the best ornament on the tree!" she pointed.

"I arranged that for you," he kidded. "happy holidays, moon girl," he whispered as he kissed her ever so tenderly.

Just then, Cat felt a drop of water on her eyelash. She was so happy. Why was she crying? Oh. She looked up and realized that a few fat snowflakes were tumbling out of the sky. One had just melted on her eyelash. She caught one of the perfect crystals with her fingertip. She pointed her finger accusingly at Tim. "Did you arrange for this too?"

"I think it's us, our energy. Amazing things seem to happen when we're together."

Suddenly, Cat knew that the moment was right. Exactly right. Although, there were only a few stragglers still on the ice, she tugged Tim to the center of the rink where the two of them wouldn't be in the way. "I have an early Christmas present for you," she breathed huskily.

Tim looked genuinely confused. "In the middle of Rockefeller Center?"

Cat looked up at him framed by the halo of the tree lights. "Everything about tonight has been more than I could have dreamed of. In fact, pretty much every minute that we have spent together has been more than I could have imagined—from the fire tower, to skating with the snowflakes under the tree. Anyhow, I know I told you that I needed to stay open and see other people because I needed to know more about who I am, what I like, who is out there. But tonight

I realized that I don't need to know any more. I don't want to see anyone else. I'm all in."

It seemed to take Tim a minute to digest her words. Then, a Cheshire Cat grin spread from ear to ear on his face. "You know, I planned an early gift for you too. I realized that more than anything, I was hoping that you would spend time with me and my boys during the holidays."

"Oh, Tim. I want to meet them more than anything."

"I decided that I didn't even care if you were seeing other 'people' because I've known since the beginning that we are something special."

Cat threw her arms around Tim. They kissed for all they were worth.

A group of tourists watching them from above the rink started clapping and whistling.

Eventually, Tim and Cat realized they were the object of the group's approval and waved back at them.

Cat murmured, "I thought you might be interested to know that I turned down a trip to Rome for you."

"You what?"

"Suffice it to say that I realized that a fantasy of mine, going to Rome, was not worth it without you. So I said, no thank you. And—goodbye."

Cat could tell that Tim was impressed. "You're crazier than I thought."

"No, I'm not. I'm only catching up to you. Thank you for trusting in us, the power of us."

"You know, I touch people for a living. I knew the minute I touched you at the diner that we made fireworks."

"I guess, it's what they call chemistry."

Tim looked her in the eyes. "Chemistry is an understatement. I call it *PFM*."

"What?"

"Pure Fucking Magic."

THE LAST WORD

Totally sated, totally loved, Cat woke up much later that night. She curled up next to Tim's deliciously warm and toned body. She replayed everything that had happened tonight. She was filled with incredible joy and gratitude.

Well, he nailed it, didn't he?

What? Are you being crude again?

No. He said it, Pure Fucking Magic. I think you're the luckiest woman alive.

I know. I am. But it's not just Tim and me. The whole year has been PFM. I truly thought that my life was over when I got divorced. I thought divorce was a death sentence. And I suppose, in a way I was right. My life, as I knew it, was over. But what I didn't realize were the infinite possibilities that were just waiting to fill in for all the parts that were gone. Little by little, from the Omega catalog flipping open, to meeting Pat, to getting transformed with Dr. Martin, to finding tango, to becoming Moonrise on Match, to meeting Tim in the diner—a new life, a new me has come to be.

You've become Cat. Meow.

I don't know how or why it happened. It was just PFM.

So, with PFM, does that mean you won't need me anymore?

I wish I could say yes, but—I doubt it.

You got that right, girlfriend. We have only just begun.

Do you always have to have the last word?

Pretty much. I am the you—deep inside of you—who is more you than you.

You are the you who is so unbelievably full of herself.

Is that so bad?

(SIGHS) Now you're just fishing for compliments. You know perfectly well that you have pushed me and pushed me—and ...

Transformed you from a sniveling chimney sweep into Cinderella? I am damn good, aren't I?

That's enough. I was never a "sniveling chimney sweep."

Talk about revisionist history. What about the morning after that fiasco of a dinner with Herr Professor and a whole bottle of wine? What about those pathetic Saturday nights? What about that pile of shapeless hundred-year-old dresses that filled your closet? Now look at you, resplendent in your strapless red gown and fabulous new body—skating under the full moon with your prince.

Okay, okay. You're right. Thank you.

You're welcome. Stick with me, baby.

ACKNOWLEDGMENTS

First of all, I have to thank all the women who have shared their stories with me, especially the ladies of my book club. For thirty years, we have been through it all—together.

I am so grateful for the synchronicity that brought Dory, Paul and Colin of Epigraph to me. They have been unendingly helpful in their support. I also cannot forget to thank Judy and Cynthia who believed in me first.

I feel truly blessed to be a baby boomer. What a lucky run we've had. Who knew that when we started with silver charm bracelets complete with wedding bands and baby carriages that the ceiling would shatter and that we could and would become anything.

And then there's Argentine tango. Dancing has brought a joy and vibrancy to my life that I could never have imagined. I swear I think it's the secret to youth. I know some people truly believe that they have "two left feet." But, if you aren't convinced of that, give it a try. The music, the movement, the socializing, the physical connection—what a romantic formula. I still have to pinch myself that it worked that way for me.

Of course, at the root of everything is family and love. When I was just out of college, flush with the promise of the women's movement, I wanted to have it all. Fifteen years later, exhausted with two young children and a high-pressure job, I wanted to admit myself to the local hospital every time I drove by. There were damages along the way. And, I am delighted that it's not going to be so hard for my children and grandchildren. But, I have to say now, it was all worth it.

Finally, I am in awe of the magic that is around every corner. I have learned late in life that if I just pay attention to the possibilities that cross my path, unbelievable things happen. It's PFM.

CPSIA information can be obtained
at www.ICGtesting.com
Printed in the USA
FSHW012234290720
72015FS